Three-times Golden Heart® finalist **Tina Beckett** learned to pack her suitcases almost before she learned to read. Born to a military family, she has lived in the United States, Puerto Rico, Portugal and Brazil. In addition to travelling, Tina loves to cuddle with her pug, Alex, spend time with her family, and hit the trails on her horse. Learn more about Tina from her website, or 'friend' her on Facebook.

Also by Tina Beckett

The Doctors' Baby Miracle
Tempted by Dr Patera
The Billionaire's Christmas Wish
One Night to Change Their Lives
The Surgeon's Surprise Baby

Hot Brazilian Docs! miniseries

To Play with Fire
The Dangers of Dating Dr Carvalho
The Doctor's Forbidden Temptation
From Passion to Pregnancy

Discover more at millsandboon.co.uk.

A FAMILY TO HEAL HIS HEART

TINA BECKETT

MILLS & BOON

First published in Great Britain 2019
by Mills & Boon, an imprint of HarperCollins*Publishers*
1 London Bridge Street, London, SE1 9GF

Large Print edition 2020

© 2019 Tina Beckett

ISBN: 978-0-263-08539-6

MIX
Paper from
responsible sources
FSC
www.fsc.org   FSC™ C007454

This book is produced from independently certified
FSC™ paper to ensure responsible forest management. For
more information visit www.harpercollins.co.uk/green.

Printed and bound in Great Britain
by CPI Group (UK) Ltd, Croydon, CR0 4YY

To my children,
who put up with my crazy schedule
and who love me in spite of it.

CHAPTER ONE

LINDY FRANKLIN'S PULSE HAMMERED, and she swiped at the alarm clock to silence it, just as she had every morning for the last two years, before falling back onto the bed in relief. Six o'clock. Just like always. Only now there was no reason to leap up and try to rush to Daisy before she woke up and started to cry. No reason to make omelets and toast for her husband. But she still needed to get up, or her mom would arrive, and she'd be late for her new job.

An actual paying job this time.

Moving back to Savannah had been the right thing to do. Even if admitting she'd been wrong was one of the hardest things she'd ever done. So had realizing that most of her old friends had moved on with their lives. And who could blame them?

Climbing out of bed and sliding her feet into a pair of fuzzy slippers, she went into the bathroom, where the words taped to her mirror caught her eye.

"New beginnings, Lindy. New beginnings." She recited the phrase just as she had every morning. Ever since the judge had told her she was free to leave Fresno—and her old life—behind.

Today really was a new beginning for her. For the first time since the move to California she'd be able to practice medicine again. Her marriage had closed the door to a lot of things. Her release from it was slowly opening them back up again.

Mouthing her mantra one more time, she hurriedly showered and got dressed and fixed Daisy's breakfast.

The doorbell rang, and she froze for a pained second. Then she laughed. It was just her mom coming to pick up Daisy.

She swung it open and there stood Rachel Anderson, as tall and elegant as ever.

"You're early. I was just about to get her up."

"I know. I wanted to make sure I was here in plenty of time."

"You always are." She grinned and drew her mom into the house. "I don't think you've been late a day in your life."

Unlike Lindy, who tended to run just a few minutes behind no matter how hard she pushed herself. It had been one of those "failings" that had been used as a hammer.

New beginnings.

"I'm not sure that's true, sweetheart."

She was pretty sure it was. But her mom's sweet southern drawl spelled home the way nothing else ever had. She wrapped her in a tight hug.

"What was that for?"

"Just for being you."

Her mother had been a huge help in making sure she got back on her feet, first by watching Daisy while Lindy had volunteered at the women's crisis center. And now by insisting she apply for the nursing position at Mid Savannah Medical Center.

Lindy drew a deep breath. "I'll get Daisy. And I've just put breakfast on the table. Do you want something?"

"No, and I told you I could fix Daisy breakfast at the house."

"I know you did. But I want to try to keep things as normal as possible for her, since I'll be away from home a lot longer than I was before."

Normal. What a beautiful word. She'd only recently realized just how beautiful it was.

"And you will." Rachel peered into her daughter's face. "How are you holding up?"

"Good, Mom. Good. It's just been crazy, trying to get settled in the new house. I didn't expect to get an answer on the job so soon."

Her husband had left her one good thing: a life insurance policy that had helped her coast along. It had made her squirm to take the money, but that money had also paid for therapy and sundry other things.

Mid Savannah Medical Center had asked about the three-year lapse since her last position in Georgia, but she'd covered by saying she'd taken some time off to be home with her daughter. Not exactly a lie. She'd gotten a surprise phone call the next day telling her she had her dream job as a surgical nurse in the pediatric ward. Her parents had cosigned for the loan on her little starter home—since she hadn't had a job at the time. She'd vowed to herself that she'd make them proud.

"I told you it wouldn't take long. Maybe you should have waited a little while longer before getting back out there. I'm sorry if I rushed you into applying."

She gave her mom's hand a squeeze. "You didn't. I needed to do something, and this was the perfect opportunity."

Her mom was a music professor at one of the local colleges. She'd been alarmed when

Lindy had told her she wasn't going back to work after getting married. She'd been right to be concerned, because Luke had wanted to pack up and move to Fresno almost immediately, effectively isolating her from everyone and everything she'd known.

But that was all water under the bridge. She was back, and she intended to stay back. Nothing or no one would ever change that again.

"Why don't you let me get Daisy ready? I promise I'll lock the doors behind me when I leave."

She hesitated. Locking the doors herself had become her own personal ritual. One she wasn't sure she was ready to give up. But she'd have to sometime. And the last thing she wanted was to give her mom more cause to worry. "Are you sure you don't mind?"

"No. It'll give me and my granddaughter some time to bond before heading out."

Lindy's chest ached. Living on the other

side of the country meant that her mom hadn't seen Daisy until she'd moved back home. Not for lack of trying. Luke had thought of every reason under the sun why her parents couldn't come to see them, though: the house was too small; the trip would be too hard on them; he couldn't spare the time away from work.

Those days were behind her now. And her parents had already spent the last two years getting to know Daisy. And Daisy—maybe because of how young she was—had adapted to her new life quickly. Her daughter hadn't asked once about her father, for which Lindy was truly grateful.

"I think you bonded the moment she saw you and Daddy. But thank you." She glanced at her phone. She still had twenty-five minutes to get to work, but Savannah traffic could be unpredictable. "Maybe I can be on time for once in my life. Hopefully they'll like me."

"Just be yourself, honey. They're all going to love you. How could they not?"

And with those words ringing in her ears, she scooped up her keys, gave her mom a kiss on the cheek and hurried out the door.

Zeke Bruen was not loving the new surgical nurse. She'd done nothing wrong and was on top of every request almost before he asked, but he'd seen her eyes repeatedly stray toward the big clock on the wall. Counting down the hours until she was with her husband? Boyfriend?

Gritting his teeth, he ignored those thoughts. Some people did have a life outside the hospital. He certainly didn't expect everyone on his team to be like he was. But when they were here, he expected them to be present. Especially when it was a certain person's first day on the job.

Things had been so rushed getting into the surgical suite that he hadn't had a chance to introduce himself, although he'd been told the new nurse's name as he'd scrubbed in: Lindolynn Franklin. So maybe someone had told her his as well. Well, it wouldn't hurt to have a little chat with her after they were done here.

And do what, Zeke? Confront her about looking at the clock?

He looked too, but it was to keep track of whether things were going as expected.

Maybe Nurse Franklin was doing the same thing. Somehow he didn't think so. Those glances had seemed furtive and once, when she'd caught his eye afterward, color had flooded into the portion of her face visible above her surgical mask. The sight had turned his stomach inside out. That certainly hadn't helped.

Returning his attention to his patient with an irritated shrug, he busied himself with reconnecting the pulmonary artery, making sure each tiny stitch he placed was secure. The last thing he needed was to close this little girl's chest and have the repair leak.

A half-hour later he was done, giving a nod to each of his team with murmured thanks. Then he left the room and stripped off his gloves, relief washing through him. He'd done this particular surgery dozens of times, but each time he cracked open a child's chest, a moment of doubt threatened to paralyze him. He'd always gotten over it, his muscle memory taking over until he could get his mind back in the game. Maybe that's what had happened with the new nurse. The only thing to do was feel her out.

He propped a shoulder against the wall outside the double doors as the surgical team slowly filed out, many of them congratulating him. That wasn't what he was waiting for, however. He was searching for an unfamiliar face.

There. Her eyes connected with his for an instant before she attempted to veer off in the other direction. Good try. He fell into step beside her. "Sorry. I didn't get a chance to introduce myself before we got started."

He held out a hand. "Ezekiel Bruen."

"Oh, um, I'm Lindy Franklin. I'm new here."

Lindy. That fit. As did the rest of her face, now that her mask was gone. Delicate bones and the subtle curve of her cheeks gave her a breakable air that made him uneasy, and he had no idea why.

"So I've heard." He thought for a second she was going to ignore his outstretched hand, but then she stopped walking and placed hers in it, the light squeeze reaffirming his musings and making him hesitate. Maybe he shouldn't say anything.

And if it had been another member of his team?

He stiffened his resolve, determined to keep things professional. "I noticed you were in a rush to get out of surgery. Not happy with where the administration placed you?"

"What? Oh…no. I mean yes." That vibrant color he'd seen in the operating room reappeared, only this time he was actually able to watch as it flowed up her cheeks before receding like an ocean wave. "Why would you think I was in a hurry to get out of there?"

He ignored the quick tightening of his gut. "You were watching that clock pretty closely."

The pink returned, darker this time, and white teeth sank into a full lower lip. "I was just…" She paused as if trying to figure out how to explain herself. "I didn't realize I was. And I'm perfectly happy with where I've been placed."

So she wasn't going to let him in on whatever had kept her mind so occupied.

Well, if that's the way she wanted to play it… "As long as you're up to the demands of working with the surgical staff."

Her back stiffened, and her chin angled up. Light brown eyes rimmed with dark lashes met his head on. "I am quite up to the demands. Thank you for your concern, though."

That show of strength made him smile.

It wasn't a true thank you, and they both knew it. But he'd gotten his message across. Time to revert to his normal, friendly self. If it even existed anymore.

"Have you been in town long?"

"I was born and raised here in Savannah." The slightest flicker of her eyelids said there was something more to that story.

"So was I." He studied her for a second. "Did you transfer here from one of the other hospitals?"

"No."

So much for being friendly. He guessed it was none of his business where she'd come from. She could have just graduated from nursing school for all he knew. But the way she'd handled those instruments said she knew her way around an operating room. That kind of self-assurance only came with experience. But if she hadn't transferred from one of the local hospitals, where had she gained that experience? Unless she actually did have something to hide. Some kind of mistake that hadn't shown up on her résumé? He didn't want to go digging through her past or call her previous place of employment, but maybe he should. Just so he'd be aware of any issues before they cropped up and became a problem here. Or maybe he should just ask her outright.

"Where did you practice before this, then?" He could have asked Human Resources, but he wanted to see if she would balk about answering.

She named a place in the heart of Savannah.

"I thought you said you didn't transfer."

"I didn't." She gave a quick shrug. "I took a few years off and then decided I couldn't live without nursing."

She'd taken a few years off...

It hit him all of a sudden. His glance went to her ring finger. It was empty, but he was pretty sure there was an indentation there where a ring had once been. So she'd been married, but wasn't any longer? She could have taken some time off during that relationship, but he had a feeling he knew what had caused her inordinate interest in that clock. "I take it you have a child."

Her mouth popped open and then closed again, the color that had seeped into her face disappearing completely. "How did you know?"

"Just a hunch. The clock-watching had to be for a reason. And you took 'a few years off.' I wasn't trying to pry."

"It's okay. She's three. It's my first time leaving her with anyone for this length of time."

Including the child's father? Something about that made the hair on the back of his neck stand up, although it was ridiculous. Maybe the man had traveled so much that there'd never been time to leave her with him or with anyone else. Or maybe the mark on her finger was a figment of his imagination.

It was also none of his business.

She gave a quick shake of her head as if reading his thoughts before meeting his gaze again. "Well, it was nice working with you, Dr. Bruen—"

"Call me Zeke. Everyone does."

"Okay…" She drew the word out like it made her uncomfortable. Did she think he was hitting on her? Damn. Nothing could be further from the truth, despite that quick jerk to his senses after seeing her without her surgical mask for the first time. He hadn't felt that since… Well, in quite a while.

Time to put her mind at ease, if that were the case.

"We're pretty informal here at Mid Savannah."

"I guess I'm not used to that. You can call me Lindy, then."

"What's your daughter's name?" He had no idea why he asked that, and the last thing he should be doing was talking about baby girls with anyone. He never encouraged his colleagues to talk about their children, and most of the old-timers knew why. Maybe it was because of how reticent she'd been to talk to him. About anything.

"Her name is Daisy."

Daisy. He liked that. His own daughter's name had been Marina.

A shaft of pain arced through him and then was gone.

"Nice name."

"Thank you."

His glance went past her to see Nancy, one of the OR nurses, coming up the corridor, heading for them. She touched Lindy on the shoulder, only to have her give a squeak and nearly jump out of her skin. She whirled to the side, face white, eyes wide. She seemed to go slack when she saw who it was.

Her fellow nurse frowned. "Sorry. I didn't mean to scare you." She held up a phone. "Is this yours? It was left on the desk."

"Oh! Yes, it is. Thank you." She suddenly grinned, her nose crinkling on either side.

That smile made her face light up in a way that made his gut jerk even harder. He kicked the sensation away, irritated with himself.

"And you didn't scare me."

He wasn't sure he believed her, but he'd already shown far too much interest in her life—and her—than he should have. The last thing he needed was to have the new nurse get any wrong ideas.

Because there weren't any to have.

And if he was going to get out of here, now was the time to do it without feeling like he'd abandoned her. "Well, I have a few other patients to see, so if you two will excuse me."

"Of course." Nancy sent him a smile, while Lindy seemed to take her time looking at him, her phone now in her hand, her expression wary once again.

"I'll try to do a little less clock watching the next time we work together." As if she couldn't help herself, her lips soon turned up at the edges and those tiny lines beside her nose reappeared.

He swallowed. "Not a problem. If you have any questions about the hospital or how we do things, I'm sure Nancy, myself or any of the other staff members can steer you in the right direction."

"I appreciate that."

With that he gave the pair a quick wave, before turning around and heading in the opposite direction. Part of him wanted to solve the mystery of the newest staff member and part of him wanted nothing to do with those kinds of guessing games. Especially if it involved someone who'd recently broken up with their spouse or significant other.

Or who had a young daughter.

Better just to do his job and pretend not to notice what Lindy Franklin did or didn't do. As long as she did her job, he had no complaints.

And even if he did, he was going to keep them to himself.

For his own good. And maybe for hers too.

CHAPTER TWO

LINDY WASN'T TOO sure about bringing her mom and Daisy to the hospital for lunch. Especially not after what had happened with Dr.… Zeke. Would he think she was distracted again?

She was off duty, so it was really none of his business.

Besides, she hadn't been distracted per se. She'd been well aware of what she was doing and what she was supposed to be doing. And none of that involved the hunky surgeon.

Hunky? Really, Lindy? She gave an internal roll of her eyes.

Besides, her mom wanted to see the hospital, and she could think of no good reason to tell her no. And Daisy had seemed excited about eating somewhere other than at her or Mimi's house.

"It's hospital food, so don't get your hopes up."

Her mom laughed. "I don't have to cook, so I'm sure it'll be great."

"Poor Dad. Is he fending for himself today?"

"No. He's headed to the lodge to see his buddies. Which leaves me with time to spend with my favorite daughter."

"I'm your only daughter, Mom." She flashed a quick smile. "But I'll take whatever time with you I can get."

Especially since she hadn't seen her parents for the duration of her marriage, something that should have sent up a red flag. Luke had supposedly landed a fabulous job across the country almost as soon as the ceremony was over. But, looking back, she wondered if quitting his job in Savannah had been the plan all along. There'd actually been quite a few flags that she'd missed along the way. All because she'd "fallen in love" and hadn't taken precautions. Then, when she'd realized she was pregnant, she'd been too quick to say yes when he'd asked her to marry him.

But no more. If she ever found herself in a relationship again, she was going to make sure she let her mind do most of the work, rather than putting her heart in charge.

She had no desire to jump into that particular lake again. Maybe she'd wait until Daisy was grown up before dating. When she thought about what could have happened the last night she and Luke had been together…

She swallowed, her hand going to her throat as a phantom ache threatened to interfere with her breathing.

Stop it, Lindy. Daisy is fine. You're fine.

Leading the way through the door to the cafeteria, she frowned when she spied the doctor she'd thought of as "hunky" just a few minutes ago. Great. Just what she needed.

She hadn't had to work with him for the last several days, thank God. But she hadn't really expected to see him here either.

Why not? The man had to eat, just like everyone else.

Just as she was ready to shepherd her mom and daughter back the way they'd come with a manufactured excuse, Zeke's eyes met hers, narrowing slightly before moving from her to her mom and then to Daisy.

Then he frowned, deep furrows giving his face an ominous look that made her shiver.

Her chin went up. She wasn't cowering ever again. She had as much of a right to be in here as anyone. She changed her mind about leaving and ushered her mom and Daisy over to the line and got behind them, swinging Daisy up into her arms. "What do you want to eat, honey?"

"Sheeshburger."

"A cheeseburger? How many of those have you had recently?"

Her mom shook her head. "Hey, don't look

at me. We had plenty of fruits and vegetables to go with yesterday's burger."

Lindy's dad loved to cook out on the grill, and his meals were always delicious. "I was teasing."

Against her volition, her gaze slid back to Zeke, who she found was still watching her from the coffee bar. The frown was gone, and in its place... Another shiver went through her, this time for a completely different reason. When he snapped the lid onto whatever he'd just poured in his cup, he didn't move away from them like she'd hoped. Instead, he headed their way.

The shivery awareness died a quick death. She had no desire for her daughter to meet any of her male colleagues. Especially not Zeke.

She wanted her daughter to have a good long stretch of stability to hopefully counteract anything she might have seen sensed or heard during her mother's disastrous marriage.

Then Zeke was in line with them. "Hi. You must be off today."

This time it was her brows that came together, until she realized she wasn't dressed in scrubs. Although there were people who did bring their street clothes to work and changed into them after their shift. "I am. I thought I'd show my mom and Daisy around."

"Good idea."

There was an awkward pause, which her mom was quick to fill. "I'm Rachel Anderson. I take it you and my daughter know each other?" She shot Lindy a glance filled with curiosity.

Oh, no, Mom. Not you too.

"He's one of the pediatric surgeons here at the hospital." The words came out a little gruffer than she'd meant for them to.

Zeke held out his hand and introduced himself, making her realize that she should have at least told her mom his name. But the momentary awareness she'd felt a few minutes ago had left her flustered, and Lindy didn't like it. She'd been flustered by Luke as well and look how that had turned out.

"Why don't you join us?" her mom said as Lindy just stood there, staring at him. Damn. Soon Zeke was going to think he'd been right when he'd said she seemed distracted. She was. And this time it wasn't by thoughts of her daughter.

It was by the surgeon himself.

"That's up to Lindy."

What? Why was it up to her? She did not want to cast the deciding vote. "It's fine with me." She shifted Daisy a little higher on her hip, keeping her close. But thankfully Zeke hadn't shown much interest in her daughter. And Lindy would rather keep it that way.

They somehow made it through the line, although she no longer felt like eating. And it wasn't due to the quality of the food on offer in front of them. She tried to take one of the two trays her mom was wrestling with, only to have Zeke take it instead. "I'm not eating much, so I'll put mine on your tray, if that's okay."

Great. She guessed it didn't matter since she'd already said he could join them. "It's fine. No surgeries this afternoon?"

"I had one in the middle of the night and ended up staying. As soon as I eat, I'm heading home to crash."

A surgery in the middle of the night was never a good thing. "Was it bad?"

He nodded, a muscle in his jaw tight. "Very bad. A teenager hung herself."

"Oh, God." Her mom was thankfully ahead of them, since her lungs had suddenly seized as remembered sensations washed over her. The cramping of muscles starved of oxygen. The blackening of her vision. The realization that if she passed out, it was all over.

Somehow she got hold of herself and swallowed several times to rid herself of the memories. She cleared her throat, somehow needing to ask the question. "Did she make it?"

"Yes. Her trachea suffered a partial separation, and we had to do a tracheotomy and then go in and repair the damage. But she'll be fine physically. And hopefully she'll get the emotional help for whatever caused her to do this."

"How terrible." Lindy had been fortunate that there'd been no permanent damage to her throat. Nothing to repair. Except her heart. And she was still dealing with some of the fallout from that. Like when Nancy had tapped her on the shoulder. Even after two years of freedom, she was sometimes easily startled. And she tended to walk on eggshells around people, afraid of making someone angry, even though she knew that fear was irrational. But, like her therapist had said, it would take time.

Lindy picked out an egg salad sandwich and a small cup of fruit, while her mom put Daisy's picks on her own tray. And, yes, there was a cheeseburger. That made her smile.

She still had her daughter. There'd been no custody battles. No lengthy court cases. There'd been no need for anything, other than a coffin, in the end. Daisy would never know her father. But she couldn't help but think that was for the best.

A minute or two later they were seated at one of the small tables. Zeke yawned and downed a healthy portion of his coffee.

"Sorry. I'll try not to fall asleep on you."

A pang of compassion went through her. Anyone who saw medicine as a glamorous profession hadn't seen the toll it took on those in the field. Zeke had probably been uprooted from his bed to come in and do the surgery. And then he'd probably gone on rounds this morning and dealt with his own caseload of patients. "Were you scheduled for today?"

"Yes. But I wasn't slated to come in until seven."

"And your surgery was when?"

"Two."

"You have to be exhausted. Are you off tomorrow?" She wasn't sure why she cared. Plenty of healthcare professionals went through the same thing on a daily basis. But she could see the tired lines bracketing his mouth and eyes. Maybe that's what had made his earlier frown seem so fierce.

"Yes."

Her mom laid Daisy's food out on a napkin and put a straw in her cup of juice. "I remember the days when you pulled those kinds of hours before you got…" Her voice faded away.

Thankful her mother had caught herself. Lindy nodded and forced herself to smile. "I'm sure you pulled your share of all-nighters when I was a kid."

"Of course. But that's different from what you and Dr. Bruen do. And you were a pretty healthy child."

As was Daisy, thank goodness.

"Call me Zeke, please."

Lindy's brows went up. So it wasn't just the staff who were allowed to call him by his given name. That privilege evidently extended to their immediate relatives.

He took another gulp of his coffee, bloodshot eyes glancing at her for a second before moving over to Daisy. Then they closed, and he pinched the bridge of his nose as if suddenly sporting a massive headache.

"You don't have to stay here and keep us company. Why don't you go home and get some sleep?" This time her smile wasn't as difficult to find. "Besides, if you drink too much of that stuff you won't be able to do anything but stare at the ceiling."

"Said as if you've done exactly that."

"I have. And it wasn't fun." It also wasn't for the reasons he thought. It had been when her marriage had been at its lowest point, and she'd been worrying about Daisy's future and the hard decision ahead of her. That choice had been taken out of her hands a day later.

At least Daisy would never have to decide whether or not she wanted to see her father in the future.

Zeke pushed his cup away. "I'll take your word for it. And sleep sounds like heaven right now." He stood. "I think I'll try to do just that. Thanks for letting me join you."

"You're welcome."

Daisy lifted her cheeseburger and waved it at him. "Bye-bye."

He looked like he wasn't sure what to do for a second, then he gave a half-smile. "Goodbye to you too. And nice meeting you, Mrs. Anderson."

"Call me Rachel, since I'm calling you Zeke."

"Okay. It was nice meeting you… Rachel."

"You as well."

Once he was gone, her mother looked at her. "The doctors here are a lot cuter than at your last hospital."

"Mom!" It wasn't like she hadn't noticed how good looking Zeke was. The word *hunk*—of all things—wasn't something she threw around every day. But the last thing she needed was to fantasize about the man.

Oh, Lord, no. You are not having fantasies. About anyone!

"Don't you 'Mom' me. You can't let one bad experience turn you off love forever."

"It was a little more than a bad experience, don't you think?" She worded it carefully. Even though Daisy didn't know exactly what had happened, she might be able to understand more than Lindy thought.

"I know, but not all men are like Luke. Take your father, for example."

"I know, but I'm not ready to date. I honestly don't know if I'll ever want to again." Even Mr. Hunk himself would have a hard time moving her off that mark. Even if he wanted to. Which he didn't.

Her mom reached over to squeeze her

hand. "I understand. Really, I do. When the time is right, you'll change your mind."

This time Lindy let it go. There was no use arguing over her decisions about dating. And as much as her mom said she understood, how could she possibly know what it had been like to live with someone like Luke? A good chunk of his life insurance policy had gone to pay off credit cards he had taken out in her name. Her discovery of those cards had been what had set him off that last time. It was no wonder she was now leery of relationships. And Daisy had to come first at this point in her life.

"*If* I change my mind, you'll be one of the first to know."

Rachel gave her daughter's hand one last squeeze and then withdrew. "That's my cue to change the subject. Are you getting used to living on your own?"

Lindy's quaint little cottage wasn't all that far from the hospital. It was within walking distance, which was nice. And it overlooked a nearby park, which was even nicer. She and Daisy had strolled through it on more than one occasion already. "I am. Thank you so much for helping me find the house. We're making it a home, little by little, aren't we, Daisy? She loves the princess stickers you got for her wall. We've already put them up."

"Princess!" Daisy said the word in a loud voice.

"I saw them. She is my little princess, aren't you?" Her mom tweaked Daisy's nose.

The tyke repeated the word like a battle cry, stretching her arms out as if showing her grandmother just how much of a princess she was.

They laughed and suddenly Lindy was fiercely glad she'd decided to return to Savannah when she had. She was back among familiar landmarks and people she loved. It made the odd little pangs in her chest bearable.

She couldn't change the past, but she could

make the future something her daughter could look forward to without fear. And if she'd never met Luke, Daisy might not be here at all. Didn't that make it worth it?

Worth it? Lindy hadn't deserved what she'd gotten, but she did love her daughter more than life itself. And, yes, she was glad that at least something good had come out of their marriage.

"I guess I know what she might want to be for Halloween."

Lindy's chest swelled with love. Her mom hadn't showered her with recriminations or accusations. She'd been truly glad that her daughter had come back. If she'd known how the marriage would turn out, she'd kept that declaration to herself. Both of her parents had. They loved Daisy like she did, unconditionally, insisting that they be the ones to provide childcare rather than Lindy finding a daycare center. And Daisy was thriving. Finally. She hadn't noticed the pale fear in her baby's eyes while she'd been in the situation, but now that they were out? Oh, yes, she could see nuances she'd never known were there. It made the guilt that much worse. She'd thought she'd protected Daisy from the worst parts of her marriage, and she had. But, even as an infant, had she been able to pick up on the subtle emotions Lindy thought she'd hidden?

She'd probably never know.

New beginnings.

No more staring in the rearview mirror. There was nothing back there she needed to see. She was supposed to be looking to the future.

And if her glance strayed to places it shouldn't?

Like Zeke Bruen?

Yes. She could acknowledge that he'd caught her eye. But if she was smart, Lindy would make sure that was all he caught: her glance. Because a glance was temporary. A gaze, however…well, that carried a lot more permanence. And that was going to be reserved for Daisy and Daisy only.

No matter how difficult that might prove to be.

Zeke could see Lindy standing by the nurses' station, staring at the patient board.

Lunch the other day had been a blur of exhaustion and depleted emotions. Suicide attempts were always difficult, but this was one life they'd saved.

For how long, though?

The kicker was that these teens thought they wanted to die. Zeke's daughter, on the other hand, had wanted to live. Only she hadn't gotten to choose.

He glanced at the board. Two of those up there were his patients. Lindy would be one of the surgical nurses. He'd asked for her and wasn't sure why. He suspected some of it had to do with seeing the object of her clock-watching up close and personal. Small and full of smiles, Lindy's daughter was a miniature version of her. Only Lindy's smile seemed much more elusive than her child's. And something Rachel had said stayed with him over the last couple of days. And he couldn't even remember exactly what it had been. It was more her tone of voice.

He should turn around and walk away before he found himself caught up in something he wanted no part of. But to do so might make her think it was because of her. And she'd be right.

Better that he go over and talk to her as if she were any other member of the team. "Off to an early start?"

She whirled around, a hand pressed to her chest, face draining of all color. When she focused on him, she gave a nervous laugh and leaned back against the counter. "Oh, God, sorry. You startled me."

Startled? That was the second time he'd seen her react like that.

"I didn't mean to. Did you think I was the hospital administrator or something?"

"No." She shook her head. "I was just lost in thought. Didn't anyone ever tell you not to sneak up on people?"

"They did. I just wasn't aware that I was sneaking."

"No, of course you weren't." She sucked down a deep breath and blew it out. "Sorry. Anyway, did you catch up on your sleep?"

He couldn't remember the last time he'd scared someone like that, and he was pretty sure that time it had been on purpose. But her explanation was reasonable.

"I did, thanks. Just checking in about the surgeries I have scheduled. You'll be scrubbing in on both of them?" Since he'd put her name in as someone he wanted on those cases, the question was more rhetorical than anything.

Her glance went back to the board. "Ledbetter and Brewster? Yes. Anything I should know?"

"Ledbetter has had a reaction to anesthesia before, so they're tweaking the ratios.

Just wanted you to be aware in case we have to make a sudden shift in care."

"Okay, got it. And Brewster?"

"We're doing her first. Pneumothorax. Routine."

Lindy gave a visible swallow and looked back up at the board. "She's only five? Since when is a collapsed lung in a child that age considered routine?"

"When that child has been kicked by her father. And I worded that badly. It's never routine." Just saying the words made a jet of anger spurt through Zeke's chest. What kind of monster hurt his own child? Or any child?

"That's horrible." Her voice came out as a whisper.

The boards listed names and ages and team members, but nothing more.

"I know. I thought maybe you'd looked at the charts."

She reached behind her and gripped the edge of the desk. "I just got here. I was going to look at them once I figured out which cases I'd be working on."

The hospital had code numbers for staffing the surgical suites, with the surgeons sometimes handpicking their crews, and other times it was the luck of the draw, depending on scheduling.

Zeke had asked for her, telling himself he wanted to see her in action now that he knew a little more about her. There were a few surgical nurses that he preferred not to work with, either because they were difficult or because they were slow to hand over instruments. Every surgeon had their own style and not everyone meshed with his. He knew he could sometimes be demanding.

Like confronting Lindy about being distracted that first time working together?

It had nothing to do with idle interest and everything to do with watching her work. She definitely had compassion, judging from her reaction to the patient with the collapsed lung.

"These kinds of cases are always difficult."

"Yes. Yes, they are."

The thread of resignation in her voice gave him pause. Maybe her other hospital saw more cases involving domestic violence than Mid Savannah did, although even one case was too many.

"We'll get her patched up, and hopefully the system will do what it's supposed to do and keep her out of that home. I think the dad is in jail right now."

"As well he should be. And her mother?"

"She said she was at work when the incident happened."

"The incident. That's one way to put it." Her tight voice spoke volumes. Then she sighed. "Sorry. I didn't mean to snap. The wheels of justice just never seem to turn fast enough."

"I didn't think you were, and you're right, they don't. But those wheels can't move on their own. There has to be that initial push."

First she'd jumped when he'd come up behind her, now this. Was she just out of sorts today or was something else going on?

"Those situations are just so hard. I actually volunteered at a center helping victims of domestic violence, so it's just straying a bit too close to home."

"That's interesting. I sat in on a meeting of department heads a couple of weeks ago. The hospital has discussed putting together a center for victims of domestic violence or abuse. They already have a grant from a private donor, but they need someone to jump start things. So far no one has stepped up to volunteer."

Lindy's head came up. "Really? I would love to be involved."

"Are you still volunteering somewhere?"

"Not at the moment. I took a leave of absence so I could focus on this job. I thought once I got established I could go back at some point."

An alarm sounded in one of the rooms

and a light flashed in the panel of monitors behind her. She glanced back.

"Go," he said. "I'll see you in surgery as soon as our patient is prepped. If you're serious about helping out with the center, let the administrator know. I'm sure they could use someone who already knows the ropes."

"Thanks. I might just do that." With that, she walked away, headed for the nearby room, leaving Zeke with more questions than answers. He was usually pretty adept at figuring people out after talking with them a time or two. But she was proving to be an enigma.

There was part of him, though, that wondered if he wasn't missing something obvious.

Like what?

He had no idea. And he was definitely not going to start asking her a bunch of questions. He barely knew her. Maybe he should drop in on the hospital administrator himself and let the cat out of the bag about her experience. Not everyone could stomach what went on behind closed doors. The fact that she could...

How did one decide to volunteer for something like that? Especially if you had no first-hand knowledge?

Something kicked up in the back of his head. Lindy had never mentioned a husband.

So? That meant nothing.

Or did it?

Back at the cafeteria it had been Daisy and her mother with no mention of anyone else being involved in her life.

Again, it might not be significant.

And if it was?

Then helping with the program might be the best thing that Lindy could do. Not only for the hospital's sake. But if the weird feelings he had going on were true, then it might do Lindy some good as well.

CHAPTER THREE

FIVE DAYS AFTER helping to re-inflate a little girl's damaged lung, Lindy went and talked to the administrator about the program and offered to help. In doing so, she told him about her past, including the truth behind Luke's death. As she did so, a weight lifted off her chest. He asked if she'd be willing to speak at an informal Q&A about the program that was already in the works. If there was interest, they would move forward. If not, they wouldn't. He would leave it up to her as far as how much she shared.

Could she do it? Well, it was too late now, since she'd already agreed. She just had to figure out what she was going to say.

By concealing her past from her colleagues, she'd wondered if she wasn't contributing to a culture that encouraged people to hide behind a mask of normalcy.

In fact, she'd almost told Zeke in front of the schedule board as they'd talked about the little girl's injuries but had chickened out. If he was at the meeting, he would probably soon know, anyway. And that scared her to death. Would he look at her differently? Feel pity for her?

She didn't know why it mattered, but it did.

As painful as it was to look back at what had happened, Zeke's words about the wheels needing a push to start them turning made a lot of sense. In fact, they'd played over and over in her head all weekend long, and they were still going strong today. Even if it was just manning a phone on a helpline for an hour or two a week after her shift, she could help to be that push that changed someone's life for the better. And it fit right in with her "new beginnings" motto.

She might not be a trained psychologist,

but she was a medical professional. She also had first-hand knowledge of the excuses that kept someone from leaving a deplorable relationship. She'd used those same excuses. Luke's gambling problems—which she hadn't known about when they'd dated—had been spiraling out of control for years.

That was probably part of the reason for the job change right after their marriage, although she didn't know that for sure. He'd gone to great lengths to hide the truth, his behavior becoming more and more erratic and threatening. Once she'd found out about the credit cards he'd taken out in her name, it was all over. Lindy had almost lost her life. But in the end, it was Luke who'd paid the ultimate price.

She still had nightmares about the last day they'd been together. In fact, the night before Zeke had startled her, she'd woken up in a cold sweat and had lain awake for hours. So when Zeke's voice had come out of nowhere at the desk that day, her hands had curled into fists out of instinct.

There'd been no danger, though. Not from him.

But it also made her aware of how she'd changed in the years since the police had come to arrest her husband. She'd dropped her guard in some ways, but in other ways those walls were just as tall and as thick as they'd ever been. Time did dull the fear, but it hadn't obliterated it completely.

And maybe that was a good thing. It kept her wary of what could happen if she didn't stay vigilant. She'd made a vow to herself never to put her daughter in a situation like that again.

Would Zeke be interested in volunteering, if the hospital program did get underway?

What had even brought that to mind?

Maybe the memory of the way he'd operated on five-year-old Meredith Brewster. That man had been a study in compassion that brought tears to her eyes. He'd been worried about an injury to her spleen. Something that was insidious, often having few symptoms as the organ slowly filled with blood. But if it ruptured, the effects could be catastrophic. Luckily everything had come back normal, aside from the collapsed lung and a fractured rib.

Normal?

Nothing about it had been normal.

But she could be the change that started that wheel turning. And maybe asking Zeke to help could be part of that initial push.

Besides, she was curious about what his response would be.

She was sure her parents wouldn't mind watching Daisy for an hour while she talked to the group. Even if it meant exposing scars that weren't completely healed?

If not now, then when?

That was the question and one she had no answer to. So it was time to jump in and make sure that terrible period in her life did some good. Even if it meant she and Zeke might be seeing a lot more of each other.

She wasn't watching the clock. It appeared Lindy had been able to settle into her role of surgical nurse without worrying about her daughter.

Not much of her face was visible with the mask and surgical cap. But those light brown eyes were there. And they were still wreaking havoc with his insides. They came up unexpectedly and caught him looking. Damn. He needed to pay more attention to what he was about to do and less attention to the way she was affecting him.

This might be a routine 'scope, but the child deserved every ounce of his attention. He jerked his glance to the anesthesiologist, who was standing at her head. "She's ready for the procedure," the man said.

The twilight sedation would allow his patient to swallow and follow instructions, but she would have little or no memory of doing so when they were done with the procedure.

Zeke pulled the loupes down over his eyes. "Okay, Tessa, open your mouth."

It always amazed him that part of the brain was still aware and could obey simple commands even while the patient's conscious self was wandering through a gray haze. He slid the endoscope into place. "Big swallow."

Tessa complied, gagging slightly as the scope was introduced. Then it was all business.

"Suction."

Lindy was right there, clearing excess moisture from the child's mouth.

He relayed his observations, knowing the microphone that hung overhead would pick up his words, which he could transcribe later. "Pink mucosa with no abnormalities. Advancing to the sphincter."

He then slid past it, moving into the main part of Tessa's stomach. This was where he needed to take his time. "How's the patient doing, Steve?"

"Everything looks good."

He adjusted the focus of the 'scope and went over the surface of the stomach. "Normal appearance of the fundus and the lesser curvature." But when he turned the 'scope to face the other direction he pulled up short. There was a large eroded section of the lining and a mass about the size of a golf ball. "I'm seeing a nodule with irregular borders in the middle of the greater curvature. There is a moderate amount of erosion of the surrounding tissue. Going to attempt a biopsy of the mass."

He moved in closer and changed the setting, snapping several pictures, and then grabbed a piece of the tissue with the pincers. He cut and cauterized in one fluid motion. "I've got it. Bleeding is negligible."

He surveyed the rest of the stomach but didn't see anything else abnormal, so he eased the 'scope out, his chest tight. He had only seen one other growth similar to this one and the outcome hadn't been good. He could only hope the pathology findings were different in this case and would allow the child to go on with her life.

This time it was Lindy's eyes who were on him, the narrow furrow between her brows saying that she'd had the same suspicion. But now wasn't the time to dwell on that. He needed to finish the procedure and make sure Tessa was okay. Then they could worry about the other stuff.

Fifteen minutes later, she was waking up, lids fluttering as her awareness returned. "Am I okay?" Her voice was raspy, which was normal.

"You did just fine." It wasn't exactly what she'd asked, but close enough. He forced a smile, pulling down his mask so she could see his face. "That wasn't so bad, was it?"

But what was coming might very well prove to be.

"No, I didn't feel anything."

"That's what I like to hear. Dr. Black is pretty good at his job." He glanced at Steve, whose face was as solemn as everyone else's.

"I do my best." The other doctor laid his hand on her head, ignoring the surgical cap. "You did a good job too, kiddo."

Yes, she had. And she'd been stoic every time he'd met with her parents, although they described her pain levels as varying between moderate and debilitating. And now he had to go out and talk to them. The procedure itself had gone like clockwork. Everything else? Well, they would know that soon enough.

"I'm going to go see your mom and dad and let them know you're awake, okay? They'll be able to see you once we get you into your room."

He motioned for Lindy to follow him out. "You said you wanted to talk to me?" She'd mentioned wanting to meet with him after the procedure.

"It can wait."

He frowned at her. Maybe it could, but with the way his day had been he might not have many opportunities to come find her later on. "Follow me down to the waiting room. We can discuss whatever it is afterward."

"Seriously, it's nothing important. Not like…" Her voice trailed away, but he knew what she meant.

"Maybe not, but I think I need something else to think about once this is over."

"It's a hard case."

"Yes, it is." She had no idea how hard. And he hadn't been joking when he'd said he needed something else to think about. Cases like Tessa's brought back memories that were still raw and painful, even after five years. He remembered all too well the pain of that diagnosis, of the symptoms he felt he should have seen. Of the fear that had followed him all the way down to the bitter end.

Did Lindy ever wonder about Daisy when she went into that operating room? Did she think about what it would be like to…lose her? He swallowed hard to control his emotions, forcing himself back to the here and now.

Heading toward the waiting room, Lindy took out her phone and trailed behind a few steps. Texting to see how her daughter was? If it had been him, that's exactly what he would have been doing. Instead, he was pushing through the door to the waiting room to address two people who still had their daughter.

For now, at least.

"Mr. and Mrs. Williams?" He turned his thoughts to his patient's care. The family deserved that.

Tessa's mom and dad separated themselves from a group of people who had been huddled in the back. Zeke was glad he'd stripped his surgical gown and cap off, although he wasn't sure why. He normally left them on, choosing to notify the family as soon as possible. But he'd wanted to face them as a human being first and a doctor second.

Mr. Williams clasped his wife's hands in his. "How is she?"

"The procedure went very well. Tessa is already awake and will be anxious to see you, although her throat will be sore, and she may still be a little bit groggy." He paused. "Can we sit for a minute?"

He motioned to a bank of chairs that were a little removed from the group, sensing they would rather hear the details in private. He glanced at Lindy and gave a slight nod to indicate that she was welcome to join them. He hoped she did, in fact. "This is Lindy Franklin, she's a surgical nurse who assisted me."

"Tessa is a very sweet girl," Lindy said.

Mrs. Williams already had tears streaming down her face, maybe sensing what was to come. "Do either of you have children?"

Zeke froze, the way he did every time he was asked that question. What did he say? Yes, he had a child? Because saying he'd had a daughter who had died of an insidious disease would do nothing to help reassure the two people in front of him.

Lindy saved him from having to say anything. "I have a little girl. She's three. Her name is Daisy."

Tessa's mom nodded and then turned her gaze to him. "It's bad, isn't it?"

"We did find a mass in her stomach. We biopsied it but won't know exactly what we're dealing with until the pathology results come back."

Mr. Williams put his arm around his wife's shoulders. "What do you *think* it is?"

"I don't really want to speculate. It could be benign." He leaned forward, planting his elbows on his knees. "Let's just take this one step at a time, shall we?"

Tessa's father dragged a hand through his hair, his eyes closing for a second. Then he looked at Zeke with a steady gaze. Steadier than Zeke's had been when he'd heard a piece of devastating news. "How long before the results are back?"

"I'm thinking they should be in by Monday. I'll call you as soon as we hear anything."

Mr. Williams drew his wife closer as tears silently tracked down her face. "Thank you for everything." He glanced at Lindy. "And you as well."

"I was happy to be there." The sincerity in her voice was unmistakable. A zip of pride went through him at the great team they had at Mid Savannah. And that included Lindy. Two weeks ago he hadn't even been sure he was going to like her, and now he was sitting here glad she'd come with him to notify the parents. Glad that she'd worked beside him in that operating room. There was something about her that...

Maybe it was the fact that she had a child almost the same age as his would have been.

His eyes skimmed down her profile as she quietly talked to Mrs. Williams about the joys of having a daughter.

He'd once known that same joy.

But there were joys in the memories, weren't there?

Yes, but not enough to want to go on that particular journey again. He'd seen enough in his days as a doctor to make him realize how very tenuous life was and all the things that could go wrong. He saw it day in and day out. Even sitting here talking to Tessa's parents. He had no idea what they were facing.

And Zeke wasn't sure he could face those kinds of odds again in his own life.

As glad as he was to have Lindy here for moral support, he'd better make sure it stayed on a professional footing. Having lunch with her mom and daughter last week had been harder than he'd thought it would be. He dealt with kids every day, but for the most part he was able to compartmentalize that. But interacting on a social level was something else entirely. By the end of the meal, he'd found himself avoiding the child's glance in order to make it through until the end. Hopefully he'd hidden it well enough that they hadn't guessed.

They finished up their conversation and the parents looked at him as if waiting for him to make another statement. "You're welcome to go see her now. And as soon as the discharge papers are ready, you can take her home." He forced a smile. "I'm sure she's more than ready. You'll be hearing from us early next week."

They thanked him again and headed over to be with their family. Tessa's mom was immediately caught up in the embrace of an older woman. Her mother, maybe? He was glad this family could support each other through the good times and the not so good—something he hadn't had.

Lindy met him outside the doors. "Are you okay?" she asked.

"Fine." He leaned against the wall and faced her. Had she seen something in his expression back there? Hell, he hoped not. "Now, what was it you wanted to say to me?"

He hadn't meant it to sound brusque, but when her eyes flickered and glanced away he realized the rough edge hadn't gone unnoticed. Dammit, why did he always do this? He'd done it with Janice too, pushing her away when they should have been clinging to each other.

Turning toward her, he let his fingers trail over hers in apology. The warmth of her skin, even with that brief contact, awoke an answering warmth within him that quickly spread. Big mistake. Big honking mistake.

"Sorry, Lindy. It's been a long, hard day."

"I know, and I don't mean to add to it. Like I said, it can wait."

The warmth evaporated, a sudden chill sending prickles over his scalp. A thought hit him, and his gut lurched sideways. "Are you quitting?"

"What? No." She wore scrubs adorned in balloons today, the multicolored bunches that danced across her red top looking almost obscenely cheerful after the procedure they'd just taken part in. Worse was the fact that his touch hadn't seemed to hijack her senses the way it had his. Except, when he looked closer, her pupils were large and bottomless, handing back his reflection in a way that made him wonder.

She bit her lip. And, dammit, that act sent his thoughts careening in a completely different direction.

"You don't *want* me to quit, do you?" she asked.

He forced his eyes back up. No. He didn't. And he wasn't sure how he felt about that.

"No, of course not. You handled things with Tessa's parents admirably. Better than I did, actually."

She grinned, looking relieved. "Doctors don't always have the best reputation as far as that goes."

Thankful for the lighter tone, he feigned offense. "We don't?"

This time she laughed. "You know you don't."

"Well, on that note, let's change the subject to something a bit more positive."

"Okay, so I did something." She reached into the pocket of her scrubs and pulled out a sheet of printer paper with something typed on it. "I took your advice and went to see the hospital administrator."

He focused on her words, not quite sure what they meant for a second. Then his gaze shifted to the sheet, more notably the hand holding it. It was shaking.

So much for a lighter tone. He started to ask about it, but a group of residents walked by, laughing about something one of them had done earlier today.

"Let's go back to my office. We can talk there."

They arrived, and Lindy dropped into one of the leather chairs.

He rounded the desk and sat as well. "You talked to the hospital administrator about…" Their earlier conversation came flooding back. "About the women's crisis center?"

"Yes."

"What did he say?"

"Well, I remembered what you said about a wheel needing a push to get it turning—"

"I said that?"

She leaned forward in her chair, seeming more at ease now. "You did, actually. And so I went in and gave a little push. I volunteered to help with it."

That shocked him. He hadn't really expected her to go in, even though he'd been the one to suggest it. Or that his words had been what had spurred her to action. He wasn't sure whether to feel guilty or glad.

"And?"

"He's planning on having an informal Q&A on Friday. And he wants me to do one of the presentations."

Lindy? He knew she'd volunteered for a

period of time, but it almost sounded like she'd done more than that. "Wow. That's great. What are you presenting?"

"About why the community needs something like this so much."

"It does, of course." He still wasn't quite sure what was happening. "The hard part seems to be getting women in those situations to leave...to get away from the person or situation."

"I know." She shook her head before he had a chance to say anything else. "No, Zeke. I *really* know."

The emphasis on that word made him stare. "Oh, hell, Lindy. You?"

"Yes, unfortunately. That's what Neil wants me to talk about. I was one of the ones who stayed. Until I realized it wasn't just about me anymore. It was also about my daughter."

His jaw tightened until it sent a warning. He would never understand it. What kind of man hurt the people he was supposed to love?

Well, he might as well point that finger back at himself. Hadn't he hurt Janice by refusing to acknowledge her requests to talk? By not budging when she asked him to redirect his professional life to something that didn't involve kids? But he'd never in a million years raised a hand to her or any other woman.

It didn't make any sense to him. And what kind of person stayed?

Lindy had, evidently. An ache settled in his chest.

"And if Daisy hadn't come along?" The thought of her cowering in a corner while some piece of scum stood over her, glorying in what he'd made her do, made Zeke want to do some serious damage to the man.

"I think I eventually would have left. At least I hope I would have."

The ache spread to the backs of his eyes.

"Is he in prison?"

"No."

Shock roiled through him. Had she not pressed charges?

"He's still out there? They didn't prosecute?"

"He's not out there."

"But I thought you said—"

"I did." She shut her eyes for a second before fixing him with a look that made his blood run cold. "He's dead. And before you ask, no, I didn't pull the trigger. The police did."

He hadn't expected that. Then again, he hadn't expected Lindy to just admit that she'd once been one of those that Mid Savannah hoped to help.

"God. I'm sorry."

"Don't be. The only people I'm sorry for is his family. His parents had no idea what was going on. And I said nothing. I know exactly what it's like to cake on makeup and present a smiling face to hide the damage."

"How long were you with him?"

"A year. I left him two years ago."

Daisy would have been, what, one at the time? Hopefully too young to remember anything.

"I'll say it again… I'm sorry. Not that he's dead, but that you went through any of it."

"I wish I'd left sooner. But there came a point when I didn't have a choice. When I realized that if I didn't get out right then, I probably wasn't going to live to see another day."

She'd almost died? Hell, what had the man done to her?

He reached across and put his hand over the one holding the flyer. "I'm glad."

"You're glad…?"

"That you left."

"So am I. The kicker is that he died before I could get a divorce. So according to legal documents I'm a widow, not a divorcee."

The irony wasn't lost on him.

"At least he's out of your life."

"Not entirely, I'm afraid. Luke had a gambling problem. Some of the debts he incurred affected my credit, even though I paid them off."

This was one of the things that people didn't think of: the financial ramifications of leaving and how to navigate those waters. No wonder Neil wanted her to speak.

"Did you see an attorney?"

"Yep. He helped me negotiate with the credit bureaus to wipe out some of the ones Luke defaulted on. But I couldn't prove that all of them were his."

"Do you need help?"

"What?" Her eyes widened, then flashed with anger. "No. I can manage just fine on my own."

Realizing he'd offended her, he rephrased slightly. "I didn't mean to imply that you couldn't. Sorry if it sounded that way."

"It's okay." She smiled. "Maybe I haven't come as far as I thought I had. I still get defensive from time to time. And having people come up behind me can still make me jumpy."

He'd witnessed that a couple of times. He let go of her hand and came around the front of the desk, sitting on the edge of it. "That's why you took a few years off. It wasn't just because of Daisy."

Another thing that was none of his business. But he was curious.

"Yes. He didn't want me to work…wanted me there when he got home. At first I convinced myself that it was sweet, and that I would be perfectly happy as a housewife and mother. Lots of women are, and I think that's their path. But I have always enjoyed my job. I'm glad to be back in the thick of it."

"Well, we're happy to have you."

This made her laugh. "Are you? That's quite a turnaround from my first day on the job."

An extra little cleft appeared in her left cheek when she smiled. Not a dimple exactly but more of a line caused by her smile pulling more to one side than the other.

Whatever it was, it was damned attractive. As was that glossy head of dark hair.

Easy, Bruen. You don't need to be noticing things like that. Especially not on someone who's suffered so much hurt at the hands of another man.

Maybe his reaction was just a misplaced sense of needing to protect someone.

Whatever it was, he was glad she'd landed at Mid Savannah Medical Center.

"I guess it is a little bit of a turnaround." And he wasn't exactly sure what had made the difference. Maybe it was that smile. Or maybe it had nothing to do with the ridiculous way he seemed to be noticing everything about her. Much better to attribute it to the dedication he saw in her after that first wobbly start.

And he couldn't fault her for worrying or staring at the clock that day.

Weren't there days when his lungs still slammed shut in grief over a loss he might have been able to prevent had he recognized the signs? Yes, there were. More of them than he cared to admit.

It was strange how death could be at opposite ends of the spectrum. To one person, it meant freedom from abuse. To another, it meant the loss of something irretrievable and precious. Like his daughter. And the trust of his ex-wife.

"So this is my cue to ask you that question I mentioned."

"Question? I thought you wanted to tell me that you went to the hospital administrator."

"Yes, that, but I also wanted to see if you'd be interested in volunteering."

His eyes widened. "You want *me* to volunteer? In the program? I thought that's what I was asking you to do?"

"You did. And I am. But you're the head of pediatric surgery. You can bring another side to this. There are a lot of women who were in the same position I was. Women with children. Women who stay, in spite of those children." He watched her take a deep breath. "Remember Meredith Brewster?"

"The pneumothorax case?"

"Yes. There are thousands of Meredith Brewsters out there, who get hurt because women stayed in terrible relationships. You could speak about that. Tell hurting women what you've seen over the years. Maybe you can change someone's mind."

He frowned. "I'm not sure about that. Would I have changed your mind?"

The answer was suddenly very important to him. Especially in light of what he'd just learned about her.

Her eyes met his, staring at him for a long second. "Yes. I think you might have." Her index finger wrapped around his. "This feels right, Zeke. I'm glad I'm here."

Glad she was at Mid Savannah? Or glad she was in his office, practically holding his hand?

Because hell if he wasn't glad of both of those things.

The swirling in his head started again, maybe in reaction to her words. Or the light scent that her movements sent his way. Whatever it was, it was making him want to do something crazy. Something more than what they were currently doing.

"I'm glad you are too." He turned his palm and caught her hand, drawing her to her feet. "And it does feel right. Very, very right."

Her eyes held his, a growing warmth in their depths he hadn't noticed when this conversation had started.

He tightened his grip slightly and the muscles in his biceps tightened as he drew her hand closer. Except it wasn't just her hand that answered the request. Her whole body did, taking a step toward him.

Sliding off his desk, he found himself standing within inches of her. He willed himself to let go of her, and he succeeded in uncurling his fingers. Except his hand seemed to have a mind of its own, lifting to cup her face.

"Yes. I think you could have talked me into almost anything."

As soon as she said the words he was lost, his mouth coming down to meet hers and finding her lips so much softer than he expected. And when she kissed him back, his world exploded—a million fragments flying in all directions. And for once in his life he didn't care which pieces he found. Or which ones were lost forever.

CHAPTER FOUR

SHE'D THOUGHT SHE'D never enjoy another kiss.

But, God, when Zeke asked if he could have made her change her mind, she'd melted inside. He acted like it mattered. Said that her being here did feel right.

And so did this.

The heady warmth of his mouth filled her senses, and she couldn't get enough of the taste of him, of the smooth slide of skin against skin. It all melded together into a luscious blend she would never get out of her head. The second he'd come around that desk, she'd started wondering what it would be like if he touched her.

It was so much better than she imagined.

Maybe that was what had made her curl

her finger around his. Curiosity. What she hadn't expected was the jolt of need that rocked her world and nearly made her gasp aloud. Had she ever experienced that before? She didn't think so.

Then he'd done the unthinkable and wrapped his whole hand around hers. Her senses had been swamped. A tsunami striking shore and wiping out every rational thought in its path.

She was still caught in its grip.

A tiny sound came out of her throat, and she inched closer, his hard chest brushing her breasts. Her nipples tightened instantly.

She wanted him with everything that she had.

The hands that had been cupping her face moved to her hips, and she thought he was going to haul her against him completely, but he didn't. His grip was tight, but it was as if he were holding her in place, keeping her still. Was he trying to torture her?

Something warred inside her, telling her

to take another step and test that theory…
see just how strong his resolve was, and just
how much this kiss was affecting him.

Surely he'd been swept along by the same
wave.

I dare you, Lindy. Do it.

She opened her mouth, dumbfounded by
the fact that it was something she'd never
done before. Would never have thought of
doing.

Ever.

The thought awoke some rational part of
her brain, and she froze.

What was she doing here? Wasn't this exactly what she'd warned herself about: im-
pulsively jumping into something she should
avoid?

Maybe. But for now…

She closed her eyes, realizing this was
about to end. Just one more second. Then
she would move away.

As if he'd read her thoughts, the pressure
on her hips increased. Only instead of eas-

ing her closer, he propelled her a step backward, removing all points of contact—right before his head lifted.

There was a glazed look in his eyes, that said stopping hadn't been easy.

Well, join the club, mister.

Only in the end he'd been stronger than she had, and that bothered her on a level she didn't want to explore.

He spoke up first. "Damn." He pulled in an audible breath and let it hiss back out. "I'm sorry, Lindy. I have no idea where that came from."

She did, but she wasn't about to shoulder the blame by herself. At least not out loud. Inside, it was a whole different matter. She was the one who'd started down this road, but she wasn't quite sure why. Maybe the realization that she wasn't afraid of him, at least not physically.

Emotionally?

Lord. This man could destroy her, if she let him.

She needed to make sure something like this didn't happen again. She'd been so proud of her resolve, telling herself she would turn down any and all offers to date if they came about, which they hadn't.

Would I have changed your mind?

His earlier words whispered through her head, and suddenly she wasn't sure she could have been as strong as she'd thought. If he'd asked her out, could she have refused?

Hadn't that kiss answered that question? It had.

And that scared her on a completely different level.

She went with the first thing that came to mind. "Domestic violence is an emotional subject. You didn't know about my past— and, honestly, I had no intention of saying anything until the Q&A. The last thing I need is anyone's pity."

Oh, God, was that why he'd kissed her? Because he felt sorry for her?

"You think that came out of pity?"

This time he took hold of her hips and tugged her against him, making her very aware of where things stood between them. "This has nothing to do with pity."

Then he was gone, this time back behind the refuge of his desk, leaving her standing there…her breathing not completely normal yet. Neither was the rest of her. Little charges of electricity were still zapping between neurons, hoping to be reignited.

Not a chance.

She needed to get out of there. Before she did something she'd regret.

"I should go."

He pushed the flyer across the desk to her. "If you still want me to be there on Friday, I will. How long does my part of the presentation have to be?"

She was tempted to tell him to stay away. But surely by the end of the week she'd be able to put out the rest of today's embers.

And if she couldn't?

Then she was in big trouble.

"Around ten minutes. Do you want me to put you down?"

His thumb tapped out a rhythm on the surface of his desk, and she held her breath. As scary as this was, she really did think he could make a difference in the program.

And if he ended up making a difference in her instead?

Well, she would have to deal with that when and if it came up.

"Yes. Put me down."

"Okay, I will. And thank you."

She didn't say what she was thanking him for. Instead, she just turned around and hightailed it out of there, all the while praying that tomorrow would find her strong enough to put this all behind her.

Because the last thing she needed was to get involved with someone, especially someone she worked with. Because if things went south…

Lindy, they've already gone so far south they've jumped off the bottom of the globe.

Ha! Well, then, it was up to her to reel them back in until her feet were standing on firm ground.

No more talk of tsunamis. Or electrical charges.

And, most of all, no more kissing of hunky surgeons.

Who was she kidding? The truth was she would probably be reliving that kiss in her dreams. Tonight. Tomorrow night. And any number of unnamed nights in the future.

And although Friday might seem like quite a way off right now, it would come long before she was ready for it to.

So all she could do was regroup, and hope she could pretend she'd recovered from their encounter. Even if it was a complete and utter lie.

Tessa's results were in. Zeke counted to five before opening the digital file. Either her parents would be referred to an oncologist, or he would schedule her for surgery to remove a benign tumor. He certainly knew what he hoped for. But what he hoped for didn't always come to pass.

He clicked on the folder, his glance skipping through everything but the meat of the report: *...atypical cells...noninvasive...*

He almost went slack with relief. It wasn't quite benign, but it wasn't cancerous either and more than likely confined to the area in which it was found. That was good news. Great news, in fact.

The tumor would still have to be removed, and Zeke would need to get clean margins so that the growth didn't come back, but there would be no need for radiation or chemo treatments.

His fingers went to his cellphone to tell Lindy the good news, then he stopped. He didn't usually call his surgical team individually and relay test results. They normally found out, but that was because of follow-up surgery or treatment.

The truth was he just wanted to hear her voice. Maybe to make sure she was okay.

His oath as a doctor was to do no harm. And he wasn't quite sure he'd lived up to that in this case.

He still wasn't sure what had caused that kiss the other day, even though he had repeatedly micro-analyzed everything that had led up to it. To the point that it kept him awake at night and had ended with him standing under a cold blast of water on one occasion.

Not that he was any closer to an answer now than he had been the day it happened. It had changed the way he scheduled his surgeries, though. Whereas where he might have requested her as part of his team before, he was now loath to attach her name to anything connected with him. She'd probably noticed, but if she was smart, she'd be relieved by it.

Of course, there was the little matter of her wanting him to help with the Q&A on Friday and with the program itself, but surely that wouldn't require a lot of time together.

He picked up the phone again. But this time it was because he remembered her asking to be kept in the loop regarding Tessa's results. But maybe he would simply text her rather than call.

He punched in the words as quickly as he could, as if it would limit his contact with her. Tessa's results are in. Atypical cells, but no malignancy. Will follow up with surgery at a later date. He then hit "send" and set the phone down again, forcing himself to go back to work, rather than worry about whether or not she would get the message and/or respond. He'd almost succeeded when a little *ding* told him he had an incoming message.

From Lindy?

Just leave it.

Too late. His glance was already on the

screen. It was from Lindy, but the message was short and succinct. So glad!

And that was that.

The next thing he knew, the phone was ringing. He swallowed when he saw it was from the same person.

This time his subconscious didn't argue with him. He picked it up and punched the button. "Bruen here."

As if she wouldn't know who was on the line.

"Hi, um… I was just checking to see if you know when surgery will be."

"I haven't scheduled it yet. I just got the report."

"Oh, okay." She hesitated, then said, "I'd like to be on the surgical team, if I could."

"Of course." He wasn't sure why she felt she had to ask. His heart clenched. Maybe because he'd avoided putting her on the schedule. It had probably made something that wasn't really a big deal into something more than it was. Except to him it had been a very big deal. He'd never kissed a woman in his office before. And certainly not someone he worked with.

"I was already planning on it."

"It just seemed as if…"

He could almost hear the shrug on the other end of the line. Not willing to confirm that he was avoiding her, he countered by finishing her sentence in a completely different way. "It just seemed as if the schedules have changed? They have. I feel like I've been overtaxing some of the nurses and am trying to make things a little more equitable. Spread the load out among more people."

It wasn't exactly the truth, but it was better than saying he didn't want to work with her anymore. Because he did. He just wasn't sure it was a good idea.

"Okay. I just didn't want what happened to change our working relationship."

He assumed she was speaking somewhere where she couldn't be overheard. Maybe she wasn't even at the hospital today. "It won't as long as neither of us lets it."

Hadn't he already done that?

"Thank you. I, um… I promise I wasn't throwing myself at you."

That was the last thing he would expect from her. "I know. I promise I wasn't throwing myself at you either." He couldn't stop the smile that formed at those words. "Like you said, Lindy, it was an emotional subject. I think it just caught us both off guard. I'm glad you told me, though. I do think you'll be a great asset to the new program."

"I think you will be as well. You still want to come, don't you?"

Hmm…that was probably going to be a yes on more than one level. But he wasn't going there.

"I do. And like I said, you're the perfect person to talk about what it's like to survive domestic violence. Not everyone there has been through what you have."

"I'm very glad of that." He thought he

heard a sigh. "I'd appreciate it if you'd keep this between the two of us."

Was she talking about the kiss or her background? It didn't matter. He'd never been one for indulging in workplace gossip—or workplace romances, for that matter—and he wasn't about to start now. "Don't worry about it. I've told no one. It's no one's business but yours."

"Thank you. I know I'm talking about it at the meeting, but I'd rather control how much is shared."

"Completely understandable." He picked up a pencil and wiggled it between his fingers, surprised by how comfortable he felt talking to her, even after what had happened. What he'd expected had been awkward silences on both ends of the line. It was nice. As was hearing her voice again.

A little too nice.

"Well, I'll let you go."

The pencil went still. "Okay. I'll let you know when Tessa's surgery is."

They said their goodbyes and then she was gone, leaving him to wonder if the next face-to-face meeting would prove to be just as easy as that phone conversation had been.

Somehow, he doubted it. But if they could do it once, they could do it again. At least he hoped so. Because it would make work—and his life—that much easier.

Why had he thought this would be easy? He scheduled Lindy on his next surgical day and the second he saw her brown eyes peering at him from above that mask, he knew he should have waited a few more days. Because his glance had slid over her and remembered exactly what her lips looked like. What they felt like.

How they tasted.

Damn. But the only thing he could do was stick to the plan of getting past that memory. It would get easier with time.

Lindy, on the other hand, seemed fine. Her eyes twinkled when she saw him, and he knew she was smiling beneath the mask, her nose crinkling in that adorable way that went straight to his gut. "This looks like an interesting case."

It was going to be interesting all right. And that wasn't including the case.

"The infection hasn't responded to antibiotics, like we'd hoped." These pulmonary cases actually were interesting, but they were also nerve-racking. There was always the possibility of spreading the bacteria to other parts of the lung. This time, though, the pocket of infection was encapsulated and hopefully it could be removed and the lung re-sectioned, barring any complications.

That wasn't the only reason they were nerve-racking. They also brought up a lot of unwanted memories. His ex-wife had wanted him to change specialties for just this reason. Pulmonary cases almost always sent him home in a stupor that had nothing to do with drugs or alcohol.

That first year had been the worst. He would spend weeks either not speaking or lashing out in anger if Janice tried to talk to him. Not physically, but he'd made it clear he didn't want to interact. In failing his daughter, he'd also failed his wife. She'd needed him. And he hadn't been there. She'd rightfully filed for divorce on the anniversary of Marina's death.

"Zeke?"

Lindy had asked him a question.

"Sorry, what?"

"How many of these have you done?"

He told the truth. "Too many." He'd saved a lot of lives, but he'd also lost the one he'd needed to save the most.

His daughter had died of childhood interstitial lung disease, only he hadn't recognized it for what it was. Not at first. Not until it had been far too late.

The guilt of that had almost killed him. He was a surgeon, supposedly one of the top in his field, and still he'd missed it.

He could remember the times when Marina's cough had turned into something worse, the recurrent bouts of bronchitis and pneumonia visiting their neck of the woods time and time again.

By the time they realized what they were dealing with, they'd been unable to stop it. The fluid in her lungs that last time had been virulent and aggressive, and her tired body could no longer fight the ravages of her disease. Marina had died, obliterating his heart with one swift blow. And his marriage had imploded a year later, when he'd refused to leave his field of medicine.

His wife had protested his decision, saying, "It won't bring Marina back."

It hadn't. But what it had done was destroy any possibility of saving his marriage.

At the time, he'd felt he had no choice. As if his penance was in trying to save other people's children. Even if doing so carved out another little piece of his heart.

Lindy shifted beside him, reminding him that he had a job to do.

So he took a deep breath. "Ready, people? Let's get to work."

And work they did. The patch of infection was the size of a baseball, bigger than he'd originally thought, and it required cutting away more tissue than he'd anticipated. But he wanted to get it all, otherwise it might come back, and none of them wanted that.

Lindy was right beside him, having instruments at hand almost before he asked for them. It was what separated a good surgical nurse from a great one. And she was definitely one of the great ones. Even after having been out of the game for...what had she said? A little over three years?

"Looks like we've gotten it all. We'll ship the tissue off to Pathology and have another culture done."

"It looks good. Really good." Lindy murmured the words over his shoulder.

Her praise sent a burst of warmth through

him that had nothing to do with a job well done and everything to do with the stuff that had led to that crazy kiss.

He'd better put a stop to those thoughts right now.

Soon they'd closed the wound, and Zeke breathed a sigh of relief. Part of the patient's aftercare would be IV antibiotics, and the culture would help determine what this particular strain would respond to, although they'd tried most of the broad-spectrum ones already. The ball of infection had lain there unchanged by anything they'd thrown at it. Hopefully manually removing it would make any microbe that remained lose its hold on her.

One of the other nurses took the specimen cup and marked it with their patient's number and date of birth and hand-carried it down to the pathology lab. She called up saying the lab was going to put a rush on the results. "Tell them I said thanks. They can ping my cell when they get it."

"I'll let them know."

Zeke waited until his patient came round, while other members of the team worked on getting their instruments packed away for sterilization.

When they were done, he turned to Lindy. "I could use a coffee. How about you?"

At her slight frown he realized, given the circumstances, he probably shouldn't have asked, but he'd done it out of habit. How many times had he invited whoever happened to be standing around if they wanted to go for coffee? It didn't mean anything, but she evidently thought differently. And maybe it did. But he wasn't going to attempt any big explanations. If she wanted to say no, that was fine.

"Sounds good."

He blinked in surprise but couldn't say he was disappointed by her answer. He liked having company after a difficult surgery. No one had ever taken those invitations to mean anything other than what they were.

The camaraderie of teamwork. Sometimes there were seven staff members seated around that table in the hospital cafeteria. And sometimes there were two. He looked around, but the room had basically emptied now that the patient had been wheeled to Recovery, so there was no one else to invite.

He could do this. They were both grown-ups, both capable of getting past one little mistake. Little? Hmm, not according to the dreams that still plagued him at night.

Saying that, he'd rather not have a bunch of people see him having coffee with the new nurse, especially in light of what had happened. So, yes, he'd been stupid to ask. But maybe if they went somewhere else, there would be less cause for tongues to wag.

"I know a coffee shop just down the road from the hospital. It'll get us out in the fresh air for a bit, if you can spare the time."

"I'm due for a half-hour break, so it's fine." But she didn't sound quite as sure as she had a moment ago. Did she think he was asking her out on a date? He didn't want to set her straight and embarrass her, although he had a feeling she had no such illusions.

"Are you up for walking?"

She glanced down at her shoes, which looked comfortable. "I'm good."

Soon they were out the door. "Is it Mulroney's just down the street?"

"Yes. I forgot you're from the area."

He stuffed his hands in his pockets as the full force of the Savannah heat hit him.

"I might need to worry more about melting than what kind of footwear I have on." She laughed as she said it, though.

"I take it you'd rather not have your coffee on the shop's patio?"

"I'd prefer my air to be conditioned, if you don't mind. The cooler the better."

This time he was the one who laughed. "I admit I didn't think this out as well as I might have."

Thankfully, it didn't take long to reach

their destination, and the interior of the shop was indeed blessedly cool.

He found a table in a secluded corner of the coffee bar and motioned her to take a seat. A minute later, one of the servers came over and asked for their order. "Go ahead," he said.

"I'd actually like an iced coffee, please, with extra sugar."

His brows went up, but he said nothing, instead ordering his own coffee black and waiting until the server moved away to another customer.

"Would you have ordered that at the hospital cafeteria?"

She smiled. "Have you actually had the coffee there?"

"Have you?"

"No." Her teeth came down on her lip. "I just assumed it was the same as most hospital cafeteria meals. I've come here the last two times I've had a break. I even brought

Daisy here once and ordered her a hot chocolate."

"Your husband never…?"

She didn't ask what he was talking about. "No, never."

There was a tight set to her lips that warned him not to push his luck, so he moved on to a less volatile subject. "Did Mulroney's chocolate get Daisy's stamp of approval?"

"She loved it. My mom actually brought her to meet me that day. She's been great about watching Daisy for me. She insists, actually. I don't blame her. She missed out on a lot."

So had his mom.

His mom had loved Marina, had loved every second of the time they'd spent together. And then after her diagnosis everything had changed.

They'd no longer had entire days to simply let her visit with her grandparents. By that time Marina had been sick more often than not. Their lives had been taken up with fighting an enemy that refused to let go. In the end that enemy had won, and Zeke had lost everything.

His parents had been devastated when they lost not only their granddaughter but also their daughter-in-law. Janice had told them she was sorry, but it hurt too much to stay in contact with them, so she'd dropped out of their lives completely, moving out west.

His mom never said anything directly, but every once in a while she hinted about him remarrying one day. Her ultimate dream was probably another grandchild, especially since she was now alone, his father having died a year ago. She was still grieving his passing.

As for marriage, Zeke didn't see that happening.

After the way he'd shut Janice out during his grief, he'd been wary of relationships. He hadn't liked who he'd become after Marina's death. He'd been selfish and unsupportive, basically crawling into a dark emotional tunnel that only had room for one occupant: him. His wife had been out of luck.

It had been ugly and wrong, and he didn't trust himself to do things differently if faced with a similar crisis. So he didn't try. He wasn't willing to risk someone else's happiness.

And that kiss with Lindy?

It had been a momentary surge of lust. Nothing more. Nothing less. He'd already nipped that in the bud.

"What about you?" Lindy said. "It seems we're always discussing my personal life. What do you do when you're not at the hospital? You're not married…right?"

She was fishing. It made him smile.

"Don't worry, Lindy. You didn't break up a marriage with that kiss. I did that all by myself quite a while ago."

"So you were married?"

"Yep." He already knew what was coming and braced himself for it, although he was surprised she hadn't already heard. There were still some people at the hospital who'd been there at the time of his daughter's illness.

"Any kids?" Her eyes were curious, but there was still no hint that she knew anything about Marina.

What did he tell her? The truth. After all, look at what she'd shared with him.

"I did have. She died five years ago."

"Oh, Zeke, I'm sorry. What happened, if you don't mind my asking?"

"Not at all. She had an incurable lung disease. She died when she was three and a half."

Her hand touched his, but this time it wasn't out of anything other than sympathy. "I didn't know."

"It's not something that comes up in most casual conversations." Was he saying this wasn't that type of conversation? Maybe. Either he was slipping in his old age, or she had a knack for inviting confidences.

Before he could say anything else, their coffees came, and the discussion soon turned to work, and Tessa's case. "Any idea yet when surgery will be?"

"Soon. The hospital is trying to sync their schedules with our open time slots. I imagine it will be sometime this next week after the open house on the women's crisis center."

"She's a sweet little girl."

"Yes. She reminds me of Marina a little bit."

And just like that, he'd circled back around to the subject of his daughter.

"Tell me about her. What was she like?"

"She was a sweet baby. Janice—my wife—and I knew each other in high school and fell in love. Then came med school and all the pressures that came with it. By the time I was done with that and we were ready to have children, nothing seemed to work. We finally went in for fertility treatments and along came Marina. Everything seemed good. At first."

"You said she had a lung condition. Was it asthma?"

"No, an interstitial lung disease. ChILD, to be exact. She had a type called crypto-genic organizing pneumonia, which is just what it sounds like. She had repeated bouts of lung infections until she couldn't fight them off any longer."

"Did you and your wife split over that?"

"About a year after Marina's death. I wasn't a very nice person during that time."

Lindy's head cocked to the side. "What do you mean?"

He could almost see the wheels in her head turning. "I found out too late that I don't react well to crises. I shut down. Not a trait most women want in a life partner."

"There are worse things."

Looking at it from her point of view, he guessed there were. "Maybe, but in our case it meant the end of our marriage."

"Does it hurt? Treating other people's children, I mean?"

Today's case had been hard. "Sometimes. Especially when the patients are the same age or have a similar illness."

"I can imagine. I'm surprised you still opt to treat those patients."

He shrugged. "How fair would it be of me to refuse to treat a patient simply because it made me sad? Or uncomfortable?"

"I get it." She paused as if thinking. "I get it, but it can't make it any easier."

"No, it doesn't."

They sat in silence for a minute or two, then Lindy sighed and closed her eyes. "They do have great coffee here."

No more confessions? Maybe she was right. There'd been enough soul-baring for one coffee session. And it was probably time to get back.

"I'm not sure about calling a drink with ice 'coffee.'" He smiled to show it wasn't meant as a true criticism.

"Hey, it's made from the same bean that yours is. Like iced tea or hot tea."

He couldn't really argue with that.

The door opened and two nurses from the hospital came in. Lindy recognized them and waved. It served to officially mark the end of personal conversations. And thank God she'd taken her hand off his when their drinks had come. That was all he needed… for the hospital gossip chain to decide to do a little matchmaking based on mistaken assumptions. It was why he hadn't wanted to go to the hospital cafeteria.

Talking about Marina had brought back memories he'd rather have left buried. And to get involved with someone who had a child that was almost the same age as his when she'd died, well, he couldn't imagine it would be good. Or that he wouldn't wonder, year after year, what Marina would have been like at each of those year markers.

Hadn't he already wondered that? His daughter would have been almost nine years old by now. He'd actually looked up a program that could "age" the subject of a photograph. He'd done it with his daughter's picture last year to see what she might have looked like at different stages of her life. He'd printed the images off as a keepsake, but it had been a mistake. The passage of time on those faces had haunted him for months afterward, and he preferred to remember the flesh and blood child, rather than some hazy possibility that would never come to pass. He'd finally had to bury those prints deep inside one of his desk drawers at home. He probably should throw them away, except the thought of doing so felt wrong, like he was throwing away everything that could have been. So he'd kept them. He hadn't thought about those photos for months.

He'd be better off not thinking about them now either.

"My mom is planning to come to the

Q&A, even though I told her it was no big deal."

"I don't blame her. She must be proud of how far you've come."

Lindy shrugged. "I'm only mentioning it because she'll want to bring Daisy. Are you planning to show anything graphic?"

"I haven't actually thought about what I'll say, but no. No graphic shots of wounds or anything upsetting."

Although the fact that they even had to have a center like this should be upsetting.

"The hospital has a daycare center for employees. I wasn't sure if you were aware of it. I imagine it will be operating for the Q&A as well, if she wants to drop her off there."

"That's a great idea. It might free up time for my mom, if they take kids on a part-time basis as well. Thanks. And speaking of people in the medical field, I'd probably better get going, I imagine my break is just about up."

"And I need to check on today's surgery patient, so I'd better head back as well." He picked up their trash and tossed it into a nearby waste bin. "And I'll let you know as soon as Tessa's surgery date is set."

"Thanks." She smiled, settling the strap to her purse on her shoulder. "And thanks for suggesting coffee. It was good to get away from the hospital, if only for a few minutes."

"Yes, it was."

And with that, they headed back toward the big white building and the reality that came with it.

CHAPTER FIVE

JUST AS SHE'D SUSPECTED, Lindy's mom had insisted on coming to the Q&A, promising she'd whisk Daisy to the daycare center as soon as the actual meeting started, just in case the conversations became too much for little ears.

Lindy wasn't planning on sharing the worst of the worst, but still it made her nervous to have her mom there.

"Just pretend I'm not here."

"Oh, sure." She smoothed her skirt down over her legs. If she knew her mom, she'd be waving from the audience, which would make it almost impossible to pretend anything.

"And if you want to go out with friends

afterward, I can always keep Daisy for the night."

Friends? Was her mom serious?

She barely knew any of these people.

Um…hadn't she kissed one of them?

That didn't count. Besides, she didn't know Zeke any more than she knew anyone else.

Didn't she? She'd told him things that no one else knew, except her parents, and Zeke had shared things about his daughter that he said didn't get thrown around in casual conversations.

Well, after today everyone in the room would know the basics of what had happened to her, but she certainly wasn't going to get it tattooed across her forehead.

She glanced at the clock and saw there were only ten minutes until she was on.

"Okay, Mom, I should probably go."

"Love you. I'll take our girl out in a few minutes." Rachel kissed her on the cheek and settled into a chair with Daisy on her lap.

By the time Lindy got to the front, Zeke was already beside the podium, talking to a group of people. So was Neil, the hospital administrator. He waved her over.

Taking a deep breath, she smiled and joined them. Were they already volunteers, or were they new to the program like she was?

Dressed in tan khakis and a snug black polo that hugged his biceps, Zeke looked confident and unruffled. A world away from the nervous slosh of stomach acid she was currently dealing with.

"You look nice," he murmured.

A rush of warmth flooded her face. Great. Just what she needed.

"So do you."

And her mom, right on cue, was holding Daisy up and using her hand to move her granddaughter's in the semblance of a wave.

Ugh. So much for presenting a professional appearance.

She pulled herself up short. This wasn't about professionalism. This was about helping women. Women like she'd once been.

Neil nodded at the podium. "Once people take their seats, I'll open with some introductions and then you're on, okay?"

"That's fine." She was as ready as she'd ever be.

"Princess!" Daisy's voice rang out across the gathering, causing a quick burst of laughter.

Oh, brother. Why had she ever thought having her mom here was a good idea? Oh, wait. She hadn't thought that. Not once.

If that wasn't bad enough, her mom was suddenly up front, mingling with the other hospital employees. "Look, Daisy, there's the man you ate lunch with." Rachel turned to Lindy and whispered, "Isn't his name Zeke, or something like that?"

"Yes, but—"

Zeke had moved a short distance away to talk to someone else.

"Let's go say hi. You can tell him about your new princess castle."

"Princess!"

Lindy broke into her daughter's mounting excitement before it got out of hand. "I don't think that's a good idea. I'm sure he's busy."

"Nonsense. I'm sure he'll be happy to see Daisy again." And before Lindy could say anything else, the pair sauntered off, leaving her to groan out loud.

"Mothers."

"Ain't it the truth?" A voice to her side made her look. Nancy, a glass of some type of cola in her hand, smiled at the consternation on her face. "They drive you crazy, but you wouldn't trade them for the world."

"I don't know. Today might be the day..."

They both laughed, and Lindy glanced at her. Maybe the thing about not having made any friends wasn't entirely true. She and Nancy had shared a few moments of chitchat here and there. "Are you interested in volunteering if the center opens?"

"Yep. I have a vested interest, since my baby sister is in a bad relationship and won't leave."

"I'm so sorry." Lindy bit her lip. Not to stop herself from sharing her story but out of embarrassment. She'd once been like that baby sister. And Nancy was going to hear her talk about it soon enough.

"I'm hoping one day she'll realize."

"I do too."

She glanced up to see Zeke staring at her and realized he was holding Daisy. Oh, no. She'd never seen a man look any more uncomfortable than he did right now.

Then it hit her. He no longer had a daughter to hold. And to have Daisy thrust at him like a sack of potatoes…

Her mom had no idea, though, because her mouth was moving a mile a minute just as Daisy threw her arms around Zeke's neck and squeezed.

That was her cue.

"Will you excuse me? I think I have to rescue Dr. Bruen before he passes out."

Nancy giggled. "He does look a little odd. His face is beet red."

"Yes, it is." She made her way through the small groups of people who were conversing, hoping she could get up there before Zeke made some kind of "no-kids" rule for any future meetings, not that he made those kinds of decisions.

She arrived and held her arms out. "Sorry, Zeke. I'll take her."

"It's okay. Your mom was just telling me about your new place. It sounds charming."

She turned toward her mom and gave her a hard look. "It is. But I'm sure you must have other things to do than chat about my living conditions."

"On the contrary. I'm way down on the program so I have plenty of time to kill. Besides, Rachel and Daisy are keeping me from becoming too nervous."

That was the funniest thing she'd heard all day. He was a well-respected surgeon who commanded the operating room the way a ship's captain commanded his vessel. There was no way he would be scared to face a group and talk about what he did on a daily basis.

"I have my doubts about that."

He smiled. "Now, Daisy, on the other hand, wants me to dress up as a princess with her. That does make me nervous."

Oh, Lord. She should have known. How many times had she had to dress in one of her best party dresses in order to have tea with her pint-sized daughter?

"I'm sure. Although that could be an interesting look." She smiled at Zeke, letting her nerves settle. Maybe the look he'd thrown her hadn't been one of horror after all. She'd offered to take Daisy and he hadn't taken her up on it. Although he was right. Lindy was the first one to present.

Lindy's mom chimed in. "We'll have to

have you over for dinner sometime. I'm sure both Daisy and Lindy would love that."

It seemed that with every word she uttered her mom was digging her daughter into a hole and had no idea she was throwing another shovelful of dirt on the growing pile.

"I'm sure Daisy would. I'm not so sure about Lindy," was all Zeke said, throwing a quick smile in her direction.

"Well, I guess this princess had better find her way to the daycare center." Her mom held out her arms. "I'll have Lindy get with you about a date for dinner."

"Do that."

Oh, Lord, why did her mom have to have that ingrained Southern hospitality? And she was so gently insistent that it was the rare person who got offended by it. It was just the way she was. Lindy had learned to appreciate it, for the most part, even if she hadn't quite embraced the trait.

By the time her mom moved away, Neil was asking everyone to find a seat. He presented the basics about what the hospital hoped to do, going over the funding that had already been secured, then went over the list of presenters, which included herself, two of the hospital's resident psychiatrists and Zeke. Once they'd finished, the floor would be open to questions.

Her mom slid back in the room and took a seat in the back just as Neil was finishing up.

"A sign-up sheet will be in the back for anyone interested in giving a few hours of their time. The ultimate fate of the program rests in your hands. And on that note, I'll turn the floor over to Lindy Franklin, who is new to Mid Savannah but certainly not new to working in this type of program." He nodded at her. "Lindy?"

The nerves that had been settled suddenly rose to her throat and threatened to choke her. Then she caught sight of Zeke. Maybe he saw the hint of panic in her face because he edged forward until he was standing just behind her elbow. But far enough away that those around them would simply think he was waiting for his turn.

Just knowing he was there helped her get through the rough patch and she cleared her throat. "Hello, everyone."

A spatter of returned greetings made her smile, and then she was fine. "As Neil said, my name is Lindy Franklin and I am indeed new here. But what he didn't tell you is that I was once the victim of domestic violence."

She watched people shift in their seats as they took in her words. Nancy looked shocked, as did some of the other nurses she worked with. "Most of you didn't know that about me, and that's at the heart of the problem. Most victims will never speak out about what is happening. They rarely seek help. But if they know help is there, it becomes a safety net. One that people like I was desperately need."

She talked about some of the things she

wished she'd known when she'd been with Luke and ways to get the word out to others.

Lindy ended by saying, "We want Savannah to know that help is available. It's free. It's confidential. And we can help you get out. Thank you."

Applause went up and Nancy gave her a thumbs-up sign, while her mom was dabbing at her eyes with a tissue.

Both of the hospital's psychiatrists came up and took her place, discussing between them the psychology of abuse, referencing several things she'd said and using them as illustrations.

"Good job, Lind." Zeke's low voice filtered through, carrying with it a note of admiration. "If what I saw out there is any indication, this program is really going to take off. I'd be surprised if we didn't get fifty volunteers right off the bat."

She'd spoken from her heart, but surely it hadn't made that much of a difference.

You just need to give that wheel a push to get it moving.

Then it was Zeke's turn. And wow. Just wow. He told the story of Meredith Brewster's injuries, being careful to keep any identifying elements out of his speech. But listening to him, she remembered the horror she'd felt on learning a five-year-old child had had to deal with a horrific injury at the hands of a parent. She looked around the room. No one was shifting or looking around. Even her mom was totally caught up in what he was saying. True to his word, he didn't give any of the gory details, but he still got his point across. At the end of his speech, the applause was almost deafening.

Neil moved forward, shaking Zeke's hand and murmuring something to him before turning to the audience. "Thank you to our staff for taking time out of their busy schedules to talk to us. And thank you for being here. We'd like to hear any questions or comments you might have. If you like what you've heard, there are packets stacked at the door that have a list of helpful numbers. And as I mentioned earlier, there's also a sign-up sheet, if you'd like to help this program get off the ground." He glanced at Lindy. "Let me say one more thing. If you feel someone's life is in immediate danger, I would urge you not to wait but to call 911."

The presenters fielded questions between them, with Lindy getting more than her share. She answered as best she could, grateful that everyone was respectful about not asking specifics about her own situation. Twenty minutes later there were no more lifted hands.

"Any other questions?" Neil asked, scanning the group for hands. She kept hers firmly down, even as his eyes slid over her and kept going. "Well, I guess that's it. There are refreshments at the back. Help yourselves and thanks again for letting us take up your time. If you're due back on the floor, please make your way there."

And then it was over. Zeke bumped her shoulder and gave her a smile. "Thanks for asking me to come. I think the hospital is going to do some great things with the program."

"I do too." The casual nudge had made her feel warm and tingly inside. It felt like they were finding their way back to where they'd started. Before that kiss had derailed things.

She spotted her mom, who'd evidently already picked Daisy up from daycare, coming through the door. She glanced back, to see that Zeke was just behind her. "I wanted to say bye to your mom and Daisy."

She smiled. "I'm sure they'll like that."

Rachel spoke up when they got there. "I was just about to suggest Lindy and Daisy come to the house for popcorn and a movie later tonight. You're invited as well."

Well, since she hadn't even given Lindy a chance to say yes or no to her own invitation, it was a bit forward of her to start inviting other people.

"I can't tonight, I'm sorry. I have other plans, but I'd like a raincheck on that dinner invitation you talked about earlier."

"Of course. That's a given. Well, I guess we'll have to watch *The Princess Bride* without you."

"Princess, huh? Looks like I'm missing out. By the way, a little girl gave me a packet of princess stickers that I think Daisy will probably get more use out of than I will."

"Princess!"

"I'll be kind of glad when we move into the martial arts stage," Lindy muttered.

He tilted his head. "Martial arts?"

Lindy laughed. "Basically anything other than princesses. But I'm sure she would love the stickers, thanks for thinking of her."

"I don't have anyone else to entrust them to." A brief shadow went through his dark eyes before it was gone. Remembering his own daughter?

A shard of pain went through her chest. She didn't know what she would do if she ever lost Daisy…didn't even want to think of that possibility. But she wasn't immune from tragedy, she'd already proven that. But surely she had been through the worst that life had to throw at her. Hadn't she?

She knew no one could guarantee that they'd be exempt from tragedy, but she was pretty sure most parents would trade places in a second if they could take away the pain from their child. She imagined Zeke had made all kinds of promises to God, asking Him to spare his daughter. He'd probably even offered his own life up instead.

Except Lindy couldn't imagine a world where Zeke didn't exist, even though she'd only known him a matter of weeks.

Did he still have contact with his ex-wife? Had they divided Marina's things or pictures to remember her by? How heartbreaking would that be during a divorce? Had they squabbled about what things the other could have and what they wanted to keep for themselves?

Lindy hadn't had to go through that. Even if Luke had lived, he'd have been in prison. And the courts would have made sure he had no contact with his daughter ever again.

"Anyway, she'll love them, thank you. I'll get a sticker book for her to put them in."

"I forgot they had books. I'd like to pick one up if I could."

A dangerous prickling started behind her eyes. She blinked it away, but when she found her voice she was horrified to hear a slight waver in it. "You don't have to do that." She didn't want to be the cause of stirring up painful memories. Her parents had tiptoed around the subject of Luke since she'd been home. They knew kind of what had happened, but she'd never told them about the choking incident.

The only people who knew were the police, actually. And the medical professionals that had checked her trachea for damage and swelling. And the bruising... She'd waited for it to subside before she'd packed her things and headed home. For her parents to see that would have been too much. Her dad would have blamed himself for not coming after her. But she might not have left any earlier than she had, and it could have put him in danger as well.

"I'd like to, unless you'd rather I didn't."

"Of course not." She tried to tell him with her eyes that it wasn't necessary, but he simply smiled her concern away. And then her mom kissed Daisy on the cheek and with a quick glance at both of them said she wanted to stop at the store and get some popcorn for their movie night.

"Mom, I can do that."

"No, I'm sure you need to finalize things here." She looked at Zeke. "If you change your mind about coming, have Lindy give you the address. If you've never seen *The Princess Bride* you're missing out. It's quite funny, even for adults."

"I'll keep that in mind. And thank you again for the invitation."

No mention this time of having plans. Had that all been a crock?

"I'll see you in about an hour, Lindy."

Knowing it would do no good to argue with her mother, she nodded.

Once they were out of earshot, Lindy looked at him with what she hoped was a rueful expression. "I am so sorry about that. She doesn't get that not everyone is all about watching movies with her granddaughter."

"She's proud of her, as she should be."

He was right, of course. "Well, I am sorry she pressured you into coming over to the house. She won't be offended if you don't come, especially since you have plans." It was meant as a gentle reminder of what he'd said earlier.

"I did have something planned, but I think I've changed my mind about doing it."

He gave no more explanation than that, so she didn't know if the plans had involved someone else. A date, maybe?

That thought made her heart cramp as a

million images marched past her mind's eye, each worse than the one before it. Zeke kissing other women, trailing his fingers over their bodies. Moving over them as he...

Stop it! Of course the man dated. He'd be crazy not to.

Hmm...*she* didn't date. Did that make her crazy?

That was different.

Before she could respond, Zeke went on, "If the offer is still open, I think I might like to see this famed movie."

"Y-you do?" She'd gotten the impression he wasn't eager to spend time with her outside work, so what had changed? And did she even want it to change? But she couldn't very well retract the offer without having some kind of explanation available, and right now those were in short supply. "Um, okay, Daisy will be ecstatic. If she can even stay awake. She tends to nod off halfway through."

He gave her a quick look. "Are you okay

with it? I don't want to intrude. These meetings are always hard to get through. The reality of what people go through..." He stopped as if realizing who he was talking to. "I'm glad you got away."

"Thank you. I am too. I'm swearing off relationships, though, for a long time."

"I've sworn them off too, so we're even. So, are we good? A movie as colleagues and friends?"

Friends? Wow. A warm mushy feeling crept up from somewhere deep inside her. She'd just been thinking about the fact that she didn't have many friends here yet...that she hadn't had time to develop any, and now Zeke and Nancy had both stepped a little closer. And as much as she didn't want to, she found that she liked it. A little too much.

CHAPTER SIX

ZEKE KNEW EXACTLY why he'd accepted Rachel's invitation. His plans for that evening had revolved around a resolution he'd made as he held Daisy before the open house. He'd originally been pretty horrified when Lindy's mom had thrust the little girl into his arms, but nothing had prepared him for the feeling that erupted when Daisy threw her arms around his neck.

Since Lindy said she'd walked to work that day, they drove to buy popcorn together. The plan was for Zeke to drop her and Daisy off at her house when they were done with the movie. It was on his way home anyway. And Lindy had said if an emergency came up and he needed to leave, she'd just stay with her folks and have them take her home the next day.

"Daisy's in the kitchen with her Mimi" said the man who'd opened the door.

Lindy made quick introductions and her dad, Harold, shook his hand.

"Nice to meet you."

Letting Lindy lead the way, he entered a home.

Not just a house, like his and Janice's had been on too many occasions, even after Marina was born, but a genuine home, filled with warmth and pictures and memorabilia of Lindy's time as a child.

It was much like the home he'd grown up in.

Why had he and Janice done so little of that? He wasn't sure, but it made him wonder if there hadn't been a crack in the foundation of their relationship even before Marina had come along. Her death had just split it wide open and exposed it for what it was.

Looking back, he wondered if he should have taken his ex-wife's advice and kept some of his daughter's belongings. Instead, he had little more than a few ragged photos and several age progression images. Which was what his so-called plans had originally involved this evening. He'd been going to search for them until he found them, and then he was going to shred them.

And that made him a coward. Because the only reason he'd come here was to avoid doing something he probably should have done long ago. Because thinking of all the might-have-beens had eaten at him for the last five years.

And yet here he was, spending time with a family that highlighted everything he'd lost. Wasn't that adding torture to torture?

He didn't know, but it was too late to back out now. He could feign an emergency at the hospital, but he'd already committed to staying for the movie and he wasn't willing to throw the invitation back in Rachel's face after she'd seemed so happy that he'd changed his mind.

He felt a little ludicrous sitting on a couch with a family he didn't really know, watching a film and eating popcorn. But it was ludicrous in a good kind of way. He ate a bite, and then another, and watched the crazy antics of the characters on the screen. In the end it was a movie about falling in love, just like a million other movies he'd watched over his lifetime. But this time it was different somehow.

Daisy stretched out and pushed her socked feet against the arm of the sofa, forcing Lindy over until her leg was pressed against his. "Sorry," she whispered, trying to pull away.

Except she couldn't. And he was against his side of the couch with nowhere else to go. The temptation to slide his arm around her came and went without incident. But not without a trickle of awareness that went almost unnoticed at first. Almost. But not entirely.

She might be sorry, but he wasn't. At least not yet. Right now he was enjoying that low steady hum. The one that lingered just below the surface of his mind, waiting for permission to grow and become bolder. Zeke had no intention of granting that permission, but it was nice to imagine what might happen if he did.

The banter between two of the characters made Daisy chortle loudly. Lindy gave a choked giggle in return. "Sorry," she whispered again. "She loves this movie, especially the sword fight."

"Sword fight, huh?"

He couldn't hold back a smile. And suddenly the hum grew in intensity, egged on by her whispered words and how they were meant for his ears and his alone. Despite being in the middle of her parents' living room, it was as if they were cocooned in their own little bubble of a world. He could see her folks sitting in their chairs, facing away from them as they watched the movie, but they were like so much background noise. As was Daisy, despite her laugh.

Was he the only one who felt it? Or did Lindy sense it as well?

He hoped so, because he was going to feel incredibly stupid if he was the only one who was getting an emotional buzz out of her proximity.

Then a slight sonorous noise came from beside him. He glanced at Lindy, wondering how she could have fallen asleep. But it wasn't her. It was Daisy. She was lying half across her mother's lap, mouth open, making tiny gargling sounds. He chuckled. A second ago, the child had been wide awake.

"Told you," Lindy whispered again, and his innards ratcheted another notch tighter.

"Yes, you did." He kept his own voice just as quiet, not wanting her parents to turn around and see them with their heads close, talking in quiet whispers. Heaven only knew what kind of ideas they would get from that.

Heaven only knew what kind of ideas *he* was going to get.

And that continued pressure of her thigh against his wasn't helping matters. If he wasn't careful, he was going to give them some concrete evidence that he'd rather they not see. The physical attraction was there without a doubt, but Zeke had no intention of letting it go any further than that. Because juxtaposed against the sweet, sweet press of her leg was the reality of Daisy and how it made him ache for Marina. And would likely continue to make him ache with the passing of years.

Someday he was going to have to face throwing away those age progression pictures he'd made. But today was evidently not the day.

"How long is this movie?" he asked.

"We're about halfway through. Everything okay?" She again tried to shift her leg away, but Daisy's feet were still firmly planted against the arm. It looked like she wouldn't budge.

"Fine. And don't worry about moving her."

"I thought you might be getting claustrophobic."

He was getting something, but it definitely wasn't claustrophobia."

"No." On the other side of the attraction issue was the sense that it felt right having her against him, and Zeke didn't want that at all. Because it wasn't "right." None of it was. It was an illusion that would go up in a puff of smoke as soon as they were back in their respective homes.

At least that's what he told himself. It was the only thing currently keeping him sane.

Time to concentrate on the movie. Then he realized that Harold's head had canted sideways, and a sound louder than Daisy's assailed his ears. He glanced at Lindy and she nodded. "Yep. He always falls asleep. I think that's where Daisy gets it from."

And that did it. Zeke put his arm around her, and Lindy melted against him as if she'd been waiting for that all evening.

Had she?

All too soon, the couple got their weird, but happy, ending and he unhooked his arm, pulling it back to his side before they got caught and had to give some kind of explanation. As it was, no one noticed.

Rachel was too busy shaking Harold awake. He grumbled and acted like he'd been watching the film all along. Lindy giggled. "Something else that happens all the time."

Okay. And that was his sign to get up.

In a minute. His right leg had fallen asleep from the way they'd been sitting, but he hadn't wanted to make her move. He still didn't.

Lindy's mom stretched. "Why don't you all stay the night?"

His gut seized. What was she saying? She

wanted him to spend the night with Lindy and the rest of the brood?

As in the same room?

"Mom, Zeke has his own house." Lindy smiled to take the sting out of it. "And so do I."

"Yes, I'll take Daisy and Lindy home and then head back to my place."

"Are you sure?" Rachel insisted.

Lindy saved him from answering. "Yes, we are, aren't we, Zeke?"

Well, she didn't save him entirely.

"Lindy's right on my way so yes. Thank you for the hospitality, though. And the popcorn." He held up his mostly empty bowl. "Where do you want me to put this?"

"I'll take it." Rachel held her hand out. "And thank you for coming. We're really glad you changed your mind."

Zeke stood, pushing his khakis down over his legs.

Harold nodded and shook his hand, grip

firm, even after falling asleep. "Come back any time."

"Thank you, sir. I will."

Lindy was still sitting on the sofa, pinned beneath Daisy's slight frame. Rachel moved forward as if to help, but Zeke got there first. "Here, let me take her."

He hefted the child into his arms, surprised that someone so small could feel so solid. It was good. Felt right.

There were those words again. Words he needed to banish from his vocabulary.

Lindy stood, stretching her back. "I think my whole right side is asleep."

The same thing he'd thought about his leg. It made him smile. "This little thing cut off your circulation?"

"You try holding her for a two-hour movie and see how you feel afterward. Although I wouldn't trade it for the world."

He remembered those days. In fact, the memories of those days had helped him get through the worst of his grief.

"Are you sure about driving us home? I'm sure one of my parents could."

"Like I said, it's on my way. And it'll save your mom a trip there and back."

Lindy switched the car seat from Rachel's car and installed it in his while he held Daisy. "I'll give it back to her tomorrow when she picks us up."

He lowered Daisy into her car seat and carefully buckled her in. Despite the passing of years, he still remembered how to secure a child in their seat.

They were soon on their way, getting onto the highway.

"Thanks again, Zeke. I hope we weren't too boring for you. I'm sure your Friday nights are normally much more exciting."

"Not really. My plans weren't with friends, just myself. I had some things I wanted to catch up on. But that can happen another time. The movie was cute."

"It's a classic. Kind of slapstick humor, but it grows on you."

Kind of like having her beside him had grown on him. A little too much actually.

She leaned back and stretched, the act making her breasts jut out. "I have about a thousand kinks in my spine."

He swallowed, hoping he wasn't about to get a kink in something else. Having her plastered against him had been the best kind of torture. His nerve endings hadn't completely recovered. Maybe they wouldn't until she was out of the car.

"You've been on your feet most of the day, then had the question and answer session and then movie night. It's no wonder."

"Hmm...and your day has been so much lighter?" The words came with a smile and raised brows.

"Okay, we've both had a full day."

"At least I'm off tomorrow. You?"

"I am as well. I try not to work Sundays if I don't have to."

She turned to look at him. "You go to church?"

"Sometimes. My taking off Sundays isn't for religious reasons, though. It's more personal."

When she tilted her head, he knew he was going to tell her, although he wasn't exactly sure why. Maybe it was the time spent at her parents'. Maybe it was the arm he'd draped around her shoulders. But right now he felt connected to her in a way that made him trust her.

"Marina died on a Sunday. It's been long enough ago that I could probably work now, but it's just become a habit. So I've continued it."

A sense of relief whooshed over him when she didn't react in a way that made him feel ridiculous. Instead she covered his hand with hers as it lay on the gear shift. "I think that's a great idea. We all need rest. And it kind of makes her day sacred and ensures she's remembered. I think Marina would like it."

"Thanks." A lump formed in his throat

that had nothing to do with his daughter's death. Lindy had endured her own tragedy and yet she was able to see past it to other people's suffering. Maybe he should try being a little more like her.

She glanced behind her to the back seat. "I can't believe she's still asleep. I hope this doesn't mean she'll be up at the crack of dawn. I wouldn't mind sleeping in for once."

An image of Lindy waking up slid into his mind. Brown eyes blinking open, a slow smile on her face as she peered up sleepily…

At him.

And there it was. The stupidity that he couldn't seem to shake. With each instance it seemed to embed itself deeper into his brain, making it harder and harder to shake.

Hell, he was a surgeon. Shouldn't he be able to cut it out, the same way he was going to dissect the mass in Tessa's stomach?

That was evidently beyond his purview. He could operate on real people, but not on himself.

He suddenly realized Lindy was looking at him—waiting for an answer to her statement.

"Daisy's had a pretty big day. We all have."

They arrived at her house a few minutes later. When he started to get out of the car, she said, "I can get her."

"I'm sure you can, but it'll be easier if I help. Plus we have the car seat."

"Oh, that's right."

Exiting the vehicle, he opened the passenger door and undid the straps of Daisy's car seat. "Do you want me to get her or the seat?"

She hesitated. "You decide."

"How about if you unlock the door and I'll carry her in and then come back out and get the car seat?"

"Are you sure?"

He was already lifting the sleeping child out of the seat. Lindy watched for a second, then suddenly spun around and headed up the walk, digging in her purse for something. Probably her keys.

By the time he got to the door, it was standing open, with Lindy beckoning him inside. "It's this way."

He followed her into the house and down a hallway. She turned on lights as they went. Then she opened a door and pressed a switch, but the lights must have been on a dimmer switch because the room didn't erupt in a blast of light. Instead it was soft and muted. He saw a toddler bed over to the right and headed there as Lindy pulled down the covers.

He padded over to the bed and carefully laid Daisy down. If this had been Marina, he would have kissed her goodnight. But it wasn't, and it wasn't for him to tuck her in. He took a step back and let Lindy do the honors. And just as he would have expected, she leaned down and kissed her daughter on the forehead before tucking the light covers around her. She put a finger to her lips.

Ha! He wasn't about to say anything, so no worries there.

She tiptoed out of the room and shut the door behind her.

"Is she a light sleeper?"

She smiled. "No. That girl could sleep through a hurricane, I believe."

"That makes it nice for you."

"Yes. She's always been a good sleeper, even as a baby."

Then she shut her eyes. "Sorry. You don't need to hear about that."

"About what?"

"Nothing. Can I get you some coffee? A glass of wine?"

"No wine. A beer would be nice, if you have one."

"I do, actually, although it's light. Is that okay?"

"That's actually perfect, since I'm driving home." Light beer had a lower alcohol content than the regular version. Those calories had to be cut from somewhere, didn't they?

"Why don't you sit in the living room while I get them? I could use a glass of wine to unwind."

Instead of going into the other room like she'd suggested, he followed her into the kitchen while she popped open the refrigerator and emerged with a long-necked bottle and some wine.

"Do you want yours in a glass?"

"Nope. I'll drink it straight up."

He waited for her to get a wine glass down from a tall glass-fronted cupboard and then took the bottle opener she handed him. He popped the top on his beer and the contents of the bottle made a satisfying hiss as the carbonation was released. He took a long pull and followed her into the other room.

"I haven't finished furnishing the place."

She was right. The living room consisted of a sofa, a coffee table and a television set.

Which meant he was going to have to sit next to her. Again. But at least he wouldn't have a child shoving them against each other.

He'd already been desensitized to her proximity during the movie. Right?

Somehow he didn't think so. But rather than looking like a coward for standing while she sat, he eased himself down onto the sofa, grabbing a coaster and setting his drink on it.

"Nice place."

"My parents helped me find it." Her lips twisted, and she took a sip of her wine, kicking her shoes off and tucking her feet under her. She turned toward him. "Actually, they helped me in a lot of ways. They offered to let me keep living with them until I could get back on my feet, but their house is small, and I thought I'd be in the way with Daisy. They love her dearly, but I felt they needed to be able to have some semblance of privacy, although she still takes up a lot of their lives. It's worked out, though."

He picked up his beer and took another

slug, the brew tasting good as it went down. "So you like your job at the hospital?"

"I love it more than you can know."

"Oh, I think I already know. If it's anything like the way I feel about surgery, then it's irreplaceable. It has its drawbacks and heartbreaks, but for the most part I couldn't ask for a better life."

There was a photo of her and Daisy on top of the television. Lindy was in a hospital gown and she was holding Daisy in her arms. There was no sign of her ex. Maybe he was the one who'd taken the shot, although he couldn't imagine Lindy wanting to keep the picture if that was the case.

He could remember his ex holding Marina when life had been simple and still filled with happiness. But in the end they just hadn't been able to cope with the loss as a couple.

A thought came to mind. "I got a text during the open house about Tessa's surgery.

It's scheduled for Tuesday. Do you still want to be on the roster?"

"Yes. Please." She wrapped her hand around her bare feet and tugged them in closer.

Her toes were tipped in some kind of silvery glitter polish that he hadn't noticed when she'd first taken her shoes off. It was not a color choice he would have expected her to wear, and he found himself fascinated by the way the flecks of color caught the light. "Interesting choice in nail polish."

She glanced down and smiled. "Sometimes I like to be a little wild and crazy. Just because I can."

He'd almost forgotten. There'd evidently been a time when she couldn't express herself without fear of recriminations. But over something as simple as nail polish? "Did he control that too?"

"No, not really. But there were times he'd ridicule my decisions if they didn't fit in with who he thought I should be."

"And who did he think you should be?"

"I was never quite sure. Maybe the perfect little wife. But I was the wrong person to choose, then, because I'm so far from perfect that it's not even funny."

"Oh, I don't know. I don't think you're that far off the mark."

He hadn't meant to say that. As her eyes came up and met his, he saw a flurry of emotions go by in quick succession. Then she smiled. "You obviously don't know me very well if you can say that. And I remember when you were worried that I couldn't keep up with the surgical department."

"Like you said, I obviously didn't know you back then. Because you keep up just fine."

"You didn't know me back then, but you do now?"

A strange expectancy hung in the air between them, and he wasn't sure what she wanted him to say. Or if she wanted him to say anything at all.

He was torn. He did feel like he'd gotten to know her over the last weeks. And that was part of the problem. Part of what made him keep circling back toward her, even when he wanted nothing more than to fly far away.

"I think maybe I'm coming to."

"I think maybe I'm coming to know you too. You're not quite the ogre I thought you were in the beginning."

His brows went up. "You thought I was an ogre?"

"Well…maybe ogre is too strong a word. But I was a little intimidated by you."

In the same way her husband had intimidated her? He didn't like that. He propped his arm on the back of the couch. "I don't normally have that effect on people. At least I hope I don't."

Even when he'd been at his worst, Janice hadn't been afraid of him.

"It was me. You've been great, and I appreciate it." She leaned a little closer and the heat from her body slid in and made his muscles loosen and then slowly tighten again.

He thought for a minute she might lay her head on his shoulder. He swallowed, suddenly wanting her to do exactly that. He wanted her pressed tight against him like she'd been at her parents' house. Only this time there'd be no one to see them.

Maybe that was his cue to leave.

Except she chose that very moment to tip her head back and look into his eyes. What he saw there made him stay exactly where he was, his breath stalling in his lungs long enough to make him feel woozy. Then it pumped in a full load of oxygen, sending it throughout his body in a rush of endorphins that made him want to do the unthinkable.

Time to break the spell. "Tell me it's time to go."

The fingers behind her on the sofa went to her shoulder and cupped it.

"Do you want to go?"

That was a loaded question if ever he'd

heard one. He tipped his beer from side to side. "My bottle's empty."

She licked her lips. "So is my glass. Do you want another one?"

"No. I don't."

"Then what *do* you want?"

That was a tricky question, because what he wanted didn't come in a bottle. Or a glass. He should repeat that he wanted to leave, but somehow he couldn't force the words out.

He touched a finger to the polish on one of her toes. "I want to be like this nail polish."

"I don't understand."

"I want to be wild and crazy. Just because I can. Isn't that what you said?"

"Yes," she whispered. "It is."

"So if I did something wild and crazy… what would you do?"

"It depends what it is."

His brain told him to stop right here, even as something else told him to keep on going. "'It' would be kissing you."

She gave him a slow smile. "Then I might have to do something a little wild and crazy too. Like kiss you back."

"Honey, that is what I was hoping you'd say."

And with that, he did something he'd been wanting to do ever since that day in his office. And again on her parents' sofa. He drew her close and planted his mouth on hers.

CHAPTER SEVEN

SHE'D THOUGHT THEIR first kiss had been out of this world?

Well, nothing could have prepared her for the sudden overload of sensations—the heady extravagance—of finding his lips on hers again. Why had she ever thought avoiding this was the smart thing to do?

Even as he drew her closer, her arms snaked around his neck and she gave herself fully to the kiss. It was what she wanted. What she needed. And just like her nail polish it was wild and crazy and just for her. She deserved a night of wanton sex. Sex that was offered with open arms and freely accepted.

She moaned when his tongue slid inside her mouth, the sweet friction sending goosebumps dancing across her body. A body that could rapidly grow used to his touch. His tongue eased back, and she was suddenly afraid he was going to take that away from her. Her hand went to the back of his head as if to hold him there. He surged forward again, and the burst of pleasure it brought was almost too much to bear.

Zeke was all she wanted right now.

Her fingers twined in the hair at his nape, and what she'd thought of as slightly long before became the perfect length. She tightened her fingers and felt him smile against her mouth.

When he pulled back, her eyes opened in a rush, afraid he was going to leave after all.

Instead, his thumb rubbed across her lower lip, the lip that was now hyper-sensitized to his touch. "Are you wild and crazy enough to let me stay? Just for tonight?"

"Yes."

He scooped her up in his arms and stood, his mouth descending for another swift kiss before saying, "Where?"

"I don't care. You choose."

"I would say right here, but I want complete privacy. I don't want some small visitor wandering in."

He was right. She didn't want that either. "My bedroom is the last door on the left."

That was all he needed evidently. He strode down the hallway, his steps light but sure, quick but not rushed. Was that what his lovemaking would be like?

She gulped. She wasn't sure she could wait.

And then they were inside. He pushed the door shut with his foot and turned them to face it. "Lock it, Lind."

She did, although her fingers trembled slightly as she turned the latch.

He walked to the bed and dropped her on it without warning. She bounced a time or two, making her laugh. The laughter died when he leaned over her, hands landing on either side of her on the bed.

God.

A quick flash of muscle memory made

her freeze, before her heart and mind set her straight.

She wasn't trapped. If she asked him to stand up, he would. She blinked, and Zeke's face was all she saw. He was sexy, strong and so very intense. But he was also kind and gentle. He'd asked permission every step of the way, had taken nothing for granted.

He was what she needed. What she wanted.

Her bare feet went to the backs of his knees, the fabric from his khaki slacks smooth and cool against her soles. Then his arms folded until he was down on his elbows, and he kissed her again, making all those heady sensations from the living room come roaring back to life. But only for a second, then he was up and off her again.

When she started to protest he held up a finger and then reached down to haul his shirt over his head.

The man was taut and tanned and altogether too gorgeous for his own good, and she had no idea why he'd decided she was the one he wanted to spend the night with, but she was damned glad he had.

She sat up, not wanting this to be one-sided. She wanted tonight to be about give-and-take. She unbuttoned the first two buttons of her blouse then fumbled with the third for half a second, before he came to the rescue, slowly undoing one after the other, then tugging the bottom of it out of her skirt. He peeled it off her torso, and then he swallowed with a jerky movement of his Adam's apple. "You're beautiful, Lind. So very beautiful."

The sudden prick of tears behind her eyes was altogether unexpected.

He leaned down with a frown, one of his thumbs brushing at an area of moisture and carrying it away. "What's wrong?"

"Nothing. Nothing's wrong. I promise." She reached up and cupped his face, breathing in his scent and letting it sift down to the part of her brain where her long-term memories were stored. She dropped it there, never wanting to forget tonight. Then she shrugged out of her shirt and threw it toward the footboard. "Take me to bed, Zeke."

It was kind of a ridiculous statement since they were already in bed, but she trusted him to know what she meant.

He did, because his fingers went to his belt and pulled the tab through the buckle, the metal clink of the tongue making her shiver with anticipation. He pulled his wallet out of his pocket and drew out protection, tossing it onto the bed beside her.

She hadn't had to ask. He'd just taken care of the obvious.

God. She needed to tread with care, because it wouldn't take much for her to fall for this man. And that's the last thing she needed in her life right now, just when she was starting to find herself. But for tonight she could soak in his presence and luxuriate in what he was going to do for her. Without guilt. Without recriminations.

Then he was shedding his trousers, kicking them away from him and standing there in snug black briefs that did nothing to hide what she was making him feel. What he was making *her* feel.

Her hands went to his lean hips, letting herself explore the skin above his waistband, a ripple of muscles under her touch making her smile. "Tickle?"

"Mmm, yes, but in the best kind of way." His voice was low with a hint of gravel that made her mouth water. She did that to him. And she wanted it all. Wanted to explore and taste and take everything he had to offer.

She tunneled her fingers beneath the elastic waistband and around to his butt, giving it a squeeze. A low groan from him told her he liked what she was doing.

Pushing the undergarment down, easing it over the tense flesh and letting it spring free, she couldn't help but stare. She was drunk. But it wasn't from the wine she'd had. Zeke intoxicated her, made her feel wild and free.

Her hands went back to his hips and then

she leaned forward, her mouth sliding over him in a rush, his quick epithet following soon after. But it did nothing to stop her. Instead, it drove her forward, wanting to please him in a way that went to the very heart of who she was. And yet there was a hint of greed, wanting to make him need her in a way he'd never needed anyone else.

"Lindy..." Her name was groaned in a long stream that made her heart leap in her chest.

She leaned back and licked her lips with a slow smile.

Then he was pushing her backward, undoing her slacks and tugging them off in a quick motion that left no doubt as to what his intentions were. Her bra and lacy briefs followed in quick succession until he was leaning over her, kissing her mouth then letting his lips trail down the side of her jaw, nipping at her ear, suckling at her throat and then finally reaching one of her nipples and pulling hard. She arched off the bed, a storm tearing across her nerve endings as every part of her vied for his attention all at once. It was incredible. And she was quickly moving toward the point of no return. And when that happened, she wanted him inside her.

"Zeke." She breathed his name, her hand patting the area near her hip where he'd dropped the condom. He beat her to it, ripping open the packaging and rolling it down his length in one smooth movement. Seeing his hand on himself was heady and if they'd had the time she would have tried to explore that avenue a little bit more, but for now…

He parted her knees then reached beneath her hips to drag her toward the end of the bed. He lifted her toward him but then hovered there as if thinking.

She didn't want him thinking. She wanted him doing. Wrapping her legs around his ass, she let him know in no uncertain terms what she wanted. What she expected from him.

And then he was there, thrusting inside

her with a quick move that took her breath away. He lowered her hips, following her down, and took her mouth even as he started to move. Her eyes fluttered closed, reveling in each and every sensation as it washed over her. He hadn't fully touched her, and yet she knew he wasn't going to need to. The friction of their bodies coming together was all the stimulation she needed as she pushed up, begging for more of the same.

When he changed the angle slightly, she gasped, eyes flicking back open to find him staring down at her. "Oh, God, Zeke, I've never..."

The heat in his gaze burned her alive. "Say my name again." He pushed hard inside her. "Say it."

"Zeke. Zeke... Zeke..."

He quickened his pace as she continued to whisper his name, hitting something with each thrust that made her nerve-endings burst into flame. Suddenly she was consumed in a rush that sent his name screaming from her lips, her body contracting around his. And then he was driving into her at a pace that seemed impossible before straining hard, every muscle in his face tense. Then he collapsed on top of her, his body rocking hers as tiny explosions continued to burst inside her.

Then it was over. His cheek slid against hers, and he rolled over, taking her with him. He kissed her. "What just happened here?"

The question took her aback, before she realized he wasn't really looking for an answer. He was just voicing the exact thing that she'd just thought.

And it was a good thing. Because she had no response to give him.

But the question repeated in her head. What just happened here?

And like his name during the height of passion, the question started getting louder and louder, until it was all she could hear.

She had to go to work and face this man

the day after tomorrow, and she suddenly wasn't sure she could. Not without him seeing the truth on her face. She'd meant this to be a one-time thing. A way to get him out of her head and off her mind. That plan had backfired, because right now he was all she could think about. Her new normal no longer felt so normal. She was jittery and unsure and starting to wonder if this had been such a good idea after all. She had no idea how to explain any of it to herself, much less to him.

"About Monday..." She couldn't find a single word that would get her meaning across. Especially not when she was lying on top of him, still enjoying the feeling of being connected to him.

He frowned. "What about it?"

And she heard it. A wariness in his voice that matched her thoughts and had her up and off him in an instant. He made no effort to get up and cover himself, but she sure as hell did, going into her bathroom and sliding into her robe.

When she went back into the bedroom he was sitting up, his hair sticking up in odd directions that gave him a boyish appearance that stopped at his eyes. They were old and weary, and held a resignation she'd never seen in him before.

Before she could try to assuage his fears and assure him that she didn't want things to change between them at work, he said, "I know this wasn't planned, on either of our parts, but it happened. As much as I enjoyed it, it can't change what happens in the operating room. Because if it does…if it interferes with our patients…" He took a long careful breath. "Then I don't want you there anymore."

He didn't want her there? Doing surgery with him? Or at the hospital itself.

"I'm not sure I understand."

He reached for her hand, catching it before she could pull away. "People put their lives in our hands. They trust us to have our minds fully on what needs to be done. If this changes that for either of us then we can't work together anymore."

A slice of pain went through her. Where she had just been going to say that she wanted things to be business as usual, he was saying he might not want to be associated with her at all now.

"Do…" Her voice caught, and she had to stop. Then fear was replaced with a bubble of anger. She had been about to ask him if he wanted her to quit, but that was something the old Lindy would have done when backed into a corner. The new Lindy had to grow a backbone or she would regret it. She changed the question to a statement. "I'm not quitting, if that's what you mean."

He stared at her for a second. "Hell, no. Where did you get that idea?"

"I just thought… You said we might not be able to work together anymore."

"I wasn't talking about the hospital in general." He dragged a hand through his hair and then got up. "Hold that thought for a minute."

He went into the bathroom with his briefs and when he re-emerged he was wearing them. "I don't know where you came up with that idea, but I would never ask you to quit. I just don't want what happened tonight to affect our patients. I feel I can put this into a compartment and keep it there during surgery. I hope you can too."

"Absolutely." He'd actually said what she'd been thinking much better than she could have. Relief washed over her. "It's not something that will happen again, so I vote that we just put it behind us."

"I concur." He looked a whole lot surer than she felt, but if he could adopt that certainty, she could too.

She really should thank him. It was much better to have had her first post-marriage sexual experience with someone that she instinctively trusted. Someone like Zeke.

Just thinking his name made her shiver. It had been exciting to know he liked hearing his name on her lips. And she liked hearing him call her Lind. Not many people called her that. Certainly never Luke, who'd never ever used a pet name for her. She'd liked it a little too much, and she needed to be careful not to infer anything from it.

Because what she'd said was true. She could fall for this man. Only he obviously had other ideas. Ideas that did not involve him and her together forever.

They were not a couple, and they were unlikely to ever become a couple, so she needed to get that thought right out of her head. They both needed to be on the same page about this. She didn't need to be mooning after him and wondering whether or not he felt the same. He didn't. He'd just said he could shove what had happened between them into a box and seal it up, probably for all eternity.

Lindy only hoped she was strong enough

to do the same. She wasn't stupid. She knew that the feelings he'd generated in her tonight would easily turn into a form of infatuation if she wasn't careful. One that was based on nothing more than pleasurable sensations.

Pleasurable sensations? That was such a weak way of expressing how she'd felt. Which was part of the problem. She shouldn't be looking for stronger words.

She shook herself from her mental ramblings to see him standing there with his hands on his hips. Her heart skipped a beat. He was one of the most attractive men she'd ever laid eyes on. She needed him to get dressed before she did something stupid. Like peel those briefs off and haul him back to bed. If that happened, it would be a whole lot harder for her to let him go, or compartmentalize what had happened, like he wanted her to do.

"I'm glad we're in agreement on where to go from here." She wasn't sure they were, but that was all she could think of to say to get him out of her bedroom and out of her house.

As if reading her mind, he reached for his slacks and pulled them on, one leg at a time, buckling them around his waist. Realizing she was staring, she turned away and tidied her bed and gathered her own clothes before sitting on the edge of it. Except that reminded her of the way she'd pulled him toward her and slid her mouth…

Lord! She wasn't sure there was a compartment big enough to pack all of this away. But she'd better find one, even if it meant building it with her own two hands.

But at least he now had his clothes on, and that wallet was tucked back in his pocket. No fear of repeating what had happened. At least not tonight, and hopefully not any other night. He'd already warned her. If she wanted any possibility of continuing to work with him, she'd better get her act together.

So she smiled and saw him to the door,

and kept smiling as he walked toward his car and got in, leaving her with one of the worst cases of doubt she'd ever had.

Because as easy as it might be for Zeke to erase this from his memory, Lindy wasn't at all sure that she was going to be able to follow his example. But if she couldn't then she needed to pretend. And she'd better do a damned good job of it, or he was going to see right through it and straight into her heart.

CHAPTER EIGHT

ZEKE WAS GLAD to see Lindy already gowned and inside that operating room on Monday morning.

Even though she'd said she wanted to scrub in on Tessa's case, he hadn't been entirely sure she'd be there. Especially since he'd been so damned pompous about doing what was best for their patients. As if Lindy didn't feel the same way. He wouldn't have blamed her if she'd turned around and refused to work with him, and not because of what had happened the night before last. But because he'd acted like her boss and not her coworker.

Yes, she was a nurse, but that didn't mean he was higher than she was on the hiring chart. Yes, he might command the OR, but he didn't have the power to tell nurses where they could and couldn't work. Not without a good reason.

And he wasn't about to tell anyone what had happened between them.

He only hoped she could be just as tight-lipped. Not because he felt embarrassed or ashamed. He wasn't. But the workplace wasn't the best place to let these kinds of things play out. Things got twisted out of shape, and heaven forbid something went really wrong...

There it was again. That attitude that he was the only one who knew how to keep this contained. Lindy had just as much at stake as he did, if not more. She was new to the hospital. There was no way she'd want everyone to know that she'd slept with him. And he had no desire to hurt her career, or his own for that matter. So they would just do as he'd said and keep this between the two of them. Surely he was capable of that.

He gave her a smile that was a lot warmer

than it should have been, but he was truly glad to see her. "Everything okay?"

"Yes, thank you." Her response was stilted and formal, but he could understand that. He hadn't meant to make her feel her job was in jeopardy, hadn't realized until afterward how she'd taken his words. He hoped he'd cleared that up, but maybe he hadn't entirely. But he wasn't sure at this point how to make his meaning any clearer.

Did he really think she couldn't keep her personal life and her professional life separate? No. The reality was that as he'd been lying on her bed, looking up at her, he had suddenly felt unsure whether or not *he* was going to be able to keep them separate. And that had terrified him.

There had been a sense of eager exploration on her part that had shocked him. As if the world before her was new and bright, waiting for her to go out and conquer it. It had hit him right between the eyes and moved him in a way that was alien to him.

He and his ex-wife had had a sexual relationship when they'd both been new to the game, but this had been different and new. Not that he had anything to compare it to. She was the first woman he'd been with since his divorce.

Maybe her reaction had stemmed from her abuse. The fact that she trusted Zeke to *not* be that person touched him. It humbled him, but also made him realize that he was not the best person for her. He couldn't promise to be there when she needed him. After all, he'd proven once before that he wasn't trustworthy when it came to that. Instead of working through issues, he withdrew, resisting all efforts to reach him.

But he needed to get over that and be the professional he'd claimed he could be. So he took a deep breath.

"Ready, people?" He glanced around at the individuals in the room with him and saw the nods of those who had devoted themselves to the same cause that he had: saving lives and helping children live those lives in a way that gave them the best chance at happiness and wellness.

Unlike last time, when they'd used twilight sedation, Tessa was now under general anesthesia, since this surgery would be much more invasive than the last one. He'd already mapped out his plan for removing the tumor. It would involve taking out a piece of her stomach, but this particular organ was amazing in that it could stretch and adapt to the needs of the individual.

"Let's begin. Scalpel."

As in previous surgeries, Lindy anticipated his every need, placing the instrument in his gloved hand almost before he asked for it. Except this time, he was hyperaware of her fingers connecting with his. As much as he tried to tune it out, he couldn't. So he ignored it instead.

He found the tumor on the wall of Tessa's stomach and carefully clamped the blood supply to it. "Preparing to dissect." His hand was remarkably steady as he made his way around the border of the tumor, marking positions on a chart so that he could tell how the tumor had been situated. He would need that in case the pathology came back with tumor cells within the dissected edge. If he left cells behind, there was a good chance the tumor would grow back. Then he lifted it out and placed the growth in a stainless-steel basin that Lindy held up for him. "I need that taken to Pathology to see if the margins are clean."

One of the other nurses took the specimen container. "I'll be right back."

This was the waiting game. Pathology would do a quick scan to see if they could detect abnormal cells along the border, listing where they'd found them, if they did. If that happened, he would know exactly where to remove more tissue, which would then be rechecked.

There was no music. Zeke preferred to work in a quiet space, and his team knew that, keeping all conversations minimal and in low tones so as not to distract him. Lindy's eyes met his above the mask. "It looked good."

"Thank you." He glanced up at the anesthesiologist. "Everything okay?"

"She's in good shape."

The clocked ticked down the seconds and the sound seemed to ping in Zeke's head, time dragging out until it seemed almost a surreal dream. But it wasn't. This was a girl's life and he didn't want to close her without knowing it was safe to do so.

Ten minutes later the phone to the OR rang and one of the nurses picked it up. She looked at Zeke and gave him a thumbs-up sign then hung up. "All clear."

A series of pleased murmurs went through the room. "Let's close her up."

He sutured the stomach with small careful stitches, not wanting to risk a hole or a leak that could bring with it the danger of peritonitis and a second surgery or worse.

As soon as he had that done, he sewed the abdominal muscles back in place and finally the layers of skin.

And then he was done. He glanced again at the clock. What he'd expected to take four hours had taken three. Part of that was due to the skill of his team, and specifically Lindy, who'd performed her duties brilliantly. He might have had a couple of rough patches, but she'd sailed through without a hitch.

"Good job as always, people. Let's wake her up. Anyone up for coffee?" He made sure he asked early enough that Lindy wouldn't feel put on the spot if no one else opted to go.

A couple of the other nurses indicated they could go and when he glanced at Lindy, she hesitated as if trying to decide where this fit in that whole personal versus professional discussion they'd had. Finally she nodded.

Relief washed through him like a flood. Maybe they were going to be able to get through this after all. Or at least he was. Maybe she'd misread his intentions as much as he'd thought she had. Or at least was willing to give him the benefit of the doubt.

And sometimes that was all he could ask. But from now on, no more movie nights with Lindy and her daughter, and no more nights of any kind with Lindy. For his own peace of mind.

Daisy ran down the hospital corridor and latched onto his leg before he could back away. Zeke stood stock still before looking down at the tyke who'd attached herself to him. Marina used to run up to him and do exactly the same thing, looking up at him with her sweet smile.

But this wasn't his daughter. And she never would be.

Lindy hurried down the corridor and caught up with Daisy. "I'm so sorry. I didn't realize she'd slipped away from me until it was too late."

He swallowed. The same could be said of Marina. He hadn't realized she'd slipped away either, until it had been too late. And realizing she was never coming back again had taken even longer to sink in. And when it had…

Clenching his jaw, he forced a smile that probably looked as ghastly as it felt. "It's fine."

"Daisy, you need to let go of him." She pried the child's fingers loose and then swung her up into her arms.

Daisy looked right at him. "Can Zeke come?"

"No, not tonight."

That's right. It was Friday night. A full week since the last disastrous one, when he'd taken Lindy home and made love to her.

She hadn't asked him to come. In fact, she'd made it clear she didn't want him to. It was good, because that way he wouldn't have to turn down the invitation. Which he would have. Right?

"What's the film?" he asked out of curiosity, not because he was going.

"*Princess Diaries*!" Daisy's answer was immediate, the delight in her face obvious.

He couldn't hold back his grin. "You still like princesses, huh?"

"Princess!"

When he glanced at Lindy, her face was tense. "Don't worry. I won't come."

"I didn't mean..."

"I know you didn't."

Even so, she seemed to hug Daisy tighter as if closing him out of their little circle. That stung, and he got his first whiff of what it was like to be shut out. "I don't want my parents to get any funny ideas, which they might if it became a regular thing."

His brows went up. The thought of movie night and all that went with it becoming a regular thing made something inside him perk up. He quickly put it right back in its place. Not only because of work but because of how right it felt having Daisy cling to him.

"I don't want them to get any funny ideas either." He forced himself to give Daisy's nose a light-hearted tweak. "Even though I'll miss the princesses."

Realizing how that sounded, he added, "The ones on the screen."

Well, that didn't make it much better. He seemed determined to make a mess of things, even when trying to straighten them out. All the more reason to leave things where they'd left them.

Daisy laughed and hugged her mom tight before giving a loud wheezing cough.

His chest gave a sudden squeeze. "Is she okay?"

"Yes, just an allergy or something. She gets them periodically."

An allergy. Or something. Hadn't he said those very words?

"Have you had it checked out?"

Lindy looked up at him with a sideways

grin. "I'm a nurse, remember? Yes. I checked her out. And I had her pediatrician check her out. Nothing to worry about."

A few of his muscles relaxed, even though he'd been a doctor at the time that Marina had fallen ill and had missed the signs. Another reminder of why getting involved with someone with a child was not a good idea.

He was happy the way he was, his job giving him all the love and fulfillment he needed.

At least that's what he had told himself time and time again.

Was he starting to doubt that?

Maybe he was, because he felt a little flat, knowing he wasn't going to be spending the evening in the company of Daisy and her mother.

Lindy was evidently a whole lot better at compartmentalizing than he was.

"Well, I'm glad she's okay."

"Speaking of okay..." she shifted Daisy a little higher on her hip "...how is Tessa doing? I heard that her parents were really happy about the outcome of her surgery. Any idea when she'll be discharged? I'm assuming she'll still be here tomorrow. I was hoping to run by and see her, if so."

"She won't be discharged for another day or two. I want to make sure her system reboots itself once we introduce liquids and solids back into her diet. And, yes, her parents consider themselves very lucky."

"I'm sure they do. You're a great surgeon."

He hadn't meant about that. "No, they feel very lucky that the tumor was benign." He understood the relief they must have felt, even if he hadn't experienced that first-hand.

"I'm pretty sure they feel lucky to have had you operating on her too. Don't sell yourself short."

"I'm not." He knew he was a good surgeon. But he sometimes wondered if he was lacking in the empathy department, trying to keep himself emotionally removed from his patients even as he tried his best to save them. The same way he'd kept his wife at arm's length at times. Tessa had somehow broken through that barrier, at least on some level. And Daisy had wormed her way in even further. He was going to have to be careful or pretty soon he wasn't going to have any wall of protection left.

Did he even really need one?

He used to think he did. And now?

"Well, we'd better go. Mom went down to visit a sick friend and was going to meet us back in the lobby."

"Have a good time tonight. At least you'll get to bed at a decent hour." He couldn't resist that little rejoinder. The sudden pink tinge to her face said she knew exactly what he was referring to.

"Well, I guess you will too."

That was doubtful at this point, but he wasn't about to tell her that he'd spent a few sleepless nights remembering what they'd done a week ago. And talking about it, even in a half-teasing way, wasn't going to help him in that area. Better to just drop the subject before it got any deeper. Or he changed his mind about coming to watch Daisy's latest princess movie.

Because the further he steered away from any thoughts of an after-party, the better.

Three days later, Lindy and Zeke were parked outside a neighboring hospital, where they were going to see if its helpline project would fit in with what Mid Savannah wanted to do with a women's center. They were to spend a couple of hours there and then report back to Neil and the committee later in the week. The idea was to jump in and see how things ran.

And if it came to actually answering phones?

Lindy wasn't sure she could bare her soul to a complete stranger. But she'd done it at her other volunteer job, and these were strangers who needed help. And hadn't she bared her soul to Zeke when he'd been practically a stranger? She had, and she was none the worse for wear. Not from that anyway.

Taking a deep breath, she waited for Zeke to push through the door and followed him in. They found the place empty except for two people—one of whom was seated at a desk, a phone in her hand, and the other person, who looked to be a supervisor, was leaning over her. The man scribbled something on a pad of paper and pushed it toward the person on the phone. Lindy's misgivings grew. Was that person on a tough call? She had no way of knowing.

The man motioned them over, where they waited for him to finish helping the volunteer.

The small office looked like it had actually been a large supply closet at one time, so there wasn't room for an army of people all talking at once. As it was, it was a little cramped with just the four of them.

She'd been thinking more along the lines of

something bigger. With room for two or three people working at one time. And the ability to take walk-ins off the street if it came down to it.

But one volunteer? There would be no one to pass the client to if whoever was on duty got in over their head or landed in a dangerous situation.

No. That wasn't entirely true. When Lindy had spoken with the person in charge of the service she'd been told they could get on another line and either call 911 or get in touch with one of the agencies that dealt with issues that were more complicated. Or more dangerous. That was a good point to remember when they opened their clinic. The place she used to volunteer at had a panic button that would notify the police in case an irate partner came in. A button she'd never had to push, thank God.

She glanced at Zeke and said in hushed tones, "Have you been here before?"

"No, first time, and I have to tell you this isn't what I had in mind."

"Me neither. The place I worked at had multiple lines and a place where people who were in trouble came to get help."

She went on. "I do have a line on a building that I want to check out after we leave here." She'd felt horrible calling Zeke in on his day off, especially for what had turned out to be such a small operation, but Neil had been getting pressure from some of his board who wanted to see them move on this thing quickly.

Quick didn't always equal better.

She moved toward the pair who were working together on the phone and overheard the other volunteer trying to get an address. The phone was on speaker and the woman on the other end seemed angry.

"I just want to know where I can find a good lawyer to sue my boyfriend. Like I said, he hit me."

The caller's voice sounded belligerent

rather than frightened and for Lindy, that sent up an automatic red flag.

"I can't do that, but I can get you some help, if you're in danger. What is your boyfriend's name?"

"I'm not saying." A few choice words came over the speaker, causing the volunteer to glance up at her supervisor with raised brows.

It was then that Lindy saw what he'd written on the pad.

Possible hoax.

It did sound like it and the person's speech sounded almost slurred, as if she'd been drinking or was taking something that impaired her thinking. "Then can you give me your address so that we can make sure you're safe?"

Click.

The caller had hung up. The volunteer sighed. Young, with long blond hair and baby-blue eyes, she introduced herself as Tara Sanders.

"Sorry to have called you in here for nothing," she said to the man, who introduced himself as Todd Grissom. "I've just never had a caller like that before. I thought she was suicidal at first. She didn't ask for a lawyer until just a second ago."

Todd glanced at them. "We find it's better to give people the benefit of the doubt, when possible. But as she hung up, our hands are tied. We can hand the recording over to the police department and see if there's anything in there they can use, and of course we'll keep a record of the cellphone number, just like we do with all our calls."

Zeke glanced around. "I see another desk and a phone." He nodded behind the current volunteer.

"We do have another line. Unfortunately, we don't have enough volunteers to man it. We're probably going to throw in the towel if nothing changes in the next couple of months."

Lindy didn't understand. "Were there

enough volunteers when your program started up?"

This time it was Tara who answered. "I've been volunteering for three years and we used to have a lot of people. But people get tired, you know? Burned out. It seems like there's a never-ending stream of people who need help and not enough resources to go around."

Which was exactly why Mid Savannah was interested in opening their own center. Neil said they'd had a plea from another organization saying an actual medical-based facility was needed. People could always come to the hospital, but the tangles of insurance and red tape sometimes kept them from trying to get help. They wanted an actual place with an exam room or two, along with a place to conduct group sessions or one-on-one counseling. The phones would be used as a filter and a way to direct folks to the right place on the right day.

"How many callers would you say you log in an average day?" she asked.

"You mean on this phone or both of them together?"

"Let's say both of them." Even as she said it the phone behind Tara began to ring. Todd went back to get that one, speaking in low tones as he jotted down what the caller said.

"I'd say we get around forty calls in a day."

"So in an eight-hour period there are around five calls an hour." Less than fifteen minutes per caller. "And if someone calls while you're on the line?"

"They'll get a busy signal. Todd only answers if there's no one else available. He knows how hard it can be for some of them to confide in a man. But there are no guarantees the caller will try again later."

"They'll get a busy signal."

Lindy had visions of their lobby flooded with people and not enough bodies to handle them "Great. Thanks so much for letting us come and observe."

"Do you want to try taking a call? We have a book with prompts that help a lot.

You told me you volunteered at Gretchen's Place, didn't you?"

"I did."

"Did you do phone work?"

"Yes. It was pretty busy as well."

The difference had been that their volunteers hadn't petered out.

Tara reached under her desk and hefted a large three-ring binder, setting it on the desk.

Okay, wow, that was bigger than anything they'd had at Gretchen's Place. "How do you find anything in there?"

"It's all alphabetized."

Todd was still in the background on the phone. It sounded like he was trying to get someone to turn himself in.

Lindy glanced at Zeke. "We'll go as soon as I try this, okay? Unless you want a turn as well."

Zeke shook his head. "I do better in person than on the phone."

She certainly understood that. Was that true? Or was he quickly realizing this was going to be more involved than simply empathizing with at-risk women and trying to get them help, the way she herself had once needed help?

"Gretchen's Place had a log that we entered all calls into."

Tara flipped to the first page of the binder. "We have that as well. And you'll need to record the call and notify the person on the other end that you're doing so. You'll assign the recording the next number in the sequence. Doing that will automatically save it to the computer, and we can retrieve it at a later date along with the actual recording and time stamp. It helps us cover ourselves in the event that someone challenges our version of a conversation."

She was impressed. From her initial impression and the tiny size of the office, Lindy hadn't expected the helpline to be as sophisticated as it was, but it sounded like they'd started off well and things had just fizzled out, for whatever reason. It was a good reminder that you couldn't grow complacent about the mission or it would lose its momentum.

She'd never known Mid Savannah Medical Center to do things in half-measures. Not that she'd been there all that long, but from everything she'd seen, they liked to stay on top of things. The hospital she'd worked at before her marriage had also paid attention to the little things, but it had been a much smaller facility and it was doubtful they would have had the resources to open up a place even as small as this one.

And somehow she couldn't imagine her and Zeke trapped in a tiny cubicle for two or three hours. His lanky figure already ate up a great deal of the available air space. And he was rapidly taking up a great deal of her thoughts as well. He'd once said he couldn't work with her if she couldn't maintain that separation of professional and personal. Well, it was hard enough in their huge hospital. In here, it would be impossible.

Friday night movies hadn't been quite the same without him, however, and her mom had insisted on keeping a sleeping Daisy for the night yesterday. If only she'd done that the Friday before, maybe she and Zeke would have never had their encounter. Except she had enjoyed her time with him, was glad for it no matter what else happened.

She glanced at Tara. "Anything of crucial importance inside that book?" Maybe she could treat it like her other hospital's helpline. Surely it couldn't be all that different.

She slid into the chair and looked at the open screen on the desk. Tara grabbed a second chair and sat beside her. "There is, but you won't have to deal with most of it." The other woman flipped a couple of tabs and opened the page to a list of phone numbers. "These are the organizations that you'll want to keep track of. They're also on one of the screens."

She leaned across and clicked an icon labeled "Resource Referrals." A page identical to the one in the binder popped onto the screen. "It's here, so the book doesn't have to be pulled out every time we want to give someone a phone number. And of course 911 is exactly the same."

Tara continued. "Mostly you want to listen and make sure the caller isn't in immediate danger, like we said earlier."

"If I suspect someone is in danger, even if the caller claims she isn't, can I still call and report it?"

"Absolutely. That's happened more than once, and we'd much rather be on the safe side than risk someone's life."

"Once you disconnect, the computer will ask you if you want to save or delete. You'll always want to save. Periodically, one of the other board members will go through calls that were marked non-urgent and cross-reference them to other calls. If it was a one-off and there was a satisfactory resolution, such as finding the appropriate place to send her, then we'll delete the actual recording to free up space. But the phone number and time stamp will remain to help with writing grant requests."

"Okay, got it."

She glanced up and caught Zeke's eyes on her. Damn! How was she going to concentrate on a caller when he was looking at her like that?

Like what?

She wasn't sure. But she liked it.

Their night together almost seemed like a dream now, a surreal combination of physical and emotional reactions that could have belonged to someone else. Only they didn't. They belonged to her and she did not want to give them up. Not yet.

That sexy mouth went up in a half-smile that made her stomach flip.

"What?"

"Nothing. Just anxious to see you in action."

She gave him a sharp look, but there was

nothing there to indicate the words had any other meaning.

Was she the only one having trouble wiping those memories from her skull? If only it was as easy to zap them away as it was to erase the call files from the computer. But like Tara said, even if that happened, there would probably still be some kind of record, a mental paper trail that would remain with her forever.

And that's probably the way it should be. Every experience in life brought an opportunity to learn and grow. Though she wasn't quite sure what she'd learned from that night other than to be more careful about letting her sexual urges run amok.

That made her smile, because it perfectly described what had happened. She'd let them out for the first time in ages and they'd gone a little wild and crazy on her.

Wild and crazy. Like her toenail polish. She remembered using those words. Remembered him saying them back to her. As if he knew exactly what she was thinking about, his dark eyes dropped to her mouth for a brief second before swiftly returning to her face as a whole.

Tara cocked her head. "Something funny?"

Somehow her smile had frozen in place. She wiped it away as quickly as she could. She needed to get control of herself. "No, sorry. What else do I need to know?"

Instead of Tara answering, it was Zeke. "You already know enough to get you into a whole lot of trouble. I don't think you need to know any more."

Um, what kind of trouble was he talking about?

Her mind had swung onto a detour. And he knew it. Knew what he'd done to her with those few simple words.

Tara smiled. "He's right. There's no reason to try to stuff everything in your head for one caller."

She was right. About the helpline. And about the other stuff?

What she would like to do was admit that

she wanted his mouth back on hers. But that wasn't going to happen. Not now. Maybe not ever again.

The phone suddenly rang, making her jump. Oh, Lord, could she really do this?

Tara rubbed her hands together. "Okay. It's showtime. I'll be right here if you need me."

Unfortunately, it wasn't Tara she needed. It was Zeke. And she was very afraid that he already knew exactly how he affected her. And that there was no way in heaven or on earth that she could let him know. Because Zeke wasn't offering a lifetime. He wasn't even offering to repeat their last encounter. So she picked up the phone and gave a shaky greeting and waited to see who was on the other end of the line.

CHAPTER NINE

SOMEHOW ZEKE GOT through the next two hours of visiting the call center and then a building a few blocks away. It had been one thing to be cramped in a tiny space when there'd been other people around, but to be standing in a large open warehouse with no one but a realtor, who politely waited outside while they looked around, was much worse.

At the call center he'd been a brave man teasing her when he'd known they could do nothing about it. But he'd sensed her wound so tightly in there that he'd been afraid she might burst.

Afraid to be back in that world where there was fear and denial. So he'd tried to lighten the atmosphere and had ended up almost setting himself on fire in the process.

He had a feeling that he and Lindy had something in common besides a single night of sex. And it wasn't nearly as fun.

Could she have PTSD from her experience? Of course she could. Just as any of them could from a deep-seated trauma. Including him.

That sex, though, had blotted out everything for a brief period of time. It had been like an addictive drug that when used once hooked the user for the rest of his life. Zeke already found himself wanting more. Only they'd both agreed that wasn't happening.

She finally finished looking at the building. "Well, I think this one's a possibility."

"A lot of money to revamp it to fit our purposes, though."

"I think anything will be."

They got back into her car and she switched on the ignition.

Touching her shoulder, he swiveled in his seat to face her. "Are you okay?"

"I think so. I'm pretty keyed up right now,

though. I probably won't be able to sleep for a while. Do you want me to drop you off at home or at the hospital?"

Since it was only seven o'clock, he doubted she would go home and hop right into bed. Besides, she had Daisy to deal with, unless she was sleeping over at Rachel and Harold's tonight.

"Do you have to pick up Daisy?"

"No, Mom is keeping her."

"Good. It probably would be a good idea for you to unwind."

"After sitting for the last two hours? I feel like I need to be up doing something. I need to burn off some energy."

It wouldn't be dark for a while, and he didn't really feel like going home to an empty house either. But what else could he do? Just then he saw a poster hanging on a street sign. It was the perfect solution. "I don't know if you're up for it, but Savannah hosts a jazz festival every year. I just saw a sign for it. I'm pretty sure tonight's is in Forsythe Park. It's probably partway over, but it's free, if you're interested. Otherwise drop me off at the hospital so I can get my car."

"I remember those, although it's been ages since I've been to one. You're thinking of going?"

"I thought I might. Care to join me?"

Zeke wasn't quite ready to go home, and the thought of going to the concert by himself was depressing.

He'd given up on finding Marina's age progression pictures but, then again, he hadn't really tried. He kept putting it off. And maybe that's what asking her to a concert was about as well. But sitting on a blanket listening to live music appealed to him. Like Lindy, it had been ages since he'd gone to one of the events, and tonight seemed like the perfect night. It would give the rapid firing of neurons in his head a chance to slow their pace.

And music? The perfect stress reliever.

Well, almost perfect. The only thing better would have been…

Nope, not going there. He was going to have to find his endorphin fix in a different place.

"The jazz festival sounds perfect. I think I have a blanket in the back of my car from when I took Daisy on a picnic after we moved back, if you don't mind sitting on the ground."

With her? That sounded like heaven, and he still wasn't sure why. Maybe the snatches of memories from their night together were holding him enthralled. Well, that would diminish with time. Maybe if he was with her in a non-sexual way, his body would get used to the idea that he wasn't going back to visit again, that it was firmly part of his past.

Like his ex. And Marina.

A bucket of pain sloshed over him, but he ignored it, pulling out his phone and saying, "I can't think of a better way to listen to one of those concerts. Let me just check to make sure it's at the park and not the theater." The concerts were sometimes split between the two venues. If it was inside, seating was limited. Scrolling down until he found today's date, he nodded. "It's at the park."

"Great. That settles it, then. Do you want me to drive?"

He smiled, his heart suddenly light. "How about you provide the seating, and I'll provide the transportation? Does that sound like a semi-equitable trade?"

Within five minutes they were on their way in his car, her blanket folded on the backseat. He was glad she'd agreed to come, the tiredness of mind and body dissipating almost immediately and warm anticipation taking its place. As hot and humid as it was in the summer and early fall, September was the beginning of a modicum of relief from the constant heat. And right now, with the sun starting to descend, the weather was comfortably balmy, if not cool.

Finding a place to park proved to be a bit of a challenge, since they'd arrived after things had already started. The plaintive sound of a saxophone reached them, even through the closed windows of his Jaguar, the one real luxury item he'd allowed himself.

Pulling the blanket from Lindy's more sensible car had made something inside him warm. He had imagined her and Daisy having conversations as they drove to the store or to Rachel and Harold's place. It had set up an ache in him that he'd tried to banish but he hadn't been entirely successful. He'd pushed it back, but it was there hovering in the background, waiting for another opportunity to make itself known. It actually would have been nice to bring Daisy out here, the three of them sitting together.

The ache took a step forward, but Zeke clenched his jaw and it retreated once again.

There! Someone was pulling out of a spot.

Just in time. He slid into the space and shut the car off.

"This is great. Thanks for thinking of it. I wasn't looking forward to going home to an empty house but didn't want to admit that to my mom when she suggested she keep Daisy for the night."

"That makes two of us. The thought of sitting at home staring at the walls didn't appeal to me either. So we'll enjoy some good music and even better company."

They got out of the car and he retrieved the blanket. Lindy's light floral scent clung to the fabric. Folding it over his arm set the scent free, and he breathed deeply. He almost said the words "Next time…" but somehow called them back before they left his throat.

Why would there be a next time? He might have coffee with her periodically after a shared surgery, but he wouldn't be sitting in the office of the women's center week after week. He didn't have time to, first and foremost, and secondly he was pretty sure that Lindy would find it odd if he somehow managed to appear each and every time she volunteered. So he'd better take advantage of tonight and enjoy himself. Because he wasn't sure when he would get the chance to do something like this again.

They wove their way between people, and Zeke glanced at the stage periodically. The saxophone was still playing, the light notes spiraling from the stage to their intended target, his ears absorbing the sound.

There they went…those muscles in his neck. They were starting to soften and relax, and his headache began to ease.

"How's this?" He'd found a spot big enough to toss open the blanket without hitting anyone and where they wouldn't feel like they were sitting on top of those surrounding them.

"Perfect."

Zeke shook it open and spread it on the ground, waiting while she kicked off her shoes and eased her way down, knees bent, arms wrapped around them. She arched her neck way back, while tilting her head to the right and left as if she had a few kinks of her own to get rid of. Her dark hair touched the blanket behind her, sliding back and forth as she continued to work at it.

"Sore?"

"A little. I'm not sure why."

Maybe the music had lulled him into a false sense of security, because when her hand went to her nape, as if trying to tackle the ache on her own, he couldn't resist.

"Here, let me." He toed off his loafers and sat beside her, one hand sliding under her hair and massaging the muscles he found there with firm strokes.

"Mmm, that feels good, thanks."

Focusing on the stage, he let the music wash over him as he kept ministering to her nape and the sides of her neck, his thumb gliding up and down her soft skin.

When he glanced over at her, her eyes

were closed, but she wasn't sleeping. What he hoped she was doing was enjoying the feel of his fingers pressing deep into her tight muscles and loosening them up, one section at a time. What he was doing probably wasn't obvious to anyone around them and even if it was, it wasn't any different from what any man might do for someone he loved.

Only he didn't love her. He needed to remember that. So what *were* his feelings toward her?

Hell if he knew. But one thing was for sure. The feelings weren't platonic. No matter how many times he might lecture himself or how many examples of friendship he might hold up, he knew there had to be a third option. Something he hadn't quite reached or achieved. Some deep transcendental realm that he needed to find.

As if reading his mind, she took a deep breath and let it out on a sigh before leaning to the side slightly. "Thanks. I'm good."

She stretched her legs out in front of her and leaned back on her elbows. The polish on her toes had changed. The glittery silver had been replaced by some kind of opalescent purple that seemed to shift colors each time she moved her feet, which she was now doing, one foot moving sideways, keeping time with the beat.

"More wild and crazy?"

She glanced at him and then looked at her feet and laughed. "Oh, yes. Everyone should have at least one wild and crazy side."

He'd been the recipient of another wild and crazy side, then shut that line of thought down. They were here for the music and nothing else.

Planting his hands on the blanket behind him, he forced himself to settle and relax as the quick notes continued to dance around them. Low conversations were taking place as dusk enfolded them in shadows, and as he looked, he saw all types of people, some on lawn chairs, some on blankets like they were, and some simply sitting on the grassy expanse. But one thing they all had in common was a love of a way of life that was both old and new. Savannah had a charm that he hadn't found in many other places.

And Lindy fit right into that charm. Being away from her hometown hadn't killed it, although there was a solemnity to that wild and crazy side that had probably come from what she'd endured.

As it had a couple of times before, anger rolled up his gut. How could any man do such damage to someone he was supposed to love? And worse, not care whether or not his child was around while it was happening. Thank God, Daisy had been an infant at the time. He could not imagine his daughter seeing such an ugly side of human nature, and Zeke had a hard time understanding what could generate so much rage that someone would lash out at another person.

He wouldn't. And most people he knew

wouldn't, although he did know that abusers could come across as great people when you met them on the street or worked with them. It was only those at home who saw the truth.

That was the dangerous side to compartmentalizing, the very thing he'd told himself he needed to do in regard to the night he and Lindy had spent together. But making love hadn't hurt anyone. Except maybe his "want to," which he now kept locked up. And that guy needed to stay there. At least when Lindy was around.

So he settled in to enjoy this side of being with her. And actually he had probably seen Lindy in more settings than he had any other woman at the hospital. He'd seen worried Lindy, competent Lindy, concerned Lindy…and sexy-as-hell Lindy. And those facets were all rolled into one fascinating woman. It was no wonder he wanted her.

And she'd wanted him. At least she had for one night.

"He's so good." A soft voice came from beside him and he tensed at first, confused as to what she was saying, then he realized she was referring to the musician.

What had he thought? That she was muttering something about him under her breath? Not very likely.

"Yes, he is. I don't think I've heard him before but, like I said, it's been years since I've been to one of the festivals. He might have been in diapers the last time I came."

She gave a light laugh. "You're not quite that ancient. If he was in diapers, then you probably were too. He can't be any older than thirty-five or -six."

"How did you guess my age?"

"You have that look about you."

That made him frown. "What kind of look is that?" It didn't sound exactly flattering to hear her say that.

"That crinkling around your eyes from laughter."

"So I have wrinkles, do I?"

"Not wrinkles. Crinkles. There's a big difference."

He suddenly found himself wanting to know exactly what that difference was. "Explain it to me."

"Wrinkles are caused by worry or stress. Crinkles are caused by happiness."

They were? He didn't normally feel happy. But maybe she saw a side to him that he'd missed. His job made him happy. Could that actually express itself in the way lines were woven into the fabric of someone's skin? Maybe.

"You have crinkles too."

"I do? Where?"

He leaned over and touched a finger to the bridge of her nose and let it slide down the side nearest him. "Here. When you smile, the skin here crinkles. I remember the first time I saw them."

"Really?"

"Yes. You were in the operating room and you had your surgical mask on. I could tell whether or not you were smiling by the lines—or lack thereof—on either side of your nose. It was damned attractive."

"Wow. I didn't know. And I certainly can't imagine that looking good. To anyone."

"Well, it does." He had no idea why he was admitting any of this, except that she'd brought up the subject by explaining what she thought so-called crinkles represented. He liked her thinking of him as being happy. He couldn't remember the last time someone had said that of him, even his mom, who was carrying some long-term grief herself over the death of her husband of thirty-four years. Marina and his dad had died within a few years of each other. He guessed it really was true. Grief had no expiration date.

Or maybe it could have. If he let it.

What exactly was the problem with him and Lindy being together? He'd made it into such a big thing in his head, but maybe it wasn't. As long as she didn't want promises of forever—which she'd never even implied she did—and probably didn't honestly, after what she'd been through. But maybe being with her had caused some of his wrinkles to make the shift into crinkles.

Or maybe he'd been generating them all along. But suddenly he thought that coming to the concert was the stupidest idea he could have come up with. Why hadn't he just taken her back to his place and done what he really wanted to do?

Was it because of the whole "bad idea" thing? Or was it because he'd thought she might reject him? Maybe it was a little of both, but he was about to test one of those theories. Whether the other was tested or not depended on her response.

"Lind, how interested are you in staying for the entire concert?"

That got her attention. Her eyes met his and she seemed to look at him forever, although it was probably only a few seconds. Then she smiled…and there they were: crinkles. On either side of her nose. "I think I could be talked into slipping out a little early."

He leaned over the blanket and gave her a gentle kiss. It was the only way he could think of to make his intentions known. And when she curled her fingers around his neck and held him there for a second, he had his answer. He stood, reaching a hand down to help her up and then whipping the blanket back over his arm. There were some looks of confusion from those around them, but a couple of other folks knew exactly what was going on. After all, jazz's smooth, silky notes made it the perfect intro for what was on his mind. From the moment he'd suggested coming here, things had been moving in this direction, only he'd been too stupid—or maybe too smart—to admit it to himself.

And now he didn't care.

He tossed the blanket into the back of his car. The second they were in the car his lips were on hers and it was all he could do to pull away from her and put the car in gear. He didn't want to take the time to go all the way back home, wanted to do it right here in this car. But it was very probable they'd be arrested before they got to the best stuff. And that was definitely not the stuff crinkles were made of. So he added gas and eased off the clutch and headed back the way they'd come.

His apartment was on the far side of town and it took them almost a half-hour to get there. The whole time Lindy's palm had been splayed across his right thigh, and with each shift of gears, each time his foot came off the gas pedal, it seemed to slip a little bit higher. He wasn't quite sure if he was causing it or if she was purposely moving her hand. Whatever it was, he was hot and hard and was having a godawful time concentrating on the road in front of him.

But he'd better, or they were going to crash into one of the posts along the highway, and if he survived, he'd have to explain to law enforcement exactly why he'd been driving while distracted. He didn't think Lindy's parents would approve of him putting their daughter in the hospital. So although it took a monumental effort, he glanced over at her. "You go much higher with that hand and I'm going to have to pull off the road and find a bank of trees to hide away in."

"Would that be so bad?"

"No." He laughed. "Not bad at all, but I'd rather have you in bed, where I can do anything I want to you."

Her hand edged higher. "Does that mean I can do anything I want to you too?"

"Yes, baby, you can do absolutely anything your heart desires."

And there went that hand yet again. He gritted his teeth and prayed for mercy.

They hit what must have been Zeke's apartment door with a rattle of keys and her back pressed against the solid surface as he kissed her again and again. She never would have believed she could be so turned on by a car ride where they'd barely touched, but anything and everything had been implied, even without saying it outright.

His pelvis pressed into her in the deserted corridor as he tried to fit his key into the lock beside her. She laughed and slid sideways to let him have better access.

To the lock. And to certain regions of her body that were hoping to get a little satisfaction. The door swung open without warning and she careened backward, only just barely missing falling by him grabbing hold of her wrist. That didn't stop her from knocking over a bookshelf that was next to the door. Papers and framed awards sprayed in every direction. She gave a horrified murmur and turned to clean up the mess.

"Leave it." He was still holding her hand, coming up behind her and turning her to face him. "They're just things, Lind. Nothing to worry about."

God. She wanted this man. Wrapping her arms around his neck, she went up on tiptoe. "In that case, we're either going to spend some time on the long leather sofa that I see on my right or you're going to take me to your bedroom and show me exactly what you meant earlier when you said I could do anything I wanted."

He bit her lip. "Did I say anything? That term might have been a little too sweeping."

"Uh-uh. No give-backs."

"Maybe you'd better tell me what you have in mind, then."

He leaned his head down and in a sudden boost of confidence she whispered the naughtiest thing she could think of in his ear. The thing she'd thought about last time as he'd rolled his condom over his length.

His answering laugh was rough-edged with what sounded like disbelief. "I'm pretty sure that's not going to happen. I don't intend this to be a party of one."

"But you promised…" Talking like this, freely, without shame, was the biggest turn-on of all. She couldn't wait to get this man in bed and feel him in her, over her. Once had definitely not been enough. Especially since there was some kind of raw emotion twisting its way out of her. Something that made her look at him—at everything that made Zeke who he was. And it was just…

God. Oh, *God*! She loved him.

Loved him. Loved his laugh. Loved his crinkles. Loved his wrinkles, even. Loved the way he made her feel.

How was this even possible? She didn't know, but she gloried in realizing it was possible to feel something profound. Something that felt sacred and good. And whether it worked out or not, she owed Zeke a debt of gratitude, and she intended to start paying it now.

She didn't have to wait for the bedroom.

The party could start right here. Right now. With hurried hands, she reached for his belt and undid it, and the button of his slacks, then his zipper. She was wild for him, wanted him to take her now, as all the foreplay she'd needed had happened on the way over here: in the car, in the elevator, at his front door.

Then she had him out, his hard length in her hands, glorying in the heat coming off his skin, in the hiss of his breath as she tightened her fingers around him and pumped.

"God, Lindy." He cupped her face. "What are you doing to me?"

"If you won't do it, someone has to." She stretched up and bit his lip. Hard, letting him know she was not afraid of rough, because she knew he wouldn't hurt her. Not really.

She let go of him long enough to push her own slacks down her hips, her undergarments following quickly. She needed him. Right now. They could slow it down later.

Zeke got the idea and eased her down to the floor, making short work of finding a condom and sheathing himself. But this time, instead of thrusting into her, he rolled over so that she was on top, the way they'd ended the last time. Only this time they were just beginning. Just getting started.

She lowered herself onto him, that luscious sense of fullness so very perfect. Just like him. He took hold of her hips, but instead of guiding her, he let her set the rhythm, simply gripping her as she took him all the way in and then lifted off him.

Closing her eyes, she concentrated on the sensations that were washing over her and slowly building. She picked up the pace, vaguely hearing him mutter something under his breath. Whatever it was, it sounded like he approved. Her world was spinning in on itself, becoming denser and more compressed the faster it whirled. Her hands went to his shoulders, using his body as leverage as she rose up and came down again and again, the feeling of power it gave her heady. Her movements sped up as she got closer and closer to the zenith, a searing heat growing in her belly. And then it hit. Hard and long, her brain losing its ability to process for a second or two. Zeke shouted beneath her as he followed her into oblivion.

An oblivion that was more beautiful than anything she'd ever experienced.

She loved him. God. She couldn't get enough of those words, wanted desperately to say them aloud, but she didn't dare, clenching her teeth around them and keeping them inside.

Then it was over. She pulled in a breath and then another, her fingers reaching to sift through his hair. And then he opened those gorgeous brown eyes of his, and she was lost all over again.

"That was…incredible." He reached up and cupped the back of her head, tugging her down for a kiss. And then another. "I can't seem to get enough of you."

"I think you just did."

One side of his mouth went up in a smile. "You only think I did. But that was your turn. And now it's mine."

Then he turned onto his side, dumping her off him. "Hey!" Her brief attempt at a protest ended in a laugh as he climbed to his feet and reached down a hand.

"This time we're going to bed. You don't have to go home, and I already am home, so you're going to spend the night."

He didn't ask, which made her smile. "What makes you think I'll say yes?"

"Remember that thing you wanted me to do? The one I said no to?"

A spark ignited in her belly. "Are you saying…?"

His smile grew. "Tell me you'll spend the night, and you'll find out."

"I'll spend the night. Gladly." He didn't have to coax her. She would have stayed even without the hinted promise.

"Then, my dear, you're about to get your

wish. And I'm about to get mine." With that he led her through to the bedroom and shut the door behind them.

CHAPTER TEN

ZEKE WOKE UP in a swirl of confusion, unsure of where he was. For a panicked second, he thought he'd forgotten to go to work before realizing it was still early. He glanced at the readout on his phone. Barely six.

He heard some kind of scraping noise, like furniture being dragged across the floor, and tensed before the events of the previous night came flooding back.

Lindy had stayed with him and they'd made love… He tried to count and failed. The events were pretty much a blur. Except for the fact that his muscles were loose and relaxed, so much so that he wasn't sure they were going to let him get up.

But where was Lindy?

Had she left?

He frowned before hearing the same sound he'd noticed a second ago, a little louder this time.

That had to be her. But what was she doing? Trying to leave before he woke up?

He didn't like that. Last night, just before he'd dropped off to sleep, he'd had a vague plan of getting up, cooking her breakfast and then having a long talk.

Cranking himself out of bed, protest of muscles or not, he somehow made it to his feet and headed into the other room. He was afraid that if he stopped to get dressed, she'd be gone before he could stop her.

He made it through the door and came to an abrupt halt. She'd righted the bookcase and was in the process of putting the spilled contents back on it, gathering papers and giving them a tap to neaten them.

"You don't have to do that."

She whirled around. "Good morning to you too. And I wanted to. It's a good feeling to know that I can knock over a bookcase without making someone angry."

"Never. I take it we're talking about Luke."

"Yes. That last day with him was…" Her eyes skated down his length. "It's really hard to talk to you when you're standing there naked."

He gave her a slow smile. "Okay. Give me a sec."

He went and pulled on a pair of sweat pants and then arrived back in the room. "I want to hear the rest of the story. This is the day you got away?"

"Yes. Remember I told you he opened credit cards in my name? Well, I found out and confronted him. He flew into such a rage, screaming that I knew nothing about him. I'd seen him angry before, but this was different, and I knew I had to leave. But when I went to get Daisy, he blocked my access to her. That scared me. I backed away and went into the kitchen, dialing 911 as I went.

"I barely got out my name and address when I felt him behind me. His arm wrapped around my neck and suddenly I couldn't breathe. I knew I was going to die. All I could think about was Daisy, how I should have left long ago, how I should have protected her. Then I blacked out. There must have been a police officer right around the corner, because when I came to, somehow I was alive and Luke was on the floor. There was blood everywhere. They told me he grabbed an officer's gun as he was being arrested, and they'd had no choice but to shoot."

Zeke took a step forward. "I knew it was bad. Hell, Lind, but I didn't know it was that bad. I'll be honest. I'm glad he's dead, because I'd be tempted to put him in the ground myself."

Lindy went back to picking things up, setting another stack of papers on one of the lower shelves. He went over to stop her, to make her turn around and face him, when he recognized something she had in her hand. A small pile of printer paper that was stacked together. He saw her look at it and frown, her head tilting in question.

"Who's this?"

She turned it toward him and there, facing him, was a picture of his daughter. And not just any picture, it was one of the ones he'd been avoiding looking for. They hadn't been in his desk after all, they'd been on that bookshelf.

Every ounce of pain that he'd felt after seeing that picture roll off his printer returned in full force, and he felt himself shut down, even as her question hung in the air. What the hell was wrong with him? She'd just opened up to him and told him about the worst day of her life. So why couldn't he tell her about his?

Because he couldn't.

Maybe it was some character flaw in him, maybe he was just not built like normal people, but he knew he wasn't going to talk to her about it. Wasn't going to suggest they start seeing each other. He didn't want to watch Lindy go through what he'd put Janice through. Especially not after what she'd endured with Luke. She needed someone who could be open and honest and give her that new life she deserved. That person wasn't him.

And Daisy should have someone who wouldn't constantly compare her to a ghost or wonder what his own daughter might have looked like. He'd known all along this was a bad idea, and Lindy had shown him just how bad it could get.

"It's Marina. I used an age progression program to see what she'd look like as she grew up." He took the sheaf from her and set it on top of another stack of papers. When Lindy was gone, he was going to shred them and be rid of them once and for all.

Thank God she'd found that picture before he started something he now knew he couldn't finish. So he needed to finish it in another way.

"Listen, Lindy, about last night..." He didn't want to hurt her, although he wasn't sure that what he was going to say would do more than sting. Maybe he'd been wrong, and she really didn't care about him as a person at all. Maybe she was just experimenting with something she'd never been able to experience as a married woman.

He swallowed hard. Just a few minutes ago, as he'd lain in bed, he'd actually contemplated attaching a permanence to their relationship that had been so premature it was laughable. Except no one had ever felt less like laughing than Zeke.

"What about it?" She was watching him, a wariness in her eyes that hadn't been there a minute or two ago. Then her face cleared even as all the color drained out of it. "I see."

For several seconds no one said anything. As he was formulating the words that would make the smallest burn circle possible, she beat him to it. "Were you afraid I was going to expect something out of you because of what we did here? If so, don't. You've already seen that I'm a neurotic mess. And that won't change." She pulled her hair over one shoulder. "I have no intention of getting involved with anyone ever again. I have a daughter to protect."

The use of that last word felt designed to cut and maim, which it did. Especially since part of his reason for breaking things off was Daisy herself.

What if someday he resented the fact that Daisy was alive, and she figured out why? He couldn't do that to her. Couldn't do that to Lindy. And he definitely couldn't do it to himself.

Only he didn't need to say any of it, because Lindy was telling him she had no interest in pursuing something more. Well, that was perfect. It was win-win for both of them.

"I know you do. And I was going to suggest basically the same thing. Whether it's our timing or..." He cleared his throat. "Whatever it is, it's obvious neither of us wants a steady relationship right now. This was great. I enjoyed it. But I think we were right the first time around. It's better if we keep our relationship strictly professional."

Lindy's expression had gone very still, and he wondered for a second if he'd only heard what he'd wanted to hear. No. She'd said specifically that she had no intention of getting involved with anyone. Because of Daisy.

Well, that made two of them. He couldn't get involved with her. Because of her daughter. And because of him. She thought she was a neurotic mess. Well, his neuroses beat hers hands down.

He was suddenly wishing he'd finished getting dressed. He felt naked and exposed even with the important parts covered.

"Right. Now that we've both cleared the

air and found that we're in agreement, I'm going to go. I need to pick up Daisy from Mom's house, and I have some errands to run."

Errands that didn't involve him. The sting of pain that caused made him grit his teeth for a second or two.

"I thought she was staying with your mom for the night."

"I've changed my mind."

Because of him. A wall of hurt rose up, towering over him. "I'll get dressed and take you."

"No!" She stopped and then lowered her voice. "I really don't want them to see you pull up. It'll just give Daisy an opportunity to talk to you, and I think we both know that's not a good idea. I don't want her getting attached, only to have... Only to have to tell her that she can't see you anymore."

"I understand." His heart felt as hard as a rock. She wasn't going to let him see Daisy again. Well, why would she? It was true,

Daisy had launched herself at him almost every time she'd seen him. It was better this way. For both of them. "I can at least take you to the hospital to get your car."

"Thank you, but I'd actually rather take a taxi. I've called them already, in fact. They should be here any minute. So I'm going to go down to meet them."

She glanced at the paper lying on top of the stack. "Your daughter would have been very beautiful, Zeke. I'm so sorry she's no longer with you."

And with that, she went out his front door and quietly shut it behind her.

As he stood there, staring at the space she'd once occupied, he wondered if he'd somehow just made the biggest mistake of his life. And somewhere inside the answer came: yes, he had. Only he'd realized it far too late.

Lindy got through the rest of the week in a daze. Every time she looked at the board over the nurses' desk and saw her name on cases other than Zeke's, she realized he'd shut her out. Not only out of his personal life—it also looked like he'd shut her out of his surgical life. She missed working with him. Missed talking to him. Missed making love with him.

But those were no longer viable options. So she needed to do one of two things. Suck it up and make the best of things or quit a job she'd come to love and try to find another position at one of the other hospitals in the city. It wouldn't be hard. Nurses with her qualifications were in high demand, from what she'd heard. She'd had four offers before settling on Mid Savannah Medical Center. She'd chosen the best of the best.

In more ways than one.

And it looked like she wasn't going to get to keep any of them.

What about the women's crisis center?

She'd personally asked Zeke to be involved in it. Volunteering there would be torture, although she doubted he'd put in another appearance if she were in the room.

The strange thing was, Zeke had come into that living room naked, but he'd been a much softer man than the one who'd re-emerged in briefs and affirmed every reason she'd given for them not being together. Neither of them had talked about love. She'd had to assume that Zeke felt nothing for her. That had stabbed her through the heart, and she'd been unable to catch her breath for several terrifying seconds. It was like being strangled all over again. Only this time it had been caused by her own stupidity.

She could have sworn, though…

When she'd told him she couldn't think with him standing there, he'd given her this smile. This sexy, *oh, really?* kind of grin that had given her a boost of confidence. That confidence had been short-lived. Because the next thing she'd known, his face had gone stony and cold, and she had no idea why.

It had been right after she'd picked up that picture of his daughter.

Was he mad that she'd touched it? No, it hadn't seemed that way. Shocked was more like it. Well, she'd been shocked too, because the face in the top picture on the stack had looked like Zeke. So why…? Then she realized it had to do with Daisy. She was about the same age as Marina when she'd died. But what if Zeke had realized the same thing. From the look on his face it had been a while since he'd seen those pictures. Maybe he'd thought he'd lost them. They'd been mixed in with all those scattered papers.

So? How did standing here agonizing over the whys change any of it? It didn't. So it was better just to make a decision and then stand by it. The way she had as she'd stood in his living room. She was not going to go back and beg him to be in a relationship with her. The old Lindy might have done exactly that. But the woman who looked back at her in the mirror every morning was no longer a pushover who would lie down and let people wipe their feet on her. She'd made it through a terrible ordeal. This was a walk in the park compared to that.

She had a feeling she was comparing apples to oranges, but it didn't matter. What was done was done and there was no going back. For either of them. The sooner she realized that the better. With that, she opened her computer and jumped from website to website, searching for the perfect position. One that was as far from Mid Savannah Medical Center as she could get.

CHAPTER ELEVEN

HE COULDN'T BELIEVE she would leave the hospital over what had happened between them. But who could blame her, honestly? He'd done nothing to convince her to stay. He hadn't even put her on his surgical schedule. If that wasn't him telling her she wasn't wanted, he didn't know what was. He hadn't meant it that way.

No, Zeke. You never do.

But where the hell was she? The thought of her going back to California made him feel physically ill.

Why? It should make everything a whole lot easier for him, but it didn't. He was more miserable than he'd ever been, actually.

He jiggled his pencil between his fingers and tried to reason through things. Tried to take them apart and examine them one piece at a time. When he came to the one in the middle he stopped. Stared at it with eyes that finally had the blinders stripped away. He loved her.

It was that simple. And that complicated.

That was why he'd taken her off his rotation. Why he instinctively knew that things could never go back to the way they used to be. It was far too late for that. It was either all or it was nothing. And for days now he'd teetered between two worlds. The present. And the past. He could only live in one or the other.

Which did he choose?

The possibility of living with a deep well of pain with a margin of happiness? Or living with a deep well of pain and no happiness?

Did he want wrinkles? Or crinkles?

Did it even matter? She was gone. He'd driven her away with his stupidity.

There was only one thing to do. He walked

out of the hospital, got into his car and headed home. Once there, he took the thin batch of papers and stared at them one by one, inspecting each change with a surgeon's eyes.

They weren't his daughter. They would never be his daughter. In holding on to something that wasn't real, he'd probably destroyed the best thing that had happened to him since Marina's death. Lindy. And Daisy. He loved that little girl. He didn't know how or why, but he did. And, by God, he loved her mother too.

Marina would be horrified at how long he'd held on to those fake pictures. The ones he needed to cherish were the ones that were real and depicted her as she had been. A sweet, kind soul who hadn't deserved what had happened.

And neither had Lindy. She hadn't deserved what he'd dished out. Or what he hadn't dished out, actually. His silence about the real issue had spoken volumes. And he'd been wrong.

What could he do about it now?

For one thing, he would get rid of these images. Even as he thought it, he turned on the shredder and slowly fed the manufactured photos through it.

Then he could learn to talk. Even when he was in pain. So what if he didn't want to. It was what adults did, and if he couldn't figure out how it worked, then he'd better damn well find a therapist who could help him get there.

One thing he did know. He wanted his future to include Lindy and Daisy.

And if he gave in and begged Lindy to come back, what then? What if Daisy got sick and died? What if Lindy was hit by a car? And died?

Was the hurt of that possibility worse than the hurt of losing Lindy forever?

No. It wasn't.

So he needed to find her and quickly. Before it was too late. And he knew just where to start.

* * *

Lindy sat in the waiting room of a stepdown hospital on the other side of the city from Mid Savannah. She hated it. Didn't like the people, didn't like the feeling she got when she came through those double doors. She knew it had nothing to do with the hospital, though, and everything to do with her.

Because she hadn't liked any of the other four hospitals she'd applied at either. Two of them had offered to hire her on the spot. But she'd held off. She'd know it when it was right.

Or at least that's what she'd told herself.

She wasn't as sure as she'd once been. After all, she hadn't been willing to go back and confront Zeke about what had happened in his living room a week ago. And it was too late now. She'd already resigned from her position. She doubted they would take her back, since she'd given hardly any notice. But she'd barely been scheduled for any surgeries either. She didn't want to just sit around and do nothing. That wasn't the way she operated.

Ha! So she operated by running away from her problems? Since when? Lord, she hadn't run when she should have, and now she'd run when she shouldn't have. She'd run away from a man who meant the world to her. Who had shown her life in a whole new way. He was the best thing to ever happen to her. And she'd crumpled up her broken heart and tossed any chance of getting him back out the window.

Except he didn't love her. He'd practically said it himself.

Only he hadn't. She'd ended up doing most of the talking, putting all kinds of words into his mouth, which he'd merely repeated. And she'd never said the one thing that might have made all the difference. If he didn't love her back, then she'd have to accept it.

But what if he did? What if, like her, he'd just been afraid to admit the truth?

Dammit, she should hunt the man down

and tell him how she felt about him. If he didn't feel the same way, she'd be no worse off. She could just keep job hunting and hope that she would one day get over him.

But only if she got actual closure. Only if she heard the words come out of his mouth.

A woman came out and called her name. It was her turn to be interviewed. She stood and looked at the HR person and gave her a smile and a quiet apology, and then she turned and walked back the way she'd come. For once in her life she was going to face down her fears and kick them in the butt. And then she was going to go and confront Zeke.

As she went through the exit, she was so intent on getting where she was going that she didn't see a man coming up on her right until he said her name.

The voice was familiar. Too familiar. She turned in a rush and saw Zeke standing there. How in the world…?

Maybe he was picking something up. He

might not have come looking for her. But hadn't she been about to go try to find him?

Well, here he was.

She was just going to do it and to hell with the consequences. Up went her chin and when she spoke her voice didn't quaver. Instead it was solid with conviction.

"I was actually getting ready to go see you."

He smiled. "Well, that's pretty convenient, because I was coming to see you."

"What? How?"

"What do you mean, how?"

"I mean how did you know where I was?"

He reached a hand out and then seemed to think better of it. "You weren't home and weren't taking my calls, so I went to the one person who would know where I could find you."

"My mom."

"Yes, but don't blame her. She wasn't sure about telling me at first, but Daisy vouched for me."

That made her laugh. "Of course she did. She probably ran up to you and gave you a kiss, didn't she?"

"How did you know?" He shoved his hands in his pockets. "I did something bad, though, while I was there. I told Daisy a secret."

Foreboding swept over her and then came tears, her voice breaking as she forced out the words. "Don't you make her fall for you the way you made *me* fall for you. Not unless you intend to follow through."

He frowned but didn't say anything. Okay, she'd said her piece. That was that.

"What…what did you say?" His voice was soft and laced with an intensity that sent goosebumps skittering up her spine.

She didn't care. She was going to get her closure if she had to drag it out of him. "I said I fell for you."

There. Digest that!

"What if I told you that I fell for you long before you fell for me?"

"I'd say that was impossible." Her heart warred with her mind for several long seconds before one of them came out the victor.

"Why do you say that?"

"Because I fell for you while we were sitting on a blanket at the jazz festival."

His eyes closed for a second before flicking open and staring at her. "Say that again."

"I fell in love with you." She changed the tense to present. "I *am* in love with you."

"You said you had no intention of getting involved with anyone."

"You fed me that same line."

"I lied." Their voices marched across the space in unison.

This time Lindy got there first. "But why?"

"I lost my daughter. And I was afraid of getting attached to Daisy. To you. And then losing one or both of you too. Or shutting down emotionally and then losing one or both of you. In my mind, the outcome was always the same. I lost you."

"Oh, God, Zeke. When I think of what could have happened…"

"I know. And when you left the hospital, I had visions of you running back to California and realized the real danger of losing you didn't come from the outside. It came from me. I pushed you away before you could leave. And it evidently worked."

"Not quite. Because as I was sitting here, waiting for an interview, I realized that I'm done running. Done being afraid of what might happen. Things happen, they happened to both of us, but that doesn't mean they will again."

Zeke nodded, and he cupped her face with hands that shook. "I think I finally came to terms with that over the last couple of days. I love you, Lind. I want to be with you. Only you."

She pressed her forehead to his. "Yes. I want that too. All of it."

"I don't have a ring yet. There hasn't been

time. But I do want you wearing my ring. If you'll say yes."

"Oh, Zeke, of course I will. And yes."

"I want to do it right this time. My ex-wife and I got married young. Probably too young. But you and I have both lived through some terrible circumstances. And I think we're mature enough—and smart enough—to know what we want out of life and to go after it. At least I am."

"Me too."

Lindy drew in a deep breath and held it for a second before allowing all the past hurts to flow out and disappear into the atmosphere. "So are you saying you actually *want* me as your wife, Dr. Bruen?"

"I definitely do, Surgical Nurse Franklin."

He kissed her and then drew her into his arms and held her tight. "I almost lost you."

"No, you didn't. Like I said, I was coming to find you. I was planning to tell you how I felt about you. Instead, you found me."

"Thank God we both came to our senses.

Is it too early to tell your folks? To tell Daisy?"

"To be honest, I think my mom already knows. And if I know my daughter, Daisy probably knows you're here to stay."

"And I am. Here to stay." He wrapped an arm around her waist as they walked toward the exit. "Come back to Mid Savannah. We all want you back."

"I don't know if they'll have me back."

He smiled and drew her closer. "I'm pretty sure you'll be welcomed back with open arms. By Neil. By our team. By me. *Especially* by me."

As the automatic doors swept open, dropping them right into the heat and humidity that defined Savannah, she couldn't think of any place she'd rather be than with this man. And now that she had him, she was never letting him go again.

They deserved a fresh start and a happy ending. And it looked like this gentle southern city was going to give them exactly what they wished for.

EPILOGUE

LINDY AND ZEKE, along with the hospital administrator and a few other key folks, gathered around a wide red ribbon that stretched across a white-pillared porch. What had once been a genteel old house a few blocks from the hospital was about to become the Mid Savannah Women's Crisis Center. Neil, scissors in hand to cut the ribbon, awaited a signal from somewhere off to the side.

Zeke wrapped his arm around his wife's waist, uncaring that there were photographers snapping constant pictures. His hand splayed over the side of Lindy's belly, thumb tracing over the taut surface, where a new life was rapidly making its presence known. The first three months of marriage had been exciting in more ways than one. The pink "plus" symbol that had appeared on the pregnancy test had come as quite a shock, but after a few minutes of blinding panic, he'd welcomed the news wholeheartedly.

Caleb Roger Bruen would be well loved. There were no guarantees in this life—for any of them—but Zeke had decided that fear and guilt would no longer take up residence in his heart. He had been given a second chance at love…one he probably didn't deserve, but he was not going to take it for granted, or waste a single precious minute of their time together.

"Ready?" Neil's voice called him back to the present. "One, two, three." He sheared the ribbon in two as cheers from the onlookers went up all around them.

The hospital administrator had wanted to name the place after Lindy, but she'd refused, saying that that part of her life was behind her. That while she wanted to help as many women as she could, she would rather not have a constant reminder of what she'd personally gone through. She needed to move forward with her life. Plus the fact that she wanted to be able to tell their children at a place and time of her choosing and not because they'd seen her name on a sign.

Once the pictures were done, he leaned down to her ear. "Feeling okay?"

"Perfect. You?"

"More than perfect."

She turned and faced him. "I love you, Zeke."

"I love you too."

She peered to the side, where the crisp white porch gave way to huge magnolia trees that stretched down the road almost as far as the eye could see. The blooms were magnificent. "This is my favorite time of year."

"Is it?"

"Mmm…" She put her hands on her belly. "It's the perfect time to be pregnant."

She seemed to like that word right now, and he could see why. He liked it too.

"I hadn't realized there was a perfect time."

"There isn't, but I just love the way the magnolias bloom."

He dropped a kiss on her mouth. "I love the way *you* bloom. You are glowing."

"It's the heat."

No, it wasn't, but he wasn't going to argue with her. He'd asked her to hold off working at the center until she'd had the baby, but Lindy, in her calm unruffled way, had sat him down and told him that she needed this. Needed to continue what she'd started when she'd first returned to Savannah. She promised not to take any unnecessary chances and would take a break once she hit her seventh month.

Zeke would have to trust her. He *did* trust her. She wanted this baby as much as he did. And so did Daisy. She couldn't wait to meet her new brother.

"What time do we need to be at your parents' house?"

Her head tilted to look at him as the reporters moved on to their next story and people began clearing away the ribbon and the rest of the paraphernalia that went with the grand opening.

"Not until six, why?" She gave him a smile that could only be described as wicked. "Did you have something in mind?"

He hadn't. Until she'd said that. It didn't take much to start him thinking along those lines nowadays. Then again, Lindy had been pretty amorous herself.

"Always." He glanced down at his watch. "It's three. Does that give us enough time?"

She laughed. "Are you feeling a little ambitious today?"

"I'm 'ambitious' every day, when it comes to you."

"Well, then, I'd better put all of that ambition to work." She stretched up on tiptoe and gave him a slow kiss that made something start buzzing in his skull.

He pulled away, his breathing no longer

steady. "We'd better get going if we're going to reach the house. Hopefully there are no emergencies."

She slid her fingers into his hair. "The only emergency right now…is me."

So Zeke took her hands and kissed the palm of each one, before towing her behind him on their way to the parking area. He couldn't wait to get her home. Where he could show her just how much she meant to him.

And where he would renew his vow to be the best husband he could. Because Lindy, Daisy and now Caleb deserved the best of everything. And he was going to see that they got it.

Each and every day of his life.

* * * * *

LET'S TALK

Romance

For exclusive extracts, competitions
and special offers, find us online:

f facebook.com/millsandboon

◎ @millsandboonuk

𝕐 @millsandboon

Or get in touch on 0844 844 1351*

For all the latest titles coming soon,
visit millsandboon.co.uk/nextmonth

Collins World Atlas

MINI EDITION

Collins

COLLINS WORLD ATLAS
MINI EDITION

Collins
An imprint of HarperCollins Publishers
Westerhill Road, Bishopbriggs,
Glasgow
G64 2QT

First Published as Collins Mini Atlas of the World 1999
Second edition 2004
Third Edition 2007
Fourth Edition 2009

Reprinted with changes 2012

Copyright © HarperCollins Publishers 2012
Maps © Collins Bartholomew Ltd 2012

Printed in Hong Kong

British Library Cataloguing in Publication Data.
A catalogue record for this book is available from the British Library.

ISBN 978-0-00-784960-4

All mapping in this atlas is generated from Collins Bartholomew™
digital databases. Collins Bartholomew™, the UK's leading
independent geographical information supplier, can provide a digital,
custom, and premium mapping service to a variety of markets.
For further information:
Tel: +44 (0) 208 307 4515
e-mail: collinsbartholomew@harpercollins.co.uk
or visit our website at: www.collinsbartholomew.com

Follow us on Twitter @collinsmaps

CONTENTS

AFGHANISTAN
Islamic State of Afghanistan
Capital Kābul

Area sq km	652 225	**Currency**	Afghani
Area sq miles	251 825	**Languages**	Dari, Pushtu,
Population	32 358 000		Uzbek, Turkmen

ALBANIA
Republic of Albania
Capital Tirana (Tiranë)

Area sq km	28 748	**Currency**	Lek
Area sq miles	11 100	**Languages**	Albanian, Greek
Population	3 216 000		

ALGERIA
People's Democratic Republic of Algeria
Capital Algiers (Alger)

Area sq km	2 381 741	**Currency**	Algerian dinar
Area sq miles	919 595	**Languages**	Arabic, French,
Population	35 980 000		Berber

ANDORRA
Principality of Andorra
Capital Andorra la Vella

Area sq km	465	**Currency**	Euro
Area sq miles	180	**Languages**	Spanish,
Population	86 000		Catalan, French

ANGOLA
Republic of Angola
Capital Luanda

Area sq km	1 246 700	**Currency**	Kwanza
Area sq miles	481 354	**Languages**	Portuguese,
Population	19 618 000		Bantu, local lang.

ANTIGUA AND BARBUDA
Capital St John's

Area sq km	442	**Currency**	East Caribbean
Area sq miles	171		dollar
Population	90 000	**Languages**	English, creole

ARGENTINA
Argentine Republic
Capital Buenos Aires

Area sq km	2 766 889	**Currency**	Argentinian peso
Area sq miles	1 068 302	**Languages**	Spanish, Italian,
Population	40 765 000		Amerindian lang.

ARMENIA
Republic of Armenia
Capital Yerevan (Erevan)

Area sq km	29 800	**Currency**	Dram
Area sq miles	11 506	**Languages**	Armenian, Azeri
Population	3 100 000		

AUSTRALIA
Commonwealth of Australia
Capital Canberra

Area sq km	7 692 024	**Currency**	Australian dolla
Area sq miles	2 969 907	**Languages**	English, Italian
Population	22 606 000		Greek

AUSTRIA
Republic of Austria
Capital Vienna (Wien)

Area sq km	83 855	**Currency**	Euro
Area sq miles	32 377	**Languages**	German,
Population	8 413 000		Croatian, Turki

AZERBAIJAN
Republic of Azerbaijan
Capital Baku

Area sq km	86 600	**Currency**	Azerbaijani ma
Area sq miles	33 436	**Languages**	Azeri, Armenia
Population	9 306 000		Russian, Lezgia

THE BAHAMAS
Commonwealth of The Bahamas
Capital Nassau

Area sq km	13 939	**Currency**	Bahamian dolla
Area sq miles	5 382	**Languages**	English, creole
Population	347 000		

BAHRAIN
Kingdom of Bahrain
Capital Manama (Al Manāmah)

Area sq km	691	**Currency**	Bahraini dinar
Area sq miles	267	**Languages**	Arabic, English
Population	1 324 000		

BANGLADESH
People's Republic of Bangladesh
Capital Dhaka (Dacca)

Area sq km	143 998	**Currency**	Taka
Area sq miles	55 598	**Languages**	Bengali, Englis
Population	150 494 000		

BARBADOS
Capital Bridgetown

Area sq km	430	**Currency**	Barbados dolla
Area sq miles	166	**Languages**	English, creole
Population	274 000		

BELARUS
Republic of Belarus
Capital Minsk

Area sq km	207 600	**Currency**	Belarus rouble
Area sq miles	80 155	**Languages**	Belorussian,
Population	9 559 000		Russian

BELGIUM
Kingdom of Belgium
Capital Brussels (Bruxelles)

Area sq km	30 520	**Currency**	Euro
Area sq miles	11 784	**Languages**	Dutch (Flemish),
Population	10 754 000		French (Walloon),
			German

BELIZE
Capital Belmopan

Area sq km	22 965	**Currency**	Belize dollar
Area sq miles	8 867	**Languages**	English, Spanish,
Population	318 000		Mayan, creole

BENIN
Republic of Benin
Capital Porto-Novo

Area sq km	112 620	**Currency**	CFA franc*
Area sq miles	43 483	**Languages**	French, Fon,
Population	9 100 000		Yoruba, Adja,
			local lang.

BHUTAN
Kingdom of Bhutan
Capital Thimphu

Area sq km	46 620	**Currency**	Ngultrum,
Area sq miles	18 000		Indian rupee
Population	738 000	**Languages**	Dzongkha,
			Nepali, Assamese

BOLIVIA
Plurinational State of Bolivia
Capital La Paz/Sucre

Area sq km	1 098 581	**Currency**	Boliviano
Area sq miles	424 164	**Languages**	Spanish, Quechua,
Population	10 088 000		Aymara

BOSNIA-HERZEGOVINA
Republic of Bosnia and Herzegovina
Capital Sarajevo

Area sq km	51 130	**Currency**	Marka
Area sq miles	19 741	**Languages**	Bosnian, Serbian,
Population	3 752 000		Croatian

BOTSWANA
Republic of Botswana
Capital Gaborone

Area sq km	581 370	**Currency**	Pula
Area sq miles	224 468	**Languages**	English, Setswana,
Population	2 031 000		Shona, local lang.

BRAZIL
Federative Republic of Brazil
Capital Brasília

Area sq km	8 514 879	**Currency**	Real
Area sq miles	3 287 613	**Languages**	Portuguese
Population	196 655 000		

BRUNEI
State of Brunei Darussalam
Capital Bandar Seri Begawan

Area sq km	5 765	**Currency**	Brunei dollar
Area sq miles	2 226	**Languages**	Malay, English,
Population	406 000		Chinese

BULGARIA
Republic of Bulgaria
Capital Sofia (Sofiya)

Area sq km	110 994	**Currency**	Lev
Area sq miles	42 855	**Languages**	Bulgarian,
Population	7 446 000		Turkish, Romany,
			Macedonian

BURKINA FASO
Democratic Republic of Burkina Faso
Capital Ouagadougou

Area sq km	274 200	**Currency**	CFA franc*
Area sq miles	105 869	**Languages**	French, Moore
Population	16 968 000		(Mossi), Fulani,
			local lang.

BURUNDI
Republic of Burundi
Capital Bujumbura

Area sq km	27 835	**Currency**	Burundian franc
Area sq miles	10 747	**Languages**	Kirundi (Hutu,
Population	8 575 000		Tutsi), French

CAMBODIA
Kingdom of Cambodia
Capital Phnom Penh

Area sq km	181 035	**Currency**	Riel
Area sq miles	69 884	**Languages**	Khmer,
Population	14 305 000		Vietnamese

CAMEROON
Republic of Cameroon
Capital Yaoundé

Area sq km	475 442	**Currency** CFA franc*
Area sq miles	183 569	**Languages** French, English,
Population	20 030 000	Fang, Bamileke, local lang.

CANADA
Capital Ottawa

Area sq km	9 984 670	**Currency** Canadian dollar
Area sq miles	3 855 103	**Languages** English, French
Population	34 350 000	

CAPE VERDE
Republic of Cape Verde
Capital Praia

Area sq km	4 033	**Currency** Cape Verde
Area sq niles	1 557	escudo
Population	501 000	**Languages** Portuguese, creole

CENTRAL AFRICAN REPUBLIC
Capital Bangui

Area sq km	622 436	**Currency** CFA franc*
Area sq miles	240 324	**Languages** French, Sango,
Population	4 487 000	Banda, Baya, local lang.

CHAD
Republic of Chad
Capital Ndjamena

Area sq km	1 284 000	**Currency** CFA franc*
Area sq miles	495 755	**Languages** Arabic, French,
Population	11 525 000	Sara, local lang.

CHILE
Republic of Chile
Capital Santiago

Area sq km	756 945	**Currency** Chilean peso
Area sq miles	292 258	**Languages** Spanish,
Population	17 270 000	Amerindian lang.

CHINA
People's Republic of China
Capital Beijing (Peking)

Area sq km	9 584 492	**Currency** Yuan, HK dollar,
Area sq miles	3 700 593	Macao pataca
Population	1 332 079 000	**Languages** Mandarin, Hsiang, Cantonese, Wu, regional lang.

COLOMBIA
Republic of Colombia
Capital Bogotá

Area sq km	1 141 748	**Currency** Colombian pes
Area sq miles	440 831	**Languages** Spanish,
Population	46 927 000	Amerindian la

COMOROS
United Republic of the Comoros
Capital Moroni

Area sq km	1 862	**Currency** Comoros franc
Area sq miles	719	**Languages** Shikomor
Population	754 000	(Comorian), French, Arabic

CONGO
Republic of the Congo
Capital Brazzaville

Area sq km	342 000	**Currency** CFA franc*
Area sq miles	132 047	**Languages** French, Kongo
Population	4 140 000	Monokutuba, local lang.

CONGO, DEMOCRATIC REPUBLIC OF THE
Capital Kinshasa

Area sq km	2 345 410	**Currency** Congolese frar
Area sq miles	905 568	**Languages** French, Lingala
Population	67 758 000	Swahili, Kongo local lang.

COSTA RICA
Republic of Costa Rica
Capital San José

Area sq km	51 100	**Currency** Costa Rican co
Area sq miles	19 730	**Languages** Spanish
Population	4 727 000	

CÔTE D'IVOIRE (IVORY COAST)
Republic of Côte d'Ivoire
Capital Yamoussoukro

Area sq km	322 463	**Currency** CFA franc*
Area sq miles	124 504	**Languages** French, creole,
Population	20 153 000	Akan, local lan

CROATIA
Republic of Croatia
Capital Zagreb

Area sq km	56 538	**Currency** Kuna
Area sq miles	21 829	**Languages** Croatian, Serb
Population	4 396 000	

CUBA
Republic of Cuba
Capital Havana (La Habana)

Area sq km	110 860	**Currency**	Cuban peso
Area sq miles	42 803	**Languages**	Spanish
Population	11 254 000		

EAST TIMOR
Democratic Republic of Timor-Leste
Capital Dili

Area sq km	14 874	**Currency**	US dollar
Area sq miles	5 743	**Languages**	Portuguese, Tetun, English
Population	1 154 000		

CYPRUS
Republic of Cyprus
Capital Nicosia (Lefkosia)

Area sq km	9 251	**Currency**	Euro
Area sq miles	3 572	**Languages**	Greek, Turkish, English
Population	1 117 000		

ECUADOR
Republic of Ecuador
Capital Quito

Area sq km	272 045	**Currency**	US dollar
Area sq miles	105 037	**Languages**	Spanish, Quechua, Amerindian lang.
Population	14 666 000		

CZECH REPUBLIC
Capital Prague (Praha)

Area sq km	78 864	**Currency**	Czech koruna
Area sq miles	30 450	**Languages**	Czech, Moravian, Slovakian
Population	10 534 000		

EGYPT
Arab Republic of Egypt
Capital Cairo (Al Qāhirah)

Area sq km	1 000 250	**Currency**	Egyptian pound
Area sq miles	386 199	**Languages**	Arabic
Population	82 537 000		

DENMARK
Kingdom of Denmark
Capital Copenhagen (København)

Area sq km	43 075	**Currency**	Danish krone
Area sq miles	16 631	**Languages**	Danish
Population	5 573 000		

EL SALVADOR
Republic of El Salvador
Capital San Salvador

Area sq km	21 041	**Currency**	El Salvador colón, US dollar
Area sq miles	8 124	**Languages**	Spanish
Population	6 227 000		

DJIBOUTI
Republic of Djibouti
Capital Djibouti

Area sq km	23 200	**Currency**	Djibouti franc
Area sq miles	8 958	**Languages**	Somali, Afar, French, Arabic
Population	906 000		

EQUATORIAL GUINEA
Republic of Equatorial Guinea
Capital Malabo

Area sq km	28 051	**Currency**	CFA franc*
Area sq miles	10 831	**Languages**	Spanish, French, Fang
Population	720 000		

DOMINICA
Commonwealth of Dominica
Capital Roseau

Area sq km	750	**Currency**	East Caribbean dollar
Area sq miles	290	**Languages**	English, creole
Population	68 000		

ERITREA
State of Eritrea
Capital Asmara

Area sq km	117 400	**Currency**	Nakfa
Area sq miles	45 328	**Languages**	Tigrinya, Tigre
Population	5 415 000		

DOMINICAN REPUBLIC
Capital Santo Domingo

Area sq km	48 442	**Currency**	Dominican peso
Area sq miles	18 704	**Languages**	Spanish, creole
Population	10 056 000		

ESTONIA
Republic of Estonia
Capital Tallinn

Area sq km	45 200	**Currency**	Euro
Area sq miles	17 452	**Languages**	Estonian, Russian
Population	1 341 000		

ETHIOPIA
Federal Democratic Republic of Ethiopia
Capital Addis Ababa (Ādīs Ābeba)

Area sq km	1 133 880	Currency	Birr
Area sq miles	437 794	Languages	Oromo, Amharic,
Population	84 734 000		Tigrinya,
			local lang.

GEORGIA
Republic of Georgia
Capital Tbilisi

Area sq km	69 700	Currency	Lari
Area sq miles	26 911	Languages	Georgian, Russi
Population	4 329 000		Armenian, Azeri
			Ossetian, Abkha

FIJI
Republic of Fiji
Capital Suva

Area sq km	18 330	Currency	Fiji dollar
Area sq miles	7 077	Languages	English, Fijian,
Population	868 000		Hindi

GERMANY
Federal Republic of Germany
Capital Berlin

Area sq km	357 022	Currency	Euro
Area sq miles	137 849	Languages	German, Turkis
Population	82 163 000		

FINLAND
Republic of Finland
Capital Helsinki (Helsingfors)

Area sq km	338 145	Currency	Euro
Area sq miles	130 559	Languages	Finnish, Swedish
Population	5 385 000		

GHANA
Republic of Ghana
Capital Accra

Area sq km	238 537	Currency	Cedi
Area sq miles	92 100	Languages	English, Hausa,
Population	24 966 000		Akan, local lang.

FRANCE
French Republic
Capital Paris

Area sq km	543 965	Currency	Euro
Area sq miles	210 026	Languages	French, Arabic
Population	63 126 000		

GREECE
Hellenic Republic
Capital Athens (Athina)

Area sq km	131 957	Currency	Euro
Area sq miles	50 949	Languages	Greek
Population	11 390 000		

GABON
Gabonese Republic
Capital Libreville

Area sq km	267 667	Currency	CFA franc*
Area sq miles	103 347	Languages	French, Fang,
Population	1 534 000		local lang.

GRENADA
Capital St George's

Area sq km	378	Currency	East Caribbean
Area sq miles	146		dollar
Population	105 000	Languages	English, creole

THE GAMBIA
Republic of The Gambia
Capital Banjul

Area sq km	11 295	Currency	Dalasi
Area sq miles	4 361	Languages	English, Malinke,
Population	1 776 000		Fulani, Wolof

GUATEMALA
Republic of Guatemala
Capital Guatemala City

Area sq km	108 890	Currency	Quetzal, US doll
Area sq miles	42 043	Languages	Spanish,
Population	14 757 000		Mayan lang.

Gaza
Semi-autonomous region
Capital Gaza

Area sq km	363	Currency	Israeli shekel
Area sq miles	140	Languages	Arabic
Population	1 535 120		

GUINEA
Republic of Guinea
Capital Conakry

Area sq km	245 857	Currency	Guinea franc
Area sq miles	94 926	Languages	French, Fulani,
Population	10 222 000		Malinke,
			local lang.

GUINEA-BISSAU
Republic of Guinea-Bissau
Capital Bissau

Area sq km	36 125	**Currency**	CFA franc*
Area sq miles	13 948	**Languages**	Portuguese,
Population	1 547 000		crioulo, local lang.

GUYANA
Co-operative Republic of Guyana
Capital Georgetown

Area sq km	214 969	**Currency**	Guyana dollar
Area sq miles	83 000	**Languages**	English, creole,
Population	756 000		Amerindian lang.

HAITI
Republic of Haiti
Capital Port-au-Prince

Area sq km	27 750	**Currency**	Gourde
Area sq miles	10 714	**Languages**	French, creole
Population	10 124 000		

HONDURAS
Republic of Honduras
Capital Tegucigalpa

Area sq km	112 088	**Currency**	Lempira
Area sq miles	43 277	**Languages**	Spanish,
Population	7 755 000		Amerindian lang.

HUNGARY
Republic of Hungary
Capital Budapest

Area sq km	93 030	**Currency**	Forint
Area sq miles	35 919	**Languages**	Hungarian
Population	9 966 000		

ICELAND
Republic of Iceland
Capital Reykjavík

Area sq km	102 820	**Currency**	Icelandic króna
Area sq miles	39 699	**Languages**	Icelandic
Population	324 000		

INDIA
Republic of India
Capital New Delhi

Area sq km	3 064 898	**Currency**	Indian rupee
Area sq miles	1 183 364	**Languages**	Hindi, English,
Population	1 241 492 000		many regional
			lang.

INDONESIA
Republic of Indonesia
Capital Jakarta

Area sq km	1 919 445	**Currency**	Rupiah
Area sq miles	741 102	**Languages**	Indonesian,
Population	242 326 000		local lang.

IRAN
Islamic Republic of Iran
Capital Tehrān

Area sq km	1 648 000	**Currency**	Iranian rial
Area sq miles	636 296	**Languages**	Farsi, Azeri,
Population	74 799 000		Kurdish,
			regional lang.

IRAQ
Republic of Iraq
Capital Baghdād

Area sq km	438 317	**Currency**	Iraqi dinar
Area sq miles	169 235	**Languages**	Arabic, Kurdish,
Population	32 665 000		Turkmen

IRELAND
Republic of Ireland
Capital Dublin (Baile Átha Cliath)

Area sq km	70 282	**Currency**	Euro
Area sq miles	27 136	**Languages**	English, Irish
Population	4 526 000		

ISRAEL
State of Israel
Capital Jerusalem* (Yerushalayim) (El Quds)

Area sq km	20 770	**Currency**	Shekel
Area sq miles	8 019	**Languages**	Hebrew, Arabic
Population	7 562 000		

* De facto capital. Disputed.

ITALY
Italian Republic
Capital Rome (Roma)

Area sq km	301 245	**Currency**	Euro
Area sq miles	116 311	**Languages**	Italian
Population	60 789 000		

JAMAICA
Capital Kingston

Area sq km	10 991	**Currency**	Jamaican dollar
Area sq miles	4 244	**Languages**	English, creole
Population	2 751 000		

JAPAN
Capital Tōkyō

Area sq km	377 727	**Currency**	Yen
Area sq miles	145 841	**Languages**	Japanese
Population	126 497 000		

JORDAN
Hashemite Kingdom of Jordan
Capital 'Ammān

Area sq km	89 206	**Currency**	Jordanian dinar
Area sq miles	34 443	**Languages**	Arabic
Population	6 330 000		

KAZAKHSTAN
Republic of Kazakhstan
Capital Astana (Akmola)

Area sq km	2 717 300	**Currency**	Tenge
Area sq miles	1 049 155	**Languages**	Kazakh, Russian,
Population	16 207 000		Ukrainian, German,
			Uzbek, Tatar

KENYA
Republic of Kenya
Capital Nairobi

Area sq km	582 646	**Currency**	Kenyan shilling
Area sq miles	224 961	**Languages**	Swahili, English,
Population	41 610 000		local lang.

KIRIBATI
Republic of Kiribati
Capital Bairiki

Area sq km	717	**Currency**	Australian dollar
Area sq miles	277	**Languages**	Gilbertese,
Population	101 000		English

KOSOVO
Republic of Kosovo
Capital Prishtinë (Priština)

Area sq km	10 908	**Currency**	Euro
Area sq miles	4 212	**Languages**	Albanian, Serbian
Population	2 180 686		

KUWAIT
State of Kuwait
Capital Kuwait (Al Kuwayt)

Area sq km	17 818	**Currency**	Kuwaiti dinar
Area sq miles	6 880	**Languages**	Arabic
Population	2 818 000		

KYRGYZSTAN
Kyrgyz Republic
Capital Bishkek (Frunze)

Area sq km	198 500	**Currency**	Kyrgyz som
Area sq miles	76 641	**Languages**	Kyrgyz, Russian,
Population	5 393 000		Uzbek

LAOS
Lao People's Democratic Republic
Capital Vientiane (Viangchan)

Area sq km	236 800	**Currency**	Kip
Area sq miles	91 429	**Languages**	Lao, local lang.
Population	6 288 000		

LATVIA
Republic of Latvia
Capital Riga

Area sq km	64 589	**Currency**	Lats
Area sq miles	24 938	**Languages**	Latvian, Russian
Population	2 243 000		

LEBANON
Republic of Lebanon
Capital Beirut (Beyrouth)

Area sq km	10 452	**Currency**	Lebanese pound
Area sq miles	4 036	**Languages**	Arabic, Armenian,
Population	4 259 000		French

LESOTHO
Kingdom of Lesotho
Capital Maseru

Area sq km	30 355	**Currency**	Loti,
Area sq miles	11 720		S. African rand
Population	2 194 000	**Languages**	Sesotho, English,
			Zulu

LIBERIA
Republic of Liberia
Capital Monrovia

Area sq km	111 369	**Currency**	Liberian dollar
Area sq miles	43 000	**Languages**	English, creole,
Population	4 129 000		local lang.

LIBYA
Capital Tripoli (Ṭarābulus)

Area sq km	1 759 540	**Currency**	Libyan dinar
Area sq miles	679 362	**Languages**	Arabic, Berber
Population	6 423 000		

LIECHTENSTEIN
Principality of Liechtenstein
Capital Vaduz

Area sq km	160	**Currency**	Swiss franc
Area sq miles	62	**Languages**	German
Population	36 000		

LITHUANIA
Republic of Lithuania
Capital Vilnius

Area sq km	65 200	**Currency**	Litas
Area sq miles	25 174	**Languages**	Lithuanian,
Population	3 307 000		Russian, Polish

LUXEMBOURG
Grand Duchy of Luxembourg
Capital Luxembourg

Area sq km	2 586	**Currency**	Euro
Area sq miles	998	**Languages**	Letzeburgish,
Population	516 000		German, French

MACEDONIA (F.Y.R.O.M.)
Republic of Macedonia
Capital Skopje

Area sq km	25 713	**Currency**	Macedonian denar
Area sq miles	9 928	**Languages**	Macedonian,
Population	2 064 000		Albanian, Turkish

MADAGASCAR
Republic of Madagascar
Capital Antananarivo

Area sq km	587 041	**Currency**	Malagasy franc
Area sq miles	226 658		Malagasy ariary
Population	21 315 000	**Languages**	Malagasy, French

MALAWI
Republic of Malawi
Capital Lilongwe

Area sq km	118 484	**Currency**	Malawian kwacha
Area sq miles	45 747	**Languages**	Chichewa,
Population	15 381 000		English, local lang.

MALAYSIA
Federation of Malaysia
Capital Kuala Lumpur/Putrajaya

Area sq km	332 965	**Currency**	Ringgit
Area sq miles	128 559	**Languages**	Malay, English,
Population	28 859 000		Chinese, Tamil,
			local lang.

MALDIVES
Republic of the Maldives
Capital Male

Area sq km	298	**Currency**	Rufiyaa
Area sq miles	115	**Languages**	Divehi
Population	320 000		(Maldivian)

MALI
Republic of Mali
Capital Bamako

Area sq km	1 240 140	**Currency**	CFA franc*
Area sq miles	478 821	**Languages**	French, Bambara,
Population	15 840 000		local lang.

MALTA
Republic of Malta
Capital Valletta

Area sq km	316	**Currency**	Euro
Area sq miles	122	**Languages**	Maltese, English
Population	418 000		

MARSHALL ISLANDS
Republic of the Marshall Islands
Capital Delap-Uliga-Djarrit

Area sq km	181	**Currency**	US dollar
Area sq miles	70	**Languages**	English,
Population	55 000		Marshallese

MAURITANIA
Islamic Arab and African Rep. of Mauritania
Capital Nouakchott

Area sq km	1 030 700	**Currency**	Ouguiya
Area sq miles	397 955	**Languages**	Arabic, French,
Population	3 542 000		local lang.

MAURITIUS
Republic of Mauritius
Capital Port Louis

Area sq km	2 040	**Currency**	Mauritius rupee
Area sq miles	788	**Languages**	English, creole,
Population	1 307 000		Hindi, Bhojpurī,
			French

MEXICO
United Mexican States
Capital Mexico City

Area sq km	1 972 545	**Currency**	Mexican peso
Area sq miles	761 604	**Languages**	Spanish,
Population	114 793 000		Amerindian lang.

MICRONESIA, FEDERATED STATES OF
Capital Palikir

Area sq km	701	**Currency**	US dollar
Area sq miles	271	**Languages**	English, Chuukese,
Population	112 000		Pohnpeian,
			local lang.

13

MOLDOVA
Republic of Moldova
Capital Chişinău (Kishinev)

Area sq km	33 700	**Currency**	Moldovan leu
Area sq miles	13 012	**Languages**	Romanian,
Population	3 545 000		Ukrainian,
			Gagauz, Russian

MONACO
Principality of Monaco
Capital Monaco-Ville

Area sq km	2	**Currency**	Euro
Area sq miles	1	**Languages**	French,
Population	35 000		Monégasque,
			Italian

MONGOLIA
Capital Ulan Bator (Ulaanbaatar)

Area sq km	1 565 000	**Currency**	Tugrik (tögrög)
Area sq miles	604 250	**Languages**	Khalka
Population	2 800 000		(Mongolian),
			Kazakh,
			local lang.

MONTENEGRO
Republic of Montenegro
Capital Podgorica

Area sq km	13 812	**Currency**	Euro
Area sq miles	5 333	**Languages**	Serbian
Population	632 000		(Montenegrin),
			Albanian

MOROCCO
Kingdom of Morocco
Capital Rabat

Area sq km	446 550	**Currency**	Moroccan dirham
Area sq miles	172 414	**Languages**	Arabic, Berber,
Population	32 273 000		French

MOZAMBIQUE
Republic of Mozambique
Capital Maputo

Area sq km	799 380	**Currency**	Metical
Area sq miles	308 642	**Languages**	Portuguese,
Population	23 930 000		Makua, Tsonga,
			local lang.

MYANMAR (Burma)
Republic of the Union of Myanmar
Capital Nay Pyi Taw/Rangoon (Yangôn)

Area sq km	676 577	**Currency**	Kyat
Area sq miles	261 228	**Languages**	Burmese, Shan,
Population	48 337 000		Karen, local lang.

NAMIBIA
Republic of Namibia
Capital Windhoek

Area sq km	824 292	**Currency**	Namibian dolla
Area sq miles	318 261	**Languages**	English, Afrika
Population	2 324 000		German, Ovam
			local lang.

NAURU
Republic of Nauru
Capital Yaren

Area sq km	21	**Currency**	Australian dolla
Area sq miles	8	**Languages**	Nauruan, Englis
Population	10 000		

NEPAL
Federal Democratic Republic of Nepal
Capital Kathmandu

Area sq km	147 181	**Currency**	Nepalese rupee
Area sq miles	56 827	**Languages**	Nepali, Maithil
Population	30 486 000		Bhojpuri, Engli
			local lang.

NETHERLANDS
Kingdom of the Netherlands
Capital Amsterdam/The Hague ('s-Gravenh

Area sq km	41 526	**Currency**	Euro
Area sq miles	16 033	**Languages**	Dutch, Frisian
Population	16 665 000		

NEW ZEALAND
Capital Wellington

Area sq km	270 534	**Currency**	New Zealand
Area sq miles	104 454		dollar
Population	4 415 000	**Languages**	English, Maori

NICARAGUA
Republic of Nicaragua
Capital Managua

Area sq km	130 000	**Currency**	Córdoba
Area sq miles	50 193	**Languages**	Spanish,
Population	5 870 000		Amerindian lan

NIGER
Republic of Niger
Capital Niamey

Area sq km	1 267 000	**Currency**	CFA franc*
Area sq miles	489 191	**Languages**	French, Hausa,
Population	16 069 000		Fulani, local lan

NIGERIA
Federal Republic of Nigeria
Capital Abuja

Area sq km	923 768	**Currency**	Naira
Area sq miles	356 669	**Languages**	English, Hausa,
Population	162 471 000		Yoruba, Ibo, Fulani, local lang.

NORTH KOREA
Democratic People's Republic of Korea
Capital P'yŏngyang

Area sq km	120 538	**Currency**	North Korean won
Area sq miles	46 540	**Languages**	Korean
Population	24 451 000		

NORWAY
Kingdom of Norway
Capital Oslo

Area sq km	323 878	**Currency**	Norwegian krone
Area sq miles	125 050	**Languages**	Norwegian
Population	4 925 000		

OMAN
Sultanate of Oman
Capital Muscat (Masqaṭ)

Area sq km	309 500	**Currency**	Omani riyal
Area sq miles	119 499	**Languages**	Arabic, Baluchi,
Population	2 846 000		Indian lang.

PAKISTAN
Islamic Republic of Pakistan
Capital Islamabad

Area sq km	803 940	**Currency**	Pakistani rupee
Area sq miles	310 403	**Languages**	Urdu, Punjabi,
Population	176 745 000		Sindhi, Pushtu, English

PALAU
Republic of Palau
Capital Melekeok

Area sq km	497	**Currency**	US dollar
Area sq miles	192	**Languages**	Palauan, English
Population	21 000		

PANAMA
Republic of Panama
Capital Panama City

Area sq km	77 082	**Currency**	Balboa
Area sq miles	29 762	**Languages**	Spanish, English,
Population	3 571 000		Amerindian lang.

PAPUA NEW GUINEA
Independent State of Papua New Guinea
Capital Port Moresby

Area sq km	462 840	**Currency**	Kina
Area sq miles	178 704	**Languages**	English,
Population	7 014 000		Tok Pisin (creole), local lang.

PARAGUAY
Republic of Paraguay
Capital Asunción

Area sq km	406 752	**Currency**	Guaraní
Area sq miles	157 048	**Languages**	Spanish, Guaraní
Population	6 568 000		

PERU
Republic of Peru
Capital Lima

Area sq km	1 285 216	**Currency**	Nuevo sol
Area sq miles	496 225	**Languages**	Spanish, Quechua,
Population	29 400 000		Aymara

PHILIPPINES
Republic of the Philippines
Capital Manila

Area sq km	300 000	**Currency**	Philippine peso
Area sq miles	115 831	**Languages**	English, Filipino,
Population	94 852 000		Tagalog, Cebuano, local lang.

POLAND
Polish Republic
Capital Warsaw (Warszawa)

Area sq km	312 683	**Currency**	Złoty
Area sq miles	120 728	**Languages**	Polish, German
Population	38 299 000		

PORTUGAL
Portuguese Republic
Capital Lisbon (Lisboa)

Area sq km	88 940	**Currency**	Euro
Area sq miles	34 340	**Languages**	Portuguese
Population	10 690 000		

QATAR
State of Qatar
Capital Doha (Ad Dawḥah)

Area sq km	11 437	**Currency**	Qatari riyal
Area sq miles	4 416	**Languages**	Arabic
Population	1 870 000		

ROMANIA
Capital Bucharest (Bucureşti)

Area sq km	237 500	**Currency**	Romanian leu
Area sq miles	91 699	**Languages**	Romanian,
Population	21 436 000		Hungarian

RUSSIAN FEDERATION
Capital Moscow (Moskva)

Area sq km	17 075 400	**Currency**	Russian rouble
Area sq miles	6 592 849	**Languages**	Russian, Tatar,
Population	142 836 000		Ukrainian,
			local lang.

RWANDA
Republic of Rwanda
Capital Kigali

Area sq km	26 338	**Currency**	Rwandan franc
Area sq miles	10 169	**Languages**	Kinyarwanda,
Population	10 943 000		French, English

ST KITTS AND NEVIS
Federation of St Kitts and Nevis
Capital Basseterre

Area sq km	261	**Currency**	East Caribbean
Area sq miles	101		dollar
Population	53 000	**Languages**	English, creole

ST LUCIA
Capital Castries

Area sq km	616	**Currency**	East Caribbean
Area sq miles	238		dollar
Population	176 000	**Languages**	English, creole

ST VINCENT AND THE GRENADINES
Capital Kingstown

Area sq km	389	**Currency**	East Caribbean
Area sq miles	150		dollar
Population	109 000	**Languages**	English, creole

SAMOA
Independent State of Samoa
Capital Apia

Area sq km	2 831	**Currency**	Tala
Area sq miles	1 093	**Languages**	Samoan, English
Population	184 000		

SAN MARINO
Republic of San Marino
Capital San Marino

Area sq km	61	**Currency**	Euro
Area sq miles	24	**Languages**	Italian
Population	32 000		

SÃO TOMÉ AND PRÍNCIPE
Democratic Rep. of São Tomé and Prín
Capital São Tomé

Area sq km	964	**Currency**	Dobra
Area sq miles	372	**Languages**	Portuguese, cre
Population	169 000		

SAUDI ARABIA
Kingdom of Saudi Arabia
Capital Riyadh (Ar Riyāḍ)

Area sq km	2 200 000	**Currency**	Saudi Arabian
Area sq miles	849 425		riyal
Population	28 083 000	**Languages**	Arabic

SENEGAL
Republic of Senegal
Capital Dakar

Area sq km	196 720	**Currency**	CFA franc*
Area sq miles	75 954	**Languages**	French, Wolof,
Population	12 768 000		Fulani, local la

SERBIA
Republic of Serbia
Capital Belgrade (Beograd)

Area sq km	77 453	**Currency**	Serbian dinar,
Area sq miles	29 904	**Languages**	Serbian,
Population	7 306 677		Hungarian

SEYCHELLES
Republic of Seychelles
Capital Victoria

Area sq km	455	**Currency**	Seychelles rup
Area sq miles	176	**Languages**	English, Frenc
Population	87 000		creole

SIERRA LEONE
Republic of Sierra Leone
Capital Freetown

Area sq km	71 740	**Currency**	Leone
Area sq miles	27 699	**Languages**	English, creole
Population	5 997 000		Mende, Temne
			local lang.

SINGAPORE
Republic of Singapore
Capital Singapore

Area sq km	639	**Currency**	Singapore doll
Area sq miles	247	**Languages**	Chinese, Engli
Population	5 188 000		Malay, Tamil

SLOVAKIA
Slovak Republic
Capital Bratislava

Area sq km	49 035	**Currency** Euro
Area sq miles	18 933	**Languages** Slovak,
Population	5 472 000	Hungarian, Czech

SLOVENIA
Republic of Slovenia
Capital Ljubljana

Area sq km	20 251	**Currency** Euro
Area sq miles	7 819	**Languages** Slovene, Croatian,
Population	2 035 000	Serbian

SOLOMON ISLANDS
Capital Honiara

Area sq km	28 370	**Currency** Solomon Islands
Area sq miles	10 954	dollar
Population	552 000	**Languages** English, creole, local lang.

SOMALIA
Somali Republic
Capital Mogadishu (Muqdisho)

Area sq km	637 657	**Currency** Somali shilling
Area sq miles	246 201	**Languages** Somali, Arabic
Population	9 557 000	

SOUTH AFRICA, REPUBLIC OF
Capital Pretoria (Tshwane)/Cape Town

Area sq km	1 219 090	**Currency** Rand
Area sq miles	470 693	**Languages** Afrikaans,
Population	50 460 000	English, nine official local lang.

SOUTH KOREA
Republic of Korea
Capital Seoul (Sŏul)

Area sq km	99 274	**Currency** South Korean
Area sq miles	38 330	won
Population	48 391 000	**Languages** Korean

SOUTH SUDAN
Republic of South Sudan
Capital Juba

Area sq km	644 329	**Currency** South Sudan
Area sq miles	248 775	pound
Population	8 260 490	**Languages** English, Arabic, Dinka, Nuer, local lang.

SPAIN
Kingdom of Spain
Capital Madrid

Area sq km	504 782	**Currency** Euro
Area sq miles	194 897	**Languages** Spanish, Castilian,
Population	46 455 000	Catalan, Galician, Basque

SRI LANKA
Democratic Socialist Republic of Sri Lanka
Capital Sri Jayewardenepura Kotte

Area sq km	65 610	**Currency** Sri Lankan rupee
Area sq miles	25 332	**Languages** Sinhalese,
Population	21 045 000	Tamil, English

SUDAN
Republic of the Sudan
Capital Khartoum

Area sq km	1 861 484	**Currency** Sudanese pound
Area sq miles	718 725	(Sudani)
Population	36 371 510	**Languages** Arabic, Dinka, Nubian, Beja, Nuer, local lang.

SURINAME
Republic of Suriname
Capital Paramaribo

Area sq km	163 820	**Currency** Suriname guilder
Area sq miles	63 251	**Languages** Dutch,
Population	529 000	Surinamese, English, Hindi

SWAZILAND
Kingdom of Swaziland
Capital Mbabane

Area sq km	17 364	**Currency** Emalangeni,
Area sq miles	6 704	South African
Population	1 203 000	rand
		Languages Swazi, English

SWEDEN
Kingdom of Sweden
Capital Stockholm

Area sq km	449 964	**Currency** Swedish krona
Area sq miles	173 732	**Languages** Swedish
Population	9 441 000	

SWITZERLAND
Swiss Confederation
Capital Bern (Berne)

Area sq km	41 293	**Currency** Swiss franc
Area sq miles	15 943	**Languages** German, French,
Population	7 702 000	Italian, Romansch

SYRIA
Syrian Arab Republic
Capital Damascus (Dimashq)

Area sq km	185 180	**Currency**	Syrian pound
Area sq miles	71 498	**Languages**	Arabic, Kurdish,
Population	20 766 000		Armenian

TAIWAN
Republic of China
Capital Taibei

Area sq km	36 179	**Currency**	Taiwan dollar
Area sq miles	13 969	**Languages**	Mandarin, Min,
Population	23 164 000		Hakka, local lang.

The People's Republic of China claims Taiwan as its 23rd province.

TAJIKISTAN
Republic of Tajikistan
Capital Dushanbe

Area sq km	143 100	**Currency**	Somoni
Area sq miles	55 251	**Languages**	Tajik, Uzbek,
Population	6 977 000		Russian

TANZANIA
United Republic of Tanzania
Capital Dodoma

Area sq km	945 087	**Currency**	Tanzanian shilling
Area sq miles	364 900	**Languages**	Swahili, English,
Population	46 218 000		Nyamwezi,
			local lang.

THAILAND
Kingdom of Thailand
Capital Bangkok (Krung Thep)

Area sq km	513 115	**Currency**	Baht
Area sq miles	198 115	**Languages**	Thai, Lao,
Population	69 519 000		Chinese, Malay,
			Mon-Khmer lang.

TOGO
Republic of Togo
Capital Lomé

Area sq km	56 785	**Currency**	CFA franc*
Area sq miles	21 925	**Languages**	French, Ewe,
Population	6 155 000		Kabre, local lang.

TONGA
Kingdom of Tonga
Capital Nuku'alofa

Area sq km	748	**Currency**	Pa'anga
Area sq miles	289	**Languages**	Tongan, English
Population	105 000		

TRINIDAD AND TOBAGO
Republic of Trinidad and Tobago
Capital Port of Spain

Area sq km	5 130	**Currency**	Trinidad and
Area sq miles	1 981		Tobago dollar
Population	1 346 000	**Languages**	English, creole,
			Hindi

TUNISIA
Republic of Tunisia
Capital Tunis

Area sq km	164 150	**Currency**	Tunisian dinar
Area sq miles	63 379	**Languages**	Arabic, French
Population	10 594 000		

TURKEY
Republic of Turkey
Capital Ankara

Area sq km	779 452	**Currency**	Lira
Area sq miles	300 948	**Languages**	Turkish, Kurdish
Population	73 640 000		

TURKMENISTAN
Republic of Turkmenistan
Capital Aşgabat (Ashkhabad)

Area sq km	488 100	**Currency**	Turkmen manat
Area sq miles	188 456	**Languages**	Turkmen, Uzbek,
Population	5 105 000		Russian

TUVALU
Capital Vaiaku

Area sq km	25	**Currency**	Australian dollar
Area sq miles	10	**Languages**	Tuvaluan, English
Population	10 000		

UGANDA
Republic of Uganda
Capital Kampala

Area sq km	241 038	**Currency**	Ugandan shilling
Area sq miles	93 065	**Languages**	English, Swahili,
Population	34 509 000		Luganda,
			local lang.

UKRAINE
Capital Kiev (Kyiv)

Area sq km	603 700	**Currency**	Hryvnia
Area sq miles	233 090	**Languages**	Ukrainian,
Population	45 190 000		Russian

UNITED ARAB EMIRATES
Federation of Emirates
Capital Abu Dhabi (Abū Ẓabī)

Area sq km	77 700	**Currency**	UAE dirham
Area sq miles	30 000	**Languages**	Arabic, English
Population	7 891 000		

UNITED KINGDOM
United Kingdom of Great Britain and
Northern Ireland
Capital London

Area sq km	243 609	**Currency**	Pound sterling
Area sq miles	94 058	**Languages**	English, Welsh,
Population	62 417 000		Gaelic

UNITED STATES OF AMERICA
Capital Washington D.C.

Area sq km	9 826 635	**Currency**	US dollar
Area sq miles	3 794 085	**Languages**	English, Spanish
Population	313 085 000		

URUGUAY
Oriental Republic of Uruguay
Capital Montevideo

Area sq km	176 215	**Currency**	Uruguayan peso
Area sq miles	68 037	**Languages**	Spanish
Population	3 380 000		

UZBEKISTAN
Republic of Uzbekistan
Capital Tashkent

Area sq km	447 400	**Currency**	Uzbek som
Area sq miles	172 742	**Languages**	Uzbek, Russian,
Population	27 760 000		Tajik, Kazakh

VANUATU
Republic of Vanuatu
Capital Port Vila

Area sq km	12 190	**Currency**	Vatu
Area sq miles	4 707	**Languages**	English,
Population	246 000		Bislama (creole),
			French

VATICAN CITY
Vatican City State or Holy See
Capital Vatican City

Area sq km	0.5	**Currency**	Euro
Area sq miles	0.2	**Languages**	Italian
Population	800		

VENEZUELA
Bolivarian Republic of Venezuela
Capital Caracas

Area sq km	912 050	**Currency**	Bolívar fuerte
Area sq miles	352 144	**Languages**	Spanish,
Population	29 437 000		Amerindian lang.

VIETNAM
Socialist Republic of Vietnam
Capital Ha Nôi (Hanoi)

Area sq km	329 565	**Currency**	Dong
Area sq miles	127 246	**Languages**	Vietnamese, Thai,
Population	88 792 000		Khmer, Chinese,
			local lang.

West Bank
Disputed territory

Area sq km	5 860	**Currency**	Jordanian dinar,
Area sq miles	2 263		Israeli shekel
Population	2 513 283	**Languages**	Arabic, Hebrew

Western Sahara
Disputed territory (Morocco)
Capital Laâyoune

Area sq km	266 000	**Currency**	Moroccan dirham
Area sq miles	102 703	**Languages**	Arabic
Population	548 000		

YEMEN
Republic of Yemen
Capital Şan'ā'

Area sq km	527 968	**Currency**	Yemeni riyal
Area sq miles	203 850	**Languages**	Arabic
Population	24 800 000		

ZAMBIA
Republic of Zambia
Capital Lusaka

Area sq km	752 614	**Currency**	Zambian kwacha
Area sq miles	290 586	**Languages**	English, Bemba,
Population	13 475 000		Nyanja, Tonga,
			local lang.

ZIMBABWE
Republic of Zimbabwe
Capital Harare

Area sq km	390 759	**Currency**	Zimbabwean
Area sq miles	150 873		dollar (suspended)
Population	12 754 000	**Languages**	English, Shona,
			Ndebele

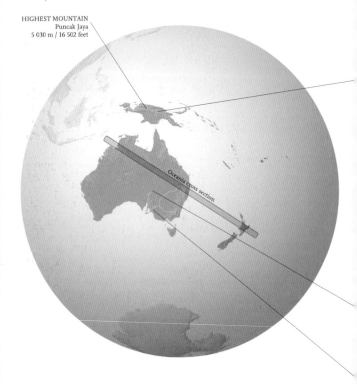

Total Land Area 8 844 516 sq km / 3 414 868 sq miles
(includes New Guinea and Pacific Island nations)

HIGHEST MOUNTAIN
Puncak Jaya
5 030 m / 16 502 feet

Oceania cross section

Joseph
Bonaparte Gulf

Arnhem Land

Gulf of
Carpentaria

Cape York
Peninsula

Great Dividing
Range

Tasman Sea

North Cape

North Island

Cook Strait

Oceania cross section and perspective view

HIGHEST MOUNTAINS	metres	feet	Map page
Puncak Jaya, Indonesia	5 030	16 502	59 D3
Puncak Trikora, Indonesia	4 730	15 518	59 D3
Puncak Mandala, Indonesia	4 700	15 420	59 D3
Puncak Yamin, Indonesia	4 595	15 075	—
Mt Wilhelm, Papua New Guinea	4 509	14 793	59 D3
Mt Kubor, Papua New Guinea	4 359	14 301	—

LARGEST ISLAND
New Guinea
808 510 sq km /
312 166 sq miles

LARGEST ISLANDS	sq km	sq miles	Map page
New Guinea	808 510	312 166	59 D3
South Island, New Zealand	151 215	58 384	54 B2
North Island, New Zealand	115 777	44 701	54 B1
Tasmania	67 800	26 178	51 D4

LONGEST RIVERS	km	miles	Map page
Murray-Darling	3 672	2 282	52 B2
Darling	2 844	1 767	52 B2
Murray	2 375	1 476	52 B3
Murrumbidgee	1 485	923	52 B2
Lachlan	1 339	832	53 C2
Cooper Creek	1 113	692	52 B1

LARGEST LAKES	sq km	sq miles	Map page
Lake Eyre	0–8 900	0–3 436	52 A1
Lake Torrens	0–5 780	0–2 232	52 A1

LARGEST LAKE AND LOWEST POINT
Lake Eyre
0–8 900 sq km / 0–3 436 sq miles
16 m / 53 feet below sea level

LONGEST RIVER AND
LARGEST DRAINAGE BASIN
Murray-Darling
3 672 km / 2 282 miles
1 058 000 sq km / 409 000 sq miles

Total Land Area 45 036 492 sq km / 17 388 589 sq miles

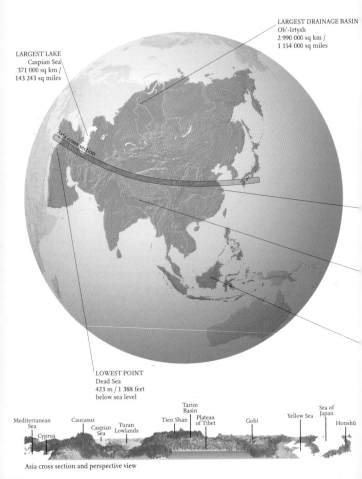

LARGEST DRAINAGE BASIN
Ob'-Irtysh
2 990 000 sq km /
1 154 000 sq miles

LARGEST LAKE
Caspian Sea
371 000 sq km /
143 243 sq miles

Asia cross section

LOWEST POINT
Dead Sea
423 m / 1 388 feet
below sea level

Mediterranean Sea — Cyprus — Caucasus — Caspian Sea — Turan Lowlands — Tien Shan — Tarim Basin — Plateau of Tibet — Gobi — Yellow Sea — Sea of Japan — Honshū

Asia cross section and perspective view

HIGHEST MOUNTAINS	metres	feet	Map page
Mt Everest (Sagarmatha/ Qomolangma Feng), China/Nepal	8 848	29 028	75 C2
K2 (Qogir Feng), China/Pakistan	8 611	28 251	74 B1
Kangchenjunga, India/Nepal	8 586	28 169	75 C2
Lhotse, China/Nepal	8 516	27 939	—
Makalu, China/Nepal	8 463	27 765	—
Cho Oyu, China/Nepal	8 201	26 906	—

LARGEST ISLANDS	sq km	sq miles	Map page
Borneo	745 561	287 861	61 C1
Sumatra (Sumatera)	473 606	182 859	60 A1
Honshū	227 414	87 805	67 B3
Celebes (Sulawesi)	189 216	73 056	58 C3
Java (Jawa)	132 188	51 038	61 B2
Luzon	104 690	40 421	64 B1

LONGEST RIVER
Yangtze (Chang Jiang)
6 380 km /
3 965 miles

LONGEST RIVERS	km	miles	Map page
Yangtze (Chang Jiang)	6 380	3 965	70 C2
Ob'-Irtysh	5 568	3 460	86 F2
Yenisey-Angara-Selenga	5 550	3 449	83 H3
Yellow (Huang He)	5 464	3 395	70 B2
Irtysh	4 440	2 759	86 F2
Mekong	4 425	2 750	63 B2

HIGHEST MOUNTAIN
Mt Everest
8 848 m / 29 028 feet

LARGEST LAKES	sq km	sq miles	Map page
Caspian Sea	371 000	143 243	81 C1
Lake Baikal (Ozero Baykal)	30 500	11 776	69 D1
Lake Balkhash (Ozero Balkash)	17 400	6 718	77 D2
Aral Sea (Aral'skoye More)	17 158	6 625	76 B2
Ysyk-Köl	6 200	2 394	77 D2

LARGEST ISLAND
Borneo
745 561 sq km /
287 861 sq miles

Total Land Area 9 908 599 sq km / 3 825 710 sq miles

LARGEST ISLAND
Great Britain
218 476 sq km /
84 354 sq miles

Europe cross section

HIGHEST MOUNTAIN
El'brus
5 642 m / 18 510 feet

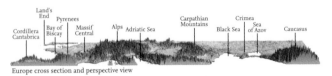

Cordillera
Cantabrica

Land's
End

Bay of
Biscay

Pyrenees

Massif
Central

Alps

Adriatic Sea

Carpathian
Mountains

Black Sea

Crimea

Sea
of Azov

Caucasus

Europe cross section and perspective view

24

HIGHEST MOUNTAINS	metres	feet	Map pages
El'brus, Russian Federation	5 642	18 510	87 D4
Gora Dykh-Tau, Russian Federation	5 204	17 073	—
Shkhara, Georgia/Russian Federation	5 201	17 063	—
Kazbek, Georgia/Russian Federation	5 047	16 558	76 A2
Mont Blanc, France/Italy	4 810	15 781	105 D2
Dufourspitze, Italy/Switzerland	4 634	15 203	—

LARGEST ISLANDS	sq km	sq miles	Map pages
Great Britain	218 476	84 354	95 C3
Iceland	102 820	39 699	92 A3
Ireland	83 045	32 064	97 C2
Ostrov Severnyy (part of Novaya Zemlya)	47 079	18 177	86 E1
Spitsbergen	37 814	14 600	82 C1

LONGEST RIVER AND
LARGEST DRAINAGE BASIN
Volga
3 688 km / 2 292 miles
1 380 000 sq km / 533 000 sq miles

LONGEST RIVERS	km	miles	Map pages
Volga	3 688	2 292	89 F2
Danube	2 850	1 771	110 A1
Dnieper	2 285	1 420	91 C2
Kama	2 028	1 260	86 E3
Don	1 931	1 200	89 E3
Pechora	1 802	1 120	86 E2

LARGEST LAKE AND LOWEST POINT
Caspian Sea
371 000 sq km / 143 243 sq miles
28m / 92 feet below sea level

LARGEST LAKES	sq km	sq miles	Map pages
Caspian Sea	371 000	143 243	81 C1
Lake Ladoga (Ladozhskoye Ozero)	18 390	7 100	86 C2
Lake Onega (Onezhskoye Ozero)	9 600	3 707	86 C2
Vänern	5 585	2 156	93 F4
Rybinskoye Vodokhranilishche	5 180	2 000	89 E2

Total Land Area 30 343 578 sq km / 11 715 655 sq miles

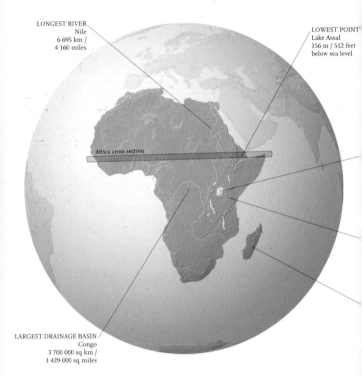

LONGEST RIVER
Nile
6 695 km /
4 160 miles

LOWEST POINT
Lake Assal
156 m / 512 feet
below sea level

Africa cross section

LARGEST DRAINAGE BASIN
Congo
3 700 000 sq km /
1 429 000 sq miles

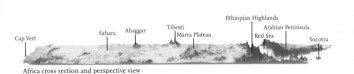

Cap Vert   Sahara   Ahaggar   Tibesti   Marra Plateau   Ethiopian Highlands   Arabian Peninsula   Red Sea   Socotra

Africa cross section and perspective view

HIGHEST MOUNTAINS	metres	feet	Map page
Kilimanjaro, Tanzania	5 892	19 330	119 D3
Mt Kenya (Kirinyaga), Kenya	5 199	17 057	119 D3
Margherita Peak, Democratic Republic of the Congo/Uganda	5 110	16 765	119 C2
Meru, Tanzania	4 565	14 977	119 D3
Ras Dejen, Ethiopia	4 533	14 872	117 B3
Mt Karisimbi, Rwanda	4 510	14 796	—

LARGEST ISLANDS	sq km	sq miles	Map page
Madagascar	587 040	226 656	121 D3

LONGEST RIVERS	km	miles	Map page
Nile	6 695	4 160	116 B1
Congo	4 667	2 900	118 B3
Niger	4 184	2 600	115 C4
Zambezi	2 736	1 700	120 C2
Webi Shabeelle	2 490	1 547	117 C4
Ubangi	2 250	1 398	118 B3

LARGEST LAKES	sq km	sq miles	Map page
Lake Victoria	68 870	26 591	52 B2
Lake Tanganyika	32 600	12 587	119 C3
Lake Nyasa (Lake Malawi)	29 500	11 390	121 C1
Lake Volta	8 482	3 275	114 C4
Lake Turkana	6 500	2 510	119 D2
Lake Albert	5 600	2 162	119 D2

LARGEST LAKE
Lake Victoria
68 870 sq km /
26 591 sq miles

HIGHEST MOUNTAIN
Kilimanjaro
5 892 m / 19 330 feet

LARGEST ISLAND
Madagascar
587 040 sq km /
226 656 sq miles

Total Land Area 24 680 331 sq km / 9 529 076 sq miles
(including Hawaiian Islands)

HIGHEST MOUNTAIN
Mt McKinley
6 194 m / 20 321 feet

LARGEST ISLAND
Greenland
2 175 600 sq km /
839 999 sq miles

North America cross section

LOWEST POINT
Death Valley
86 m / 282 feet
below sea level

Coast Ranges
Rocky Mountains
Great Plains
Lake Michigan
Lake Huron
Lake Erie
Chesapeake Bay
Appalachian Mountains
Long Island
Cape Cod
Nova Scotia

North America cross section and perspective view

HIGHEST MOUNTAINS	metres	feet	Map page
Mt McKinley, USA	6 194	20 321	124 F2
Mt Logan, Canada	5 959	19 550	126 B2
Pico de Orizaba, Mexico	5 610	18 405	145 C3
Mt St Elias, USA	5 489	18 008	126 B2
Volcán Popocatépetl, Mexico	5 452	17 887	145 C3
Mt Foraker, USA	5 303	17 398	—

LARGEST LAKE
Lake Superior
82 100 sq km /
31 699 sq miles

LARGEST ISLANDS	sq km	sq miles	Map page
Greenland	2 175 600	839 999	127 I2
Baffin Island	507 451	195 927	127 G2
Victoria Island	217 291	83 896	126 D2
Ellesmere Island	196 236	75 767	127 F1
Cuba	110 860	42 803	146 B2
Newfoundland	108 860	42 031	131 E2
Hispaniola	76 192	29 418	147 C2

LONGEST RIVERS	km	miles	Map page
Mississippi-Missouri	5 969	3 709	133 D3
Mackenzie-Peace-Finlay	4 241	2 635	126 C2
Missouri	4 086	2 539	137 E3
Mississippi	3 765	2 340	142 C3
Yukon	3 185	1 979	126 A2
St Lawrence	3 058	1 900	131 D2

LONGEST RIVER AND
LARGEST DRAINAGE BASIN
Mississippi-Missouri
5 969 km / 3 709 miles
3 250 000 sq km / 1 255 000
sq miles

LARGEST LAKES	sq km	sq miles	Map page
Lake Superior	82 100	31 699	140 B1
Lake Huron	59 600	23 012	140 C2
Lake Michigan	57 800	22 317	140 B2
Great Bear Lake	31 328	12 096	126 C2
Great Slave Lake	28 568	11 030	128 C1
Lake Erie	25 700	9 923	140 C2
Lake Winnipeg	24 387	9 416	129 E2
Lake Ontario	18 960	7 320	141 D2

Total Land Area 17 815 420 sq km / 6 878 534 sq miles

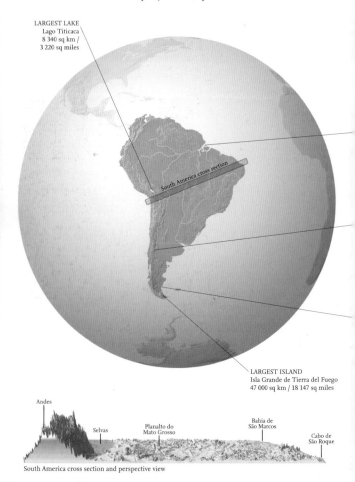

LARGEST LAKE
Lago Titicaca
8 340 sq km /
3 220 sq miles

South America cross section

LARGEST ISLAND
Isla Grande de Tierra del Fuego
47 000 sq km / 18 147 sq miles

Andes

Selvas

Planalto do
Mato Grosso

Bahia de
São Marcos

Cabo de
São Roque

South America cross section and perspective view

HIGHEST MOUNTAINS	metres	feet	Map page
Cerro Aconcagua, Argentina	6 959	22 831	153 B4
Nevado Ojos del Salado, Argentina/Chile	6 908	22 664	152 B3
Cerro Bonete, Argentina	6 872	22 546	—
Cerro Pissis, Argentina	6 858	22 500	—
Cerro Tupungato, Argentina/Chile	6 800	22 309	—
Cerro Mercedario, Argentina	6 770	22 211	—

LARGEST ISLANDS	sq km	sq miles	Map page
Isla Grande de Tierra del Fuego	47 000	18 147	153 B6
Isla de Chiloé	8 394	3 241	153 A5
East Falkland	6 760	2 610	153 C6
West Falkland	5 413	2 090	153 B6

LONGEST RIVER AND
LARGEST DRAINAGE BASIN
Amazon
8 516 km / 4 049 miles
7 050 000 sq km / 2 722 000 sq miles

LONGEST RIVERS	km	miles	Map page
Amazon (Amazonas)	6 516	4 049	150 C1
Río de la Plata-Paraná	4 500	2 796	153 C4
Purus	3 218	2 000	150 B2
Madeira	3 200	1 988	150 C2
São Francisco	2 900	1 802	151 E3
Tocantins	2 750	1 709	151 D2

HIGHEST MOUNTAIN
Cerro Aconcagua
6 959 m / 22 831 feet

LARGEST LAKES	sq km	sq miles	Map page
Lake Titicaca	8 340	3 220	152 B2

LOWEST POINT
Laguna del Carbón
105 m / 345 feet below sea level

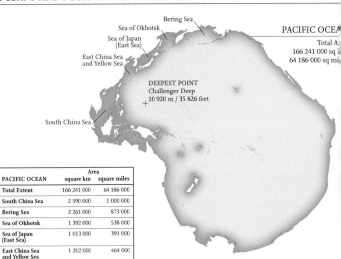

PACIFIC OCEA

Total A
166 241 000 sq
64 186 000 sq mi

Bering Sea

Sea of Okhotsk

Sea of Japan
(East Sea)

East China Sea
and Yellow Sea

DEEPEST POINT
Challenger Deep
10 920 m / 35 826 feet

South China Sea

PACIFIC OCEAN	Area square km	square miles
Total Extent	166 241 000	64 186 000
South China Sea	2 590 000	1 000 000
Bering Sea	2 261 000	873 000
Sea of Okhotsk	1 392 000	538 000
Sea of Japan (East Sea)	1 013 000	391 000
East China Sea and Yellow Sea	1 202 000	464 000

ANTARCTICA

Total Land Area 12 093 000 sq km /
4 669 107 sq miles (excluding ice shelves)

HIGHEST MOUNTAIN
Vinson Massif
4 897 m / 16 066 feet

HIGHEST MOUNTAINS	Height metres	feet
Vinson Massif	4 897	16 066
Mt Tyree	4 852	15 918
Mt Kirkpatrick	4 528	14 855
Mt Markham	4 351	14 275
Mt Jackson	4 190	13 747
Mt Sidley	4 181	13 717

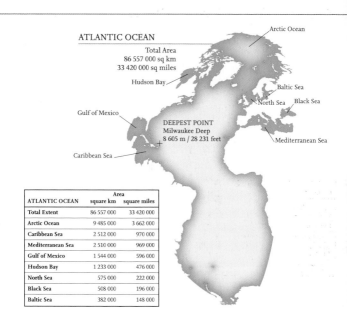

ATLANTIC OCEAN

Total Area
86 557 000 sq km
33 420 000 sq miles

Arctic Ocean

Hudson Bay

Baltic Sea

North Sea   Black Sea

Gulf of Mexico

DEEPEST POINT
Milwaukee Deep
8 605 m / 28 231 feet

Mediterranean Sea

Caribbean Sea

ATLANTIC OCEAN	Area square km	square miles
Total Extent	86 557 000	33 420 000
Arctic Ocean	9 485 000	3 662 000
Caribbean Sea	2 512 000	970 000
Mediterranean Sea	2 510 000	969 000
Gulf of Mexico	1 544 000	596 000
Hudson Bay	1 233 000	476 000
North Sea	575 000	222 000
Black Sea	508 000	196 000
Baltic Sea	382 000	148 000

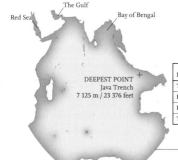

The Gulf

Red Sea

Bay of Bengal

DEEPEST POINT
Java Trench
7 125 m / 23 376 feet

INDIAN OCEAN	Area square km	square miles
Total Extent	73 427 000	28 350 000
Bay of Bengal	2 172 000	839 000
Red Sea	453 000	175 000
The Gulf	238 000	92 000

INDIAN OCEAN

Total Area
73 427 000 sq km
28 350 000 sq miles

CLIMATE

MAJOR CLIMATIC REGIONS AND SUB-TYPES
Köppen classification system
Winkel Tripel Projection
scale 1:200 000 000

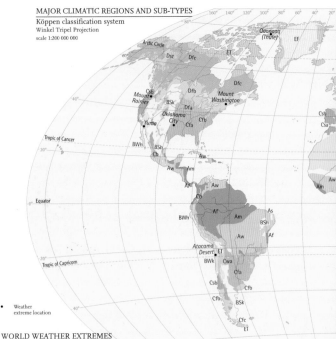

• Weather
   extreme location

WORLD WEATHER EXTREMES

	Location
Highest shade temperature	57.8°C / 136°F Al 'Azīzīyah, Libya (13 September 1922)
Hottest place – Annual mean	34.4°C / 93.9°F Dalol, Ethiopia
Driest place – Annual mean	0.1 mm / 0.004 inches Atacama Desert, Chile
Most sunshine – Annual mean	90% Yuma, Arizona, USA (over 4 000 hours)
Least sunshine	Nil for 182 days each year, South Pole
Lowest screen temperature	-89.2°C / -128.6°F Vostok Station, Antarctica (21 July 1983)
Coldest place – Annual mean	-56.6°C / -69.9°F Plateau Station, Antarctica
Wettest place – Annual mean	11 873 mm / 467.4 inches Meghalaya, India
Highest surface wind speed	
- High altitude	372 km per hour/231 miles per hour Mount Washington, New Hampshire, USA, (12 April 1934)
- Low altitude	333 km per hour/207 miles per hour Qaanaaq (Thule), Greenland (8 March 1972)
- Tornado	512 km per hour / 318 miles per hour in a tornado, Oklahoma City, Oklahoma, USA (3 May 1999)
Greatest snowfall	31 102 mm / 1 224.5 inches Mount Rainier, Washington, USA (19 February 1971 – 18 February 1972)

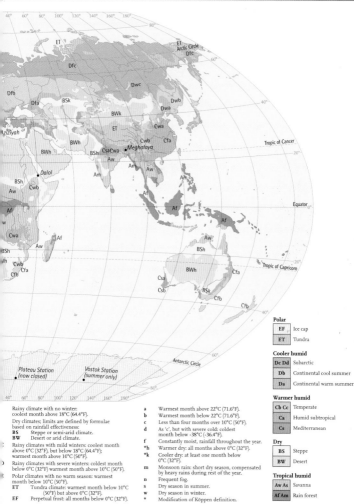

Rainy climate with no winter: coolest month above 18°C (64.4°F).

Dry climates; limits are defined by formulae based on rainfall effectiveness:
BS   Steppe or semi-arid climate.
BW   Desert or arid climate.

Rainy climates with mild winters: coolest month above 0°C (32°F), but below 18°C (64.4°F); warmest month above 10°C (50°F).

Rainy climates with severe winters: coldest month below 0°C (32°F) warmest month above 10°C (50°F).

Polar climates with no warm season: warmest month below 10°C (50°F).
ET   Tundra climate: warmest month below 10°C (50°F) but above 0°C (32°F).
EF   Perpetual frost: all months below 0°C (32°F).

a   Warmest month above 22°C (71.6°F).
b   Warmest month below 22°C (71.6°F).
c   Less than four months over 10°C (50°F).
d   As 'c', but with severe cold: coldest month below -38°C (-36.4°F).
f   Constantly moist, rainfall throughout the year.
*h   Warmer dry: all months above 0°C (32°F).
*k   Cooler dry: at least one month below 0°C (32°F).
m   Monsoon rain: short dry season, compensated by heavy rains during rest of the year.
n   Frequent fog.
s   Dry season in summer.
w   Dry season in winter.
*   Modification of Köppen definition.

Polar

EF	Ice cap
ET	Tundra

Cooler humid

Dc Dd	Subarctic
Db	Continental cool summer
Da	Continental warm summer

Warmer humid

Cb Cc	Temperate
Ca	Humid subtropical
Cs	Mediterranean

Dry

BS	Steppe
BW	Desert

Tropical humid

Aw As	Savanna
Af Am	Rain forest

© Collins Bartholomew Ltd

35

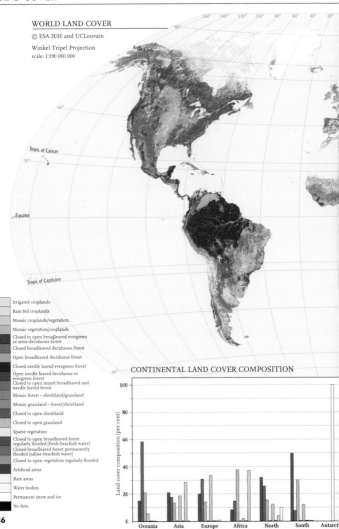

WORLD LAND COVER

© ESA 2010 and UCLouvain

Winkel Tripel Projection
scale: 1:190 000 000

Irrigated croplands
Rain fed croplands
Mosaic croplands/vegetation
Mosaic vegetation/croplands
Closed to open broadleaved evergreen or semi-deciduous forest
Closed broadleaved deciduous forest
Open broadleaved deciduous forest
Closed needle leaved evergreen forest
Open needle leaved deciduous or evergreen forest
Closed to open mixed broadleaved and needle leaved forest
Mosaic forest – shrubland/grassland
Mosaic grassland – forest/shrubland
Closed to open shrubland
Closed to open grassland
Sparse vegetation
Closed to open broadleaved forest regularly flooded (fresh-brackish water)
Closed broadleaved forest permanently flooded (saline-brackish water)
Closed to open vegetation regularly flooded
Artificial areas
Bare areas
Water bodies
Permanent snow and ice
No data

CONTINENTAL LAND COVER COMPOSITION

Land cover composition (per cent)

Oceania   Asia   Europe   Africa   North America   South America   Antarct

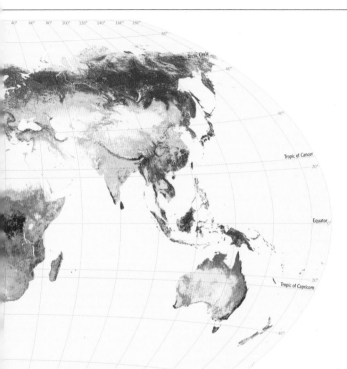

AND COVER GRAPHS - CLASSIFICATION

Class description	Map classes
Forest/Woodland	Evergreen needleleaf forest
	Evergreen broadleaf forest
	Deciduous needleleaf forest
	Deciduous broadleaf forest
	Mixed forest
Shrubland	Closed shrublands
	Open shrublands
Grass/Savanna	Woody savannas
	Savannas
	Grasslands
Wetland	Permanent wetlands
Crops/Mosaic	Croplands
	Cropland/Natural vegetation mosaic
Urban	Urban and built-up
Snow/Ice	Snow and Ice
Barren	Barren or sparsely vegetated

GLOBAL LAND COVER COMPOSITION

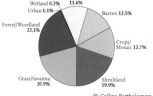

Snow/Ice 11.6%
Wetland 0.2%
Urban 0.1%
Barren 12.5%
Forest/Woodland 22.1%
Crops/Mosaic 12.7%
Grass/Savanna 20.9%
Shrubland 19.9%

© Collins Bartholomew Ltd

WORLD POPULATION DISTRIBUTION
Population Density
Winkel Tripel Projection
scale 1:190 000 000

KEY POPULATION STATISTICS FOR MAJOR REGIONS

	Population 2011 (millions)	Growth (per cent)	Infant mortality rate	Total fertility rate	Life expectancy (years)
World	6 974	1.1	42	2.45	69
More developed regions[1]	1 240	0.3	6	1.7	78
Less developed regions[2]	5 774	1.3	46	2.6	67
Africa	1 046	2.3	71	4.4	55
Asia	4 207	1.0	37	2.2	70
Europe[3]	739	0.1	6	1.6	77
Latin America and the Caribbean[4]	597	1.1	19	2.2	75
North America	348	0.9	6	2.0	79
Oceania	37	1.5	19	2.5	78

1. Europe, North America, Australia, New Zealand and Japan.

2. Africa, Asia (excluding Japan), Latin America and the Caribbean and Oceania (excluding Australia and New Zealand).

3. Includes Russian Federation.

4. South America, Central America (including Mexico) and all Caribbean Islands.

Except for population (2011) the data are annual averages projected for the period 2010–2015.

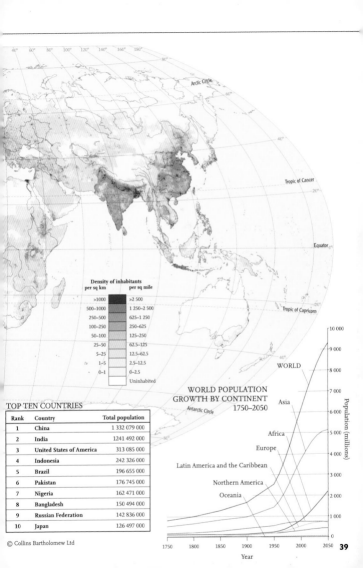

Density of inhabitants

per sq km	per sq mile
>1000	>2 500
500–1000	1 250–2 500
250–500	625–1 250
100–250	250–625
50–100	125–250
25–50	62.5–125
5–25	12.5–62.5
1–5	2.5–12.5
0–1	0–2.5
Uninhabited	

TOP TEN COUNTRIES

Rank	Country	Total population
1	China	1 332 079 000
2	India	1241 492 000
3	United States of America	313 085 000
4	Indonesia	242 326 000
5	Brazil	196 655 000
6	Pakistan	176 745 000
7	Nigeria	162 471 000
8	Bangladesh	150 494 000
9	Russian Federation	142 836 000
10	Japan	126 497 000

© Collins Bartholomew Ltd

WORLD POPULATION GROWTH BY CONTINENT 1750–2050

WORLD

Asia

Africa

Europe

Latin America and the Caribbean

Northern America

Oceania

Population (millions)

Year

THE WORLD'S MAJOR CITIES

Urban agglomerations with over
1 million inhabitants.
Winkel Tripel Projection
scale 1:190 000 000

LEVEL OF URBANIZATION BY MAJOR REGION 1970–2030
Urban population as a percentage of total population

	1970	2010	2030
World	36.1	50.5	59.0
More developed regions[1]	64.7	75.2	80.9
Less developed regions[2]	25.3	45.1	55.0
Africa	23.6	40.0	49.9
Asia	22.7	42.2	52.8
Europe[3]	62.8	72.8	78.4
Latin America and the Caribbean[4]	57.1	79.6	84.9
Northern America	73.8	82.1	86.7
Oceania	70.8	70.2	71.4

1. Europe, North America, Australia,
New Zealand and Japan.
2. Africa, Asia (excluding Japan), Latin
America and the Caribbean, and
Oceania (excluding Australia and
New Zealand).
3. Includes Russian Federation.
4. South America, Central America
(including Mexico) and all Caribbean
Islands.

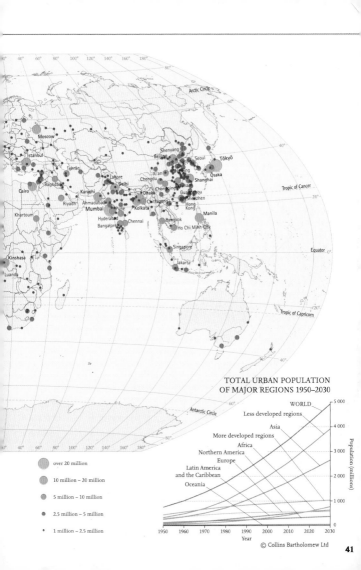

TOTAL URBAN POPULATION
OF MAJOR REGIONS 1950–2030

WORLD
Less developed regions
Asia
More developed regions
Africa
Northern America
Europe
Latin America
and the Caribbean
Oceania

Population (millions)

5 000
4 000
3 000
2 000
1 000
0

1950 1960 1970 1980 1990 2000 2010 2020 2030

Year

over 20 million

10 million – 20 million

5 million – 10 million

2.5 million – 5 million

1 million – 2.5 million

© Collins Bartholomew Ltd

41

SYMBOLS AND ABBREVIATIONS

SYMBOLS

Map symbols used on the map pages are explained here. The status of nations and their boundaries are shown in this atlas as they are in reality at time of going to press, as far as can be ascertained. Where international boundaries are subject of disputes the aim is to take a strictly neutral viewpoint, based on advice from expert consultants. Settlements are classified in terms of both population and administrative significance. The abbreviations listed are those used in place names on the map pages and within the index.

BOUNDARIES

- International boundary
- Disputed international boundary or alignment unconfirmed
- Undefined international boundary in the sea. All land within this boundary is part of state or territory named.
- Disputed territory boundary
- Administrative boundary Shown for selected countries only.
- Ceasefire line or other boundary described on the map

TRANSPORT

- Motorway
- Main road
- Track
- Main railway
- Canal
- ✈ Main airport

LAND AND WATER FEATURES

- Lake
- Impermanent lake
- Salt lake or lagoon
- Impermanent salt lake
- Dry salt lake or salt pan
- River
- Impermanent river
- Ice cap / Glacier
- ⤴ 123 Pass height in metres
- 123 △ Summit height in metres
- ∴ Site of special interest
- ᨛᨛᨛ Wall

CITIES AND TOWNS

Population	National Capital	Administrative Capital Shown for selected countries only	Other City or Town
over 10 million	**BEIJING** ▣	**São Paulo** ◉	**New York** ◉
5 to 10 million	**PARIS** ▣	**St Petersburg** ◉	**Chicago** ◉
1 to 5 million	**KUWAIT** □	**Sydney** ○	**Seattle** ○
500 000 to 1 million	**BANGUI** □	**Winnipeg** ○	**Jeddah** ○
100 000 to 500 000	WELLINGTON □	Edinburgh ○	Apucarana ○
50 000 to 100 000	PORT OF SPAIN □	Bismarck ○	Invercargill ○
under 50 000	MALABO ▫	Charlottetown ○	Ceres ○

STYLES OF LETTERING

Cities and towns are explained separately

		Physical features	
Country	**FRANCE**	Island	*Gran Canaria*
Overseas Territory/Dependency	**Guadeloupe**	Lake	*Lake Erie*
Disputed Territory	WESTERN SAHARA	Mountain	*Mt Blanc*
Administrative name Shown for selected countries only.	**SCOTLAND**	River	*Thames*
Area name	PATAGONIA	Region	*LAPPLAND*

CONTINENTAL MAPS

BOUNDARIES

——— International boundary

- - - - - - Disputed international boundary

•••••••• Ceasefire line

CITIES AND TOWNS

National capital	Other city or town
Kuwait □	Seattle ○

ABBREVIATIONS

Arch.	Archipelago			
B.	Bay			
	Bahía, Baía	Portuguese	**bay**	
	Bahía	Spanish	**bay**	
	Baie	French	**bay**	
C.	Cape			
	Cabo	Portuguese, Spanish	**cape, headland**	
	Cap	French	**cape, headland**	
Co	Cerro	Spanish	**hill, peak, summit**	
E.	East, Eastern			
Est.	Estrecho	Spanish	**strait**	
Gt	Great			
I.	Island, Isle			
	Ilha	Portuguese	**island**	
	Islas	Spanish	**island**	
Is	Islands, Isles			
	Islas	Spanish	**islands**	
Khr.	Khrebet	Russian	**mountain range**	
L.	Lake			
	Loch	(Scotland)	**lake**	
	Lough	(Ireland)	**lake**	
	Lac	French	**lake**	
	Lago	Portuguese, Spanish	**lake**	
M.	Mys	Russian	**cape, point**	
Mt	Mount			
	Mont	French	**hill, mountain**	
Mt.	Mountain			

Mts	Mountains			
	Monts	French	**hills, mountains**	
N.	North, Northern			
O.	Ostrov	Russian	**island**	
Pt	Point			
Pta	Punta	Italian, Spanish	**cape, point**	
R.	River			
	Rio	Portuguese	**river**	
	Río	Spanish	**river**	
	Rivière	French	**river**	
Ra.	Range			
S.	South, Southern			
	Salar, Salina, Salinas	Spanish	**saltpan, saltpans**	
Sa	Serra	Portuguese	**mountain range**	
	Sierra	Spanish	**mountain range**	
Sd	Sound			
S.E.	Southeast, Southeastern			
St	Saint			
	Sankt	German		
	Sint	Dutch	**saint**	
Sta	Santa	Italian, Portuguese, Spanish	**saint**	
Ste	Sainte	French	**saint**	
Str.	Strait			
W.	West, Western			
	Wadi, Wādī	Arabic	**watercourse**	

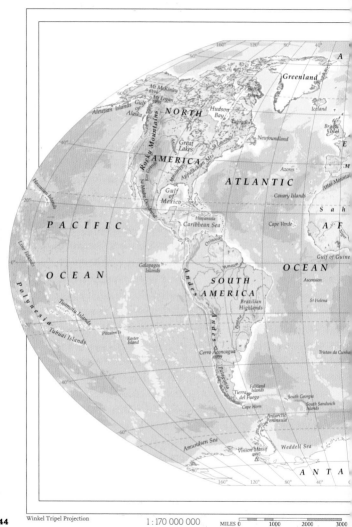

North America, South America, and surrounding oceans on a Winkel Tripel Projection, showing latitude and longitude lines at the following labeled points:

- 160°, 120°, 80°, 40° (top)
- 80°, 60°, 40°, 20°, 0°, 20°, 40°, 60°, 80° (side latitudes)
- 160°, 120°, 80°, 40° (bottom)

North America
- Mt McKinley 6194
- Mt Logan 5959
- Aleutian Islands
- Gulf of Alaska
- Rocky Mountains
- Hudson Bay
- Baffin Island
- Labrador
- Greenland
- Iceland
- Great Lakes
- St Lawrence
- Newfoundland
- British Isles
- Rio Grande
- Mississippi
- Appalachian Mts
- Sa Madre Occidental
- Gulf of Mexico
- ATLANTIC
- Azores
- Canary Islands
- Atlas Mountains
- Hispaniola
- Caribbean Sea
- Cape Verde
- S a h
- A F
- Niger
- Gulf of Guinea

South America
- Hawaiian Islands
- Line Islands
- PACIFIC
- OCEAN
- Galapagos Islands
- Orinoco
- Amazon
- SOUTH AMERICA
- Andes
- Brazilian Highlands
- Ascension
- St Helena
- Polynesia
- Tuamotu Islands
- Tubuai Islands
- Pitcairn I.
- Easter Island
- Cerro Aconcagua 6959
- Paraná
- Falkland Islands
- Tierra del Fuego
- Cape Horn
- South Georgia
- South Sandwich Islands
- Tristan da Cunha
- Antarctic Peninsula
- Amundsen Sea
- Vinson Massif 4897
- Weddell Sea
- ANTA
- OCEAN

Winkel Tripel Projection   1 : 170 000 000   MILES 0   1000   2000   3000

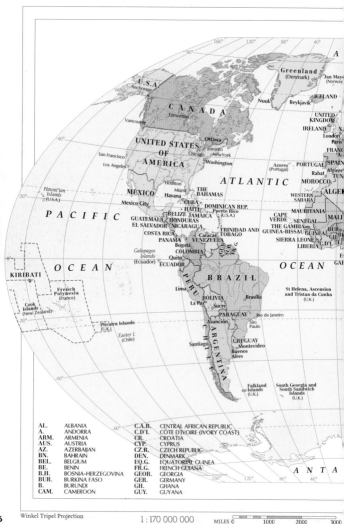

Winkel Tripel Projection   1 : 170 000 000   MILES 0   1000   2000   3000

HUN.	HUNGARY	NI.	NIGERIA
ISR.	ISRAEL	Q.	QATAR
JOR.	JORDAN	R.	RWANDA
K.	KOSOVO	S.	SERBIA
KU.	KUWAIT	SLA.	SLOVAKIA
KYR.	KYRGYZSTAN	SL.	SLOVENIA
LEB.	LEBANON	SUR.	SURINAME
LITH.	LITHUANIA	SW.	SWITZERLAND
LUX.	LUXEMBOURG	TAJIK.	TAJIKISTAN
MA.	MACEDONIA	T.	TOGO
MO.	MOLDOVA	TURKM.	TURKMENISTAN
M.	MONTENEGRO	U.A.E.	UNITED ARAB EMIRATES
NETH.	NETHERLANDS	UZBEK.	UZBEKISTAN

0   1000   2000   3000   4000   5000 KILOMETRES

© Collins Bartholomew Ltd

47

| | B | 120° | C | 135° | D | 150° | E | 165° | F |

Tropic of Cancer

Wake Island
(U.S.A.)

1

Pagan

Northern
Mariana Islands
(U.S.A.)

Saipan

**MARSHALL
ISLANDS**

15°

Guam
(U.S.A.) Capitol Hill

Hagåtña

Ralik Chain

Delap-Ulig
Djarrit

Yap

Gaferut

Chuuk

Pohnpei Palikir

Majuro

Caroline Islands

Gilbert
Islands Tar

**FEDERATED STATES
OF MICRONESIA**

2

Kosrae

ASIA

Bairiki

Kingsmi
Grou

Equator

Yaren
NAURU

Bismarck
New Ireland
Sea
Mount Rabaul
Wilhelm New
New
Guinea 4509 Britain

Bougainville I.

SOLOMON ISLANDS

PAPUA

NEW
GUINEA

Solomon
Sea

Malaita

Santa Cruz
Islands

T

Guadalcanal Honiara

Arafura
Sea

Torres Strait Port
Moresby

VANUATU

Banks
Islands

F

Espiritu Santo

3

Timor Sea

Darwin

Gulf
of
Carpentaria

Cairns

Coral Sea
Islands Territory
(Australia)

Coral
Sea

New
Caledonia
(France)

Malakula

Éfaté

Port Vila

15°

Cape Lévêque

**INDIAN
OCEAN**

Broome

Townsville

Nouméa

Îles
Loyauté

North West
Cape

Lake
Argyle

AUSTRALIA

Norfolk
Island
(Australi

Tropic of Capricorn

Uluru
867

Alice Springs

Brisbane

Lord Howe
Island
(Australia)

North Cape

4

Perth

Kalgoorlie

Lake Eyre

Lake
Torrens

Darling

Canberra Sydney

Auckla
Nor
Isla

Great
Australian Bight

Murray

Mount
2229 Kosciuszko

Tasman

Cape Leeuwin

Kangaroo
Island Adelaide

Melbourne

Welling

30°

Bass Strait

Sea

Christchurc

Tasmania

Hobart

Aoraki
3754

South
Island

Stewart Island

5

Auckland Islands
(N.Z.)

Campbell Island
(N.Z.)

Macquarie Isl
(Australia)

| | | 90° | A | 45° | 105° | B | 120° | Longitude 135° east of Greenwich 150° | E | 165° |

48

1 : 72 000 000   MILES 0   500   100

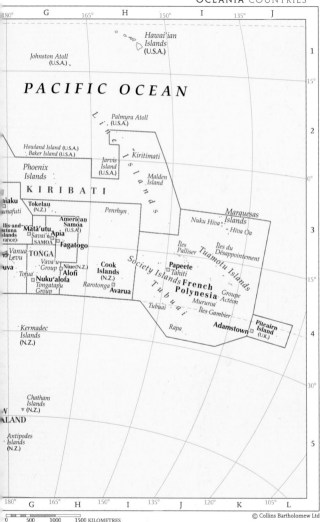

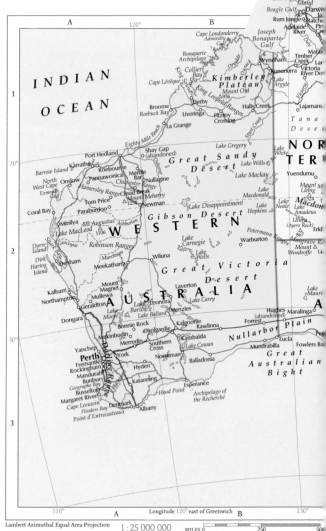

Lambert Azimuthal Equal Area Projection   1 : 25 000 000   MILES 0   250

A — 120°   **B** — Longitude 120° east of Greenwich — **B**   130°

INDIAN

OCEAN

Bathurst Island   *Melville Island*   Darwin
Beagle Gulf   Batch
Rum Jungle   Pir
Joseph   Adelaide   Cre
Bonaparte   River
Cape Londonderry   *Gulf*   Mata
Admiralty
Bonaparte   Wyndham   Timber   Lar
Archipelago   Kununurra   Creek
Collier   *Drysda*   Victoria   Do
Bay   River
Cape Lévêque   **Kimberley**   Lake
King Sound   **Plateau**   Argyle
Mount Ord   Lajamanu
Broome   Derby   936
Roebuck Bay   Halls Creek   Ta na
Liveringa   *King Leopold Ranges*   Dese
La Grange   Fitzroy
Crossing   *Sturt Creek*

NOR
Eighty Mile Beach   **TER**

Port Hedland   Shay Gap   Lake Gregory   Lake
(abandoned)   White
Barrow Island   Karratha   **Great Sandy**   Lake Wills   Yuendumu
North   Roebourne   Marble   **Desert**
West Cape   Pannawonica   Bar   Nullagine   Lake Mackay   Mount
Exmouth   Onslow   *Chichester Range*   Liebig
Gulf   *Hamersley Range*   Cloud Break   Lake   **Macdon**
Coral Bay   Tom Price   Mount Meharry   Macdonald   524   1
1250   Lake   Lake   Uluru
Paraburdoo   Newman   *Lake Disappointment*   Neale   Amadeus   Erld
Lake Hopkins   (Ayers Rock)   867
Minilya   Mt Augustus   **Gibson Desert**   Mount △   Mount
Ashburton   1106   Warburton   Musgrave Ra.   Woodroffe   14
Lake MacLeod   **WESTERN**
Dorre   *Robinson Ranges*   Lake
Island   *Gascoyne*   Carnegie   *Petermann Ranges*
Denham   *Murchison*   Wiluna
Dirk   Lake   Lake
Hartog   Wells   *Mauri*
Island   **Great Victoria**
Kalbarri   Mount   **Desert**
Northampton   Magnet   Laverton
Mullewa   **AUSTRALIA**   Lake
Geraldton   Lake   Leonora   Carey
Lake   Barlee
Dongara   Moore   Menzies   Hughes   Maralinga
Bonnie Rock   Coolgardie   Kalgoorlie   Rawlinna   Forrest   (abandoned)   **Nullarbor plain**
Mukinbudin   Southern   Kambalda   Eucla   Per
Yanchep   Merredin   Cross   Lake Cowan   Mundrabilla   Fowlers Ba
Perth   York   Norseman   **Great**
Fremantle   Hyden   Balladonia   **Australian**
Rockingham   **Bight**
Mandurah   Katanning
Bunbury   *Geographe Bay*   Esperance
Busselton   Hood Point   *Archipelago of*
Margaret River   *the Recherche*
Cape Leeuwin   Denmark
Flinders Bay   Albany
Point d'Entrecasteaux

110°   **A**

30°

20°

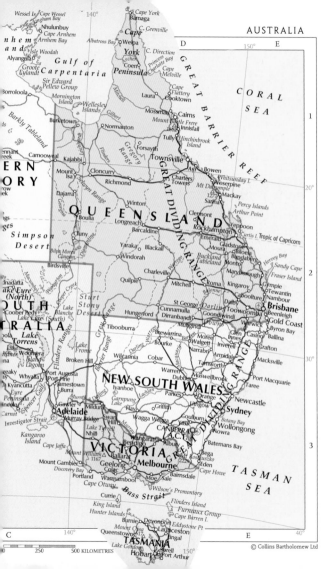

AUSTRALIA

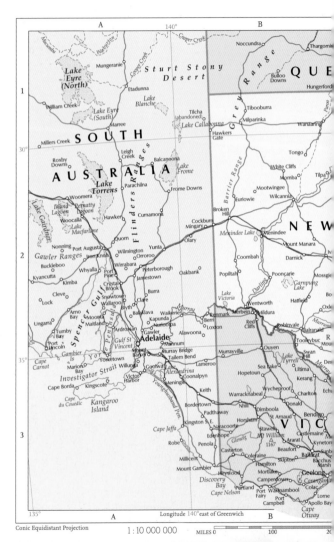

Conic Equidistant Projection   1 : 10 000 000   MILES 0   100   20

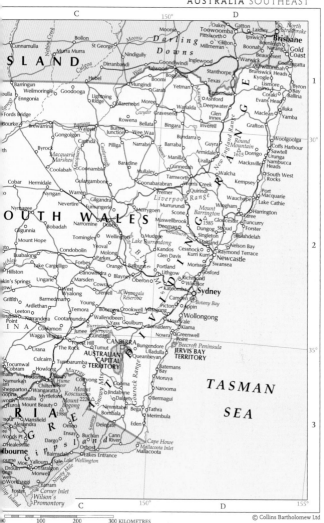

NEW ZEALAND

Te Paki   North
            Cape
North
Cape   North
Te Reinga Nine
           Mile   —35°

A 170°   B   Awanui   175°   C
                    Kaitaia
                    Kerikeri   Bay of Islands
                    Okaihau Russell
                             Kawakawa
                    Kaikohe
           Donnellys Crossing   Whangarei
           Dargaville
                    Wellsford   Great Barrier
                                         Island
                    Kaipara Harbour   Port Fitzroy
                    Takapuna Coast Bay
                              Whitianga
                    Auckland Manukau   Coromandel
                    Papakura   Peninsula
                    Waiuku Pukekohe Thames
                            Huntly   Mount
                    Ngaruawahia   Maung<i>anui</i> Hicks Bay
N O R T H   Hamilton   Tauranga
            Te Awamutu Cambridge Whakatane
I S L A N D   Te Kuiti Rotorua Kawerau Murupara Matawai
               Tokoroa Lake   Ruatahuna
                        Taupo   Rotorua
                    Nokau Mangakino   Wairoa Gisborne
            North Waitara Taumarunui Taupo
            Taranaki Bight New Plymouth Lake
                    Inglewood Taupo Turangi
T A S M A N   Mount Taranaki Mt Ruapehu Kaweka Napier
                    (Mount Egmont) 2797 Mountains Hastings
                    2518 Stratford Raetihi Mahia Havelock North
                    Opunake Waiouru   Peninsula Cape
S E A   Hawera Taihape   Hawke Kidnappers
            South Patea   Waipawa
            Taranaki Bight Wanganui Feilding Danevirke
                    Marton Palmerston North Woodville Cape Turnagain
                    Cape   Foxton Levin
                    Farewell D'Urville Otaki Masterton
            Collingwood Golden Island Paraparaumu Te Wharau
                    Bay Takaka Porirua Palmerston
                    Tasman Tasman Picton Lower Hutt
                    Mountains Bay Havelock WELLINGTON
            Karamea Richmond Nelson Blenheim
                    Wakefield Renwick Seddon
            Karamea Motueka Wairau Cape
            Bight Westport Buller Inland Kaikoura Campbell
                    Reefton Spenser Range
                    Mts Clarence
            Punakaiki Hanmer Kaikoura
            Runanga Springs Springs
            Greymouth Junction Waiau
            Hokitika Arthur's Pass Parnassus
            Kowhitirangi 920 Waipara Pegasus Bay
                    Franz Josef SOUTHERN Oxford Rangiora
                    Glacier ALPS Kaiapoi
                    Fox Glacier Aoraki Christchurch
                    3754 Lake Ellesmere Banks Peninsula
            Lake Paringa Canterbury
                    Haast Plains Geraldine
                    Mount Lake Tekapo Ashburton
            Jackson Head Aspiring Temuka
                    3030 Canterbury Timaru
            Milford Sound Twizel Bight
                    Mount Lake Pleasant
                    Aspiring Wanaka Point
                    Cook Wanaka Waimate
                    3102 Cromwell Benmore Waitaki
            Queenstown Lake Oamaru
            Te Anau Wakatipu SOUTH   P A C I F I C
            Lake
            Te Anau Alexandra I S L A N D
                    Teviot
            Lumsden Beaumont O C E A N
            Tuatapere Winton Mosgiel Port Chalmers
                    Gore Balclutha Otago Peninsula
            Orepuki Mataura Milton Dunedin
                    Ruapuke I.
            Foveaux Invercargill
            Strait Bluff Chaslands
            Halfmoon Bay Mistake Conic Equidistant Projection
            Stewart   Longitude 175° east of Greenwich
            Island   170°   B   C
                      1 : 10 000 000   MILES 0   100
                                              0   100 KILOMETRES

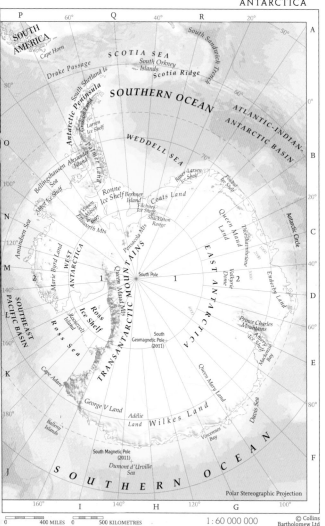

P   60°   Q   40°   R   20°   50°   A

SOUTH AMERICA

Cape Horn

SCOTIA SEA

South Sandwich Trench

South Orkney Islands

Scotia Ridge

Drake Passage

South Shetland Is

SOUTHERN OCEAN

ATLANTIC-INDIAN-ANTARCTIC BASIN

0°

Antarctic Peninsula

Larsen Ice Shelf

Graham Land

WEDDELL SEA

O

80°

Alexander Island

Palmer Land

B

70°

Bellingshausen Sea

Ronne Ice Shelf

Berkner Island

Coats Land

Riiser-Larsen Ice Shelf

Fimbul Ice Shelf

20°

100°

Abbot Ice Shelf

Vinson Massif 4897

Filchner Ice Shelf

Shackleton Range

Queen Maud Land

Thoshammerne

Antarctic Circle

N

Ellsworth Mts

Pensacola Mts

3000

Valkyrie Dome

Enderby Land

C

120°

Amundsen Sea

Marie Byrd Land

WEST ANTARCTICA

2

South Pole

EAST ANTARCTICA

2

3000

40°

M

1

1

South Geomagnetic Pole (2011)

D

140°

SOUTHEAST PACIFIC BASIN

Ross Ice Shelf

Roosevelt Island

TRANSANTARCTIC MOUNTAINS

Prince Charles Mountains

Amery Ice Shelf

Mackenzie Bay

60°

2

L

Ross Sea

Queen Alexandra Mts

Queen Mary Land

Davis Sea

E

160°

Cape Adare

George V Land

Adélie Land

Wilkes Land

Vincennes Bay

80°

K

180°

Balleny Islands

South Magnetic Pole (2011)

Dumont d'Urville Sea

SOUTHERN OCEAN

Polar Stereographic Projection

F

J

160°   I   140°   H   120°   100°

0   400 MILES   0   500 KILOMETRES   1 : 60 000 000   © Collins Bartholomew Ltd

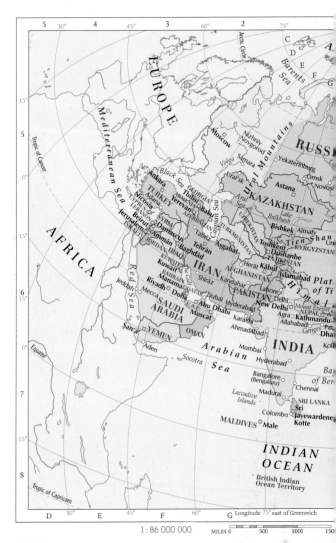

1 : 86 000 000

MILES 0   500   1000   150

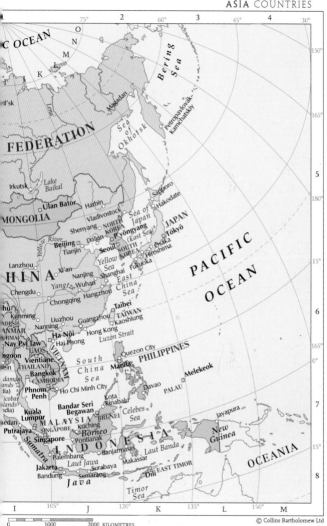

ARCTIC OCEAN

Bering Sea

Sea of Okhotsk

FEDERATION

Ril'sk

Lena

Magadan

Petropavlovsk-Kamchatskiy

MONGOLIA

Irkutsk

Lake Baikal

Ulan Bator

Harbin

Vladivostock

Sea of Japan (East Sea)

Sapporo

Hakodate

JAPAN

Shenyang

NORTH KOREA

P'yŏngyang

Tōkyō

Beijing

Dalian

Seoul

SOUTH KOREA

Ōsaka

Yellow River

Tianjin

Yellow Sea

Hiroshima

Fukuoka

Lanzhou

Xi'an

Nanjing

Shanghai

CHINA

Yangtze

Wuhan

East China Sea

Chengdu

Chongqing

Hangzhou

PACIFIC OCEAN

hu'

Kunming

Liuzhou

Guangzhou

Taibei

TAIWAN

ADESH

Nanning

Hong Kong

Kaoshiung

ANMAR

Ha-Nôi

Luzon Strait

RMA)

Hai Phong

Nay Pyi Taw

ngon

LAOS

VIETNAM

South China Sea

Quezon City

PHILIPPINES

ein

Vientiane

(THAILAND)

Manila

Bangkok

Melekeok

daman ands dia)

CAMBODIA

Ho Chi Minh City

Davao

PALAU

icobar slands ndia)

Phnom Penh

Kota Kinabalu

edan

Bandar Seri Begawan

Celebes Sea

Jayapura

Putrajaya

Kuala Lumpur

MALAYSIA

BRUNEI

Kuching

New Guinea

SINGAPORE

Borneo

Pontianak

Sumatra

INDONESIA

OCEANIA

Palembang

Banjarmasin

Laut Banda

Makassar

Jakarta

Laut Jawa

Surabaya

EAST TIMOR

Bandung

Semarang

Dili

Java

Timor Sea

0   1000   2000 KILOMETRES

© Collins Bartholomew Ltd

PHILIPPINE

SEA

PACIFIC

OCEAN

Northern
Mariana
Islands
(U.S.A.)

Pagan

135°

C

D

1

15°

CAPITOL HILL
Saipan
Tinian

Rota

Guam
(U.S.A.)

HAGÅTÑA

PHILIPPINES

Catanduanes

Sorsogon
Catarman
Samar
Catbalogan
Tacloban

Cebu

Bohol Sea
Surigao
Butuan
Cagayan de Oro
Iroquieta
Pagadian
Mindanao
Cotabato
Davao
Mati
General Santos

Ulithi
Fais

Yap
FEDERATED STATES

Ngulu
Sorol
OF MICRONESIA

Eauripik
Caroline
Islands

PALAU

MELEKEOK

2

Kepulauan
Talaud

Kepulauan
Sangir

Morotai

Equator
0°

Manado
Tomdano
Gorontalo
Halmahera
Malik
Molucca Sea
Ternate
Sau-Siu
Tobelo

Labuna

Bacan
Obi
Salawati
Waigeo

Selat Dampir
Kwoka
Manokwari
Biak

Pellelulu Is

Hermit Is

Peleng
Taliabu
Mangole
Misool
Jazirah
Numfoor
Sarmi
Jayapura
Vanimo
Aitape
Schouten Islands
Manam Is
Long

Banggai
Kepulauan
Dota
Sorong
Afanlap
Inanwatan
Yapen
Van Res
Tarataru
Sepik
Wewak
PAPUA
Madang
Hmbn

Seram

Fakfak
Babo
Nabire
Teluk
Pk Jaya
Pk
Pk
Central Ra.
4509
Goroka

Ambon
G. Binaiya
3011
Laut Seram
Kaimana
Enarotali
Nggulingm
Mdoke
5030
4730
Mendi
Hagen
Lae

Laut Banda
(Banda Sea)
Amamapare
4700
Mandala
NEW GUINEA
Kikori
Morobe

Kepulauan Kai
Tg Deyong
Digul
NEW GUINEA
Balimo
MT
Victoria

Kai Kecil
Benjina
Sia
Trangan
Pulau
Dolok
Kerema
Bereina

Kai
Besar
Kepulauan Aru
Merauke
Morehead
Danu
Gulf
PORT
MORESBY

Tg Vals
of
Papua

Kepulauan Tanimbar
Saumlakki
Selaru

Barat
Damar
Wuliaru
Pulau Romang
Babar
Kepulauan Leti
Kisar
Kepulauan Sermata
Arafura Sea

DILI
Manatuto
Leti

Kefamenanu
C. York
Bamaga

CUSSI
EAST
TIMOR
AUSTRALIA
C. Wessel

Kupang
Timor
Melville
Island
C. Wessel
Wessel Is
Gulf

Rote
Bathurst
Island
Croker I.
Van Diemen
Nhulunbuy
C. Arnhem
of
Carpentaria
Weipa

Beagle Gulf
Darwin
Jabiru
Coen

C

D

135°

0   500   1000 KILOMETRES

© Collins Bartholomew Ltd

59

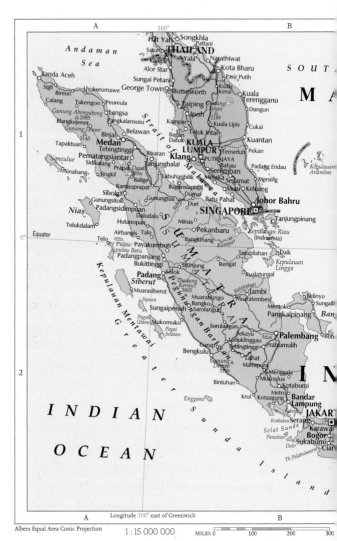

Andaman
Sea

Hat Yai
Songkhla
Pattani
Satun
THAILAND
Kangar
Alor Star
Yala
Narathiwat
Banda Aceh
Sungai Petani
Kota Bharu
Sigli
Bireun
Lhokseumawe
Pasir Putih
Calang
Takengon
Peureula
George Town
Butterworth
Kuala
Keral
Kuala
Terengganu
Langsa
Gunung Abongabong
2985
Pangkalansusu
Taiping
Gunung
Tahan
2189
Dungun
Blangkejeren
Gunung Leuser
3145
Binjai
Belawan
Ipoh
Kuala Lipis
Cukai
Tapaktuan
Medan
Tebingtinggi
Kampar
Teluk Intan
Kuantan
Simeulue
Pematangsiantar
Sidikalang
Kisaran
Bagan
Datuk
KUALA
LUMPUR
Klang
Temerluh
Pekan
Sinabang
Prapat
Danau
Toba
Tanjungbalai
PUTRAJAYA
Bahau
Padang Endau
Kepulauan
Anambas
Baliqe
Labuhanbilik
Seremban
Segamat
Mersing
Sibolga
Rantauprapat
Bagansiapiapi
Melaka
Muar
Keluang
Gunungsitoli
Padangsidimpuan
Gunungtua
Dumai
Duri
Batu Pahat
Johor Bahru
Nias
Daludalu
SUMATRA
SINGAPORE
Tanjungpinang
Hutanopan
Minas
Airbangis
Talu
Pekanbaru
Kepulauan Riau
(Indonesia)
Telukdalam
Telo
Payakumbuh
Bangkinang
Kampar
Daik
Pulau-
pulau Batu
Padangpanjang
Sijunjung
Rengat
Tembilahan
Kepulauan
Lingga
Bukittinggi
Solok
Kualatungal
Siberut
Padang
Gunung
Kerinci
3805
Batanghari
Jambi
Muarabungo
Muaratembesi
Belinyu
Muarasiberut
Bangko
Sungaili
Sipura
Sungaipenuh
Sarolangun
Mentoko
Pangkalpinang
Ban
Pagai
Utara
Mukomuko
Surulangun
Sekayu
Lubuklinggau
Musi
Palembang
Tob
Pagai
Selatan
Curup
Tebingtinggi
Prabumulih
Bengkulu
Lahat
Gunung
Dempo
3159
Martapura
Menggala
Muaradua
Kotabumi
IN
Bintuhan
Krul
Metro
Kotaagung
Bandar
Lampung
Enggano
Krakatau
Kotaagung
Serang
JAKAR
Selat Sunda
Karawar
Bogor
Panaitan
Sukabumi
Ciar
Tk Palabuhanratu
Deli

I N D I A N

O C E A N

110°

C

Banggi

*SULU
SEA*

Kudat

Kota Belud

*Gunung
Kinabalu*
4095

HINA SEA

Ranau

Sandakan

Kota
Kinabalu

AYSIA

Beaufort

SABAH

Lamag

Labuan

Kuamut

Lahad
Datu

Tawau

Pensiangan

BANDAR SERI
BEGAWAN

BRUNEI

Kuala Belait
Lutong
Miri

Seria

Lumbis

CELEBES

Tumbao

Tawau

1

Natuna Besar

Panarik

Long
Akah

Kubuang

*Pulauan
Natuna*

Bintulu

Igan Mukah

Tarakan

Tanjungselor

SARAWAK

Belaga

Sibu

Datadian

Tanjungredeb

Sarikei

Kapit

Liku

Sematan

Kota

Saratok

Kuching

Debak

Belaga

Tanjungredeb

Sambas

Semitau

Datadian

2988

Sepinang

Pemangkat

Serian

Sri Aman

Sangkulirang

gkawang

Bengkayang

Lubok
Antu

Putusibau

*dalauan
abelian*

Sanggau

Sintang

BORNEO

Bontang

empawah

Ngabang

Pontianak

Nangahpinoh

Longiram

Tenggarong

Samarinda

0°

Balaiberkuak

Muaralaung

Telukbatang

Sukadana

Nangatayap

Rantaupanjang

Muarateweh

Balikpapan

*pulau-pulau
Karimata*

Ketapang

KALIMANTAN

Tanahgrogot

Babana

Palangkaraya

Mamuju

lat Kalimata

Kendawangan

Sukaraja

Sampit

Amuntai

3074

njungpandan

Pangkalanbuun

Kandangan

Kotabaru

Bukit
Gandadiwata
Polewall

Kualapembuang

Manggar

*Tanjung
Sambar*

Martapura

Majene

Banjarmasin

litung

*Tanjung
Puting*

Pagatan

Laut

*Tanjung
Selatan*

2

DONESIA

*Kepulauan
Laut Kecil*

*LAUT JAWA
(JAVA SEA)*

*Pulau-pulau
Karimunjawa*

Sabalana

Kemujan

Bawean

wakarta

*Tanjung
Indramayu*

*Tanjung
Bugel*

bon

Tegal Pekalongan

Pati

Tuban

Bangkalan

Madura

Sumenep

*Kepulauan
Kangean*

Garut

3428

Kudus

Surabaya

Raas

*Laut Bali
(Bali Sea)*

Sumbawa

ndung

Semarang

Jombang

Pasuruan

Situbondo

emis

Surakarta

Madiun

Banyuwangi

Alas

Dompu

Raba

Temanggung

Cilacap

Kebumen

Yogyakarta

Malang

G. Raung
3142

Singaraja

Mataram

Sumbawabesar

*JAVA
(JAWA)*

Lumajang

Jember

Barung

Gianyar

Selat Lombok

Praya

Taliwang

Bali

Denpasar

Lombok

110°

C

0   250   500 KILOMETRES

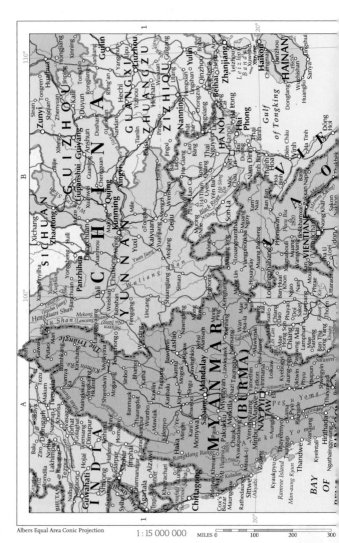

Albers Equal Area Conic Projection

1 : 15 000 000   MILES 0   100   200   300

V I E T N A M

THAILAND

CAMBODIA

MALAYSIA

INDONESIA

SOUTH CHINA SEA

Gulf of Thailand

Andaman Sea

Gulf of Martaban

Gulf of Tonkin

INDIAN OCEAN

BANGKOK (Krung Thep)

PHNOM PENH

Ho Chi Minh City (Saigon)

Da Nang
Hôi An
Quang Ngai
Quy Nhon
Tuy Hòa
Nha Trang
Phan Rang-Thap Cham
Phan Thiêt
Da Lat
Buôn Ma Thuôt
Pleiku
Kontum

Vientiane
Pakxé
Savannakhét
Salavan

Nakhon Ratchasima
Nakhon Sawan
Ubon Ratchathani
Khon Kaen
Udon Thani
Nong Khai
Roi Et
Surin
Buriram
Nakhon Phanom

Ayutthaya
Nonthaburi
Chon Buri
Pattaya
Rayong
Chanthaburi
Trat

Phetchaburi
Prachuap Khiri Khan
Chumphon
Ranong
Surat Thani
Nakhon Si Thammarat
Phatthalung
Songkhla
Hat Yai
Pattani
Yala
Narathiwat
Kota Bharu
Pasir Puteh
Alor Star
Sungai Petani
Satun

Phuket
Thalang
Krabi
Phangnga
Takua Pa

Tavoy
Mergui
Tenasserim
Myeik (Mergui) Archipelago

Mergui Archipelago

Andaman Islands (India)
Nicobar Islands (India)
Port Blair
North Andaman
Middle Andaman
South Andaman
Little Andaman
Car Nicobar
Great Nicobar
Little Nicobar
Katchall
Teressa Island
Tillanchong Island
Camorta
Nancowry

Ten Degree Channel
Preparis North Channel
Preparis South Channel
Great Coco Island
Narcondam Island

Cape Negrais
Mouths of the Irrawaddy

Battambang
Siemréab
Poŭthĭsăt
Kâmpóng Cham
Kâmpôt
Sihanoukville
Kâmpóng Saôm
Takêv
Tônlé Sap
Krâchéh
Mekong

Mouths of the Mekong
Mui Ca Mau
Ca Mau
Bac Liêu
Soc Trang
Can Tho
My Tho
Rach Gia
Vinh Long
Long Xuyên
Tây Ninh
Vung Tau

Banda Aceh

© Collins Bartholomew Ltd

63

0   250   500 KILOMETRES

Longitude 100° east of Greenwich

PHILIPPINE
SEA

PHILIPPINES

Babuyan
Calayan   Babuyan
Islands
Fuga   Camiguin

Laoag City   Aparri
Bangged   Tuguegarao
Vigan   Mount Chico
Tagudin   Bontoc   Sapoccoy   Ilagan   Palanan
San Fernando   Mount   Santiago
La Trinidad   Pulog   Bayombong
Dagupan   Baguio   LUZON
Lingayen   San Carlos
Tarlac   San Jose
Iba   Cabanatuan
Angeles   San Fernando
Olongapo   Valenzuela   Polillo Islands
Quezon City
MANILA   Pasig
Santa Cruz   Labo
Tagaytay City   San Pablo   Daet
Batangas   Lucena   Lopez   Catanduanes
Calapan   Boac   Virac
Mount   Naga
Halcon   Legazpi   Sorsogon
2555   Roxas   Irosin
San Jose   Romblon   Calamian
Mindoro   Sibuyan   Masbate
Calamian   Romblon   Masbate   Calbayog
Group   Sibuyan Sea   Samar
Culion   Pandan   Catbalogan
Roxas   Visayan
El Nido   Linapacan   Sea
Taytay   Cuyo   Iloilo   Tacloban
Islands   Panay   Pototan   Guiuan
San Jose de   Bacolod   Leyte
Dumaran   Buenavista   Cebu   Ormoc
Roxas   Negros   Talisay   Maasin
Cordillera   Dinagat
Palawan   Puerto Princesa   Cebu
Cauayan   Tagbilaran   Surigao
Quezon   Tanjay   Siargao
Mount   Bayawan   Butuan   Tandag
Mantalingajan   Aborlan   Dumaguete   Bohol Sea
2085   Brooke's Point   Presidente   Dapitan   Cagayan
Manuel A Roxas   Oroquieta   de Oro
Bugsuk   Liloy   Iligan   Malaybalay
Balabac   Ozamis   Mount
Balabac   SULU   SEA   Pagadian   Kitang   MINDANAO
Balabac Strait   Zamboanga   2815   Mount   Tagum
Peninsula   Cotabato   Apo   Davao
Cagayan de   Datu Piang   2954   Mati
Banggi   Tawi-Tawi   Zamboanga   Moro   Digos
Gulf   Banga
Kudat   Basilan   Isabela   Davao
Kota Belud   Gunung   General Santos   Gulf
Kinabalu   Jolo   Sulu
4095   Ranau   Archipelago   Sarangani Islands
Sandakan   Tawi-Tawi
MALAYSIA   Lamag   Tumindao   Kepulauan
SABAH   Kuamut   Nanusa
Lahad Datu   CELEBES   Kepulauan
Pensiangan   Karakelong   Talaud
SEA
Semporna
INDONESIA   Tawau   INDONESIA   Sangir   Kaburuang

SOUTH
CHINA
SEA

Scarborough
Shoal

Mindoro

Linapacan

SULU   SEA

MINDANAO

Longitude 120° east of Greenwich

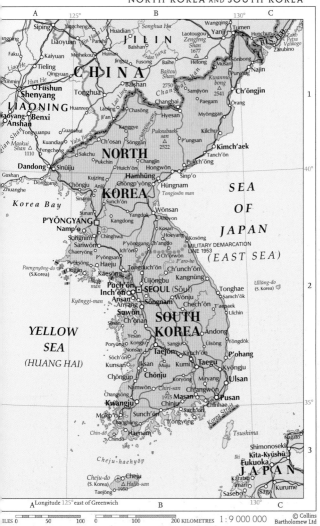

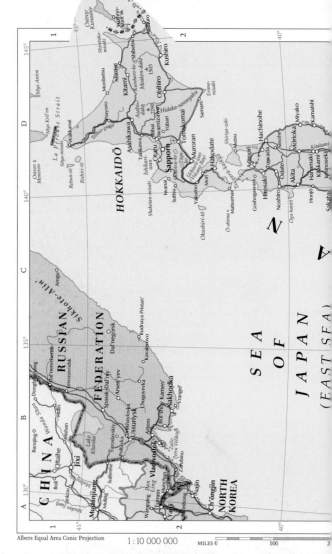

Albers Equal Area Conic Projection

1 : 10 000 000

MILES 0   100   2

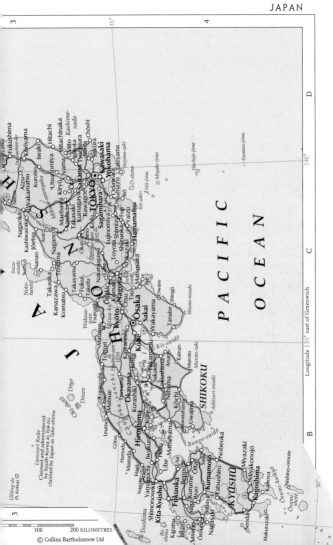

3

35°

4

D

HONSHŪ

Ullŭng-do ◇
(S. Korea)

Claimant Rocks
Claimed and administered
by South Korea but
claimed by Japan as Take-shima

Oki-shotō
Dōgo ◇
◇ Dōzen

Suzu-misaki
Noto-hantō
Suzu
Nanao

Kanazawa
Takaoka
Toyama
Komatsu

Fukui
Takefu
Tsuruga
Wakasa-wan

Tottori
Matsue
Izumo
Gōtsu
Hamada
Masuda
Hagi

Yonago
Yasugi

Kurayoshi
Tsuyama

Okayama
Kurashiki

Himeji
Kakogawa

Akashi
Kōbe
Takarazuka
Amagasaki

Kyōto
Ōtsu

Kusatsu
Ōgaki

Kashihara
Tsu

Wakayama
Ōsu

Owase

Shingū

Shimo-misaki

Tanabe

Kainan

Muroto
Muroto-zaki

SHIKOKU

Kōchi

Ashizuri-misaki

Nagaoka
Kashiwazaki
Jōetsu

Nagano

Matsumoto

Arai

Maebashi
Takasaki
Kumagaya
Kawagoe

Kiryū
Ashikaga

Utsunomiya

Ōta

Fukushima

Aizu-
wakamatsu

Kōriyama

Iwaki

Kuroiso

Kashima-
nada

Mito

Hitachi

Hitachinaka

Tsuchiura

Narita

Sakura

Chōshi

TOKYO

Yokohama

Kawasaki

Sagamihara
Fujisawa
Chiba

Atsugi
Hiratsuka

Odawara
Atami

Numazu
Mishima

Fuji

Shizuoka
Yaizu

Shimizu
Fujinomiya

Hamamatsu

Toyohashi
Okazaki

Nagoya
Ichinomiya

Kasugai

Seto

Toyota
Kariya

Kōbe

Ōsaka
Sakai

Iro-zaki

O-shima

Nii-jima

Miyake-jima

Hachijō-jima

Sumisu-jima

Inubō-saki

Neojima-zaki

Nojima-zaki

PACIFIC

OCEAN

Longitude 135° east of Greenwich

140°

C

B

Suō-nada
Shimonoseki
Iwakuni

Hiroshima
Kure
Saijō

Kudamatsu
Tokuyama
Hōfu

Yamaguchi
Ube

Nagato

Kita-Kyūshū

Fukuoka

Chōfu

Fukue

Tsushima

Iki

Karatsu

Saga

Kurume

Ōmuta

Saseho

Ōmura

Isahaya

Nagasaki

Kumamoto

KYŪSHŪ

Yatsushiro

Hitoyoshi

Kagoshima

Kanoya

Miyakonojō

Miyazaki

Nobeoka

Ōita
Beppu

Sendai

Makurazaki

Ōsumi-hantō

Ōsumi-shotō

Nishino-omote

Bungo-suidō

Uwajima

Yawatahama

Ōsu

Ōzu

Niihama

Saijō

Matsuyama
Imabari

Sakaide
Takamatsu

Marugame

Tokushima

Anan

Kii-suidō

Kaiyō

Izuhara

Nagasaki

Hirado

100   200 KILOMETRES

© Collins Bartholomew Ltd

30°

130°

Albers Equal Area Conic Projection   1 : 30 000 000   MILES 0   200   400

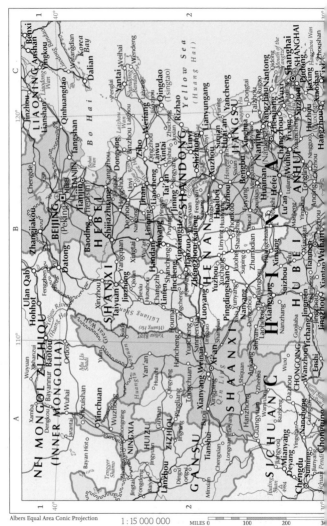

Albers Equal Area Conic Projection

1 : 15 000 000

MILES 0   100   200

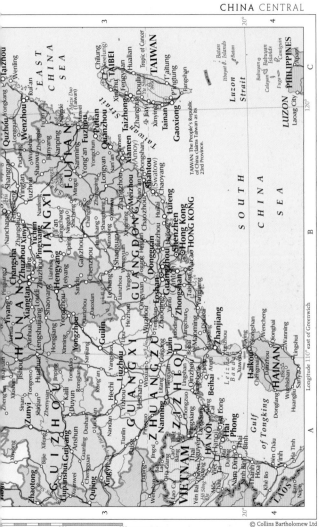

EAST CHINA SEA

Qingtian Qizhou Wenling
Wencheng Yongkang Xongkang

Rui'an
Pingyang Longquan Shangrao Nanchang

Jingdezhen

HUNAN
Changsha
Yiyang Xiangtan Zhuzhou Xinyu
Huaihua Lengshuijiang Loudi Zhuzhou Pingxiang
Shaoyang

JIANGXI

Fuzhou FUJIAN
Fuqing Putian

TAIWAN
Chilung Keelung
TAIBEI
Xinzhu Taoyuan
Taizhong Douliu Hualian
Zhanghua
Xinying Taidong
Tainan
Gaoxiong Pingtung
Fangshan

Tropic of Cancer

Hengyang Yongzhou Guzhou Sanjiang
Guilin

GUANGXI

GUANGDONG

Dongguan
Guangzhou Foshan
Zhongshan Shenzhen
Macao HONG KONG

SOUTH CHINA SEA

TAIWAN: The People's Republic
of China claims Taiwan as its
23rd Province.

Luzon Strait

LUZON
Laoag City

PHILIPPINES

ZHUANG ZIZHIQU

Nanning

HAINAN
Haikou

Zhanjiang

Gulf of Tongking

VIETNAM
HANOI

LAOS

Longitude 110° east of Greenwich

120°

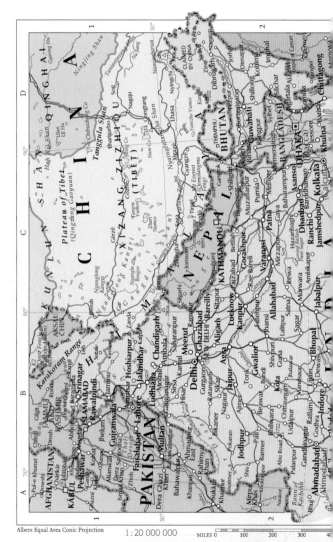

Albers Equal Area Conic Projection

1 : 20 000 000

MILES 0   100   200   300   40

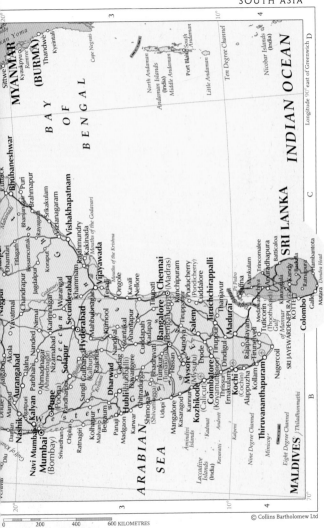

MYANMAR (BURMA)

Sittwe

kan Yoma

Kyaukpyu
Ramree
Thandwe

Kyeintali

Cape Negrais

B A Y

O F

B E N G A L

North Andaman
Andaman Islands
(India)
Middle Andaman
Port Blair
South Andaman

Little Andaman

Ten Degree Channel

Nicobar Islands
(India)

INDIAN OCEAN

Bhubaneshwar
Cuttack
Puri
Mahanadi
Bhanjanagar
Brahmapur

Dhamtari
Titlagarh
Bhawanipatna
Rayagada
Srikakulam
Koraput
Vizianagaram
Vishakhapatnam

Jagdalpur
Rajahmundry
Kakinada
Mouths of the Godavari
Khammam
Vijayawada

Warangal
Eluru
Tenali
Machilipatnam
Mouths of the Krishna

Karimnagar
Nizamabad
Secunderabad
Hyderabad
Mahbubnagar
Ongole

Nirmal
Nanded
Kavali
Nellore
Nalgonda

Parbhani
Kurnool
Cuddapah
Tirupati

Ahmadnagar
Osmanabad
Gulbarga
(Kalburgi)
Raichur
Anantapur
Kanchipuram
Chennai (Madras)

Sangli
Bijapur
(Vijapura)
Bagalkot
Bellary
Tumkur
(Tumakuru)
Bengaluru
Puducherry
(Pondicherry)

Kolhapur
Belgaum
Gadag
Davangere
Chitradurga
Bangalore
Bengaluru
Tiruppattur
Cuddalore

Panaji
Hubli
(Hubballi)
Shimoga
(Shivamogga)
Mandya
Salem
Tiruvannamalai

Karwar
Bhadravati
Hassan
Mysore
(Mysuru)
Erode
Karaikal
Tiruchirappalli
Thanjavur

Madgaon
Chikmagalur
Thrissur
(Trichur)
Coimbatore
Tiruppur
Dindigul
Karur

Mangalore
Kasaragod
Kannur
(Cannanore)
Koyambedu
Madurai
Palk Strait
Jaffna

Kozhikode
(Calicut)
Lakshadweep
Islands
(India)
Kochi
(Cochin)
Ernakulam
Rajapalayam
Tirunelveli
Pamban
Gulf of
Mannar

Amindivi
Islands
Androt
(Androth)
Alappuzha
(Alleppey)
Kollam
(Quilon)
Tuticorin
(Thoothukudi)
Trincomalee
Anuradhapura

Kavaratti
Kalpeni
Thiruvananthapuram
Nagercoil
SRI JAYEWARDENEPURA
KOTTE
Kurunegala
Kandy
Batticaloa

A R A B I A N

S E A

Nine Degree Channel

Minicoy
(India)

Eight Degree Channel

Nagercoil
Kanniyakumari
(Cape Comorin)
Colombo
Ratnapura
Badulla

SRI LANKA

Galle
Matara
Dondra Head

MALDIVES

Thiladhunmathi

Hambantota

0   200   400   600 KILOMETRES

AFGHANISTAN

Serhetabat Darya-ye Morghab Dowshi Pul-e Khumri Battura Glacier K2 Goodwin

Selseleh-ye Sefid Kuh Hari Rūd Bāmīān Charikar Bari Kot Chitral Karakoram

Kōh-e Bābā Chaghcharān Shah Fuladi Mahtar Drosh Gilgit Astor

Kōh-e Chihil 5143 Maidan Shahr Asadābād Line of Control

Abalān **KABUL** Jalalabad Dargai **JAMMU**

Dilaram Ghazni Gardez Khōst Khyber Pass Mardan Abbottabad Baramulla **AND**

HAZĀRAH JĀT Zarah Sharan **Peshawar** Nowshera **KASHMIR** Srinagar

Ginshk Qalāt Arghandāb Rūd Kohat **RAWALPINDI** Jhelum Jammu Anantnag

Lashkar Gāh Termiz Rūd Bannu Daud Khel **ISLAMABAD** Chamba Kishtwar

Kandahar Lakki Marwat Talagang Udhampur

Dasht-e Arū-ye Shamālī Tank Mianwali Khushab Sargodha Chiniot Wazirabad Sialkot Kathua

Amir Chah Chagai Hamūn-i-Lora Nushki Dera Ismail Khan Bhakkar Thal Desert Jhang Faisalabad **Lahore** **Amritsar** Ludh

Nok Kundi Dalbandin Rās Koh 3007 Zhob Layyah Khanewal Ahmadpur Sial Ravi **Multan** Burewala Okara Ferozpur Fazilka Chandiga

Hamūn-i- Māshkīl Mastung Loralai Sulaiman Range Dera Ghazi Khan Muzaffargarh Abohar Bathinda Moha

Kamarod Washuko Qilla Ladgasht Surab **PAKISTAN** Dera Bugti Rajanpur Babahpur Fort Abbas Suratgarh Hanumangarh Ganganagar Sirsa Panip

Diz Panjgur Kalat Khuzdar Sibi Rahimyar Khan Bikaner Nohar Mahajan NEW DE

Turbat Central Makran Range Bela Nagha Kandi Kot Khan Khairpur Ghotki Barsalpur Pugal Sardarshahr Ratangarh Churu Gurga

Hoshab Bazdar Larkana Sukkur Ghotaru Jaisalmer Thar Desert Nokha Sujangarh Sikar Bhar

Tump Turbat Sonmiani Dadu Nawabshah Khipro Pokaran Merta Ajmer Jaipur

Suntsar Gwadar Pasni Ormara Thano Bula Khan Hyderabad Mirpur Khas Tando Muhammad Khan Balotra Pali Deogarh Beawar Tonk Sawa Bundi

Karachi Thatta Sujawal Badin Naukot Mithi Nagar Parkar Rann of Kachchh Barmer Jodhpur Bhilwara Chittaurgarh Kota

ARABIAN SEA Mouths of the Indus Lakhpat Radhanpur Palanpur Abu Road Sirohi Udaipur Banswara Jhalaw

Tropic of Cancer Rapar Bhuj Gandhidham Mahesana Sidhpur Dungarpur **I N** Mandsaur Agar

Okha Dwarka Gulf of Kachchh Morbi Surendranagar Nadiad Gandhinagar Godhra Ratlam Ujjain Bho

Porbandar Jamnagar **Rajkot** Phasa Khambhat **Ahmadabad** **Vadodara** Narmada Rajpur Mhow Indor

Keshod Junagadh Visavadar Bhavnagar Bharuch Surat Tapti Nandurbar Jalgaon Khandwa

Veraval Mahuva Diu Gulf of Khambhat Daman Valsad Dhule Chalisgaon Bhusawa

Dahanu Nashik Godavari Aurangabad

74 Albers Equal Area Conic Projection 1 : 15 000 000 MILES 0 100 200 30

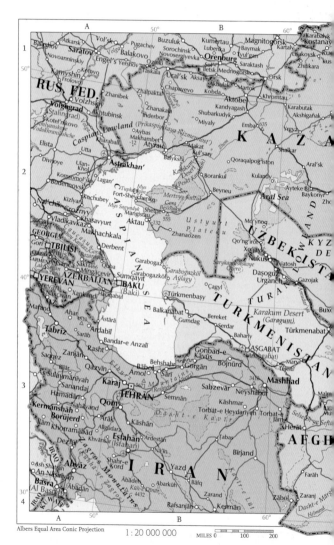

Albers Equal Area Conic Projection   1 : 20 000 000   MILES 0   100   200

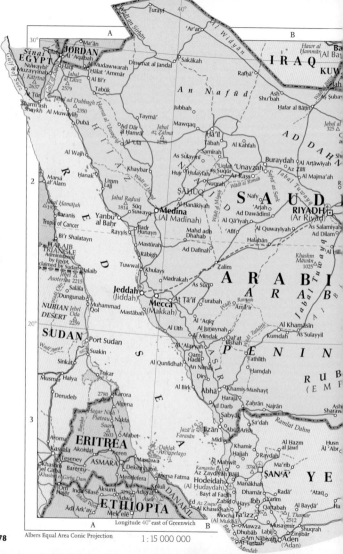

Albers Equal Area Conic Projection   1 : 15 000 000

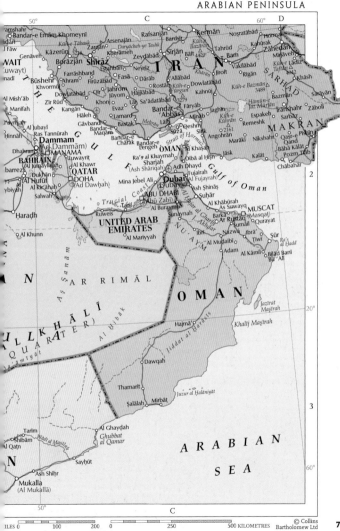

Albers Equal Area Conic Projection

1 : 15 000 000

MILES 0   100   200

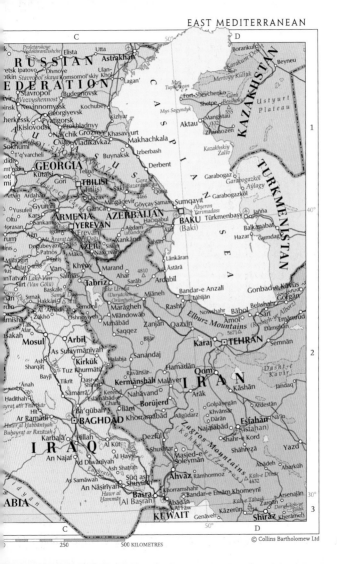

250   500 KILOMETRES

Conic Equidistant Projection   1 : 42 000 000   MILES 0   250   500   7

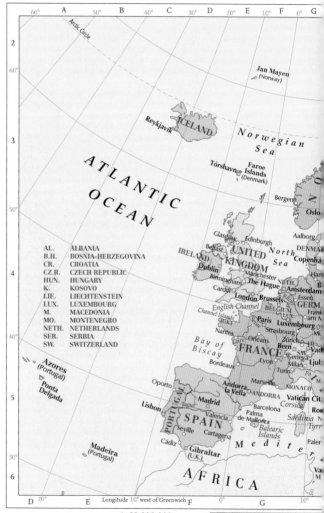

ATLANTIC

OCEAN

Arctic Circle

Jan Mayen
(Norway)

Reykjavik ICELAND

Norwegian
Sea

Tórshavn Faroe
Islands
(Denmark)

Bergen

Oslo

NO

Glasgow Edinburgh
Belfast
IRELAND UNITED
Dublin KINGDOM
Birmingham Manchester
Cardiff London

Aalborg
North DENM
Sea Copenha

The Hague NETH. Amsterdam
Brussels Essen
BELGIUM GERM.
LUX. Fran
Am N

English Channel
Channel Islands
(U.K.)

Paris Luxembourg Mu
Nantes Orleans Strasbourg LIE.
Tours Bern Zürich SW. Vad
FRANCE Geneva Ljub

Bay of
Biscay
Bordeaux
Lyon
Milan Turin

Marseille MONACO
Andorra- Corsica
la Vella ANDORRA Vatican Cit
Madrid Barcelona Rom
Oporto PORTUGAL
Lisbon Tagus
Valencia Palma
de Mallorca Sardinia
SPAIN Balearic
Seville Cartagena Islands M e d i t e
Cádiz Paler

Madeira
(Portugal)

Gibraltar
(U.K.)

A F R I C A

Va

AL. ALBANIA
B.H. BOSNIA-HERZEGOVINA
CR. CROATIA
CZ.R. CZECH REPUBLIC
HUN. HUNGARY
K. KOSOVO
LIE. LIECHTENSTEIN
LUX. LUXEMBOURG
M. MACEDONIA
MO. MONTENEGRO
NETH. NETHERLANDS
SER. SERBIA
SW. SWITZERLAND

Azores
(Portugal)

Ponta
Delgada

1 : 39 000 000   MILES 0   250   500

Longitude 10° west of Greenwich

Novaya Zemlya

Barents Sea

Vorkuta

Kola Peninsula

White Sea

Lappland

Archangel

Gulf of Bothnia

Severnaya Dvina

R U S S I A N

FINLAND

Lake Ladoga

Helsinki

St Petersburg

Izhevsk

Perm'

F E D E R A T I O N

Gulf of Finland

kholm

Tallinn

ESTONIA

Kazan'

Yaroslavl'

Nizhniy Novgorod

Ufa

tic Sea

LATVIA

Riga

Moscow

Ul'yanovsk

Samara

Orenburg

LITHUANIA

RUS. FED.

Vilnius

Tula

A S I A

ingrad

Minsk

BELARUS

Saratov

nan Warsaw

Brest

Homyel'

Voronezh

Łódź

Rivne

Kiev

Kharkiv

Volgograd

Volga

POLAND

ue

Katowice

L'viv

UKRAINE

Donets'k

Don

Rostov-na-Donu

Astrakhan

Caspian Sea

SLOVAKIA

Dniester

Dnipropetrovs'k

Bratislava

MOLDOVA

Budapest

Chişinău

Odessa

Krasnodar

Grozny

HUN.

ROMANIA

C a u c a s u s

Zagreb

Belgrade

Bucharest

Constanţa

B. H.

Danube

Black Sea

evo

SER.

BULGARIA

Prishtinë

Sofia

gorica

M.

İstanbul

Tirana

Skopje

Thessaloniki

AL.

Aegean Sea

T U R K E Y

ly

GREECE

Athens

Ionian Sea

ean Sea

Crete

Novaya Zemlya

60°

50°

40°

30°

2

3

4

5

6

20°   30°   40°   50°   60°   70°   80°

I   J   K   L   M   N   O

20°   30°   40°   50°

I   J   K

0   500   1000 KILOMETRES

© Collins Bartholomew Ltd

85

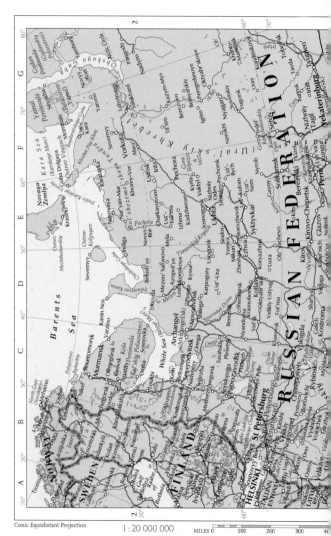

Conic Equidistant Projection

1 : 20 000 000

MILES 0   100   200   300   40

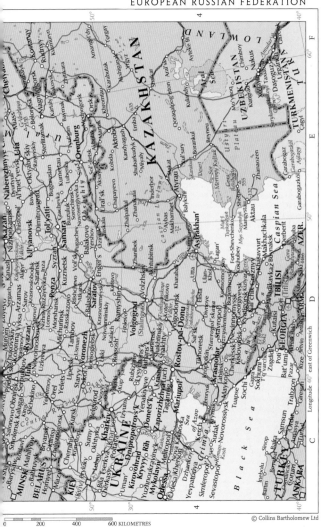

© Collins Bartholomew Ltd

0   200   400   600 KILOMETRES

Conic Equidistant Projection

Longitude 25° east of Greenwich

1 : 8 000 000

MILES 0   50   100   15

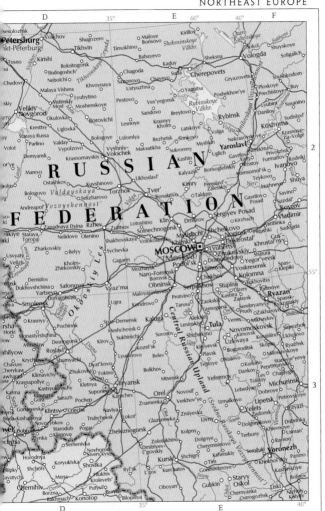

A   25°   B   30°

BELARUS

POLAND

UKR

HUNGARY

SLA

ROMANIA

MOLDOVA

WARSAW
(Warszawa)

Ostrów
Mazowiecka
Białystok   Baranavichy
Wyszków   Słonim   Asipovichy   Babruysk
Vawkavysk   LyakKavichy   Kapyl'   Slutsk   Rahachow   Zhlobin
Minsk   Klyetsk   Staraya Darohi   Buda-Kasha
Siedlce   Ivatsevichy   Hantsavichy   Mal'kavichy   Aktsyabrski   Svyetlahorsk   Hom
Mazowiecki   Byaroza   Lyuban'   Rechytsa
Zhabinka   Kobryn   Drahichyn   Luninyets   Petrykaw   Kalinkavichy
Brest   Ivanava   Pinsk   Dzyatlavichy   Zhytkavichy   Mazyr   Narowlya   Brahin
Biała   Lyubeshiv   Stolin   Lyel'chytsy   Yel'sk
Podlaska   Rathe   Zarichne   Dubrovytsya   P r i p e t   M a r s h e s
Łuków   Lyubeshiv   Prypyats (Pripet)
Lubartów   Kamin'-Kashyrs'kyy   Volodymyrets'   Rokytne   Ovruch   Narodychi   Polis'ke
Radom   Lublin   Kovel'   Manevychi   Sarny   Olevs'k   Luhyny   Vodoskhovyshche
Ostrowiec   Kuznetsovs'k   Berezne   Korosten'   Ivankiv
Świętokrzyski   Chelm   Turiys'k   Volodymyr-   Kostopil'   Volodars'k-   Malyn   Borodyanka
Sandomierz   Zamość   Volyns'kyy   Luts'k   Rivne   Volyns'kyy   Radomyshl'   Irpin'   KIEV
Stalowa   Novovolyns'k   Mlyniv   Zdolbuniv   Novohrad-Volyns'kyy   Korostyshiv   (Kyiv)
Tarnobrzeg   Wola   Sokal   Slavuta   Polonne   Brusyliv   Fastiv
Mielec   Bilgoraj   Chervonohrad   Dubno   Shepetivka   Zhytomyr   Vasyl'kiv
Rzeszów   Tomaszów   Lubelski   Radyvyliv   Izyaslav   Chudniv   Andrushivka   Bila   Kaharly
Lubaczów   Yavoriv   Buz'ka   Brody   Pochaviv   Bilohir'ya   Berdychiv   Tserk
Jaslo   Przemyśl   Lviv   Zolochiv   Starokostyantyniv   Ko
Krosno   Jaroslaw   (Lvov)   Ternopil'   Krasyliv   Kozyatyn   Tetiyiv   Zhashkiv   Myro
Sanok   Horodok   Peremyshlyany   Volochys'k   Khmel'nyts'kyy   Vinnytsya   Zvenyhoro
Sambir   Berezhany   Terebovlya   Illintsi   Khrystynivka
Drohobych   Zhydachiv   Horodok   Zhmerynka   Nemyriv   Haysyn   Monastyry
SLA   Boryslav   Stryy   Kalush   Chortkiv   Dunayivtsi   Kam''yanets'-   Sharhorod   Tul'chyn   Uman'
Humenné   Dolyna   Ivano-   Borshchiv   Podil's'kyy
Michalovce   Frankivs'k   Horodenka   Sokyryany   Mohyliv-Podil's'kyy
Uzhhorod   Mizhhir''ya   Nadvima   Kolomyya   Dnister (Dniester)   Yampil'   Bershad   Pervomays'k
Trebišov   Mukacheve   Rakhiv   Verkhovyna   Chernivtsi   Okhnytsya   Sorok   Balta   Kodyma
Nyíregyháza   Berehove   Khust   Storozhynets'   Dorohoi   Bălţi   Ribniţa   Anan'yiv   Berez
Svalyava   Sighetu   Borsa   Vatra   Suceava   Botoşani   Kotsovs'k   Pervomays'
Satu   Marmaţiei   Pietrosu   Dornei   Fălticeni   MOLDOVA
Mare   Baia   2305   Paşcani   Ungheni   Iaşi   CHIŞINĂU   Rozdil'na   Od
Carei   Mare   Zalău   Dej   Bistriţa   Piatra   Roman   Husi   Kishin   Tighina   Tiraspol'   Od
Simleu   Vârful   Reghin   Neamţ   Vaslui   Cimislia   Bilyayivka   Ilichivs'k
Silvaniei   Bihor   Gherla   Pasul   Târgu   Beiuş   Bacău   Huşi   Comrat   Bilhorod-Dnistrovs'k
Oradea   1849   Cluj-   Turda   Bucin   Vârful Harghita-Mădăras   Moineşti   Bârlad   Artsyz
Napoca   1273   1800   Miercurea-   Comăneşti   Cahul   Sarata
Aiud   Târnăveni   Ciuc   Oneşti   Adjud   Cadir-   Tatarbunary
Alba   Mediaş   Sighişoara   Tecuci   Lunca   Reni   Kiliya
Iulia   Reva   Sebeş   Agnita   Sfântu   Focşani   Galaţi   Bolhrad   Vylkove
Deva   Orăştie   Sibiu   Făgăraş   Gheorghe   Braşov   Vârful Omu   Râmnicu   Ianca   Brăila   Măcin   Izmayil
Hunedoara   Caransebeş   Petroşani   2544   Sărat   Danube   Tulcea   Danube Delta
Caracal   Lupeni   2519   Pasul   Vârful Moldoveanu   Buzău   Brăila   Lacul Razim
Vârful Svinecului   Petroşani   Vulcan   1292   2505   Câmpina   Urziceni   Cernavoda   Năvodari
1224   Strehaia   Râmnicu   Ploieşti   Slobozia   Ţăndărei
Drobeta-   Drăgăneşti   Vâlcea   Moreni   Ialomiţa   Babadag
Turnu Severin   Târgu   Piteşti   Târgovişte   Ţiţu   Urziceni   Lacul Razim
Craiova   Slatina   Costeşti   Găeşti   Videle   Buftea   BUCHAREST   (Bucureşti)
Drăgăneşti-Olt   Bolintin-Vale   Slobozia
Bals   Caracal

Longitude 25° east of Greenwich

A   B   30°

1 : 8 000 000

MILES 0   50   100   150

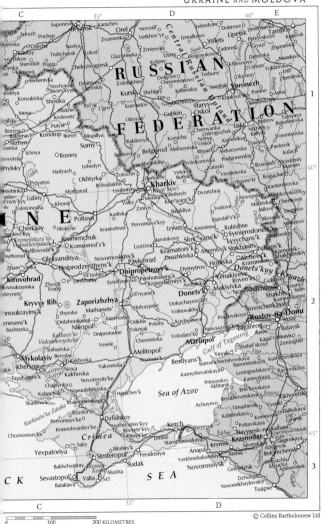

© Collins Bartholomew Ltd

0   100   200 KILOMETRES

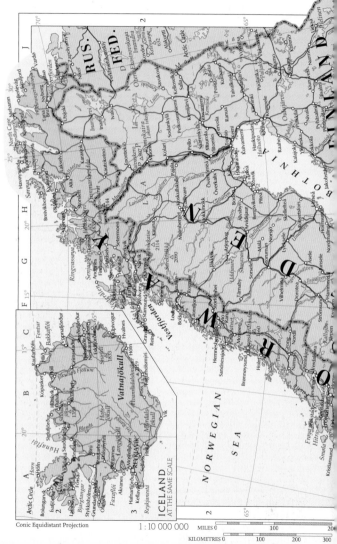

Conic Equidistant Projection

1 : 10 000 000

MILES 0   100   20

KILOMETRES 0   100   200   300

ICELAND
AT THE SAME SCALE

RUS. FED.

FINLAND

NORWAY

SWEDEN

NORWEGIAN SEA

Arctic Circle

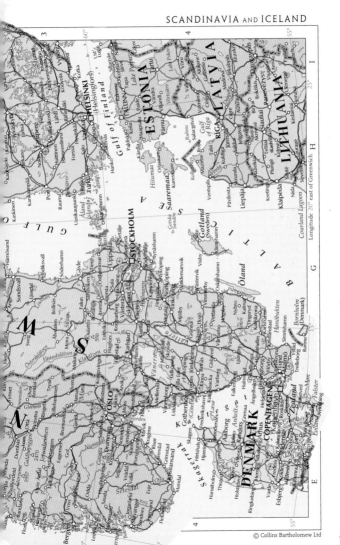

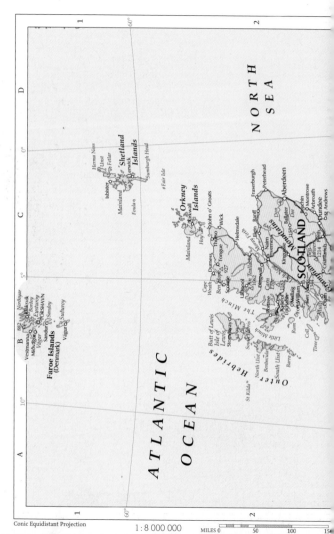

ATLANTIC

OCEAN

NORTH
SEA

Faroe Islands
(Denmark)

Nordoyar
882
Vestmanna
Bordoy
Mikladur
Eysturoy
Vagar TÓRSHAVN
Sandur Sandoy
Vágur Suduroy

Herma Ness
Unst
Fetlar
Isbister **Shetland**
Mainland **Islands**
Foula Lerwick
Sumburgh Head

Fair Isle

**Orkney
Islands**
Kirkwall
Mainland John o' Groats
Hoy Thurso Wick

Helmsdale

Butt of Lewis
Isle of
Lewis
Stornoway
Cape Kinlochbervie
Wrath Durness Tongue
Scourie
Scourie 927

Outer
Ullapool

North Uist
Benbecula
South Uist
Barra

St Kilda

The Minch

Little Minch

Hebrides

Coll
Tiree

Cairn
1062
Toridon
Kyle of
Portree Lochalsh
Skye
Mallaig
Rum Grantown
Eigg
Fort William
Ben Nevis

Durness
Bonar Bridge
Dornoch
Tain
Cromarty
Inverness
Nairn
Kingussie

Aviemore
Grampian
214 Perth
Crianlarich
Oban
Helensburgh

Grampian
Mountains

SCOTLAND

Fraserburgh
Banff Peterhead
Elgin
Huntly Aberdeen
Deveron
Ballater
Dee

Brechin
Forfar Montrose
Arbroath
Dundee
St Andrews

Conic Equidistant Projection

1 : 8 000 000

MILES 0   50   100   150

94

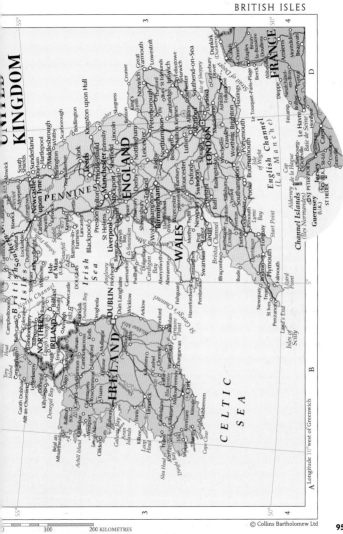

A Longitude 10° west of Greenwich

100   200 KILOMETRES

SCOTLAND

A 6° **B** 4°

North
Ronaldsay
Westray
Rousay Sanday
Loth Stronsay
Herma Ness
Unst
Orkney Mainland
Islands Kirkwall
Stromness Gritley
Ward Hill Isbister
479 Hoy St Margaret's Hope Uyea Yell Fetlar
Ronaldsay Walls
Foula Mainland
Pentland Firth Lerwick
Dunnet Head John Duncansby **Shetland** Bressay
o' Groats Head **Islands**
Cape
Wrath Thurso Sumburgh Sumburgh
Durness Wick Head
Tongue
Point Dunbeath Fair Isle
of Stoer Helmsdale
Scourie Ben More Loch
Assynt Shin 2°
998
Lochinver Lairg
Golspie
Ullapool Dornoch
An Teallach Dornoch Firth
Port of Ness 1062 Ben Wyvis Invergordon Lossiemouth
1046 Alness Elgin Banff Fraserburgh
West **Isle** Gairloch Black Isle Forres Buckie Rattray
Loch Roag **of** Achnasheen Dingwall Cairn Nairn Aberchirder Head
Stornoway **Lewis** Torridon Inverness Dufftown Huntly Peterhead
Carn Eige Monadhliath Mountains Grantown- Ellon
South 1182 Loch Ness on-Spey Inverurie DYCE
Harris Kyle of Fort Aviemore Dyce Aberdeen
North Tarbert Lochalsh Augustus Cairngorm
Uist Uig Mountains Don
Lochmaddy Portree Ben Macdui
Benbecula **Skye** Kingussie 1309 Ballater Stonehaven
Beinn Mhòr Sgurr Alasdair Garry Braemar Lochnagar
South Uist 620 1009 Fort Loch 1155 North Esk
Cuillin Sound William Laggan
Barra Rum Mallaig Blair Atholl Brechin
SCOTLAND Pitlochry Forfar Montrose
Castlebay Point of Glen Shiel Ben Nevis Blairgowrie Sidlaw Hills
Ardnamurchan Salen 1344 GRAMPIAN MOUNTAINS Arbroath
Canna Morvern Rannoch Ben Lawers Dundee
Coll Tobermory Moor 1214 Killin Firth of Tay
Arinagour **Mull** Loch Linnhe NORTH
Ben More St Andrews
Tiree 966 Crianlarich Callander Cupar Fife Ness SEA
Iona Oban Loch Awe Crieff
Fionnphort Glenrothes
Colonsay Inveraray Ben Lomond Stirling Buckhaven
978 Alloa Kirkcaldy Firth of Forth
Jura Lochgilphead Loch Dunfermline North Berwick
Sound of Jura Helensburgh Lomond Falkirk Cowdenbeath Dunbar
Port Tarbert Greenock Clydebank **Glasgow** Edinburgh St Abb's Head
Askaig Gigha Rothesay Johnstone Coatbridge Musselburgh Haddington Berwick-
Islay Largs Paisley Motherwell Penicuik Dalkeith upon-Tweed
Port Ellen East Kilbride Duns Holy Island
Mull of Oa Ardrossan Hamilton Peebles Galashiels Lindisfarne
Kilmarnock Lanark Selkirk Coldstream
Rathlin Island Goat Fell Biggar Kelso
Giant's Portrush 874 Prestwick Broad The Cheviot
Causeway Ballycastle **Arran** Ayr Law Hawick 815
Coleraine Brodick 840 Jedburgh Cheviot
Cullybackey Ballymoney Campbeltown Maybole Merrick SOUTHERN UPLANDS Hills Rothbury
Mull of Kintyre 843 Ashington
Antrim Cumnock Thornhill Moffat Morpeth
NORTHERN Kintyre Cairnryan Newton Castle Lockerbie Carter Blyth
IRELAND Stranraer Stewart Douglas Dumfries Bar Newcastle
Newtownabbey Wigtown Annan 575 Langholm upon Tyne
Ballyclare Kirkcudbright Dalbeattie Hexham Gateshead
Bangor Luce Solway Firth Longtown Consett
Whitehead Bay Whithorn Carlisle Cross Fell
Donaghadee Mull of Galloway Workington 931 Penrith Spennymoor

North
Channel
ENGLAND

Longitude 4° west of Greenwich

1 : 4 000 000

© Collins Bartholomew Ltd

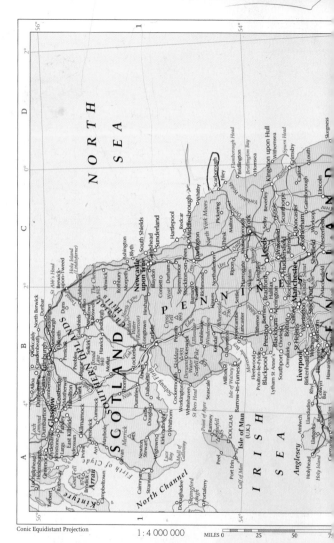

Conic Equidistant Projection

1 : 4 000 000

MILES 0   25   50   7

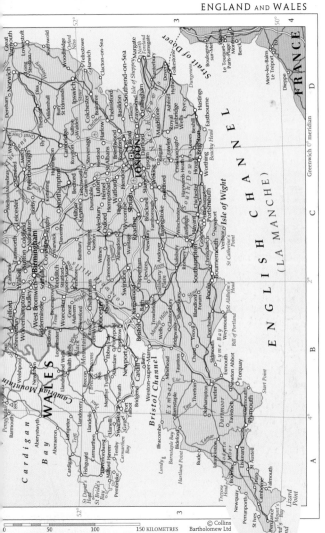

0   50   100   150 KILOMETRES

© Collins
Bartholomew Ltd

NORTH SEA

East Frisian Islands

West Frisian Islands (Waddeneilanden)

NETHERLANDS

□ AMSTERDAM

THE HAGUE ('S-Gravenhage) (Den Haag)

Rotterdam

BELGIUM

□ BRUSSELS Bruxelles

Antwerp

LUXEMBOURG

□ LUXEMBOURG

Cologne

Düsseldorf

Essen

Dortmund

F R A N C E

Conic Equidistant Projection

Longitude 6° east of Greenwich

1 : 4 000 000

MILES 0   25   50

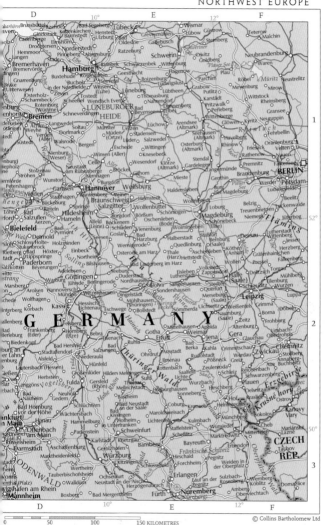

0   50   100   150 KILOMETRES

Conic Equidistant Projection   1 : 8 000 000   MILES 0   50   100   15

0   100   200 KILOMETRES

104 Conic Equidistant Projection   1 : 8 000 000   MILES 0   50   100   15

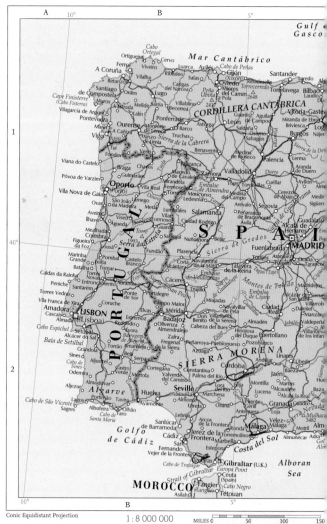

Conic Equidistant Projection

1 : 8 000 000

MILES 0   50   100   150

108

1 : 8 000 000

MILES 0 ____ 50 ____ 100 ____ 150

Longitude 10° east of Greenwich

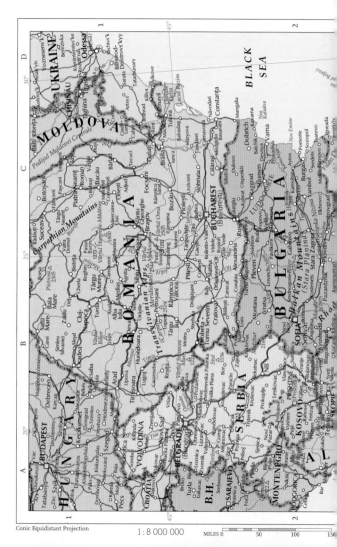

Conic Equidistant Projection

1 : 8 000 000

MILES 0   50   100   150

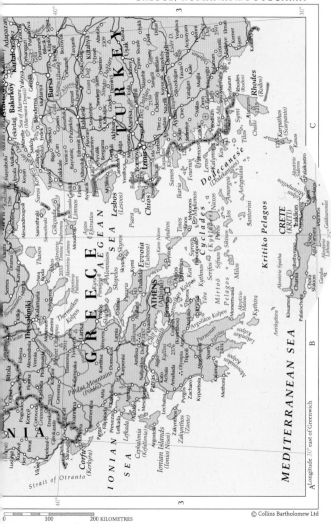

© Collins Bartholomew Ltd

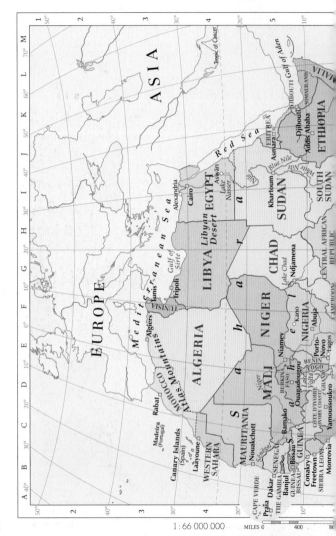

ATLANTIC OCEAN

INDIAN OCEAN

MOZAMBIQUE

Mozambique Channel

MADAGASCAR
Antananarivo

MAURITIUS
Port Louis
St-Denis
Réunion
(France)

SEYCHELLES
Victoria
Mahé

Aldabra
Islands

COMOROS
Moroni
Mayotte
Dzaoudzi
(France)

Nampula

Kilimanjaro
5199

Nairobi

Lake Victoria
Kigali
RWANDA
BURUNDI
Bujumbura

TANZANIA
Dodoma
Dar es Salaam
Zanzibar Island

DEMOCRATIC
REPUBLIC OF
THE CONGO
Kinshasa

CONG
GABON
Brazzaville

São Tomé

Lake Tanganyika

Lubumbashi

Lake Nyasa

MALAWI
Lilongwe

Zambezi

ZAMBIA
Lusaka

ZIMBABWE
Harare
Bulawayo

Maputo
Mbabane
SWAZILAND

Durban

ANGOLA

Luanda

Huambo

Cubango

Okavango
Delta

BOTSWANA
Gaborone (Tshwane)
Pretoria
Johannesburg

LESOTHO
Maseru

REPUBLIC OF
SOUTH AFRICA

Port Elizabeth

NAMIBIA

Windhoek

Namib Desert

Orange

Cape Town
Cape of
Good Hope

Cape Agulhas

Îles Crozet
(France)

Prince Edward Islands
(S. Africa)

St Helena, Ascension
and Tristan da Cunha
(UK)

Ascension

St Helena

Tristan da Cunha

Tropic of Capricorn

Longitude 20° west of Greenwich

ATLANTIC
OCEAN

INDIAN
OCEAN

500   1000   1500 KILOMETRES

© Collins Bartholomew Ltd

113

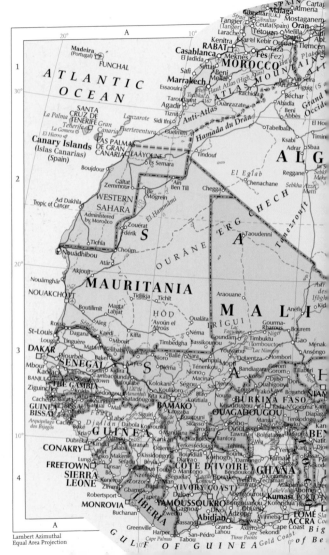

Lambert Azimuthal
Equal Area Projection

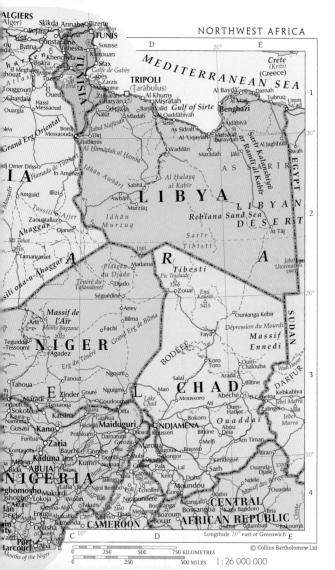

ALGIERS
(Alger)
Skikda Annaba Bizerte
Sétif Béjaïa Guelma
Batna Constantine Tébessa TUNIS
Biskra Gafsa Sousse
Khenchela Kairouan
El Meghaïer Tozeur Sfax
Touggourt Gabès Golfe de Gabès
Ghardaïa Zarzis
Ouargla Hassi Medenine
Messaoud Zuwārah TRIPOLI
Bordj Gharyān (Ṭarābulus) Al Khums
Messaouda Nālūt Banī Walīd Miṣrātah
Dirj Mizdah
Ghadāmis Al Ḥamādah al Ḥamrā Waddān
Dj Omer Driss Jabal Nafūsah Sirte
In Amenas Idhān Awbārī Marādah
Amguid Illizi Sabhā
Awbārī Murzuq
Tassili n'Ajjer
Zaouatallaz Idhān Murzuq
Djanet

MEDITERRANEAN SEA
Crete
(Kriti)
(Greece)
Al Bayḍāʾ Darnah
Tubruq Umm
Benghazi Saʿad
Ajdābiyā
As Sidrah
Al ʿUqaylah Matṣaʿ al
Buraydah
Waddān Sarīr Kalanshiyū
Maṣṣ Jalū Ṣiwah
Al Jaghbūb

LIBYA
LIBYAN
DESERT
Rebiana Sand Sea
Sarīr
Tibistī
At Tāj

S A H A R A

Ḥamada de Tinrhert
Ahaggar
At Tahat
Tamanrasset

Plateau
du Djado
Madama Tibesti
Ténéré du Pic Toussidé
Tafassâsset Séguédine Djado 3265
Zouar
Aney Emi
Bilma Koussi
Fachi 3415

Jebel
Uweinat
1893

Ounianga Kébir
Dépression du Mourdi
Massif
Ennedi

SUDAN

NIGER
Massif de
l'Aïr
Monts Bagzane
2022
Agadez
Arlit
Teguiddan-Tessoumt
Erg du Ténéré
Grand Erg de Bilma
Ngourti
Faya

Koro
Toro
Oum-
Chalouba

DARFUR
Wadi Howar
Kebkabiya
El Geneina Jebel Marra
Zalingei 3088
Jebel
Marra

Tahoua
Madaoua Zinder
Tessaoua Gouré
Maradi
Sokoto
Gusau Katsina
Kano
Funtua Zaria
Kaduna

Nguigmi
Nguru Mao
Gashua Lake
Maiduguri Chad
Dikwa Kousséri
Gwoza
Damaturu

Salal
Moussoro
Ati
Bokoro
NDJAMENA

Arada
Biltine
Oum-
Hadjer
Abéché
Abou
Deïa

L

C H A D

Ouaddaï
Am Timan
Birao

ABUJA
Minna
Bida NIGERIA

Bauchi Gombe
Kumo Mubi
Gombi
Guider
Garoua

Maroua
Bongor
Laï
Doba

Melfi
Bousso
Kélo
Sarh
Kénédougou
Ouanda-
Djallé

1330

gbomosho Makurdi Wukari
Ishogbo Lokoja Takum
Ilorin Bali
Odè Enugu Abakaliki
 city Asaba Onitsha
Awari
Port
Harcourt
Mouths of the Niger

Ngaoundéré
Ngambé Poli
Tibati Meïganga Bozoum
Bamenda Bocaranga
CAMEROON Bouar

Ndélé
Batangafo Kaga Bandoro
Bossangoa Bria
CENTRAL Bambari Bakouma
AFRICAN REPUBLIC
Sibut
Ouadda
Massif des Bongo

Longitude 20° east of Greenwich

© Collins Bartholomew Ltd

0 250 500 750 KILOMETRES
0 250 500 MILES

1 : 26 000 000

115

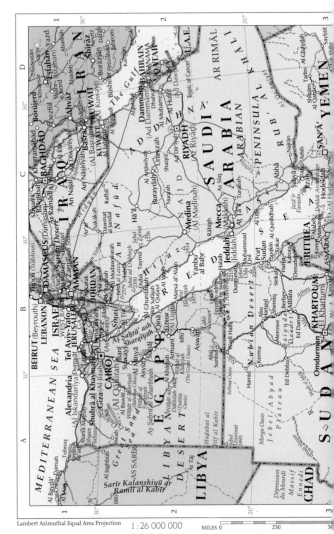

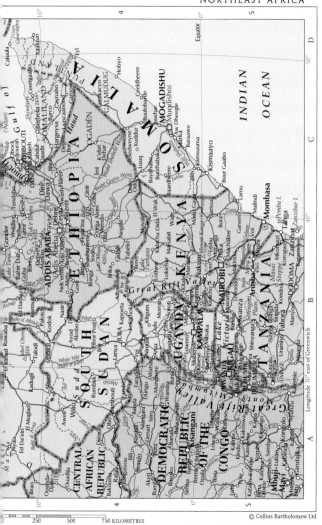

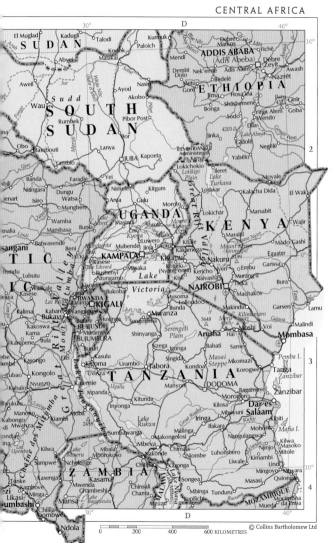

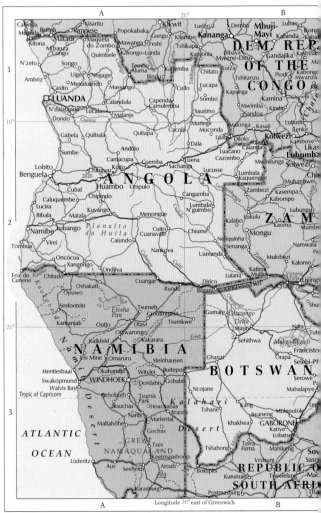

Lambert Azimuthal Equal Area Projection   1 : 20 000 000   MILES 0   100   200   300

© Collins Bartholomew Ltd

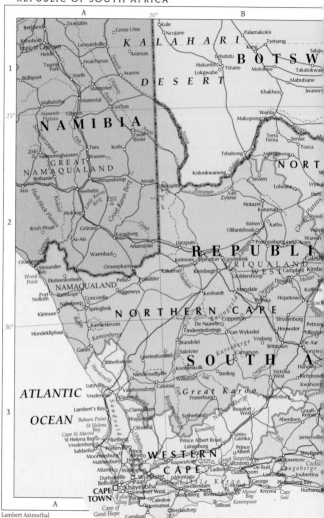

Lambert Azimuthal
Equal Area Projection

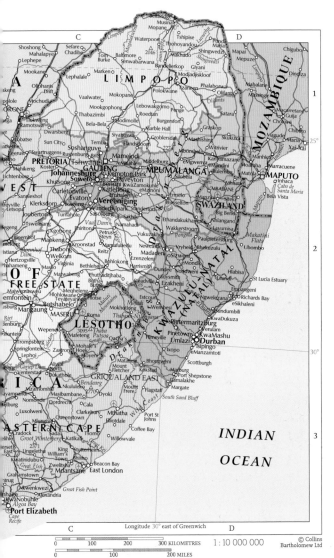

INDIAN

OCEAN

Longitude 30° east of Greenwich

0   100   200   300 KILOMETRES
0   100   200 MILES

1 : 10 000 000

© Collins
Bartholomew Ltd

123

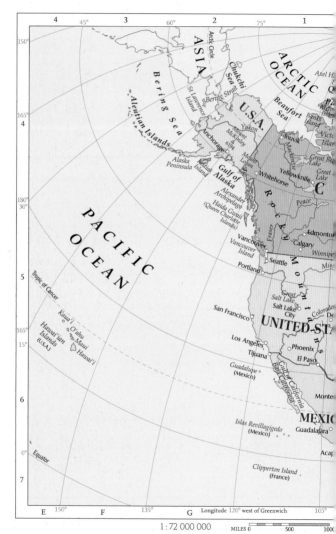

1 : 72 000 000   MILES 0   500   1000

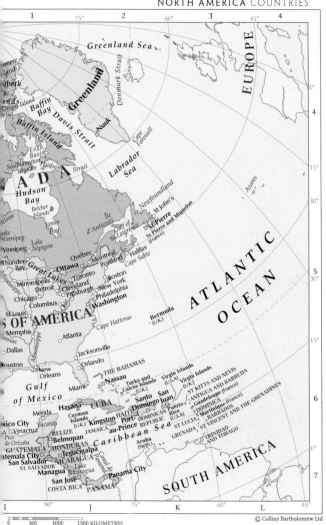

Greenland Sea

EUROPE

Greenland

Denmark Strait

Nuuk

Cape Farewell

Baffin Bay

Davis Strait

Baffin Island

Labrador Sea

Foxe Basin

Southampton Island

Hudson Strait

Newfoundland

Azores

CANADA

Hudson Bay

Belcher Islands

Nelson

James Bay

Île d'Anticosti

Gulf of St Lawrence

St John's

Lake Winnipeg

Lake Nipigon

Québec

Montreal

Portland

St-Pierre

St Pierre and Miquelon (France)

Thunder Bay

Great Lakes

Ottawa

Toronto

Halifax

Cape Sable

Minneapolis

Detroit

Cleveland

Boston

New York

Chicago

Pittsburgh

Philadelphia

Columbus

Washington

St Louis

ATLANTIC OCEAN

Memphis

UNITED STATES OF AMERICA

Cape Hatteras

Bermuda (U.K.)

Dallas

Atlanta

Houston

Jacksonville

New Orleans

Orlando

Gulf of Mexico

Miami

THE BAHAMAS

Nassau

Turks and Caicos Islands (U.K.)

Virgin Islands (U.S.A.)

Virgin Islands (U.K.)

ST KITTS AND NEVIS

Santo Domingo

San Juan

ANTIGUA AND BARBUDA

Guadeloupe (France)

Havana

CUBA

Cayman Islands (U.K.)

Kingston

HAITI

Port-au-Prince

DOMINICAN REPUBLIC

Puerto Rico (U.S.A.)

DOMINICA

Mérida

Yucatán

JAMAICA

Caribbean Sea

MARTINIQUE (France)

ST LUCIA

BARBADOS

Mexico City

Veracruz

BELIZE

Belmopan

Aruba (Neth.)

GRENADA

ST VINCENT AND THE GRENADINES

Pico de Orizaba

GUATEMALA

HONDURAS

Tegucigalpa

TRINIDAD AND TOBAGO

Guatemala City

San Salvador

NICARAGUA

EL SALVADOR

Managua

Lake Nicaragua

Canal de Panamá

San José

COSTA RICA

PANAMA

Panama City

SOUTH AMERICA

0 500 1000 1500 KILOMETRES

© Collins Bartholomew Ltd

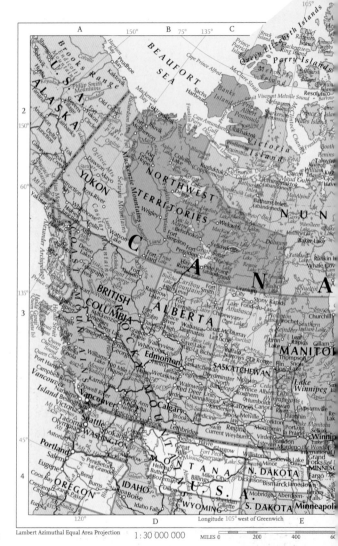

Lambert Azimuthal Equal Area Projection   1 : 30 000 000   MILES 0   200   400   60

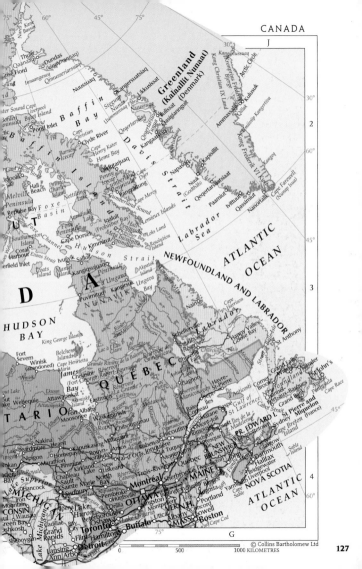

Lambert Azimuthal Equal Area Projection   1 : 15 000 000   MILES 0   100   200   30

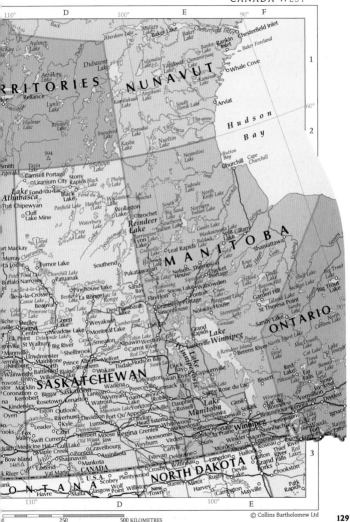

0   250   500 KILOMETRES

Lambert Azimuthal Equal Area Projection   1 : 15 000 000   MILES 0   100   200   30

© Collins Bartholomew Ltd

0   250   500 KILOMETRES

Lambert Azimuthal Equal Area Projection

1 : 25 000 000

MILES 0   250   50

Longitude 110° west of Greenwich

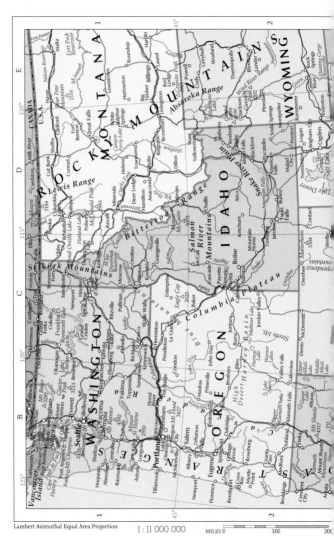

Lambert Azimuthal Equal Area Projection   1 : 11 000 000   MILES 0   100   200

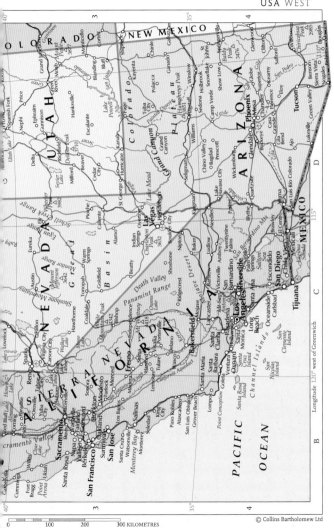

© Collins Bartholomew Ltd

0   100   200   300 KILOMETRES

Longitude 120° west of Greenwich

COLORADO

NEW MEXICO

UTAH

NEVADA

ARIZONA

CALIFORNIA

SIERRA NEVADA

MEXICO

Great Basin

Death Valley

Mojave Desert

Panamint Range

Colorado Plateau

PACIFIC OCEAN

Channel Islands

Salt Lake City

Salt Lake

Utah Lake

Provo

Nephi

Delta

Ephraim

Richfield

Escalante

Kanab

St George

Hurricane

Cedar City

Milford

Beaver

Panguitch

Lake Powell

Page

Kayenta

Chinle

Canado

Grand Canyon

Grand Canyon

Tuba City

Polacca

Winslow

Holbrook

Snowflake

Show Low

Springerville

St Johns

Flagstaff

Sedona

Camp Verde

Williams

Seligman

Chino Valley

Bagdad

Prescott

Wickenburg

Phoenix

Glendale

Mesa

Chandler

Superior

Florence

Globe

Casa Grande

Ajo

Tucson

Benson

Sierra Vista

Nogales

Bisbee

Douglas

Safford

Clifton

Kearny

San Pedro

Green Valley

Gila Bend

Sells

Yuma

San Luis Río Colorado

Mexicali

El Centro

Brawley

Calexico

Chula Vista

Tijuana

San Diego

Oceanside

Carlsbad

Escondido

San Bernardino Mtn

Twentynine Palms

Palm Springs

Indio

Blythe

Quartzsite

Parker

Lake Havasu City

Kingman

Needles

Twentynine Palms

Amboy

Ludlow

Baker

Nipton

Indian Springs

Las Vegas

Henderson

Boulder City

Lake Mead

Overton

Alamo

Warm Springs

Goldfield

Tonopah

Beatty

Shoshone

Ridgecrest

Trona

Victorville

Barstow

Lancaster

Palmdale

Santa Clarita

San Fernando

Los Angeles

Santa Monica

Long Beach

Santa Ana

Riverside

Pasadena

Glendale

Mojave

Tehachapi

Bakersfield

Delano

Porterville

Visalia

Hanford

Tulare

Corcoran

Fresno

Madera

Merced

Modesto

Stockton

Tracy

Sacramento

Davis

Vacaville

Fairfield

Napa

Vallejo

Berkeley

Oakland

San Francisco

San Jose

Santa Cruz

Watsonville

Monterey

Salinas

Soledad

King City

Paso Robles

Atascadero

San Luis Obispo

Santa Maria

Lompoc

Grover Beach

Point Conception

Santa Barbara

Ventura

Oxnard

Goleta

Santa Ynez

Santa Rosa

Petaluma

Point Reyes

Monterey Bay

Point Arena

Fort Bragg

Willits

Ukiah

Clearlake

Cloverdale

Calistoga

Red Bluff

Corning

Cummings

Garberville

Tahoe

Lake Tahoe

Reno

Sparks

Carson City

Virginia City

Minden

Hawthorne

Walker Lake

Bishop

Big Pine

Independence

Lone Pine

Mount Whitney

Owens Lake

Coaldale

Austin

Eureka

Ely

Pioche

Caliente

Fallon

Lovelock

Battle Mountain

Winnemucca

Ruby Mountains

Shoshone Mountains

Egan Range

Schell Creek Range

Toiyabe Range

Monitor Range

Quinn River

Sierra Nevada

San Clemente Island

San Nicolas Island

Santa Rosa Island

Santa Cruz Island

San Miguel Island

Santa Catalina Island

California Aqueduct

San Joaquin

Humphreys Peak 3851

Boundary Peak 4006

Telescope Peak 3368

Mount Whitney 4418

Baldy Peak 3476

White Mountain Peak 4342

Wheeler Peak 3982

Chiricahua Peak 2985

40°

35°

35°

115°

110°

3

4

B

C

D

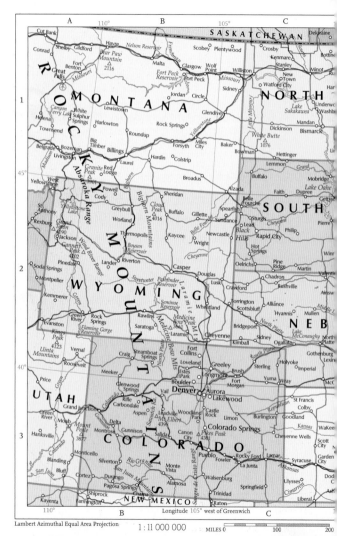

Lambert Azimuthal Equal Area Projection   1 : 11 000 000   MILES 0   100   200

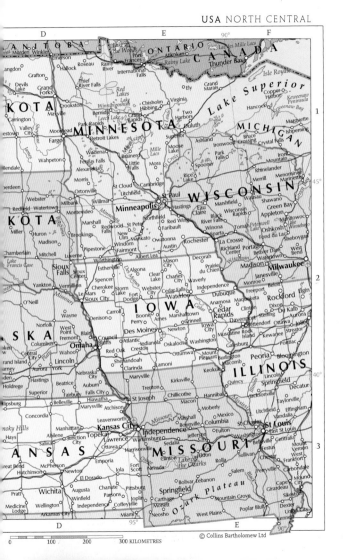

0   100   200   300 KILOMETRES

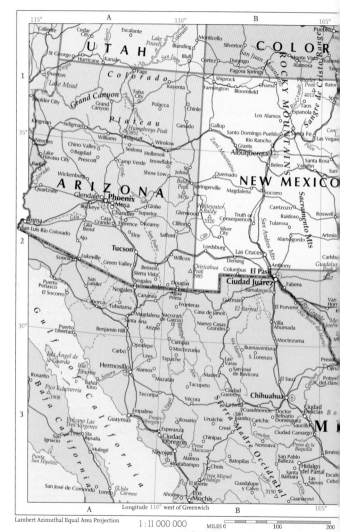

Lambert Azimuthal Equal Area Projection   1 : 11 000 000   MILES 0   100   200

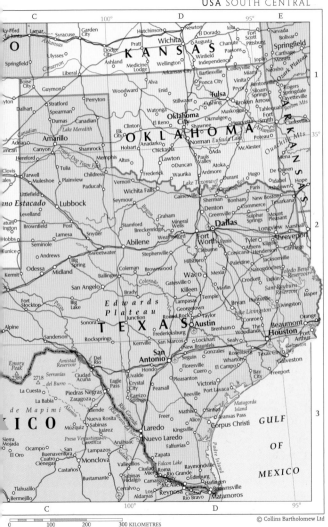

Lambert Azimuthal Equal Area Projection

1 : 11 000 000

Longitude 85° west of Greenwich

MILES 0   100   200

D   75°   E   70°   F

1

2

40°

3

D   75°   E   70°   F

0   100   200   300 KILOMETRES

© Collins Bartholomew Ltd

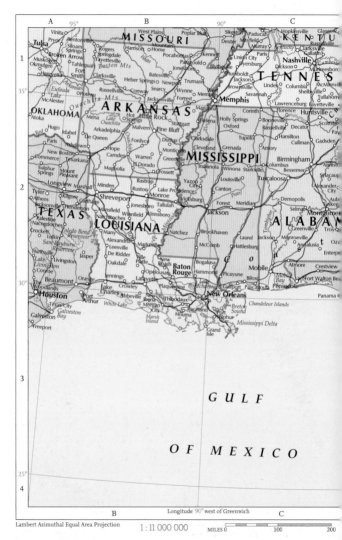

Lambert Azimuthal Equal Area Projection   1 : 11 000 000   MILES 0   100   200

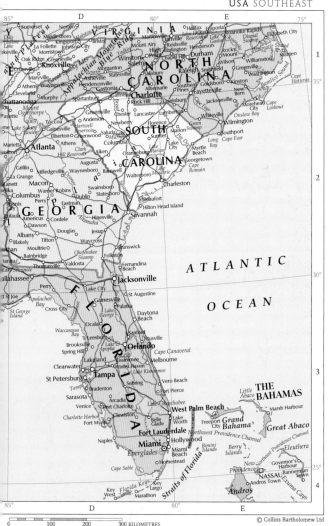

0   100   200   300 KILOMETRES

© Collins Bartholomew Ltd

A   110°   B

Mexicali
Tijuana
Ensenada
San Luis
Río Colorado
El Golfo
de Sta Clara
Ajo
Tucson
Lordsburg
NEW MEXICO
Deming Las Cruces
Carlsbad
Hobbs
Eunice
Andrews
Spr

V. Vicente
V. Vicente
Guerrero
C. San
Quintín
San Fernando
Puertecitos
San Felipe
El Socorro
Puerto
Peñasco
Sonoyta
Benson
Willcox
Chiricahua
Pk 2985
Bisbee
Douglas
El Paso
Ciudad Juárez
Guadalupe
Peak
Fabens
Pecos
Big
Midland

30°

Rosario
Isla Angel
de la Guarda
I. Tiburón
BAJA CALIFORNIA
Puerto
Libertad
Carbo
Hermosillo
Tecoripa
Chihuahua
Ciudad
Delicias
La Babia
Múzquiz

P A C I F I C

O C E A N

PACÍFICO

Longitude 110° west of Greenwich

A   B

144   Lambert Azimuthal Equal Area Projection   1 : 15 000 000   MILES 0   100   200   300

© Collins Bartholomew Ltd

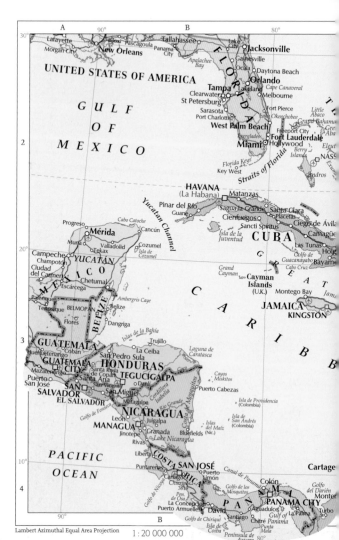

Lambert Azimuthal Equal Area Projection   1 : 20 000 000

ATLANTIC

OCEAN

Tropic of Cancer

BAHAMAS

ng Island

Island

Acklins Island

Great Inagua

Mayaguana

Turks and Caicos Islands (U.K.)
Caicos Islands
□ GRAND TURK (Cockburn Town)

W E S T   I N D I E S

Hispaniola

racoa

uantánamo Cap-Haïtien Puerto Plata **Puerto Rico** LEEWARD ISLANDS
Port-de- Paix Santiago (U.S.A.) **Virgin Is** **Anguilla**
Gonaïves **HAITI** **DOMINICAN** **SAN JUAN** (U.K.) (U.K.)
Jérémie *Île de la Gonâve* **REPUBLIC** La Romana **Virgin Is** St Maarten **ANTIGUA AND**
Les Jacmel **PORT-AU-** **SANTO** Ponce (U.S.A.) (Neth.) **BARBUDA**
Cayes **PRINCE** **DOMINGO** *St Croix* BASSETERRE ST JOHN'S
Isla Beata *Cabo Beata* **ST KITTS AND NEVIS** *Antigua*
Plymouth ◉ BRADES
(abandoned) **Montserrat** **Guadeloupe** (Fr.)
(U.K.) *Marie-Galante*

ANTILLES

BASSE-TERRE
DOMINICA
ROSEAU
Martinique **FORT-DE-**
(Fr.) **FRANCE**
CASTRIES
ST LUCIA **BARBADOS**
BRIDGETOWN
ST VINCENT AND THE Kingstown
GRENADINES

AN SEA

GRENADA
ST GEORGE'S

WINDWARD ISLANDS

Lesser   Antilles

Pta Gallinas **Aruba** **Curaçao** Scarborough
Península (Neth.) (Neth.) *Tobago*
Ríohacha *de la Guajira* WILLEMSTAD **PORT OF** **TRINIDAD**
rta Punto Fijo Coro *Bonaire* *Islas Los* La Asunción *Isla de* **SPAIN** **AND**
Golfo de Venezuela (Neth.) *Roques* *Margarita* **TOBAGO**
Isla La Tortuga Cumaná *Trinidad*
Maiquetía San Carlos Barcelona *of Paria* San
anquilla Felipe **Maracay** **CARACAS** Fernando
Maracaibo **Valencia** Los Teques Maturín
Valledupar Machiques *Tocuyo* Valle de Zaraza *Guanipa*
elejo *Lake* Acarigua la Pascua Tucupita *Delta del Orinoco*
celo San Carlos **Barquisimeto** El Tigre
El Banco del Zulia Trujillo El Baúl Calabozo *Orinoco*
angue Mérida **VENEZUELA** Ciudad Bolívar Ciudad
OLOMBIA Valera Guanare El Baúl *Guayana*
po Bello Barinas *Orinoco*

Longitude 70° west of Greenwich

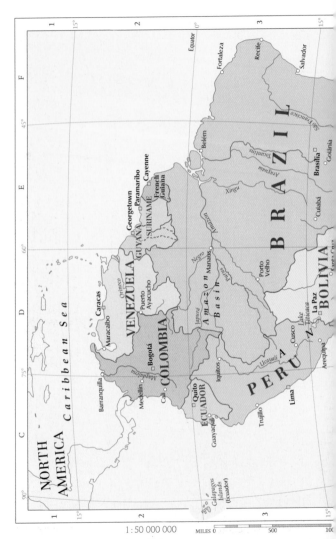

1 : 50 000 000

MILES 0   500   10

PACIFIC

OCEAN

ATLANTIC

OCEAN

Tropic of Capricorn

Rio de Janeiro

São Paulo

Curitiba

Porto Alegre

PARAGUAY

Asunción

Concordia

URUGUAY

Montevideo

Buenos Aires

Mar del Plata

Salado

Córdoba

Mendoza

ARGENTINA

Neuquén

Viedma

Comodoro Rivadavia

Falkland Islands (UK)

Stanley

Scotia Sea

South Georgia and the South Sandwich Islands (UK)

E Longitude 45° west of Greenwich

Antofagasta

Santiago

Concepción

Puerto Montt

Colorado

Negro

CHILE

Punta Arenas

Ushuaia

Isla Grande de Tierra del Fuego

Islas Desventuradas

Archipiélago Juan Fernández

Paraná

Uruguay

0   500   1000 KILOMETRES

149

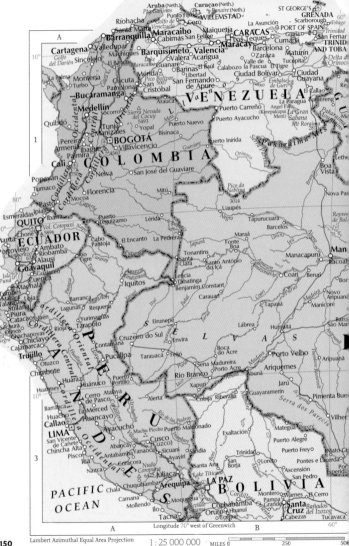

Lambert Azimuthal Equal Area Projection
Longitude 70° west of Greenwich
1 : 25 000 000   MILES 0   250   50

ATLANTIC

OCEAN

C 50° D 40° E

10°

ORGETOWN
New
Amsterdam PARAMARIBO
Nieuw
Nickerie St-Laurent-du-Maroni
Professor van
Blommestein Meer Kourou CAYENNE
URINAME French
Guiana Oiapoque 1
Pontoetoe

Serra Tumucumaque Lourenço Calçoene
Amapá Ilha de Maracá

Trombetas Porto Mouths of the Amazon
Arere Santana Macapá
ximina Óbidos Almeirim Mazagão Cabo
Chaves Norte
Baía de Marajó Equator 0°
ara Parintins Monte Breves Ilha do Marajó Salinópolis
Curituba Alegre Portel Belém Bragança
Santarém Cametá Viseu
Altamira Castanhal Baía de São Marcos 2
Itaituba Tucuruí Acará Camocim
Represa de Pinheiro São Luís
Tucuruí Viana Fortaleza
Iacundá Maraba Itapecuru Tutóia Sobral Caucaia
reacanga Araras Grajaú Mirim Parnaíba Ponta do
Manuelzinho São Imperatriz Barra Bacabal Piripiri Canindé Calcanhar
Félix do Corda Caxias Luzilândia Aracati
Tocantinópolis Codó Tianguá Mossoró Macau Touros
RAZIL Araguaína Campo Maior Crateús Natal
Conceição Carolina Balsas Timon Teresina Taua Iguatu Sousa João
do Araguaia Ajuda Boa Picos Campina Pessoa
Serra Santa Maria Jerumenha Esperança Palmeirais Floriano Grande
do Cochimbo das Barreiras Pedro Uruçuí Oeiras Juazeiro Olinda
Alonso Floresta do Norte Jaboatão Recife
dos Guararapes
Ilha do São Raimundo Nonato Garanhuns Caruaru
Gauchos Óbidos Palmas Bananal Corrente Paulo Maceió
nantino Porto São Afonso Arapiraca
Rosário Oeste Artur Nacional Barragem de Senhor do Bonfim Monte Santo
Dianópolis Sobradinho Jacobina Aracaju
Ceres Cuiabá Natividade Barreiras Ibotirama Xique- Serrinha Estância
Rondonópolis Cavalcante Xique Feira de Alagoinhas
Alto Gárças Porangatu Santana Bom Jesus Santana Salvador
Itiquira Barra do Uruaçu da Lapa Itaberaba Jequié Ubaitaba
Garças Niquelândia Correntina Guanambi Itabuna Ilhéus
Coxim Rio Verde BRASÍLIA Formosa Januária Espinosa Vitória da Una
Itumbiara Anápolis Arinos Janaúba Conquista Itapetinga Porto Seguro
Jataí Goiás Goiânia Unaí Montes Claros Salinas Almenara
Rio Verde de Mato Grosso Paraúna Viánopolis Jequitaí Teófilo
Itumbiara Patos Otoni Alcobaça
Araguari de Minas

C 50° D 40° E

0 250 500 750 KILOMETRES

© Collins Bartholomew Ltd

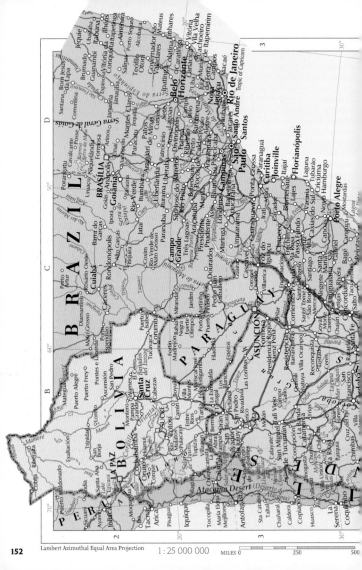

Lambert Azimuthal Equal Area Projection   1 : 25 000 000   MILES 0   250   500

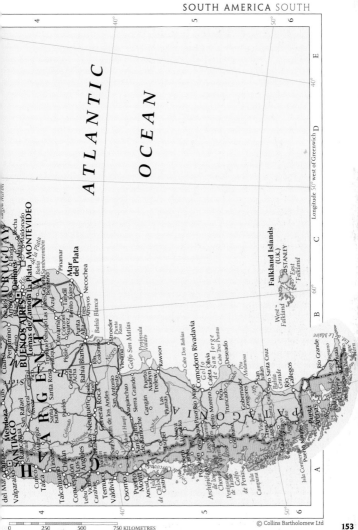

ATLANTIC

OCEAN

Falkland Islands
(U.K.)
■STANLEY
West
Falkland
East
Falkland

del Mar Chico
Valparaíso □
SANTIAGO
Rancagua San Rafael
Curicó
Talca
Talcahuano
Concepción
Lebu Los Ángeles
Cañete
Valdivia
Temuco
Osorno
Puerto
Montt
Ancud
Isla
de Chiloé
de Castro

URUGUAY
MONTEVIDEO
BUENOS AIRES
Lomas de Zamora La Plata
Quilmes

Mar del Plata
Necochea

A R G E N T I N A

Bahía Blanca

Río Colorado

Golfo San Matías
Península Valdés

Comodoro Rivadavia
Golfo San Jorge

P A T A G O N I A

Río Gallegos
Punta Arenas

Tierra del Fuego

© Collins Bartholomew Ltd

153

0   250   500   750 KILOMETRES

Lambert Azimuthal Equal Area Projection

1 : 10 000 000

MILES 0   100   200

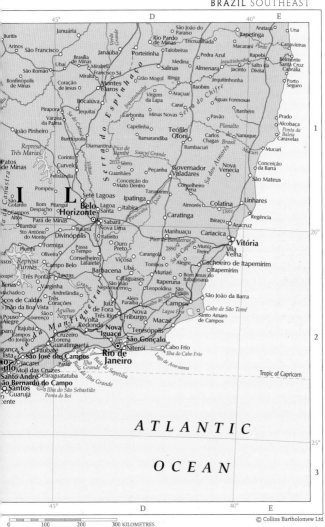

ATLANTIC

OCEAN

Tropic of Capricorn

© Collins Bartholomew Ltd

0   100   200   300 KILOMETRES

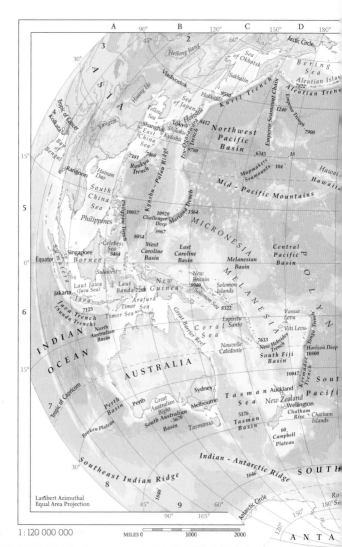

1 : 120 000 000

MILES 0   1000   2000

Lambert Azimuthal
Equal Area Projection

A 90° B 120° C 150° D 180°

3

ASIA

Heilong Jiang

Vladivostok

Sea of Okhotsk

Bering Sea

Arctic Circle

Aleutian Islands

Aleutian Trench

7822

Kuril Trench

Emperor Seamount Chain

1240

Emperor Trough

7900

Northwest Pacific Basin

Sakhalin

Hokkaido

9550

Tropic of Cancer

Kolkata

Bay of Bengal

Rangoon

Huang He

Yangtze

Yellow Sea

Sea of Japan

Honshu

Tokyo

Shanghai

East China Sea

Shikoku

Kyushu

Izu-Ogasawara Trench

8412

9780

6345

18

Mapmakers Seamounts

104

Hawaii

Hawaii

Mid - Pacific Mountains

Hainan Dao

7181

7460

Ryukyu Trench

Kyushu - Palau Ridge

South China Sea

Philippines

10057

Philippine Trench

10920

Challenger Deep

8967

Mariana Trench

1564

MICRONESIA

Central Pacific Basin

POLYN

Singapore

Sumatra

Borneo

Celebes Sea

5484

Sulawesi

8054

West Caroline Basin

East Caroline Basin

Melanesian Basin

MELANESIA

Jakarta

Java

Laut Jawa (Java Sea)

Laut Banda

7288

New Guinea

New Britain

5940

Solomon Sea

Solomon Islands

8322

Vanua Levu

Viti Levu

Tonga Trench

Java Trench (Sunda Trench)

7125

Timor Sea

Arafura Sea

North Australian Basin

Great Barrier Reef

Coral Sea

Espiritu Santo

Nouvelle Calédonie

7633

New Hebrides Trench

South Fiji Basin

Horizon Deep

10800

Equator

INDIAN OCEAN

AUSTRALIA

Tropic of Capricorn

Sydney

Tasman Sea

Auckland

New Zealand

Wellington

10047

Kermadec Trench

Sout

Pacifi

Perth Basin

Perth

Great Australian Bight

South Australian Basin

5670

Melbourne

Tasmania

5176

Tasman Basin

Chatham Rise

Chatham Islands

60

Campbell Plateau

Broken Plateau

1340

Southeast Indian Ridge

Indian - Antarctic Ridge

1646

SOUTH

Ro

80°

Antarctic Circle

ANTA

120°

150°

2

45°

60°

30°

15°

5

0°

6

15°

7

30°

45°

8

90°

105°

9

60°

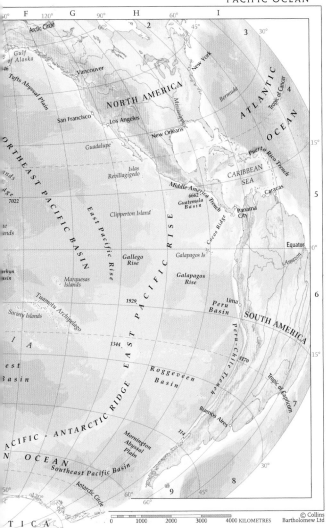

F 120° G 90° H 60° 2 45° I 3 30°

Arctic Circle

Gulf of Alaska

Tufts Abyssal Plain

46

Vancouver

New York

Bermuda

NORTH AMERICA

ATLANTIC

Tropic of Cancer 4

Mississippi

San Francisco

Los Angeles

New Orleans

OCEAN

15°

Guadalupe

ORTHEAST PACIFIC BASIN

Islas Revillagigedo

CARIBBEAN SEA

Puerto Rico Trench

lands

ge

7022

Clipperton Island

Middle America Trench
6662
Guatemala Basin

Caracas

Panama City

5

te lands

East Pacific Rise

Cocos Ridge

rhyn asin

Gallego Rise

Galapagos Is

Equator 0°

Marquesas Islands

Galapagos Rise

Amazon

Tuamotu Archipelago

1929

Lima

Peru Basin

SOUTH AMERICA

6

Society Islands

I A

EAST PACIFIC RISE

Peru-Chile Trench

est

1344

8170

15°

Basin

Roggeveen Basin

114

Buenos Aires

Tropic of Capricorn

PACIFIC - ANTARCTIC RIDGE

Mornington Abyssal Plain

N OCEAN

Southeast Pacific Basin

30°

50°

120°

Antarctic Circle

60°

9 8 45°

T I C A

0 1000 2000 3000 4000 KILOMETRES

© Collins
Bartholomew Ltd

157

A B C D E F

120° 90° 60° 30° 0° 30° 60°

NORTH AMERICA
EUROPE
AFRICA
SOUTH AMERICA

Arctic Circle
Greenland
Hudson Bay
Davis Strait
Iceland
Norwegian Basin
Norwegian Sea
Baltic Sea
Labrador Sea
Reykjanes Ridge
Iceland Basin
Rockall Bank
North Sea
British Isles
London
St Lawrence
Newfoundland
St John's
Grand Banks of Newfoundland
13
Celtic Shelf 38
New York
MID-ATLANTIC RIDGE
4938
5943
Lisbon
Mediterranean Sea
5121
Azores
Algiers
New Orleans
4556
Bermuda
Monaco Basin
Canary Is.
Tropic of Cancer
Nares Deep
5508
Sargasso Sea
6690
5491
Greater Antilles
Milwaukee Deep
8605
Puerto Rico Trench
Cayman Trench
7535
Caribbean Sea
Lesser Antilles
5523
Cape Verde
Cape Verde Basin
Dakar
Panama City
Caracas
Guiana Basin
Niger
Lagos
Equator
Amazon Cone
Amazon
Sierra Leone Basin
Gulf of Guinea
5212
Guinea Basin
Congo
Lima
SOUTH AMERICA
Brazil Basin
Ascension
5391
Luanda
St Helena
Angola Basin
Tropic of Capricorn
Paraná
Rio de Janeiro
5460
MID-ATLANTIC RIDGE
Walvis Ridge
24
Orange Cone
Orange
Rio Grande Rise
Cape of Good Hope
Cape Basin
Cape Town
Buenos Aires
Tristan da Cunha
5520
Agulhas Basin
6195
PACIFIC OCEAN
Argentine Basin
6681
Atlantic-Indian Ridge
1530
Falkland Islands
Cape Horn
Scotia Ridge
South Georgia
Scotia Sea
South Sandwich Trench
8325
Drake Passage
5750
Atlantic-Indian Antarctic Basin
Antarctic Peninsula
Antarctic Circle

45°
30°
15°
0°
30°
60°

Lambert Azimuthal Equal Area Projection
1 : 120 000 000
MILES 0   1000   2000

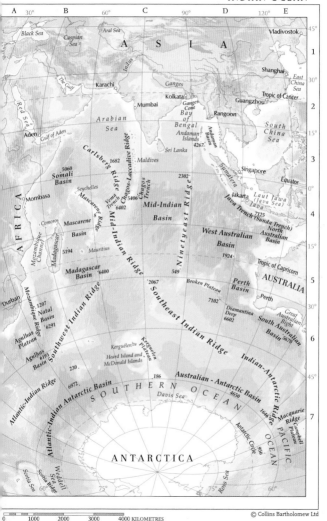

A 30° B 60° C 90° D 120° E

Black Sea *Caspian Sea* *Aral Sea* Vladivostok

A S I A

The Gulf *Indus* Shanghai *East China Sea*

Karachi *Ganges* Tropic of Cancer

Mumbai *Ganges Cone* Guangzhou

Kolkata Rangoon

Arabian Sea Bay of Bengal *South China Sea*

Aden *Andaman Islands* 4267

Gulf of Aden *Red Sea*

Carlsberg Ridge 1682 Maldives Sri Lanka

5060 Somali Basin *Seychelles* *Laccadive Ridge* *Chagos Trench* 2302 *Nineyeast Ridge* Singapore Equator

Mombasa *Mascarene Ridge* *Vema Trench* 5406 *Chagos Trench* 6402 Mid-Indian Basin *Sumatra* Jakarta *Laut Jawa (Java Sea)* *Java* *Java Trench (Sunda Trench)* 7125 North Australian Basin

A F R I C A *Comoros* Mascarene Basin Mid-Indian Ridge

5194 *Mauritius* West Australian Basin

Mozambique Channel *Madagascar* Madagascar Basin 6400 549 1924 Tropic of Capricorn

Durban *Mozambique Ridge* 1207 Natal Basin 2067 Broken Plateau Perth Basin AUSTRALIA Perth

Agulhas Plateau 6291 7102 Diamantina Deep 6602 South Australian Basin 3070 *Great Australian Bight*

Agulhas Basin 6195 Southwest Indian Ridge Southeast Indian Ridge

230 *Kerguélen* *Kerguelen Plateau* 186 Australian - Antarctic Basin 4650 Indian-Antarctic Ridge 1646 Macquarie Ridge

Atlantic-Indian Ridge 6972 *Heard Island and McDonald Islands* S O U T H E R N O C E A N Campbell Plateau

Atlantic - Antarctic Basin *Davis Sea* 956 Antarctic Circle P A C I F I C O C E A N

Antarctic Circle

A N T A R C T I C A

Scotia Sea *Scotia Ridge* *Weddell Sea* 75° 75° 60° *Ross Sea*

0 1000 2000 3000 4000 KILOMETRES

© Collins Bartholomew Ltd

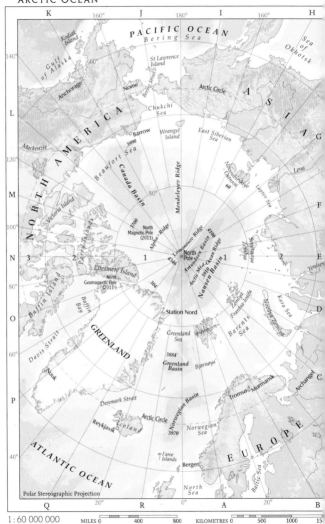

1 : 60 000 000

MILES 0   400   800

KILOMETRES 0   500   1000   15

INTRODUCTION TO THE INDEX

The index includes all names shown on the maps in the Atlas of the World. Names are referenced by page number and by a grid reference. The grid reference correlates to the alphanumeric values which appear within each map frame. Each entry also includes the country or geographical area in which the feature is located. Entries relating to names appearing on insets are indicated by a small box symbol: □, followed by a grid reference if the inset has its own alphanumeric values.

Name forms are as they appear on the maps, with additional alternative names or name forms included as cross-references which refer the user to the entry for the map form of the name. Names beginning with Mc or Mac are alphabetized exactly as they appear. The terms Saint, Sainte, etc., are abbreviated to St, Ste, etc., but alphabetized as if in the full form.

Names of physical features beginning with generic, geographical terms are permuted – the descriptive term is placed after the main part of the name. For example, Lake Superior is indexed as Superior, Lake; Mount Everest as Everest, Mount. This policy is applied to all languages.

Entries, other than those for towns and cities, include a descriptor indicating the type of geographical feature. Descriptors are not included where the type of feature is implicit in the name itself.

Administrative divisions are included to differentiate entries of the same name and feature type within the one country. In such cases, duplicate names are alphabetized in order of administrative division. Additional qualifiers are also included for names within selected geographical areas.

INDEX ABBREVIATIONS

admin. div.	administrative division	**g.**	gulf	**reg.**	region
Afgh.	Afghanistan	**Ger.**	Germany	**Rep.**	Republic
Alg.	Algeria	**Guat.**	Guatemala	**Rus. Fed.**	Russian Federation
Arg.	Argentina	**hd**	headland	**S.**	South
Austr.	Australia	**Hond.**	Honduras	**Switz.**	Switzerland
aut. reg.	autonomous region	**imp. l.**	impermanent lake	**Tajik.**	Tajikistan
aut. rep.	autonomous republic	**Indon.**	Indonesia	**Tanz.**	Tanzania
Azer.	Azerbaijan	**isth.**	isthmus	**terr.**	territory
Bangl.	Bangladesh	**Kazakh.**	Kazakhstan	**Thai.**	Thailand
Bol.	Bolivia	**Kyrg.**	Kyrgyzstan	**Trin. and Tob.**	Trinidad and Tobago
Bos.-Herz.	Bosnia Herzegovina	**lag.**	lagoon	**Turkm.**	Turkmenistan
Bulg.	Bulgaria	**Lith.**	Lithuania	**U.A.E.**	United Arab Emirates
Can.	Canada	**Lux.**	Luxembourg	**U.K.**	United Kingdom
C.A.R.	Central African Republic	**Madag.**	Madagascar	**Ukr.**	Ukraine
Col.	Colombia	**Maur.**	Mauritania	**Uru.**	Uruguay
Czech Rep.	Czech Republic	**Mex.**	Mexico	**U.S.A.**	United States of America
Dem. Rep. Congo	Democratic Republic of the Congo	**Moz.**	Mozambique	**Uzbek.**	Uzbekistan
		mun.	municipality	**val.**	valley
depr.	depression	**N.**	North	**Venez.**	Venezuela
des.	desert	**Neth.**	Netherlands		
Dom. Rep.	Dominican Republic	**Nic.**	Nicaragua		
esc.	escarpment	**N.Z.**	New Zealand		
est.	estuary	**Pak.**	Pakistan		
Eth.	Ethiopia	**Para.**	Paraguay		
Fin.	Finland	**Phil.**	Philippines		
for.	forest	**plat.**	plateau		
		P.N.G.	Papua New Guinea		
		Pol.	Poland		
		Port.	Portugal		
		prov.	province		

1

128 B2 100 Mile House Can.

A

93 E4 Aabenraa Denmark
100 C2 Aachen Ger.
93 E4 Aalborg Denmark
100 B2 Aalst Belgium
100 B2 Aarschot Belgium
68 C2 Aba China
115 C4 Aba Nigeria
81 C2 Ābādān Iran
81 D2 Ābādeh Iran
114 B1 Abadla Alg.
115 C4 Abakaliki Nigeria
83 H3 Abakan Rus. Fed.
150 A3 Abancay Peru
81 D2 Abarkūh Iran
66 D2 Abashiri Japan
117 B4 Abaya, Lake Eth.
    Ābay Wenz r. Eth./Sudan see
    Blue Nile
82 G3 Abaza Rus. Fed.
108 A2 Abbasanta Sardegna Italy
104 C1 Abbeville France
142 B3 Abbeville U.S.A.
55 O2 Abbot Ice Shelf Antarctica
74 B1 Abbottabad Pak.
115 E3 Abéché Chad
114 B4 Abengourou Côte d'Ivoire
114 C4 Abeokuta Nigeria
99 A2 Aberaeron U.K.
96 C2 Aberchirder U.K.
99 B3 Aberdare U.K.
99 A2 Aberdaron U.K.
122 B3 Aberdeen S. Africa
96 C2 Aberdeen U.K.
141 D3 Aberdeen MD U.S.A.
137 D1 Aberdeen SD U.S.A.
134 B1 Aberdeen WA U.S.A.
129 E1 Aberdeen Lake Can.
134 B2 Aberfeldy U.K.
99 A2 Aberystwyth U.K.
86 F2 Abez' Rus. Fed.
78 B3 Abhā Saudi Arabia
    Abiad, Bahr el r. Sudan/
    Uganda see White Nile
114 B4 Abidjan Côte d'Ivoire
137 D3 Abilene KS U.S.A.
139 D2 Abilene TX U.S.A.
99 C3 Abingdon U.K.
91 D3 Abinsk Rus. Fed.
130 B2 Abitibi, Lake Can.
    Åbo Fin. see Turku
74 B1 Abohar India
114 C4 Abomey Benin
60 A1 Abongabong, Gunung mt.
    Indon.
118 B2 Abong Mbang Cameroon
64 A2 Aborlan Phil.
115 D3 Abou Déia Chad
106 B2 Abrantes Port.
152 B3 Abra Pampa Arg.
136 A2 Absaroka Range mts U.S.A.
81 C1 Abşeron Yarımadası pen. Azer.
78 B3 Abū 'Arīsh Saudi Arabia
79 C2 Abu Dhabi U.A.E.
116 B3 Abu Hamed Sudan
115 C4 Abuja Nigeria
81 C2 Abū Kamāl Syria
152 B1 Abunã r. Bol./Brazil
150 B2 Abunã Brazil

74 B2 Abu Road India
116 B2 Abū Sunbul Egypt
117 A3 Abu Zabad Sudan
    Abū Zabī U.A.E. see Abu Dhabi
117 A4 Abyei Sudan
145 B2 Acambaro Mex.
106 B1 A Cañiza Spain
144 B2 Acaponeta Mex.
145 C3 Acapulco Mex.
151 D2 Acará Brazil
150 B1 Acarigua Venez.
145 C3 Acatlán Mex.
145 C3 Acayucán Mex.
114 B4 Accra Ghana
98 B2 Accrington U.K.
97 A2 Achill Island Ireland
101 D1 Achim Ger.
96 B2 Achnasheen U.K.
91 D2 Achuyevo Rus. Fed.
111 C3 Acıpayam Turkey
109 C3 Acireale Sicilia Italy
147 C2 Acklins Island Bahamas
153 B4 Aconcagua, Cerro mt. Arg.
106 B1 A Coruña Spain
108 A2 Acqui Terme Italy
103 D2 Ács Hungary
145 C2 Actopán Mex.
139 D2 Ada U.S.A.
79 C2 Adam Oman
    Adam Mountains Pitcairn Is.
49 J4 'Adam Yemen see Aden
80 B2 Adana Turkey
111 D2 Adapazarı Turkey
    Adapazarı Turkey see
    Adapazarı
108 A1 Adda r. Italy
78 B2 Ad Dafinah Saudi Arabia
78 B2 Ad Dahnā' des. Saudi Arabia
78 B2 Ad Dahnā' des. Saudi Arabia
114 A2 Ad Dakhla Western Sahara
    Ad Dammām Saudi Arabia see
    Dammam
78 A2 Ad Dār al Ḥamrā'
    Saudi Arabia
78 B3 Ad Darb Saudi Arabia
78 B2 Ad Dawādimī Saudi Arabia
78 B2 Ad Dawḥah Qatar see Doha
78 B2 Ad Dilam Saudi Arabia
116 C2 Ad Dir'īyah Saudi Arabia
117 B4 Addis Ababa Eth.
81 C2 Ad Dīwānīyah Iraq
52 A2 Adelaide Austr.
50 C1 Adelaide River Austr.
101 D2 Adelebsen Ger.
55 J2 Adélie Land Antarctica
78 B3 Aden Yemen
117 C3 Aden, Gulf of Somalia/Yemen
100 C2 Adenau Ger.
79 C2 Adh Dhayd U.A.E.
59 C3 Adi i. Indon.
78 A3 Ādī Ark'ay Eth.
116 B3 Ādīgrat Eth.
75 B3 Adilabad India
141 E2 Adirondack Mountains U.S.A.
    Ādīs Ābeba Eth. see Addis Ababa
117 B4 Ādīs Alem Eth.
110 C1 Adjud Romania
50 B1 Admiralty Gulf Austr.
128 A2 Admiralty Island U.S.A.
104 B3 Adour r. France
106 C2 Adra Spain
114 B2 Adrar Alg.
140 C2 Adrian MI U.S.A.
139 C1 Adrian TX U.S.A.
108 B2 Adriatic Sea Europe

116 B3 Ādwa Eth.
83 K2 Adycha r. Rus. Fed.
91 D3 Adygeysk Rus. Fed.
114 B4 Adzopé Côte d'Ivoire
111 B3 Aegean Sea Greece/Turkey
101 D1 Aerzen Ger.
106 B1 A Estrada Spain
116 B3 Afabet Eritrea
76 C3 Afghanistan country Asia
78 B2 'Afīf Saudi Arabia
80 B2 Afyon Turkey
115 C3 Agadez Niger
114 B1 Agadir Morocco
74 B2 Agar India
75 D2 Agartala India
81 C2 Ağdam (abandoned) Azer.
105 C3 Agde France
104 C3 Agen France
122 A2 Aggeneys S. Africa
111 C3 Agia Varvara Greece
111 B3 Agios Dimitrios Greece
111 C3 Agios Efstratios i. Greece
111 C3 Agios Nikolaos Greece
110 B1 Agnita Romania
75 B2 Agra India
81 C2 Ağrı Turkey
    Ağrı Dağı mt. Turkey see
    Ararat, Mount
108 B3 Agrigento Sicilia Italy
111 B3 Agrinio Greece
109 B2 Agropoli Italy
154 B2 Agua Clara Brazil
146 B4 Aguadulce Panama
144 B2 Aguanaval r. Mex.
144 B1 Agua Prieta Mex.
155 D1 Aguas Formosas Brazil
106 B1 Agueda Port.
106 C1 Aguilar de Campoo Spain
107 C2 Aguilas Spain
144 B3 Aguililla Mex.
122 B3 Agulhas, Cape S. Africa
155 D2 Agulhas Negras mt. Brazil
111 C2 Ağva Turkey
115 C2 Ahaggar plat. Alg.
115 C2 Ahaggar, Tassili oua-n-
    plat. Alg.
81 C2 Ahar Iran
100 C1 Ahaus Ger.
81 C2 Ahlat Turkey
100 C2 Ahlen Ger.
74 B2 Ahmadabad India
73 B3 Ahmadnagar India
74 B2 Ahmadpur East Pak.
74 B1 Ahmadpur Sial Pak.
    Ahmedabad India see
    Ahmadabad
    Ahmednagar India see
    Ahmadnagar
144 B2 Ahome Mex.
79 C2 Ahram Iran
101 E1 Ahrensburg Ger.
104 C2 Ahun France
81 C2 Ahvāz Iran
122 A2 Ai-Ais Namibia
80 B2 Aigialousa Cyprus
111 B3 Aigio Greece
143 D2 Aiken U.S.A.
97 B1 Ailt an Chorráin Ireland
155 D1 Aimorés Brazil
155 D1 Aimorés, Serra dos hills Brazil
114 B2 'Aïn Ben Tili Maur.
107 D2 Aïn Defla Alg.
114 B1 Aïn Sefra Alg.
136 D2 Ainsworth U.S.A.
    Aintab Turkey see Gaziantep

107 D2	Aïn Taya Alg.	
107 D2	Ain Tédélès Alg.	
115 C3	Aïr, Massif de l' *mts* Niger	
60 A1	Airbangis Indon.	
128 C2	Airdrie Can.	
104 B3	Aire-sur-l'Adour France	
101 E3	Aisch *r.* Ger.	
128 A1	Aishihik Lake Can.	
59 D3	Aisne *r.* France	
110 B1	Aiud Romania	
105 D3	Aix-en-Provence France	
105 D2	Aix-les-Bains France	
62 A1	Aizawl India	
88 C2	Aizkraukle Latvia	
67 C3	Aizu-Wakamatsu Japan	
105 D3	Ajaccio *Corse* France	
115 E1	Ajdābiyā Libya	
115 C2	Ajjer, Tassili n' *plat.* Alg.	
74 B2	Ajmer India	
138 A2	Ajo U.S.A.	
77 D2	Akadyr Kazakh.	
87 E3	Akbulak Rus. Fed.	
80 B2	Akçakale Turkey	
80 B2	Akdağmadeni Turkey	
66 D3	Akita Japan	
114 A3	Akjoujt Maur.	
77 D1	Akkol' Kazakh.	
88 B2	Akmenrags *pt* Latvia	
	Akmola Kazakh. *see* Astana	
117 B4	Akobo S. Sudan	
74 B2	Akola India	
78 A3	Akordat Eritrea	
127 G2	Akpatok Island Can.	
92 □A3	Akranes Iceland	
140 C2	Akron U.S.A.	
75 B1	Aksai Chin *terr.* Asia	
80 B2	Aksaray Turkey	
76 B1	Aksay Kazakh.	
91 D2	Aksay Rus. Fed.	
80 B2	Akşehir Turkey	
76 C2	Akshiganak Kazakh.	
77 E2	Aksu China	
78 A3	Aksum Eth.	
76 B2	Aktau Kazakh.	
76 B1	Aktobe Kazakh.	
88 C3	Aktsyabrski Belarus	
115 C4	Akure Nigeria	
92 □B2	Akureyri Iceland	
142 C2	Alabama *r.* U.S.A.	
142 C2	Alabama *state* U.S.A.	
111 C3	Alaçatı Turkey	
81 C1	Alagir Rus. Fed.	
151 E3	Alagoinhas Brazil	
107 C1	Alagón Spain	
79 B2	Al Aḥmadī Kuwait	
77 E2	Alakol', Ozero *salt l.* Kazakh.	
92 J2	Alakurtti Rus. Fed.	
78 B3	Al 'Alayyah Saudi Arabia	
81 C2	Al 'Amādīyah Iraq	
80 A2	Al 'Āmirīyah Egypt	
135 C3	Alamo U.S.A.	
138 B2	Alamogordo U.S.A.	
144 A2	Alamos *Sonora* Mex.	
144 B2	Alamos *Sonora* Mex.	
144 B2	Alamos *r.* Mex.	
136 B3	Alamosa U.S.A.	
93 G3	Åland Islands Fin.	

80 B2	Alanya Turkey	
73 B4	Alappuzha India	
80 B3	Al 'Aqabah Jordan	
78 B2	Al 'Aqīq Saudi Arabia	
107 C2	Alarcón, Embalse de *resr* Spain	
80 B2	Al 'Arīsh Egypt	
78 B2	Al Arṭāwīyah Saudi Arabia	
61 C2	Alas Indon.	
111 C3	Alaşehir Turkey	
128 A2	Alaska *state* U.S.A.	
124 F3	Alaska, Gulf of U.S.A.	
81 C2	Ālāt Azer.	
87 D3	Alatyr' Rus. Fed.	
150 A2	Alausí Ecuador	
93 H3	Alavus Fin.	
52 B2	Alawoona Austr.	
108 A2	Alba Italy	
107 C2	Albacete Spain	
110 B1	Alba Iulia Romania	
109 C2	Albania *country* Europe	
50 A3	Albany Austr.	
130 B1	Albany *r.* Can.	
143 D2	Albany GA U.S.A.	
141 E2	Albany NY U.S.A.	
134 B2	Albany OR U.S.A.	
51 D1	Al Başrah Iraq *see* Basra	
51 D1	Albatross Bay Austr.	
116 A2	Al Bawītī Egypt	
115 E1	Al Baydā' Libya	
78 B3	Al Baydā' Yemen	
143 D1	Albemarle U.S.A.	
143 E1	Albemarle Sound *sea chan.* U.S.A.	
108 A2	Albenga Italy	
51 C2	Alberga *watercourse* Austr.	
119 D2	Albert, Lake Dem. Rep. Congo/Uganda	
128 C2	Alberta *prov.* Can.	
100 B2	Albert Kanaal *canal* Belgium	
137 E2	Albert Lea U.S.A.	
104 C3	Albi France	
78 A2	Al Bi'r Saudi Arabia	
78 B3	Al Birk Saudi Arabia	
78 B2	Al Biyāḍh *reg.* Saudi Arabia	
106 C2	Alboran Sea Europe	
	Alborz, Reshteh-ye *mts* Iran *see* Elburz Mountains	
106 B2	Albufeira Port.	
138 B1	Albuquerque U.S.A.	
79 C2	Al Buraymī Oman	
53 C3	Albury Austr.	
106 B2	Alcácer do Sal Port.	
106 C1	Alcalá de Henares Spain	
106 C2	Alcalá la Real Spain	
108 B3	Alcamo *Sicilia* Italy	
107 C1	Alcañiz Spain	
106 B2	Alcántara Spain	
106 C2	Alcaraz Spain	
106 C2	Alcaraz, Sierra de *mts* Spain	
106 C2	Alcázar de San Juan Spain	
91 D2	Alchevs'k Ukr.	
155 E1	Alcobaça Brazil	
107 C2	Alcoy-Alcoi Spain	
107 D2	Alcúdia Spain	
145 C2	Aldama Mex.	
83 J3	Aldan Rus. Fed.	
83 J2	Aldan *r.* Rus. Fed.	
95 C4	Alderney *i.* Channel Is	
114 A3	Aleg Maur.	
155 D2	Alegre Brazil	
152 C3	Alegrete Brazil	
83 K3	Aleksandrovsk-Sakhalinskiy Rus. Fed.	
91 D1	Alekseyevka *Belgorodskaya Oblast'* Rus. Fed.	

91 D1	Alekseyevka *Belgorodskaya Oblast'* Rus. Fed.	
89 E3	Aleksin Rus. Fed.	
109 D2	Aleksinac Serbia	
118 B3	Alèmbé Gabon	
155 D2	Além Paraíba Brazil	
93 F3	Ålen Norway	
104 C2	Alençon France	
80 B2	Aleppo Syria	
150 A3	Alerta Peru	
128 B2	Alert Bay Can.	
105 C3	Alès France	
110 B1	Aleşd Romania	
108 A2	Alessandria Italy	
93 E3	Ålesund Norway	
124 C3	Aleutian Islands U.S.A.	
83 L3	Alevina, Mys *c.* Rus. Fed.	
124 C3	Alexander Archipelago *is* U.S.A.	
122 A2	Alexander Bay S. Africa	
142 C2	Alexander City U.S.A.	
55 O2	Alexander Island Antarctica	
53 C3	Alexandra Austr.	
54 A3	Alexandra N.Z.	
111 B2	Alexandreia Greece	
	Alexandretta Turkey *see* Iskenderun	
116 A1	Alexandria Egypt	
110 C2	Alexandria Romania	
123 C3	Alexandria S. Africa	
142 B2	Alexandria LA U.S.A.	
137 D1	Alexandria MN U.S.A.	
141 D3	Alexandria VA U.S.A.	
52 A3	Alexandrina, Lake Austr.	
111 C2	Alexandroupoli Greece	
131 E1	Alexis *r.* Can.	
128 B2	Alexis Creek Can.	
77 E1	Aleysk Rus. Fed.	
107 C1	Alfaro Spain	
81 C3	Al Fāw Iraq	
101 D2	Alfeld (Leine) Ger.	
155 C2	Alfenas Brazil	
	Al Fujayrah U.A.E. *see* Fujairah	
	Al Furāt *r.* Iraq/Syria *see* Euphrates	
106 B2	Algeciras Spain	
107 C2	Algemesí Spain	
78 A3	Algena Eritrea	
	Alger Alg. *see* Algiers	
114 C2	Algeria *country* Africa	
79 C3	Al Ghaydah Yemen	
108 A2	Alghero *Sardegna* Italy	
116 B2	Al Ghurdaqah Egypt	
79 B2	Al Ghwaybiyah Saudi Arabia	
115 C1	Algiers Alg.	
123 C3	Algoa Bay S. Africa	
137 E2	Algona U.S.A.	
106 C1	Algorta Spain	
81 C2	Al Ḥadīthah Iraq	
79 C2	Al Ḥajar al Gharbī *mts* Oman	
107 C2	Alhama de Murcia Spain	
80 A2	Al Ḥammām Egypt	
78 B2	Al Ḥanākīyah Saudi Arabia	
81 C2	Al Ḥasakah Syria	
81 C2	Al Ḥayy Iraq	
78 B3	Al Ḥazm al Jawf Yemen	
79 C3	Al Ḥibāk *des.* Saudi Arabia	
78 B2	Al Ḥillah Saudi Arabia	
79 B3	Al Ḥinnāh Saudi Arabia	
	Al Ḥudaydah Yemen *see* Hodeidah	
79 B2	Al Hufūf Saudi Arabia	
115 D2	Al Ḥulayq al Kabīr *hills* Libya	
79 C2	'Alīābād Iran	
111 C3	Aliağa Turkey	
111 B2	Aliakmonas *r.* Greece	

Babar

Bastrop

142 B2 **Bastrop** U.S.A.
    Basuo China see **Dongfang**
118 A2 **Bata** Equat. Guinea
83 J2 **Batagay** Rus. Fed.
154 B2 **Bataguassu** Brazil
106 B2 **Batalha** Port.
71 C3 **Batan** i. Phil.
118 B2 **Batangafo** C.A.R.
64 B1 **Batangas** Phil.
60 B2 **Batanghari** r. Indon.
71 C3 **Batan Islands** Phil.
141 D2 **Batavia** U.S.A.
91 D2 **Bataysk** Rus. Fed.
130 B2 **Batchawana Mountain** h. Can.
50 C1 **Batchelor** Austr.
63 B2 **Bătdâmbâng** Cambodia
53 D3 **Batemans Bay** Austr.
142 B1 **Batesville** U.S.A.
89 D2 **Batetskiy** Rus. Fed.
99 B3 **Bath** U.K.
74 B1 **Bathinda** India
53 C2 **Bathurst** Austr.
131 D2 **Bathurst** Can.
126 D2 **Bathurst Inlet** Can.
126 D2 **Bathurst Inlet (abandoned)** Can.
50 C1 **Bathurst Island** Austr.
126 E1 **Bathurst Island** Can.
78 B1 **Bāṭin, Wādī al** watercourse Asia
81 C2 **Batman** Turkey
115 C1 **Batna** Alg.
142 B2 **Baton Rouge** U.S.A.
144 B2 **Batopilas** Mex.
118 B2 **Batouri** Cameroon
154 B1 **Batovi** Brazil
92 I1 **Båtsfjord** Norway
73 C4 **Batticaloa** Sri Lanka
109 B2 **Battipaglia** Italy
129 D2 **Battle** r. Can.
140 B2 **Battle Creek** U.S.A.
135 C2 **Battle Mountain** U.S.A.
74 B1 **Battura Glacier** Pak.
117 B4 **Bati** mt. Eth.
60 A2 **Batu, Pulau-pulau** is Indon.
81 C1 **Bat'umi** Georgia
60 B1 **Batu Pahat** Malaysia
59 C3 **Baubau** Indon.
115 C1 **Bauchi** Nigeria
104 B2 **Baugé** France
105 D2 **Baume-les-Dames** France
154 C2 **Bauru** Brazil
154 B1 **Baús** Brazil
88 B2 **Bauska** Latvia
102 C1 **Bautzen** Ger.
144 B2 **Bavispe** r. Mex.
87 E3 **Bavly** Rus. Fed.
62 A1 **Bawdwin** Myanmar
60 A1 **Bawean** i. Indon.
114 B3 **Bawku** Ghana
146 C2 **Bayamo** Cuba
68 C1 **Bayanhongor** Mongolia
70 A2 **Bayan Hot** China
70 A1 **Bayannur** China
69 D2 **Bayan Shutu** China
69 D1 **Bayan-Uul** Mongolia
64 B1 **Bayawan** Phil.
80 C1 **Bayburt** Turkey
140 C2 **Bay City** MI U.S.A.
139 D3 **Bay City** TX U.S.A.
86 F2 **Baydaratskaya Guba** Rus. Fed.
117 C4 **Baydhabo** Somalia
81 C2 **Bayji** Iraq
    Baykal, Ozero l. Rus. Fed. see **Baikal, Lake**
83 I3 **Baykal'skiy Khrebet** mts Rus. Fed.

76 C2 **Baykonyr** Kazakh.
87 E3 **Baymak** Rus. Fed.
64 B1 **Bayombong** Phil.
104 B3 **Bayonne** France
111 C3 **Bayramiç** Turkey
101 E3 **Bayreuth** Ger.
78 B3 **Bayt al Faqih** Yemen
106 C2 **Baza** Spain
106 C2 **Baza, Sierra de** mts Spain
74 A1 **Bāzārak** Afgh.
76 A2 **Bazardyuzyu, Gora** mt. Azer./...
99 D3 **Beachy Head** U.K.
123 C3 **Beacon Bay** S. Africa
50 B1 **Beagle Gulf** Austr.
121 □D2 **Bealanana** Madag.
97 B1 **Béal an Mhuirthead** Ireland
130 C2 **Beardmore** Can.
    Bear Island Arctic Ocean see **Bjørnøya**
134 E1 **Bear Paw Mountain** U.S.A.
147 C3 **Beata, Cabo** c. Dom. Rep.
147 C3 **Beata, Isla** i. Dom. Rep.
137 D2 **Beatrice** U.S.A.
135 C3 **Beatty** U.S.A.
53 D1 **Beaudesert** Austr.
52 B1 **Beaufort** Austr.
61 C1 **Beaufort** Sabah Malaysia
143 D2 **Beaufort** U.S.A.
160 L2 **Beaufort Sea** Can./U.S.A.
122 B3 **Beaufort West** S. Africa
96 B2 **Beauly** r. U.K.
100 B2 **Beaumont** Belgium
54 A3 **Beaumont** N.Z.
139 E2 **Beaumont** U.S.A.
105 C2 **Beaune** France
100 B2 **Beauraing** Belgium
129 E2 **Beauséjour** Can.
104 C2 **Beauvais** France
129 D2 **Beauval** Can.
129 D2 **Beaver** r. Can.
135 D3 **Beaver** U.S.A.
126 B2 **Beaver Creek** Can.
140 B2 **Beaver Dam** U.S.A.
129 E2 **Beaver Hill Lake** Can.
140 B1 **Beaver Island** U.S.A.
128 C2 **Beaverlodge** Can.
74 B2 **Beawar** India
154 C2 **Bebedouro** Brazil
101 D2 **Bebra** Ger.
106 B1 **Becerreá** Spain
114 B1 **Béchar** Alg.
140 C3 **Beckley** U.S.A.
117 B4 **Bedelé** Eth.
99 C2 **Bedford** U.K.
140 B3 **Bedford** U.S.A.
100 C1 **Bedum** Neth.
53 D2 **Beecroft Peninsula** Austr.
101 F1 **Beelitz** Ger.
53 D1 **Beenleigh** Austr.
80 B2 **Beersheba** Israel
139 D3 **Beeville** U.S.A.
53 C3 **Bega** Austr.
107 D1 **Begur, Cap de** c. Spain
128 C1 **Behchokò** Can.
81 D2 **Behshahr** Iran
69 E1 **Bei'an** China
71 A3 **Beihai** China
70 B2 **Beijing** China
100 C1 **Beilen** Neth.
96 A2 **Beinn Mhòr** h. U.K.

121 C2 **Beira** Moz.
80 B2 **Beirut** Lebanon
123 C1 **Beitbridge** Zimbabwe
106 B2 **Beja** Port.
115 C1 **Bejaïa** Alg.
106 B1 **Béjar** Spain
74 A2 **Beji** r. Pak.
103 E2 **Békés** Hungary
103 E2 **Békéscsaba** Hungary
121 □D3 **Bekily** Madag.
74 A2 **Bela** Pak.
118 B3 **Bela-Bela** S. Africa
118 B2 **Bélabo** Cameroon
109 D2 **Bela Crkva** Serbia
61 C1 **Belaga** Sarawak Malaysia
88 C3 **Belarus** country Europe
    Belau country N. Pacific Ocean see **Palau**
123 D2 **Bela Vista** Moz.
60 A1 **Belawan** Indon.
83 M2 **Belaya** r. Rus. Fed.
103 D1 **Bełchatów** Pol.
130 C1 **Belcher Islands** Can.
117 C4 **Beledweyne** Somalia
151 D2 **Belém** Brazil
138 B2 **Belen** U.S.A.
89 E3 **Belev** Rus. Fed.
97 D1 **Belfast** U.K.
141 F2 **Belfast** U.S.A.
105 D2 **Belfort** France
73 B3 **Belgaum** India
100 B2 **Belgium** country Europe
91 D1 **Belgorod** Rus. Fed.
109 D2 **Belgrade** Serbia
134 D1 **Belgrade** U.S.A.
60 B2 **Belinyu** Indon.
61 B2 **Belitung** i. Indon.
146 B3 **Belize** Belize
146 B3 **Belize** country Central America
83 K1 **Bel'kovskiy, Ostrov** i. Rus. Fed.
52 B2 **Bella Bella** Can.
104 C2 **Bellac** France
128 B2 **Bella Coola** Can.
53 C1 **Bellata** Austr.
136 C2 **Belle Fourche** U.S.A.
136 C2 **Belle Fourche** r. U.S.A.
143 D3 **Belle Glade** U.S.A.
104 B2 **Belle-Île** i. France
131 E1 **Belle Isle** i. Can.
131 E1 **Belle Isle, Strait of** Can.
130 C2 **Belleville** Can.
140 B3 **Belleville** IL U.S.A.
137 D3 **Belleville** KS U.S.A.
134 B1 **Bellevue** U.S.A.
134 B1 **Bellingham** U.S.A.
55 O2 **Bellingshausen Sea** Antarctica
105 D2 **Bellinzona** Switz.
108 B1 **Belluno** Italy
122 A3 **Bellville** S. Africa
155 E1 **Belmonte** Brazil
146 B3 **Belmopan** Belize
69 E1 **Belogorsk** Rus. Fed.
121 □D3 **Beloha** Madag.
155 D1 **Belo Horizonte** Brazil
140 B2 **Beloit** U.S.A.
86 C2 **Belomorsk** Rus. Fed.
91 D3 **Belorechensk** Rus. Fed.
87 E3 **Beloretsk** Rus. Fed.
    Belorussia country Europe see **Belarus**
86 F2 **Beloyarskiy** Rus. Fed.
86 C2 **Beloye, Ozero** l. Rus. Fed.
    Beloye More sea Rus. Fed. see **White Sea**
86 C2 **Belozersk** Rus. Fed.
77 E2 **Belukha, Gora** mt. Kazakh./Rus. Fed.

Bikin

Brady

62	A1	**Bumhkang** Myanmar
118	B3	**Buna** Dem. Rep. Congo
50	A3	**Bunbury** Austr.
97	C1	**Buncrana** Ireland
119	D3	**Bunda** Tanz.
51	E2	**Bundaberg** Austr.
53	D2	**Bundarra** Austr.
74	B2	**Bundi** India
97	B1	**Bundoran** Ireland
53	C3	**Bungendore** Austr.
67	B4	**Bungo-suidō** *sea chan.* Japan
119	D2	**Bunia** Dem. Rep. Congo
118	C3	**Bunianga** Dem. Rep. Congo
63	B2	**Buôn Ma Thuột** Vietnam
119	D3	**Bura** Kenya
78	B2	**Buraydah** Saudi Arabia
100	D2	**Burbach** Ger.
117	C4	**Burco** Somalia
100	B1	**Burdaard** Neth.
80	B2	**Burdur** Turkey
117	B3	**Burē** Eth.
99	D2	**Bure** r. U.K.
74	B1	**Burewala** Pak.
110	C2	**Burgas** Bulg.
101	E1	**Burg bei Magdeburg** Ger.
101	E1	**Burgdorf** *Niedersachsen* Ger.
101	E1	**Burgdorf** *Niedersachsen* Ger.
131	E2	**Burgeo** Can.
123	D1	**Burgersdorp** S. Africa
100	A2	**Burgh-Haamstede** Neth.
145	C2	**Burgos** Mex.
106	C1	**Burgos** Spain
111	C3	**Burhaniye** Turkey
74	B2	**Burhanpur** India
101	D1	**Burhave (Butjadingen)** Ger.
131	E2	**Burin** Can.
151	D2	**Buriti Bravo** Brazil
155	C1	**Buritis** Brazil
51	C1	**Burketown** Austr.
114	B3	**Burkina Faso** *country* Africa
134	D2	**Burley** U.S.A.
136	C3	**Burlington** CO U.S.A.
137	E2	**Burlington** IA U.S.A.
143	E1	**Burlington** NC U.S.A.
141	E2	**Burlington** VT U.S.A.
		Burma *country* Asia *see* Myanmar
134	B2	**Burney** U.S.A.
51	D4	**Burnie** Austr.
98	B2	**Burnley** U.K.
134	C2	**Burns** U.S.A.
128	B2	**Burns Lake** Can.
77	E2	**Burqin** China
52	A2	**Burra** Austr.
109	D2	**Burrel** Albania
97	B2	**Burren** *reg.* Ireland
53	C2	**Burrendong, Lake** resr Austr.
53	C2	**Burren Junction** Austr.
107	C2	**Burriana** Spain
53	C2	**Burrinjuck Reservoir** Austr.
144	B2	**Burro, Serranías del** mts Mex.
111	C2	**Bursa** Turkey
116	B2	**Bür Safājah** Egypt
		Bür Sa'īd Egypt *see* Port Said
130	C1	**Burton, Lac** l. Can.
99	C2	**Burton upon Trent** U.K.
59	C3	**Buru** i. Indon.
119	C3	**Burundi** *country* Africa
119	C3	**Bururi** Burundi
91	C1	**Buryn'** Ukr.
99	D2	**Bury St Edmunds** U.K.
118	C3	**Busanga** Dem. Rep. Congo
81	C2	**Būshehr** Iran
119	D3	**Bushenyi** Uganda
118	C2	**Businga** Dem. Rep. Congo
50	A3	**Busselton** Austr.
145	C3	**Bustamante** Mex.

118	C2	**Buta** Dem. Rep. Congo
119	C3	**Butare** Rwanda
123	C2	**Butha-Buthe** Lesotho
140	D2	**Butler** U.S.A.
59	C3	**Buton** i. Indon.
134	D1	**Butte** U.S.A.
60	B1	**Butterworth** Malaysia
96	A1	**Butt of Lewis** hd U.K.
129	E2	**Button Bay** Can.
64	B2	**Butuan** Phil.
91	E1	**Buturlinovka** Rus. Fed.
75	C2	**Butwal** Nepal
101	D2	**Butzbach** Ger.
117	C4	**Buulobarde** Somalia
117	C5	**Buur Gaabo** Somalia
117	C4	**Buurhabaka** Somalia
76	C3	**Buxoro** Uzbek.
101	D1	**Buxtehude** Ger.
89	F2	**Buy** Rus. Fed.
87	D4	**Buynaksk** Rus. Fed.
111	C3	**Büyükmenderes** r. Turkey
110	C1	**Buzău** Romania
121	C2	**Búzi** Moz.
87	E3	**Buzuluk** Rus. Fed.
88	C3	**Byala** Bulg.
88	C3	**Byalynichy** Belarus
88	D3	**Byarezina** r. Belarus
88	B3	**Byaroza** Belarus
103	D1	**Bydgoszcz** Pol.
88	C3	**Byerazino** Belarus
88	C2	**Byeshankovichy** Belarus
89	D3	**Bykhaw** Belarus
127	F2	**Bylot Island** Can.
53	C2	**Byrock** Austr.
53	D1	**Byron Bay** Austr.
83	J2	**Bytantay** r. Rus. Fed.
103	D1	**Bytom** Pol.
103	D1	**Bytów** Pol.

C

154	B2	**Caarapó** Brazil
64	B1	**Cabanatuan** Phil.
117	C3	**Cabdul Qaadir** Somalia
106	B2	**Cabeza del Buey** Spain
152	B2	**Cabezas** Bol.
150	A1	**Cabimas** Venez.
120	A1	**Cabinda** Angola
118	B3	**Cabinda** prov. Angola
155	D2	**Cabo Frio** Brazil
155	D2	**Cabo Frio, Ilha do** i. Brazil
130	C2	**Cabonga, Réservoir** resr Can.
51	E2	**Caboolture** Austr.
150	A2	**Cabo Pantoja** Peru
144	A1	**Caborca** Mex.
144	B2	**Cabo San Lucas** Mex.
131	D2	**Cabot Strait** Can.
155	D1	**Cabral, Serra do** mts Brazil
107	D2	**Cabrera, Illa de** i. Spain
106	B1	**Cabrera, Sierra de** mts Spain
129	D2	**Cabri** Can.
107	C2	**Cabriel** r. Spain
152	C3	**Caçador** Brazil
109	D2	**Čačak** Serbia
108	A2	**Caccia, Capo** c. *Sardegna* Italy
151	C3	**Cáceres** Brazil
106	B2	**Cáceres** Spain
128	B2	**Cache Creek** Can.
114	A3	**Cacheu** Guinea-Bissau
151	C3	**Cachimbo, Serra do** hills Brazil
155	D1	**Cachoeira Alta** Brazil
155	D2	**Cachoeiro de Itapemirim** Brazil
114	A3	**Cacine** Guinea-Bissau
120	A2	**Cacolo** Angola

154	B1	**Caçu** Brazil
103	D2	**Čadca** Slovakia
101	D1	**Cadenberge** Ger.
145	B2	**Cadereyta** Mex.
140	B2	**Cadillac** U.S.A.
106	B2	**Cádiz** Spain
106	B2	**Cádiz, Golfo de** g. Spain
128	C2	**Cadotte Lake** Can.
104	B2	**Caen** France
98	A2	**Caernarfon** U.K.
98	A2	**Caernarfon Bay** U.K.
152	B3	**Cafayate** Arg.
66	C2	**Cagayan de Oro** Phil.
64	A2	**Cagayan de Tawi-Tawi** i. Phil.
108	B2	**Cagli** Italy
108	A3	**Cagliari** *Sardegna* Italy
108	A3	**Cagliari, Golfo di** b. *Sardegna* Italy
76	B2	**Çagyl** Turkm.
97	B3	**Caha Mountains** hills Ireland
97	A3	**Cahermore** Ireland
97	C2	**Cahir** Ireland
97	A3	**Cahirsiveen** Ireland
104	C3	**Cahore Point** Ireland
104	C3	**Cahors** France
90	B2	**Cahul** Moldova
121	C2	**Caia** Moz.
151	C3	**Caiabis, Serra dos** hills Brazil
120	B2	**Caianda** Angola
154	B1	**Caiapó, Serra do** mts Brazil
154	B1	**Caiapônia** Brazil
147	C2	**Caicos Islands** Turks and Caicos Is
96	C2	**Cairngorm Mountains** U.K.
98	A1	**Cairnryan** U.K.
51	D1	**Cairns** Austr.
116	B1	**Cairo** Egypt
98	C2	**Caistor** U.K.
120	A2	**Caiundo** Angola
150	A2	**Cajamarca** Peru
123	C3	**Cala** S. Africa
150	B1	**Calabozo** Venez.
110	C2	**Calafat** Romania
153	A6	**Calafate** Arg.
107	C1	**Calahorra** Spain
104	C1	**Calais** France
141	F1	**Calais** U.S.A.
152	B3	**Calama** Chile
64	A1	**Calamian Group** is Phil.
107	C1	**Calamocha** Spain
120	A1	**Calandula** Angola
60	A1	**Calang** Indon.
64	B1	**Calapan** Phil.
110	C2	**Călăraşi** Romania
107	C1	**Calatayud** Spain
64	B1	**Calayan** i. Phil.
64	B1	**Calbayog** Phil.
151	E2	**Calcanhar, Ponta do** pt Brazil
151	C1	**Calçoene** Brazil
		Calcutta India see Kolkata
106	B2	**Caldas da Rainha** Port.
154	C1	**Caldas Novas** Brazil
152	A3	**Caldera** Chile
134	C2	**Caldwell** U.S.A.
123	C3	**Caledon** r. Lesotho/S. Africa
123	C3	**Caledon** S. Africa
153	B5	**Caleta Olivia** Arg.
98	A1	**Calf of Man** i. Isle of Man
128	C2	**Calgary** Can.
150	A1	**Cali** Col.
		Calicut India see Kozhikode
135	D3	**Caliente** U.S.A.
135	B2	**California** state U.S.A.
144	A1	**California, Gulf of** Mex.
135	B3	**California Aqueduct** canal U.S.A.

Calitzdorp

122	B3	Calitzdorp S. Africa
145	C2	Calkini Mex.
52	B1	Callabonna, Lake imp. l. Austr.
96	B2	Callander U.K.
150	A3	Callao Peru
108	B3	Caltagirone Sicilia Italy
108	B3	Caltanissetta Sicilia Italy
120	A2	Caluquembe Angola
117	D3	Caluula Somalia
105	B3	Calvi Corse France
107	D2	Calvià Spain
144	B2	Calvillo Mex.
122	A3	Calvinia S. Africa
109	C2	Calvo, Monte mt. Italy
120	A2	Camacupa Angola
146	C2	Camagüey Cuba
150	A3	Camana Peru
154	B1	Camapuã Brazil
145	C2	Camargo Mex.
63	B3	Ca Mau Vietnam
63	B3	Ca Mau, Mui c. Vietnam
63	B2	Cambodia country Asia
99	A3	Camborne U.K.
105	C1	Cambrai France
99	B3	Cambrian Mountains hills U.K.
54	C1	Cambridge N.Z.
99	D2	Cambridge U.K.
141	E2	Cambridge MA U.S.A.
141	D3	Cambridge MD U.S.A.
137	E1	Cambridge MN U.S.A.
140	C2	Cambridge OH U.S.A.
131	D1	Cambrien, Lac l. Can.
53	D2	Camden Austr.
142	B2	Camden AR U.S.A.
141	F2	Camden ME U.S.A.
118	B2	Cameroon country Africa
118	B2	Cameroon Highlands slope Cameroon/Nigeria
151	D2	Cametá Brazil
64	B1	Camiguin i. Phil.
152	B3	Camiri Bol.
151	D2	Camocim Brazil
51	C1	Camooweal Austr.
63	A3	Camorta i. India
153	A5	Campana, Isla i. Chile
122	B2	Campbell S. Africa
54	B2	Campbell, Cape N.Z.
48	F6	Campbell Island N.Z.
128	B2	Campbell River Can.
140	B3	Campbellsville U.S.A.
131	D2	Campbellton Can.
96	B3	Campbeltown U.K.
145	C3	Campeche Mex.
145	C3	Campeche, Bahía de g. Mex.
52	B3	Camperdown Austr.
110	C1	Câmpina Romania
151	E2	Campina Grande Brazil
154	C2	Campinas Brazil
154	C1	Campina Verde Brazil
108	B2	Campobasso Italy
155	C2	Campo Belo Brazil
154	C1	Campo Florido Brazil
152	B3	Campo Gallo Arg.
154	B2	Campo Grande Brazil
151	D2	Campo Maior Brazil
106	B2	Campo Maior Port.
154	B2	Campo Mourão Brazil
155	D2	Campos Brazil
155	C1	Campos Altos Brazil
155	D2	Campos do Jordão Brazil
110	C1	Câmpulung Romania
138	A2	Camp Verde U.S.A.
128	C2	Camrose Can.
129	D2	Camsell Portage Can.
111	C2	Çan Turkey
126	F2	Canada country N. America

139	C1	Canadian U.S.A.
139	D1	Canadian r. U.S.A.
111	C2	Çanakkale Turkey
144	A1	Cananea Mex.
154	C2	Cananéia Brazil
		Canarias, Islas terr. N. Atlantic Ocean see Canary Islands
114	A2	Canary Islands terr. N. Atlantic Ocean
155	C1	Canastra, Serra da mts Brazil
144	B2	Canatlán Mex.
143	D3	Canaveral, Cape U.S.A.
155	E1	Canavieiras Brazil
53	C3	Canberra Austr.
145	D2	Cancún Mex.
111	C3	Çandarlı Turkey
145	C3	Candelaria Mex.
129	D2	Candle Lake Can.
120	A2	Cangamba Angola
106	B1	Cangas del Narcea Spain
152	C4	Canguçu Brazil
70	B2	Cangzhou China
131	D1	Caniapiscau Can.
131	D1	Caniapiscau Can.
131	C1	Caniapiscau, Réservoir de resr Can.
108	B3	Canicattì Sicilia Italy
151	E2	Canindé Brazil
144	B2	Cañitas de Felipe Pescador Mex.
80	B1	Çankırı Turkey
128	C2	Canmore Can.
96	A2	Canna i. U.K.
105	D3	Cannes France
99	B2	Cannock U.K.
53	C3	Cann River Austr.
152	C3	Canoas Brazil
129	D2	Canoe Lake Can.
154	B3	Canoinhas Brazil
136	B3	Canon City U.S.A.
129	D2	Canora Can.
53	C2	Canowindra Austr.
106	C1	Cantábrica, Cordillera mts Spain
106	B1	Cantábrico, Mar sea Spain
99	D3	Canterbury U.K.
54	B2	Canterbury Bight b. N.Z.
54	B2	Canterbury Plains N.Z.
63	B2	Cần Thơ Vietnam
151	D2	Canto do Buriti Brazil
		Canton China see Guangzhou
142	C2	Canton MS U.S.A.
140	C2	Canton OH U.S.A.
139	C1	Canyon U.S.A.
134	D1	Canyon Ferry Lake U.S.A.
62	B1	Cao Bằng Vietnam
154	C2	Capão Bonito Brazil
155	D2	Caparaó, Serra do mts Brazil
51	D4	Cape Barren Island Austr.
52	A3	Cape Borda Austr.
131	D2	Cape Breton Island Can.
114	B4	Cape Coast Ghana
141	E2	Cape Cod Bay U.S.A.
127	F2	Cape Dorset Can.
143	E2	Cape Fear r. U.S.A.
137	F3	Cape Girardeau U.S.A.
155	D1	Capelinha Brazil
100	B2	Capelle aan de IJssel Neth.
120	A1	Capenda-Camulemba Angola
122	A3	Cape Town S. Africa
112	C5	Cape Verde country N. Atlantic Ocean
51	D1	Cape York Peninsula Austr.
147	C3	Cap-Haïtien Haiti
151	D2	Capim r. Brazil
58	D1	Capitol Hill N. Mariana Is
109	C2	Čapljina Bos.-Herz.

109	B3	Capo d'Orlando Sicilia Italy
108	A2	Capraia, Isola di i. Italy
108	A2	Caprara, Punta pt Sardegna Italy
108	B2	Capri, Isola di i. Italy
120	B2	Caprivi Strip reg. Namibia
150	B2	Caquetá r. Col.
110	B2	Caracal Romania
150	B1	Caracas Venez.
151	D2	Caracol Brazil
155	C2	Caraguatatuba Brazil
153	A4	Carahue Chile
155	D1	Caraí Brazil
155	D2	Carangola Brazil
110	B1	Caransebeş Romania
131	D2	Caraquet Can.
146	B3	Caratasca, Laguna de lag. Hond.
155	D1	Caratinga Brazil
150	B2	Carauari Brazil
107	C2	Caravaca de la Cruz Spain
155	E1	Caravelas Brazil
129	E3	Carberry Can.
144	A2	Carbó Mex.
107	C2	Carbon, Cap c. Alg.
153	B5	Carbón, Laguna del l. Arg.
108	A3	Carbonara, Capo c. Sardegna Italy
136	B3	Carbondale CO U.S.A.
140	B3	Carbondale IL U.S.A.
131	E2	Carbonear Can.
155	D1	Carbonita Brazil
107	C2	Carcaixent Spain
104	C3	Carcassonne France
128	A1	Carcross Can.
145	C3	Cárdenas Mex.
99	B3	Cardiff U.K.
99	A2	Cardigan U.K.
99	A2	Cardigan Bay U.K.
128	C3	Cardston Can.
110	B1	Carei Romania
104	B2	Carentan France
50	B2	Carey, Lake imp. l. Austr.
155	D2	Cariacica Brazil
146	B3	Caribbean Sea N. Atlantic Ocean
141	F1	Caribou U.S.A.
130	B1	Caribou Lake Can.
128	C2	Caribou Mountains Can.
144	B2	Carichic Mex.
100	B3	Carignan France
53	C2	Carinda Austr.
107	C1	Cariñena Spain
130	C2	Carleton Place Can.
123	C2	Carletonville S. Africa
98	B1	Carlisle U.K.
141	D2	Carlisle U.S.A.
155	D1	Carlos Chagas Brazil
97	C2	Carlow Ireland
135	C4	Carlsbad CA U.S.A.
138	C2	Carlsbad NM U.S.A.
129	D3	Carlyle Can.
128	A1	Carmacks Can.
129	E3	Carman Can.
99	A3	Carmarthen U.K.
99	A3	Carmarthen Bay U.K.
104	C3	Carmaux France
145	C3	Carmelita Guat.
144	A2	Carmen, Isla i. Mex.
104	B2	Carnac France
122	B3	Carnarvon S. Africa
97	C1	Carndonagh Ireland
50	A2	Carnegie, Lake imp. l. Austr.
96	B2	Carn Eige mt. U.K.
63	A3	Car Nicobar i. India

176

65 B2	Chinghwa N. Korea	
120 B2	Chingola Zambia	
120 A2	Chinguar Angola	
65 B2	Chinhae S. Korea	
121 C2	Chinhoyi Zimbabwe	
74 B1	Chiniot Pak.	
144 B2	Chinipas Mex.	
65 B2	Chinju S. Korea	
118 C2	Chinko r. C.A.R.	
138 B1	Chinle U.S.A.	
71 B3	Chinmen Taiwan	
67 C3	Chino Japan	
104 C2	Chinon France	
138 A2	Chino Valley U.S.A.	
121 C2	Chinsali Zambia	
108 B1	Chioggia Italy	
111 C3	Chios Greece	
111 C3	Chios i. Greece	
121 C2	Chipata Zambia	
120 A2	Chipindo Angola	
121 C3	Chipinge Zimbabwe	
73 B3	Chiplun India	
99 B3	Chippenham U.K.	
99 C3	Chipping Norton U.K.	
77 C2	Chirchiq Uzbek.	
121 C2	Chiredzi Zimbabwe	
138 B2	Chiricahua Peak U.S.A.	
146 B4	Chiriquí, Golfo de b. Panama	
65 B2	Chiri-san mt. S. Korea	
146 B4	Chirripó mt. Costa Rica	
121 B2	Chirundu Zimbabwe	
130 C1	Chisasibi Can.	
137 E1	Chisholm U.S.A.	
90 B2	Chişinău Moldova	
87 E3	Chistopol' Rus. Fed.	
69 D1	Chita Rus. Fed.	
120 A2	Chitado Angola	
121 C2	Chitambo Zambia	
120 B1	Chitato Angola	
121 C1	Chitipa Malawi	
74 B1	Chitral Pak.	
146 B4	Chitré Panama	
75 D2	Chittagong Bangl.	
74 B2	Chittaurgarh India	
121 C2	Chitungwiza Zimbabwe	
120 B2	Chiume Angola	
121 C2	Chivhu Zimbabwe	
70 B2	Chizhou China	
114 C1	Chlef Alg.	
107 D2	Chlef, Oued r. Alg.	
153 B4	Choele Choel Arg.	
144 B2	Choix Mex.	
103 D1	Chojnice Pol.	
117 B3	Ch'ok'ē Mountains Eth.	
117 B4	Ch'ok'ē Terara mt. Eth.	
83 K2	Chokurdakh Rus. Fed.	
121 C3	Chókwé Moz.	
104 B2	Cholet France	
102 C1	Chomutov Czech Rep.	
83 I2	Chona r. Rus. Fed.	
65 B2	Ch'ŏnan S. Korea	
150 A2	Chone Ecuador	
65 B1	Ch'ŏngjin N. Korea	
65 B2	Ch'ŏngju N. Korea	
65 B2	Ch'ŏngju S. Korea	
65 B2	Chŏngp'yŏng N. Korea	
70 A3	Chongqing China	
70 A2	Chongqing mun. China	
71 A3	Chongzuo China	
65 B2	Chŏnju S. Korea	
153 A5	Chonos, Archipiélago de los is Chile	
154 B3	Chopimzinho Brazil	
111 B3	Chora Sfakion Greece	
98 B2	Chorley U.K.	
91 C2	Chornomors'ke Ukr.	
90 B2	Chortkiv Ukr.	

65 B2	Ch'ŏrwŏn S. Korea	
65 B1	Ch'osan N. Korea	
67 D3	Chōshi Japan	
103 D1	Choszczno Pol.	
114 A2	Choûm Maur.	
69 D1	Choybalsan Mongolia	
69 D1	Choyr Mongolia	
54 B2	Christchurch N.Z.	
99 C3	Christchurch U.K.	
127 G2	Christian, Cape Can.	
123 C2	Christiana S. Africa	
54 A2	Christina, Mount N.Z.	
153 B5	Chubut r. Arg.	
90 B1	Chudniv Ukr.	
89 D2	Chudovo Rus. Fed.	
	Chudskoye Ozero l. Estonia/ Rus. Fed. see Peipus, Lake	
126 B2	Chugach Mountains U.S.A.	
67 B4	Chūgoku-sanchi mts Japan	
66 B2	Chuguyevka Rus. Fed.	
91 D2	Chuhuyiv Ukr.	
160 J3	Chukchi Sea Rus. Fed./U.S.A.	
83 N2	Chukotskiy Poluostrov pen. Rus. Fed.	
135 C4	Chula Vista U.S.A.	
82 G3	Chulym Rus. Fed.	
152 B3	Chumbicha Arg.	
83 K3	Chumikan Rus. Fed.	
63 A2	Chumphon Thai.	
65 B2	Ch'unch'ŏn S. Korea	
	Chungking China see Chongqing	
83 H2	Chunya r. Rus. Fed.	
150 A3	Chuquibamba Peru	
152 B3	Chuquicamata Chile	
105 D2	Chur Switz.	
62 A1	Churachandpur India	
129 E2	Churchill Can.	
129 E2	Churchill r. Man. Can.	
131 D1	Churchill r. Nfld. and Lab. Can.	
129 E2	Churchill, Cape Can.	
131 D1	Churchill Falls Can.	
129 D2	Churchill Lake Can.	
74 B2	Churu India	
131 C2	Chute-des-Passes Can.	
62 B1	Chuxiong China	
90 B2	Ciadîr-Lunga Moldova	
61 B2	Ciamis Indon.	
60 B2	Cianjur Indon.	
154 B2	Cianorte Brazil	
103 E1	Ciechanów Pol.	
146 C2	Ciego de Ávila Cuba	
146 B2	Cienfuegos Cuba	
107 C2	Cieza Spain	
106 C2	Cigüela r. Spain	
80 B2	Cihanbeyli Turkey	
144 B3	Cihuatlán Mex.	
106 C2	Cíjara, Embalse de resr Spain	
61 B2	Cilacap Indon.	
139 C1	Cimarron r. U.S.A.	
90 B2	Cimişlia Moldova	
108 B2	Cimone, Monte mt. Italy	
140 C3	Cincinnati U.S.A.	
111 C3	Çine Turkey	
100 B2	Ciney Belgium	
145 C3	Cintalapa Mex.	
71 B3	Ciping China	
126 B2	Circle AK U.S.A.	
136 B1	Circle MT U.S.A.	
58 B3	Cirebon Indon.	
99 C3	Cirencester U.K.	
108 A1	Cirié Italy	
109 C3	Cirò Marina Italy	
109 C2	Čitluk Bos.-Herz.	
122 A3	Citrusdal S. Africa	
145 B2	Ciudad Acuña Mex.	
145 B3	Ciudad Altamirano Mex.	

150 B1	Ciudad Bolívar Venez.	
144 B2	Ciudad Camargo Mex.	
144 A2	Ciudad Constitución Mex.	
145 C3	Ciudad del Carmen Mex.	
144 B2	Ciudad Delicias Mex.	
145 C2	Ciudad de Valles Mex.	
150 B1	Ciudad Guayana Venez.	
138 B3	Ciudad Guerrero Mex.	
144 B3	Ciudad Guzmán Mex.	
145 C3	Ciudad Hidalgo Mex.	
145 C3	Ciudad Ixtepec Mex.	
144 B1	Ciudad Juárez Mex.	
145 C2	Ciudad Mante Mex.	
145 C2	Ciudad Mier Mex.	
144 B2	Ciudad Obregón Mex.	
106 C2	Ciudad Real Spain	
106 B1	Ciudad Río Bravo Mex.	
106 B1	Ciudad Rodrigo Spain	
145 C2	Ciudad Victoria Mex.	
107 D1	Ciutadella Spain	
111 C3	Civan Dağ mt. Turkey	
108 B1	Cividale del Friuli Italy	
108 B2	Civitanova Marche Italy	
108 B2	Civitavecchia Italy	
104 C2	Civray France	
111 C3	Çivril Turkey	
70 C2	Cixi China	
79 D3	Clacton-on-Sea U.K.	
128 C2	Claire, Lake Can.	
105 C2	Clamecy France	
122 A3	Clanwilliam S. Africa	
52 A2	Clare Austr.	
97 A2	Clare Island Ireland	
141 E2	Claremont U.S.A.	
97 B2	Claremorris Ireland	
54 B2	Clarence N.Z.	
131 E2	Clarenville Can.	
128 C2	Claresholm Can.	
137 D2	Clarinda U.S.A.	
123 C3	Clarkebury S. Africa	
134 C1	Clark Fork r. U.S.A.	
143 D2	Clark Hill Reservoir U.S.A.	
140 C3	Clarksburg U.S.A.	
142 B2	Clarksdale U.S.A.	
142 B1	Clarksville AR U.S.A.	
142 C1	Clarksville TN U.S.A.	
154 B1	Claro r. Brazil	
139 C1	Clayton U.S.A.	
97 B3	Clear, Cape Ireland	
137 E2	Clear Lake U.S.A.	
135 B3	Clear Lake U.S.A.	
128 C2	Clearwater Can.	
129 C2	Clearwater r. Can.	
143 D3	Clearwater U.S.A.	
134 C1	Clearwater r. U.S.A.	
51 D2	Cleburne U.S.A.	
51 D2	Clermont Austr.	
105 C2	Clermont-Ferrand France	
52 A2	Cleve Austr.	
142 B2	Cleveland MS U.S.A.	
140 C2	Cleveland OH U.S.A.	
143 D1	Cleveland TN U.S.A.	
134 D1	Cleveland, Mount U.S.A.	
143 D3	Clewiston U.S.A.	
97 A2	Clifden Ireland	
53 D1	Clifton Austr.	
138 B2	Clifton U.S.A.	
97 C2	Clinton Can.	
137 E2	Clinton IA U.S.A.	
137 E3	Clinton MO U.S.A.	
139 D1	Clinton OK U.S.A.	
96 A2	Clisham h. U.K.	
98 B2	Clitheroe U.K.	
97 B3	Clonakilty Ireland	
51 D2	Concurry Austr.	
97 C1	Clones Ireland	
97 C2	Clonmel Ireland	

Cloppenburg

100 D1	Cloppenburg Ger.	
50 A2	Cloud Break Austr.	
136 B2	Cloud Peak U.S.A.	
139 C2	Clovis U.S.A.	
129 D2	Cluff Lake Mine Can.	
110 B1	Cluj-Napoca Romania	
51 C2	Cluny Austr.	
105 D2	Cluses France	
54 A3	Clutha r. N.Z.	
96 B3	Clyde r. U.K.	
96 B3	Clyde, Firth of est. U.K.	
96 B3	Clydebank U.K.	
127 G2	Clyde River Can.	
144 B3	Coalcomán Mex.	
135 C3	Coaldale U.S.A.	
128 B2	Coal River Can.	
150 B2	Coari Brazil	
150 B2	Coari r. Brazil	
142 B2	Coastal Plain U.S.A.	
128 B2	Coast Mountains Can.	
135 B2	Coast Ranges mts U.S.A.	
96 B3	Coatbridge U.K.	
127 F2	Coats Island Can.	
55 K2	Coats Land reg. Antarctica	
145 C3	Coatzacoalcos Mex.	
146 A3	Cobán Guat.	
53 C2	Cobar Austr.	
97 B3	Cobh Ireland	
152 B2	Cobija Bol.	
141 D2	Cobourg Can.	
50 C1	Cobourg Peninsula Austr.	
53 C3	Cobram Austr.	
101 E2	Coburg Ger.	
152 B2	Cochabamba Bol.	
100 C2	Cochem Ger.	
	Cochin India see Kochi	
128 C2	Cochrane Alta Can.	
130 B2	Cochrane Ont. Can.	
153 A5	Cochrane Chile	
52 B2	Cockburn Austr.	
	Cockburn Town Turks and	
	Caicos Is see Grand Turk	
98 B1	Cockermouth U.K.	
122 B3	Cockscomb mt. S. Africa	
146 B3	Coco r. Hond./Nic.	
144 B3	Cocula Mex.	
150 A1	Cocuy, Sierra Nevada del	
	mt. Col.	
141 E2	Cod, Cape U.S.A.	
108 B2	Codigoro Italy	
131 D1	Cod Island Can.	
151 D2	Codó Brazil	
136 B2	Cody U.S.A.	
51 D1	Coen Austr.	
100 C2	Coesfeld Ger.	
134 C1	Coeur d'Alene U.S.A.	
123 C3	Coffee Bay S. Africa	
137 D3	Coffeyville U.S.A.	
53 D2	Coffs Harbour Austr.	
104 B2	Cognac France	
118 A2	Cogo Equat. Guinea	
52 B3	Cohuna Austr.	
146 B4	Coiba, Isla de i. Panama	
153 A5	Coihaique Chile	
73 B3	Coimbatore India	
106 B1	Coimbra Port.	
52 B3	Colac Austr.	
155 D1	Colatina Brazil	
136 C3	Colby U.S.A.	
99 D3	Colchester U.K.	
129 C2	Cold Lake Can.	
96 C3	Coldstream U.K.	
139 D2	Coleman U.S.A.	
97 C1	Coleraine U.K.	
52 B3	Coleraine Austr.	
123 C3	Colesberg S. Africa	
144 B3	Colima Mex.	

144 B3	Colima, Nevado de vol. Mex.	
96 A2	Coll i. U.K.	
53 C1	Collarenebri Austr.	
50 B1	Collier Bay Austr.	
54 B2	Collingwood N.Z.	
97 B1	Collooney Ireland	
105 D2	Colmar France	
100 C2	Cologne Ger.	
154 C2	Colômbia Brazil	
150 A1	Colombia country S. America	
73 B4	Colombo Sri Lanka	
104 C3	Colomiers France	
152 C4	Colón Arg.	
146 C4	Colón Panama	
109 C3	Colonna, Capo c. Italy	
96 A2	Colonsay i. U.K.	
153 B4	Colorado r. Arg.	
138 A2	Colorado r. Mex./U.S.A.	
139 D3	Colorado r. U.S.A.	
136 B3	Colorado state U.S.A.	
135 E3	Colorado Plateau U.S.A.	
136 C3	Colorado Springs U.S.A.	
144 B2	Cototlán Mex.	
136 B1	Colstrip U.S.A.	
137 E3	Columbia MO U.S.A.	
143 D2	Columbia SC U.S.A.	
142 C1	Columbia TN U.S.A.	
134 B1	Columbia r. U.S.A.	
128 C2	Columbia, Mount Can.	
142 C2	Columbia Falls U.S.A.	
128 C2	Columbia Mountains Can.	
134 C1	Columbia Plateau U.S.A.	
143 D2	Columbus GA U.S.A.	
140 B3	Columbus IN U.S.A.	
142 C2	Columbus MS U.S.A.	
137 D2	Columbus NE U.S.A.	
138 B2	Columbus NM U.S.A.	
140 C3	Columbus OH U.S.A.	
134 C1	Colville U.S.A.	
126 A2	Colville r. U.S.A.	
126 C2	Colville Lake Can.	
98 B2	Colwyn Bay U.K.	
108 B2	Comacchio Italy	
145 C3	Comalcalco Mex.	
110 C1	Comănești Romania	
130 C1	Comencho, Lac l. Can.	
97 C2	Comeragh Mountains hills	
	Ireland	
75 D2	Comilla Bangl.	
108 A2	Comino, Capo c. Sardegna Italy	
145 C3	Comitán de Domínguez Mex.	
104 C2	Commentry France	
139 D2	Commerce U.S.A.	
127 F2	Committee Bay Can.	
108 A1	Como Italy	
153 B5	Comodoro Rivadavia Arg.	
121 D2	Comoros country Africa	
104 C2	Compiègne France	
144 B2	Compostela Mex.	
90 B2	Comrat Moldova	
114 A4	Conakry Guinea	
155 L1	Conceição da Barra Brazil	
151 D2	Conceição do Araguaia Brazil	
155 D1	Conceição do Mato Dentro	
	Brazil	
152 B3	Concepción Arg.	
153 A4	Concepción Chile	
144 B2	Concepción Mex.	
135 B4	Conception, Point U.S.A.	
154 C2	Conchas Brazil	
138 C1	Conchas Lake U.S.A.	
144 B2	Conchos r. Chihuahua Mex.	
145 C2	Conchos r. Nuevo León/	
	Tamaulipas Mex.	
135 B3	Concord CA U.S.A.	
141 E2	Concord NH U.S.A.	
152 C4	Concordia Arg.	

122 A2	Concordia S. Africa	
137 D3	Concordia U.S.A.	
53 C2	Condobolin Austr.	
104 C3	Condom France	
134 B1	Condon U.S.A.	
108 B1	Conegliano Italy	
104 C2	Confolens France	
75 C2	Congdü China	
118 B3	Congo country Africa	
118 B3	Congo r. Congo/Dem. Rep.	
	Congo	
118 C3	Congo, Democratic Republic	
	of the country Africa	
129 C2	Conklin Can.	
97 B1	Conn, Lough l. Ireland	
97 B2	Connaught reg. Ireland	
141 E2	Connecticut r. U.S.A.	
141 E2	Connecticut state U.S.A.	
97 B2	Connemara reg. Ireland	
134 D1	Conrad U.S.A.	
139 D2	Conroe U.S.A.	
155 D2	Conselheiro Lafaiete Brazil	
155 D1	Conselheiro Pena Brazil	
98 C1	Consett U.K.	
63 B3	Côn Sơn, Đao i. Vietnam	
110 C2	Constanţa Romania	
106 B2	Constantina Spain	
115 C1	Constantine Alg.	
134 D2	Contact U.S.A.	
150 A2	Contamana Peru	
153 A6	Contreras, Isla i. Chile	
126 D2	Contwoyto Lake Can.	
142 B1	Conway AR U.S.A.	
141 E2	Conway NH U.S.A.	
51 C2	Coober Pedy Austr.	
	Cook, Mount mt. N.Z. see	
	Aoraki	
143 C1	Cookeville U.S.A.	
49 H4	Cook Islands S. Pacific Ocean	
131 E1	Cook's Harbour Can.	
97 C1	Cookstown U.K.	
54 B2	Cook Strait N.Z.	
51 D1	Cooktown Austr.	
53 C2	Coolabah Austr.	
53 C2	Coolamon Austr.	
53 D1	Coolangatta Austr.	
50 B3	Coolgardie Austr.	
53 C3	Cooma Austr.	
52 B2	Coombah Austr.	
53 C2	Coonabarabran Austr.	
52 A3	Coonalpyn Austr.	
53 C2	Coonamble Austr.	
52 A1	Cooper Creek watercourse	
	Austr.	
134 B2	Coos Bay U.S.A.	
53 C2	Cootamundra Austr.	
145 C3	Copainalá Mex.	
145 C3	Copala Mex.	
93 F4	Copenhagen Denmark	
109 C2	Copertino Italy	
152 A3	Copiapó Chile	
140 B1	Copper Harbor U.S.A.	
	Coppermine Can. see	
	Kugluktuk	
126 D2	Coppermine r. Can.	
122 B2	Copperton S. Africa	
152 A3	Coquimbo Chile	
110 B2	Corabia Romania	
155 D1	Coração de Jesus Brazil	
150 A3	Coracora Peru	
53 D1	Coraki Austr.	
50 A2	Coral Bay Austr.	
127 F2	Coral Harbour Can.	
156 D7	Coral Sea S. Pacific Ocean	
48 D4	Coral Sea Islands Territory	
	Austr.	
52 B3	Corangamite, Lake Austr.	
99 C2	Corby U.K.	

180

51 D3 Currie Austr.
51 E2 Curtis Island Austr.
151 C1 Curuá r. Brazil
60 B2 Curup Indon.
151 C2 Cururupu Brazil
155 D1 Curvelo Brazil
150 A3 Cusco Peru
139 D1 Cushing U.S.A.
134 C1 Cut Bank U.S.A.
75 C2 Cuttack India
101 D1 Cuxhaven Ger.
64 B1 Cuyo Islands Phil.
Cuzco Peru see Cusco
119 C3 Cyangugu Rwanda
111 B3 Cyclades is Greece
129 C3 Cypress Hills Can.
80 B2 Cyprus country Asia
102 C2 Czech Republic country Europe
103 D1 Czersk Pol.
103 D1 Częstochowa Pol.

D

Đa, Sông r. Vietnam see
Black River
69 D2 Daban China
114 A4 Dabola Guinea
Dacca Bangl. see Dhaka
102 C2 Dachau Ger.
74 A2 Dadu Pak.
64 B1 Daet Phil.
114 A3 Dagana Senegal
64 B1 Dagupan Phil.
74 B3 Dahanu India
69 D2 Da Hinggan Ling mts China
116 C3 Dahlak Archipelago is Eritrea
100 C2 Dahlem Ger.
78 B3 Dahm, Ramlat des.
audi Arabia/Yemen
60 B2 Daik Indon.
106 C2 Daimiel Spain
51 C2 Dajarra Austr.
114 A3 Dakar Senegal
116 A2 Dākhilah, Wāḥāt ad oasis Egypt
Dakhla Oasis Egypt see Dākhilah, Wāḥāt ad
63 A3 Dakoank India
88 C3 Dakol'ka r. Belarus
109 C1 Đakovica Kosovo see Gjakovë
109 C1 Đakovo Croatia
120 B2 Dala Angola
68 C2 Dalain Hob China
93 G3 Dalälven r. Sweden
111 C3 Dalaman Turkey
111 C3 Dalaman r. Turkey
69 C2 Dalandzadgad Mongolia
63 B2 Đa Lat Vietnam
74 A2 Dalbandin Pak.
96 C3 Dalbeattie U.K.
51 E2 Dalby Austr.
143 C1 Dale Hollow Lake U.S.A.
53 C3 Dalgety Austr.
139 C1 Dalhart U.S.A.
131 D2 Dalhousie Can.
62 B1 Dali China
70 C2 Dalian China
96 C3 Dalkeith U.K.
139 D2 Dallas U.S.A.
128 A2 Dall Island U.S.A.
109 C2 Dalmatia reg. Bos.-Herz./ Croatia
66 C2 Dal'negorsk Rus. Fed.
66 B1 Dal'nerechensk Rus. Fed.
114 B4 Daloa Côte d'Ivoire

51 D2 Dalrymple, Mount Austr.
92 □A3 Dalsmynni Iceland
75 C2 Daltenganj India
143 D2 Dalton U.S.A.
60 B1 Daludalu Indon.
92 □B2 Dalvík Iceland
50 C1 Daly r. Austr.
51 C1 Daly Waters Austr.
74 B2 Daman India
116 B2 Damanhūr Egypt
59 C3 Damar i. Indon.
80 B2 Damascus Syria
115 D3 Damaturu Nigeria
76 B3 Damāvand, Qolleh-ye mt. Iran
81 D2 Dāmghān Iran
79 C2 Dammam Saudi Arabia
101 D1 Damme Ger.
75 B2 Damoh India
114 B4 Damongo Ghana
59 C3 Dampir, Selat sea chan. Indon.
75 C2 Damqoq Zangbo r. China
117 C3 Danakil reg. Africa
114 B4 Danané Côte d'Ivoire
63 B2 Đa Năng Vietnam
141 E2 Danbury U.S.A.
65 A1 Dandong China
146 B3 Dangriga Belize
70 B2 Dangshan China
89 F2 Danilov Rus. Fed.
89 E2 Danilovskaya Vozvyshennost' hills Rus. Fed.
70 B2 Danjiangkou China
89 E3 Dankov Rus. Fed.
146 B3 Danlí Hond.
101 E1 Dannenberg (Elbe) Ger.
54 C2 Dannevirke N.Z.
62 B2 Dan Sai Thai.
Dantu China see Zhenjiang
110 A1 Danube r. Europe
110 C1 Danube Delta Romania/Ukr.
140 B2 Danville IL. U.S.A.
140 C3 Danville KY U.S.A.
141 D3 Danville VA U.S.A.
71 A4 Danzhou China
71 B3 Daoxian China
114 C4 Dapaong Togo
64 C2 Dapitan Phil.
68 C2 Da Qaidam China
69 E1 Daqing China
80 B2 Dar'ā Syria
79 C2 Dārāb Iran
81 D2 Dārān Iran
75 C2 Darbhanga India
119 D3 Dar es Salaam Tanz.
117 A3 Darfur reg. Sudan
74 B1 Dargai Pak.
54 B1 Dargaville N.Z.
53 C3 Dargo Austr.
69 D1 Darhan Mongolia
150 A1 Darién, Golfo del g. Col.
75 C2 Darjiling India
52 B2 Darling r. Austr.
53 C1 Darling Downs hills Austr.
50 A3 Darling Range hills Austr.
98 C1 Darlington U.K.
53 C2 Darlington Point Austr.
103 D1 Darłowo Pol.
101 D3 Darmstadt Ger.
115 E1 Darnah Libya
52 B2 Darnick Austr.
107 C1 Daroca Spain
99 D3 Dartford U.K.
99 A3 Dartmoor hills U.K.
131 D2 Dartmouth Can.
99 B3 Dartmouth U.K.
59 D3 Daru P.N.G.
50 C1 Darwin Austr.

74 A2 Dasht r. Pak.
76 B2 Daşoguz Turkm.
61 C1 Datadian Indon.
111 C3 Datça Turkey
70 B1 Datong China
71 B3 Datu Piang Phil.
74 B1 Daud Khel Pak.
88 B2 Daugava r. Latvia
88 C2 Daugavpils Latvia
100 C2 Daun Ger.
129 C2 Dauphin Can.
129 E2 Dauphin Lake Can.
73 B3 Davangere India
64 B2 Davao Phil.
64 B2 Davao Gulf Phil.
137 C2 Davenport U.S.A.
99 C2 Daventry U.K.
123 C2 Daveyton S. Africa
146 B4 David Panama
129 C2 Davidson Can.
126 E3 Davidson Lake Can.
135 B3 Davis U.S.A.
131 D1 Davis Inlet (abandoned) Can.
159 F3 Davis Sea Antarctica
160 P3 Davis Strait Can./Greenland
105 D2 Davos Switz.
78 A2 Dawmat al Jandal Saudi Arabia
79 C3 Dawqah Oman
126 B2 Dawson Can.
143 D3 Dawson U.S.A.
128 B2 Dawson Creek Can.
128 B2 Dawsons Landing Can.
68 C2 Dawu China
Dawukou China see Shizuishan
104 B3 Dax France
68 C2 Da Xueshan mts China
80 C2 Dayr az Zawr Syria
140 C3 Dayton U.S.A.
143 D3 Daytona Beach U.S.A.
70 A2 Dazhou China
122 B3 De Aar S. Africa
80 B2 Dead Sea salt l. Asia
71 B3 De'an China
152 B4 Deán Funes Arg.
128 B2 Dease Lake Can.
126 D2 Dease Strait Can.
135 C3 Death Valley depr. U.S.A.
104 C2 Deauville France
61 C1 Debak Sarawak Malaysia
109 D2 Debar Macedonia
103 E2 Debrecen Hungary
117 B3 Debre Markos Eth.
117 B4 Debre Zeyit Eth.
142 C2 Decatur AL U.S.A.
140 B3 Decatur IL U.S.A.
73 B3 Deccan plat. India
102 C1 Děčín Czech Rep.
137 E2 Decorah U.S.A.
88 C2 Dedovichi Rus. Fed.
121 C2 Dedza Malawi
98 B2 Dee r. England/Wales U.K.
96 C2 Dee r. Scotland U.K.
53 D1 Deepwater Austr.
131 E2 Deer Lake Can.
134 D1 Deer Lodge U.S.A.
140 C2 Defiance U.S.A.
68 C2 Dêgê China
117 C4 Degeh Bur Eth.
102 C2 Deggendorf Ger.
91 E2 Degtevo Rus. Fed.
75 B1 Dehra Dun India
75 C2 Dehri India
69 E2 Dehui China
100 A2 Deinze Belgium
110 B1 Dej Romania

Elandsdoorn

F

Gäncä

54	C1	Gisborne N.Z.
93	F4	Gislaved Sweden
119	C3	Gitarama Rwanda
108	B2	Giulianova Italy
110	C2	Giurgiu Romania
110	C1	Giuvala, Pasul pass Romania
105	C2	Givors France
123	D1	Giyani S. Africa
116	B2	Giza Egypt
109	D2	Gjakovë Kosovo
109	D2	Gjilan Kosovo
109	D2	Gjirokastër Albania
126	E2	Gjoa Haven Can.
93	F3	Gjøvik Norway
131	E2	Glace Bay Can.
134	B1	Glacier Peak vol. U.S.A.
51	E2	Gladstone Austr.
92	□A2	Gláma mts Iceland
100	C3	Glan r. Ger.
97	B2	Glanaruddery Mountains hills Ireland
96	B3	Glasgow U.K.
140	B3	Glasgow KY U.S.A.
136	B1	Glasgow MT U.S.A.
99	B3	Glastonbury U.K.
101	F2	Glauchau Ger.
85	E3	Glazov Rus. Fed.
89	E3	Glazunovka Rus. Fed.
96	B2	Glen Coe val. U.K.
138	A2	Glendale U.S.A.
53	D2	Glen Davis Austr.
136	C1	Glendive U.S.A.
52	B3	Glenelg r. Austr.
53	D1	Glen Innes Austr.
126	B2	Glennallen U.S.A.
96	C2	Glenrothes U.K.
141	E2	Glens Falls U.S.A.
96	C2	Glen Shee val. U.K.
97	B1	Glenties Ireland
138	B2	Glenwood U.S.A.
136	B3	Glenwood Springs U.S.A.
103	D1	Gliwice Pol.
100	C1	Glückstadt Ger.
103	D1	Głogów Pol.
92	F2	Glomfjord Norway
93	F4	Glomma r. Norway
53	D2	Gloucester Austr.
99	B3	Gloucester U.K.
101	F1	Glöwen Ger.
77	E1	Glubokoye Kazakh.
101	D1	Glückstadt Ger.
103	C2	Gmünd Austria
102	C2	Gmunden Austria
101	D1	Gnarrenburg Ger.
103	D1	Gniezno Pol.
75	D2	Goalpara India
96	B3	Goat Fell h. U.K.
117	C4	Goba Eth.
120	A3	Gobabis Namibia
153	A5	Gobernador Gregores Arg.
69	D2	Gobi des. China/Mongolia
100	C2	Goch Ger.
122	A1	Gochas Namibia
74	B3	Godavari r. India
73	C3	Godavari, Mouths of the India
130	B2	Goderich Can.
74	B2	Godhra India
129	E2	Gods r. Can.
129	E2	Gods Lake Can.
		Godthåb Greenland see Nuuk
		Godwin-Austen, Mount China/Pakistan see K2
130	C2	Goéland, Lac au l. Can.
131	D1	Goélands, Lac aux l. Can.
100	A2	Goes Neth.
154	C1	Goiandira Brazil
154	C1	Goiânia Brazil
154	B1	Goiás Brazil
154	B2	Goiás state Brazil
111	C2	Gökçeada i. Turkey
111	C3	Gökçedağ Turkey
121	B2	Gokwe Zimbabwe
93	E3	Gol Norway
62	A1	Golaghat India
111	C2	Gölcük Turkey
103	E1	Gołdap Pol.
101	F1	Goldberg Ger.
53	D1	Gold Coast Austr.
114	B4	Gold Coast Ghana
128	C2	Golden Can.
54	B2	Golden Bay N.Z.
128	B3	Golden Hinde mt. Can.
97	B2	Golden Vale lowland Ireland
135	C3	Goldfield U.S.A.
128	B3	Gold River Can.
143	E1	Goldsboro U.S.A.
135	C4	Goleta U.S.A.
68	C2	Golmud China
81	D2	Golpäyegän Iran
96	C2	Golspie U.K.
119	C3	Goma Dem. Rep. Congo
75	C2	Gomati r. India
115	D3	Gombe Nigeria
115	D3	Gombi Nigeria
		Gomel' Belarus see Homyel'
144	B2	Gómez Palacio Mex.
147	C3	Gonaïves Haiti
147	C3	Gonâve, Île de la i. Haiti
81	D2	Gonbad-e Kävüs Iran
117	B3	Gonder Eth.
75	C2	Gondia India
111	C2	Gönen Turkey
115	D4	Gongola r. Nigeria
53	C2	Gongolgon Austr.
75	D1	Gongtang China
145	C2	Gonzáles Mex.
139	D3	Gonzales U.S.A.
122	A3	Good Hope, Cape of S. Africa
134	D2	Gooding U.S.A.
136	C3	Goodland U.S.A.
53	C1	Goodooga Austr.
98	C2	Goole U.K.
53	C2	Goolgowi Austr.
52	A3	Goolwa Austr.
53	D1	Goondiwindi Austr.
134	B2	Goose Lake U.S.A.
102	B2	Göppingen Ger.
75	C2	Gorakhpur India
109	C2	Goražde Bos.-Herz.
111	C3	Gördes Turkey
89	D3	Gordeyevka Rus. Fed.
51	D4	Gordon, Lake Austr.
115	D4	Goré Chad
117	B4	Gorē Eth.
54	A3	Gore N.Z.
97	C2	Gorey Ireland
81	D2	Gorgän Iran
81	C1	Gori Georgia
108	B1	Gorizia Italy
		Gor'kiy Rus. Fed. see Nizhniy Novgorod
103	D1	Gorlice Pol.
103	C1	Görlitz Ger.
109	D2	Gornji Milanovac Serbia
109	C2	Gornji Vakuf Bos.-Herz.
77	E1	Gorno-Altaysk Rus. Fed.
110	C2	Gornotrakiyska Nizina lowland Bulg.
77	E1	Gornyak Rus. Fed.
59	D3	Goroka P.N.G.
114	B3	Gorom Gorom Burkina Faso
59	C2	Gorontalo Indon.
89	E3	Gorshechnoye Rus. Fed.
97	B2	Gorumna Island Ireland
91	D3	Goryachiy Klyuch Rus. Fed.
103	D1	Górzów Wielkopolski Pol.
53	D2	Gosford Austr.
66	D2	Goshogawara Japan
101	E2	Goslar Ger.
109	C2	Gospić Croatia
99	C3	Gosport U.K.
109	D2	Gostivar Macedonia
		Göteborg Sweden see Gothenburg
101	E2	Gotha Ger.
93	F4	Gothenburg Sweden
136	C2	Gothenburg U.S.A.
93	G4	Gotland i. Sweden
111	B2	Gotse Delchev Bulg.
93	G4	Gotska Sandön i. Sweden
67	B4	Götsu Japan
101	D2	Göttingen Ger.
128	B2	Gott Peak Can.
100	B1	Gouda Neth.
114	A3	Goudiri Senegal
115	D3	Goudoumaria Niger
130	C2	Gouin, Réservoir resr Can.
53	C2	Goulburn Austr.
53	B3	Goulburn r. N.S.W. Austr.
53	B3	Goulburn r. Vic. Austr.
114	B3	Goundam Mali
107	D2	Gouraya Alg.
105	C2	Gourdon France
115	D3	Gouré Niger
122	B3	Gourits r. S. Africa
114	B3	Gourma-Rharous Mali
53	C3	Gourock Range mts Austr.
155	D1	Governador Valadares Brazil
143	E3	Governor's Harbour Bahamas
68	C2	Govĭ Altayn Nuruu mts Mongolia
75	C2	Govind Ballash Pant Sagar resr India
99	A3	Gower pen. U.K.
152	C3	Goya Arg.
81	C1	Göyçay Azer.
75	C1	Gozha Co salt l. China
122	B3	Graaff-Reinet S. Africa
101	E1	Grabow Ger.
109	C2	Gračac Croatia
87	E3	Grachevka Rus. Fed.
101	F2	Gräfenhainichen Ger.
53	D1	Grafton Austr.
137	D1	Grafton U.S.A.
139	D2	Graham U.S.A.
128	A2	Graham Island Can.
55	P3	Graham Land pen. Antarctica
123	C3	Grahamstown S. Africa
151	D2	Grajaú Brazil
111	B2	Grammos mt. Greece
96	B2	Grampian Mountains U.K.
146	B3	Granada Nic.
106	C2	Granada Spain
141	E1	Granby Can.
114	A2	Gran Canaria i. Islas Canarias
152	B3	Gran Chaco reg. Arg./Para.
136	C1	Grand r. U.S.A.
146	C2	Grand Bahama i. Bahamas
131	E2	Grand Bank Can.
158	C2	Grand Banks of Newfoundland N. Atlantic Ocean
138	A1	Grand Canyon U.S.A.
138	A1	Grand Canyon gorge U.S.A.
146	B3	Grand Cayman i. Cayman Is
129	C2	Grand Centre Can.
134	C1	Grand Coulee U.S.A.
152	B2	Grande r. Bol.
154	B2	Grande r. Brazil
153	B6	Grande, Bahía b. Arg.

194

Hope Mountains

131	D1	Hope Mountains Can.
52	B3	Hopetoun Austr.
122	B2	Hopetown S. Africa
141	D3	Hopewell U.S.A.
130	C1	Hopewell Islands Can.
50	B2	Hopkins, Lake *imp. l.* Austr.
140	B3	Hopkinsville U.S.A.
134	B1	Hoquiam U.S.A.
81	C1	Horasan Turkey
93	F4	Hörby Sweden
89	D3	Horki Belarus
91	D2	Horlivka Ukr.
79	D2	Hormak Iran
79	C2	Hormuz, Strait of Iran/Oman
103	D2	Horn Austria
92	□A2	Horn *c.* Iceland
153	B6	Horn, Cape Chile
141	D2	Hornell U.S.A.
130	B2	Hornepayne Can.
98	C2	Hornsea U.K.
90	B2	Horodenka Ukr.
91	C1	Horodnya Ukr.
90	B2	Horodok *Khmel'nyts'ka Oblast'* Ukr.
90	A2	Horodok *L'vivs'ka Oblast'* Ukr.
90	A1	Horokhiv Ukr.
		Horqin Youyi Qianqi China *see* Ulanhot
131	E1	Horse Islands Can.
52	B3	Horsham Austr.
126	C2	Horton *r.* Can.
117	B4	Hosa'ina Eth.
74	A2	Hoshab Pak.
74	B1	Hoshiarpur India
77	E3	Hotan China
122	B2	Hotazel S. Africa
142	B2	Hot Springs *AR* U.S.A.
136	C2	Hot Springs *SD* U.S.A.
128	C1	Hottah Lake Can.
62	B1	Houayxay Laos
100	B2	Houffalize Belgium
70	B2	Houma China
143	D3	Houma U.S.A.
128	B2	Houston Can.
139	D3	Houston U.S.A.
122	B3	Houwater S. Africa
68	C1	Hovd Mongolia
99	C3	Hove U.K.
68	C1	Hövsgöl Nuur *l.* Mongolia
116	A3	Howar, Wadi *watercourse* Sudan
53	C3	Howe, Cape Austr.
49	G2	Howland Island N. Pacific Ocean
53	C3	Howlong Austr.
101	D2	Höxter Ger.
96	C1	Hoy *i.* U.K.
93	E3	Høyanger Norway
102	C1	Hoyerswerda Ger.
62	A2	Hpapun Myanmar
103	D1	Hradec Králové Czech Rep.
109	C2	Hrasnica Bos.-Herz.
91	C1	Hrebinka Ukr.
88	B3	Hrodna Belarus
62	A1	Hsi-hseng Myanmar
62	A1	Hsipaw Myanmar
70	A2	Huachi China
150	A3	Huacho Peru
69	D2	Huade China
65	B1	Huadian China
70	B2	Huai'an China
70	B2	Huaibei China
71	A3	Huaihua China
70	B2	Huainan China
70	B2	Huaiyang China
145	C3	Huajuápan de León Mex.
59	C3	Huaki Indon.
71	C3	Hualian Taiwan
150	A2	Huallaga *r.* Peru
120	A2	Huambo Angola
150	A3	Huancayo Peru
		Huangcaoba China *see* Xingyi
70	B2	Huangchuan China
		Huang Hai *sea* N. Pacific Ocean *see* Yellow Sea
		Huang He *r.* China *see* Yellow River
71	B3	Huangliu China
70	B3	Huangshan China
70	B2	Huangshi China
70	A2	Huangtu Gaoyuan *plat.* China
71	C3	Huangyan China
65	B1	Huanren China
150	A2	Huánuco Peru
152	B2	Huanuni Bol.
150	A2	Huaráz Peru
150	A3	Huarmey Peru
152	A3	Huasco Chile
152	A3	Huasco *r.* Chile
144	B2	Huatabampo Mex.
145	C3	Huatusco Mex.
71	A3	Huayuan China
		Hubballi India *see* Hubli
70	B2	Hubei *prov.* China
73	B3	Hubli India
100	C2	Hückelhoven Ger.
98	C2	Hucknall U.K.
98	C2	Huddersfield U.K.
93	G3	Hudiksvall Sweden
141	E2	Hudson *r.* U.S.A.
127	F3	Hudson Bay Can.
128	B2	Hudson's Hope Can.
127	G2	Hudson Strait Can.
63	B2	Huê Vietnam
146	A3	Huehuetenango Guat.
144	B2	Huehueto, Cerro *mt.* Mex.
145	C2	Huejutla Mex.
106	B2	Huelva Spain
107	C2	Huércal-Overa Spain
107	C1	Huesca Spain
106	C2	Huéscar Spain
50	B3	Hughes (abandoned) Austr.
139	D2	Hugo U.S.A.
122	B2	Huhudi S. Africa
122	A2	Huib-Hoch Plateau Namibia
71	B3	Huichang China
65	B1	Huich'ŏn N. Korea
120	A2	Huíla, Planalto da Angola
71	B3	Huilai China
62	B1	Huili China
59	C3	Huinan China
93	H3	Huittinen Fin.
145	C3	Huixtla Mex.
		Huiyang China *see* Huizhou
62	B1	Huize China
71	B3	Huizhou China
78	B2	Hujr Saudi Arabia
122	B1	Hukuntsi Botswana
78	B2	Ḩulayfah Saudi Arabia
66	B1	Hulin China
130	C2	Hull Can.
		Hull China *see* Hulun Buir
69	D1	Hulun Buir China
69	D1	Hulun Nur *l.* China
91	D2	Hulyaypole Ukr.
69	E1	Huma China
150	B2	Humaitá Brazil
122	B3	Humansdorp S. Africa
		Humber *est.* U.K.
135	C2	Humboldt Can.
135	C2	Humboldt U.S.A.
103	E2	Humenné Slovakia
53	C3	Hume Reservoir Austr.
138	A1	Humphreys Peak U.S.A.
92	□A2	Húnaflói *b.* Iceland
71	B3	Hunan *prov.* China
65	C1	Hunchun China
110	B1	Hunedoara Romania
101	D2	Hünfeld Ger.
103	D2	Hungary *country* Europe
52	B1	Hungerford Austr.
65	B2	Hŭngnam N. Korea
99	D2	Hunstanton U.K.
101	D1	Hunte *r.* Ger.
51	D4	Hunter Islands Austr.
99	C2	Huntingdon U.K.
140	B2	Huntington *IN* U.S.A.
140	C3	Huntington *WV* U.S.A.
54	C1	Huntly N.Z.
96	C2	Huntly U.K.
130	C2	Huntsville Can.
142	C2	Huntsville *AL* U.S.A.
139	D2	Huntsville *TX* U.S.A.
59	D3	Huon Peninsula P.N.G.
70	B2	Huozhou China
137	D2	Huron U.S.A.
140	C2	Huron, Lake Can./U.S.A.
135	D3	Hurricane U.S.A.
92	□B2	Húsavík Iceland
110	C1	Huşi Romania
126	A2	Huslia U.S.A.
78	B3	Ḩuşn Al Abr Yemen
102	B1	Husum Ger.
69	C1	Hutag-Öndör Mongolia
60	A1	Hutanopan Indon.
137	D3	Hutchinson U.S.A.
70	C2	Huzhou China
92	□C3	Hvalnes Iceland
92	□B2	Hvannadalshnúkur *vol.* Iceland
109	C2	Hvar *i.* Croatia
121	B2	Hwange Zimbabwe
136	C2	Hyannis U.S.A.
68	C1	Hyargas Nuur *salt l.* Mongolia
50	A3	Hyden Austr.
73	B3	Hyderabad India
74	A2	Hyderabad Pak.
105	D3	Hyères France
105	D3	Hyères, Îles d' *is* France
65	B1	Hyesan N. Korea
128	B2	Hyland Post Can.
67	B3	Hyōno-sen *mt.* Japan
99	D3	Hythe U.K.
93	H3	Hyvinkää Fin.

I

150	B2	Iaco *r.* Brazil
110	C2	Ialomița *r.* Romania
110	C1	Ianca Romania
110	C1	Iași Romania
64	A1	Iba Phil.
115	C4	Ibadan Nigeria
150	A1	Ibagué Col.
150	A1	Ibarra Ecuador
78	B3	Ibb Yemen
100	C1	Ibbenbüren Ger.
115	C4	Ibi Nigeria
155	C1	Ibiá Brazil
155	D1	Ibiraçu Brazil
107	D2	Ibiza Spain
107	D2	Ibiza *i.* Spain
151	D3	Ibotirama Brazil
79	C2	Ibrā' Oman
79	C2	Ibri Oman
150	A3	Ica Peru
92	□B2	Iceland *country* Europe
66	D3	Ichinoseki Japan

J

154 B2 **Jaraguari** Brazil
70 A2 **Jarantai** China
152 C3 **Jardim** Brazil
103 D1 **Jarocin** Pol.
103 E1 **Jarosław** Pol.
92 F3 **Järpen** Sweden
150 B3 **Järup** Brazil
    Jarud China *see* **Lubei**
49 H3 **Jarvis Island**
    S. Pacific Ocean
79 C2 **Jāsk** Iran
103 E2 **Jasło** Pol.
128 C2 **Jasper** Can.
140 B3 **Jasper** IN U.S.A.
139 F2 **Jasper** TX U.S.A.
103 D2 **Jastrzębie-Zdrój** Pol.
103 D2 **Jászberény** Hungary
154 B1 **Jataí** Brazil
74 A2 **Jati** Pak.
154 C2 **Jaú** Brazil
154 C2 **Jaú** r. Brazil
145 C2 **Jaumave** Mex.
75 C2 **Jaunpur** India
154 B1 **Jauru** Brazil
61 B2 **Java** i. Indon.
    Java Sea Indon. *see* **Jawa, Laut**
    Jawa i. Indon. *see* **Java**
159 D4 **Jawa, Laut** sea Indon.
117 C4 **Jawhar** Somalia
103 D1 **Jawor** Pol.
103 D1 **Jaworzno** Pol.
59 D3 **Jaya, Puncak** mt. Indon.
59 D3 **Jayapura** Indon.
79 C2 **Jaz Mūrīān, Hāmūn-e** imp. l.
    Iran
128 B1 **Jean Marie River** Can.
131 D1 **Jeannin, Lac** l. Can.
116 A3 **Jebel Abyad Plateau** Sudan
96 C3 **Jedburgh** U.K.
78 A2 **Jeddah** Saudi Arabia
101 E1 **Jeetze** r. Ger.
135 C3 **Jefferson, Mount** U.S.A.
137 E3 **Jefferson City** U.S.A.
88 C2 **Jēkabpils** Latvia
103 D1 **Jelenia Góra** Pol.
88 B2 **Jelgava** Latvia
61 C2 **Jember** Indon.
101 E2 **Jena** Ger.
    Jengish Chokusu mt. China/
    Kyrg. *see* **Pobeda Peak**
80 B2 **Jenin** West Bank
142 B2 **Jennings** U.S.A.
151 B3 **Jequié** Brazil
155 D1 **Jequitaí** Brazil
155 D1 **Jequitinhonha** Brazil
155 E1 **Jequitinhonha** r. Brazil
147 C3 **Jérémie** Haiti
144 B2 **Jerez** Mex.
106 B2 **Jerez de la Frontera** Spain
109 D3 **Jergucat** Albania
115 C1 **Jerid, Chott el** salt l.
    Tunisia
134 D2 **Jerome** U.S.A.
95 C4 **Jersey** terr. Channel Is
151 B2 **Jerumenha** Brazil
80 B2 **Jerusalem** Israel/West Bank
53 D3 **Jervis Bay Territory** admin. div.
    Austr.
108 B1 **Jesenice** Slovenia
108 B2 **Jesi** Italy
101 F2 **Jessen** Ger.
75 C2 **Jessore** Bangl.
143 D2 **Jesup** U.S.A.
145 C3 **Jesús Carranza** Mex.
109 C2 **Jezercë, Maja** mt. Albania
74 B2 **Jhalawar** India
74 B1 **Jhang** Pak.

75 B2 **Jhansi** India
75 C2 **Jharsuguda** India
74 B1 **Jhelum** Pak.
70 C2 **Jiading** China
69 E1 **Jiamusi** China
71 B3 **Ji'an** *Jiangxi* China
65 B1 **Ji'an** *Jilin* China
62 A1 **Jianchuan** China
    Jiandaoyu China *see* **Guojiaba**
70 B2 **Jiangsu** prov. China
71 B3 **Jiangxi** prov. China
70 A2 **Jiangyou** China
70 B3 **Jianli** China
70 C2 **Jianqiao** China
71 B3 **Jianyang** *Fujian* China
70 A2 **Jianyang** *Sichuan* China
70 C2 **Jiaozhou** China
70 B2 **Jiaozuo** China
70 C2 **Jiaxing** China
71 C3 **Jiayi** Taiwan
68 C2 **Jiayuguan** China
    Jiddah Saudi Arabia *see* **Jeddah**
92 G2 **Jiehkkevárri** mt. Norway
70 B2 **Jiexiu** China
68 C2 **Jigzhi** China
103 D2 **Jihlava** Czech Rep.
116 A2 **Jilf al Kabīr, Haḍabat al** plat.
    Egypt
117 C4 **Jilib** Somalia
69 E2 **Jilin** China
65 B1 **Jilin** prov. China
65 A1 **Jilin Hada Ling** mts China
117 B4 **Jima** Eth.
144 B2 **Jiménez** *Chihuahua* Mex.
145 C2 **Jiménez** *Tamaulipas* Mex.
70 B2 **Jinan** China
70 B2 **Jincheng** China
53 C3 **Jindabyne** Austr.
103 D2 **Jindřichův Hradec** Czech Rep.
71 B3 **Jingdezhen** China
70 B2 **Jinghang Yunhe** canal China
    Jinghang Yunhe canal China
    see **Jinghang Yunhe**
62 B1 **Jinghong** China
70 B2 **Jingmen** China
70 A2 **Jingning** China
70 B2 **Jingtai** China
71 A3 **Jingxi** China
71 B3 **Jingyu** China
70 A2 **Jingyuan** China
70 B2 **Jingzhou** China
70 B2 **Jingzhou** China
71 B3 **Jinhua** China
    Jining *Shandong* China
119 D2 **Jinja** Uganda
117 B3 **Jinka** Eth.
146 B3 **Jinotepe** Nic.
71 A3 **Jinping** China
    Jinsha Jiang r. China *see*
    Yangtze
70 B3 **Jinshi** China
70 C1 **Jinzhou** China
150 B2 **Jiparaná** r. Brazil
79 C2 **Jiroft** Iran
71 A3 **Jishou** China
110 B2 **Jiu** r. Romania
70 A2 **Jiuding Shan** mt. China
70 B3 **Jiujiang** China
66 B1 **Jixi** China
78 B3 **Jīzān** Saudi Arabia
77 C2 **Jizzax** Uzbek.
151 E2 **João Pessoa** Brazil
155 C1 **João Pinheiro** Brazil
74 B2 **Jodhpur** India

92 I3 **Joensuu** Fin.
67 C3 **Jōetsu** Japan
121 C3 **Jofane** Moz.
88 C2 **Jõgeva** Estonia
123 C2 **Johannesburg** S. Africa
134 C2 **John Day** U.S.A.
134 B1 **John Day** r. U.S.A.
131 D1 **John D'Or Prairie** Can.
143 E1 **John H. Kerr Reservoir** U.S.A.
96 C1 **John o' Groats** U.K.
143 D1 **Johnson City** U.S.A.
128 A1 **Johnson's Crossing** Can.
49 H1 **Johnston Atoll** N. Pacific
    Ocean
96 B3 **Johnstone** U.K.
141 D2 **Johnstown** U.S.A.
60 B1 **Johor Bahru** Malaysia
88 C2 **Jõhvi** Estonia
154 C3 **Joinville** Brazil
105 D2 **Joinville** France
92 □B2 **Jökulsá á Fjöllum** r. Iceland
140 B2 **Joliet** U.S.A.
130 C2 **Joliette** Can.
64 B2 **Jolo** Phil.
64 B2 **Jolo** i. Phil.
61 C2 **Jombang** Indon.
75 C2 **Jomsom** Nepal
88 B2 **Jonava** Lith.
142 B1 **Jonesboro** AR U.S.A.
142 B1 **Jonesboro** LA U.S.A.
127 F1 **Jones Sound** sea chan. Can.
93 F4 **Jönköping** Sweden
131 C2 **Jonquière** Can.
145 C3 **Jonuta** Mex.
137 E3 **Joplin** U.S.A.
131 D1 **Joseph, Lac** l. Can.
50 B2 **Joseph Bonaparte Gulf** Austr.
115 C4 **Jos Plateau** Nigeria
93 E3 **Jotunheimen** mts Norway
122 B3 **Joubertina** S. Africa
123 C2 **Jouberton** S. Africa
93 I3 **Joutseno** Fin.
134 B1 **Juan de Fuca Strait**
    Can./U.S.A.
    Juanshui China *see*
    Tongcheng
145 C2 **Juárez** Mex.
151 D2 **Juazeiro** Brazil
151 E2 **Juazeiro do Norte** Brazil
117 B4 **Juba** r. S. Sudan
117 C5 **Jubba** r. Somalia
78 A2 **Jubbah** Saudi Arabia
145 C3 **Juchitán** Mex.
102 C2 **Judenburg** Austria
101 D2 **Jühnde** Ger.
146 B3 **Juigalpa** Nic.
100 C1 **Juist** i. Ger.
155 D2 **Juiz de Fora** Brazil
150 A3 **Juliaca** Peru
75 C2 **Jumla** Nepal
74 B2 **Junagadh** India
137 D3 **Junction** U.S.A.
137 D3 **Junction City** U.S.A.
154 C2 **Jundiaí** Brazil
128 A2 **Juneau** U.S.A.
53 C2 **Junee** Austr.
105 D2 **Jungfrau** mt. Switz.
141 D2 **Juniata** r. U.S.A.

Junsele

76 B1 **Khromtau** Kazakh.
90 B2 **Khrystynivka** Ukr.
77 C2 **Khŭjand** Tajik.
63 B2 **Khu Khan** Thai.
78 A2 **Khulays** Saudi Arabia
75 C2 **Khulna** Bangl.
78 A2 **Khurays** Saudi Arabia
74 B1 **Khushāb** Pak.
90 A2 **Khust** Ukr.
123 C2 **Khutsong** S. Africa
74 A2 **Khuzdar** Pak.
81 D2 **Khvänsär** Iran
79 C2 **Khvormūj** Iran
81 C2 **Khvoy** Iran
89 D2 **Khvoynaya** Rus. Fed.
77 D3 **Khyber Pass** Afgh./Pak.
53 D2 **Kiama** Austr.
119 C3 **Kiambi** Dem. Rep. Congo
119 D3 **Kibiti** Tanz.
109 D2 **Kičevo** Macedonia
114 C3 **Kidal** Mali
59 C3 **Kidderminster** U.K.
114 A3 **Kidira** Senegal
54 C1 **Kidnappers, Cape** N.Z.
102 C1 **Kiel** Ger.
103 E1 **Kielce** Pol.
98 B1 **Kielder Water** U.K.
90 C1 **Kiev** Ukr.
114 A3 **Kiffa** Maur.
119 D3 **Kigali** Rwanda
119 C3 **Kigoma** Tanz.
88 B2 **Kihnu** i. Estonia
92 I2 **Kiiminki** Fin.
67 B4 **Kii-suidō** sea chan. Japan
109 D1 **Kikinda** Serbia
119 C3 **Kikondja** Dem. Rep. Congo
59 D3 **Kikori** P.N.G.
59 D3 **Kikori** r. P.N.G.
118 B3 **Kikwit** Dem. Rep. Congo
65 B1 **Kilchu** N. Korea
118 B3 **Kilembe** Dem. Rep. Congo
139 E2 **Kilgore** U.S.A.
119 D3 **Kilimanjaro** vol. Tanz.
80 B2 **Kilis** Turkey
90 B2 **Kiliya** Ukr.
97 B2 **Kilkee** Ireland
97 D1 **Kilkeel** U.K.
97 C2 **Kilkenny** Ireland
111 B2 **Kilkis** Greece
97 B1 **Killala Bay** Ireland
97 B2 **Killaloe** Ireland
129 C2 **Killam** Can.
97 B2 **Killarney** Ireland
139 D2 **Killeen** U.S.A.
96 B2 **Killin** U.K.
97 B1 **Killybegs** Ireland
96 B3 **Kilmarnock** U.K.
53 B3 **Kilmore** Austr.
119 C3 **Kilosa** Tanz.
97 B2 **Kilrush** Ireland
119 C3 **Kilwa** Dem. Rep. Congo
119 D3 **Kilwa Masoko** Tanz.
119 C3 **Kimambi** Tanz.
52 A2 **Kimba** Austr.
136 C2 **Kimball** U.S.A.
128 C3 **Kimberley** Can.
122 B2 **Kimberley** S. Africa
50 B1 **Kimberley Plateau** Austr.
65 B1 **Kimch'aek** N. Korea
65 B2 **Kimch'ŏn** S. Korea
127 G2 **Kimmirut** Can.
89 E3 **Kimovsk** Rus. Fed.
118 B3 **Kimpese** Dem. Rep. Congo
89 E2 **Kimry** Rus. Fed.
61 C1 **Kinabalu, Gunung** mt. Sabah
        Malaysia
128 C2 **Kinbasket Lake** Can.

130 B2 **Kincardine** Can.
62 A1 **Kinchang** Myanmar
119 C3 **Kinda** Dem. Rep. Congo
98 C2 **Kinder Scout** h. U.K.
129 D2 **Kindersley** Can.
114 A3 **Kindia** Guinea
119 C3 **Kindu** Dem. Rep. Congo
86 D3 **Kineshma** Rus. Fed.
51 E2 **Kingaroy** Austr.
135 B3 **King City** U.S.A.
130 C1 **King George Islands** Can.
88 C2 **Kingisepp** Rus. Fed.
51 D3 **King Island** Austr.
50 B1 **King Leopold Ranges** hills
        Austr.
138 A1 **Kingman** U.S.A.
135 B3 **Kings** r. U.S.A.
52 A3 **Kingscote** Austr.
99 D2 **King's Lynn** U.K.
48 F3 **Kingsmill Group** is Kiribati
50 B1 **King Sound** b. Austr.
134 D2 **Kings Peak** U.S.A.
143 D1 **Kingsport** U.S.A.
130 C2 **Kingston** Can.
146 C3 **Kingston** Jamaica
141 E2 **Kingston** U.S.A.
52 A3 **Kingston South East** Austr.
98 C2 **Kingston upon Hull** U.K.
147 D3 **Kingstown** St Vincent
139 D3 **Kingsville** U.S.A.
99 B3 **Kingswood** U.K.
96 B2 **Kingussie** U.K.
126 E2 **King William Island** Can.
123 C3 **King William's Town** S. Africa
67 D3 **Kinka-san** i. Japan
93 F4 **Kinna** Sweden
97 B3 **Kinsale** Ireland
118 B3 **Kinshasa** Dem. Rep. Congo
143 E1 **Kinston** U.S.A.
88 B2 **Kintai** Lith.
114 B4 **Kintampo** Ghana
96 B3 **Kintyre** pen. U.K.
62 A1 **Kin-U** Myanmar
130 C2 **Kipawa, Lac** l. Can.
83 I3 **Kirensk** Rus. Fed.
89 E3 **Kireyevsk** Rus. Fed.
        Kirghizia country Asia see
        Kyrgyzstan
49 G3 **Kiribati** country Pacific Ocean
80 B2 **Kırıkkale** Turkey
89 E2 **Kirillov** Rus. Fed.
        Kirin China see **Jilin**
        Kirinyaga mt. Kenya see
        Kenya, Mount
89 D2 **Kirishi** Rus. Fed.
49 H2 **Kiritimati** atoll Kiribati
111 C3 **Kırkağaç** Turkey
96 C2 **Kirkcaldy** U.K.
96 B3 **Kirkcudbright** U.K.
92 J2 **Kirkenes** Norway
130 B2 **Kirkland Lake** Can.
137 E2 **Kirksville** U.S.A.
81 C2 **Kirkūk** Iraq
96 C1 **Kirkwall** U.K.
89 D3 **Kirov** Kaluzhskaya Oblast'
        Rus. Fed.
86 D3 **Kirov** Rus. Fed.
        Kirovabad Azer. see **Gäncä**
86 E3 **Kirovo-Chepetsk** Rus. Fed.
91 C2 **Kirovohrad** Ukr.
86 C2 **Kirovsk** Rus. Fed.
91 D2 **Kirovs'ke** Ukr.
96 C2 **Kirriemuir** U.K.
86 E3 **Kirs** Rus. Fed.
74 A2 **Kirthar Range** mts Pak.
92 H2 **Kiruna** Sweden
67 C3 **Kiryū** Japan

89 E2 **Kirzhach** Rus. Fed.
119 C2 **Kisangani** Dem. Rep. Congo
118 B3 **Kisantu** Dem. Rep. Congo
60 A1 **Kisaran** Indon.
82 G3 **Kiselevsk** Rus. Fed.
75 A2 **Kishanganj** India
115 C4 **Kishi** Nigeria
        Kishinev Moldova see **Chişinău**
77 D1 **Kishkenekol'** Kazakh.
74 B1 **Kishtwar** India
119 D3 **Kisii** Kenya
103 D2 **Kiskunfélegyháza** Hungary
103 D2 **Kiskunhalas** Hungary
87 D4 **Kislovodsk** Rus. Fed.
117 C5 **Kismaayo** Somalia
119 C3 **Kisoro** Uganda
111 B3 **Kissamos** Greece
114 A4 **Kissidougou** Guinea
143 D3 **Kissimmee** U.S.A.
143 D3 **Kissimmee, Lake** U.S.A.
119 D3 **Kisumu** Kenya
114 B3 **Kita** Mali
66 D3 **Kitakami** Japan
66 D3 **Kitakami-gawa** r. Japan
67 B4 **Kita-Kyūshū** Japan
119 D2 **Kitale** Kenya
66 D2 **Kitami** Japan
130 B2 **Kitchener** Can.
93 J3 **Kitee** Fin.
119 D2 **Kitgum** Uganda
128 B2 **Kitimat** Can.
118 B3 **Kitona** Dem. Rep. Congo
119 D3 **Kitunda** Tanz.
128 B2 **Kitwanga** Can.
121 B2 **Kitwe** Zambia
101 E3 **Kitzingen** Ger.
92 I3 **Kiurruvesi** Fin.
119 C3 **Kivu, Lac** Dem. Rep.
        Congo/Rwanda
110 C2 **Kıyıköy** Turkey
86 E3 **Kizel** Rus. Fed.
111 C3 **Kızılca Dağ** mt. Turkey
87 D4 **Kizlyar** Rus. Fed.
92 I1 **Kjøllefjord** Norway
92 G2 **Kjøpsvik** Norway
102 C1 **Kladno** Czech Rep.
102 C2 **Klagenfurt** Austria
88 B2 **Klaipėda** Lith.
94 □ **Klaksvík** Faroe Is.
134 B2 **Klamath** r. U.S.A.
134 B2 **Klamath Falls** U.S.A.
134 B2 **Klamath Mountains** U.S.A.
60 B1 **Klang** Malaysia
102 C2 **Klatovy** Czech Rep.
122 A3 **Klawer** S. Africa
128 A2 **Klawock** U.S.A.
122 B3 **Kleena Kleene** Can.
122 B3 **Kleinbegin** S. Africa
122 A2 **Kleinsee** S. Africa
123 C2 **Klerksdorp** S. Africa
89 D3 **Kletnya** Rus. Fed.
100 C2 **Kleve** Ger.
88 C3 **Klimavichy** Belarus
89 D3 **Klimovo** Rus. Fed.
89 E2 **Klimovsk** Rus. Fed.
89 E2 **Klin** Rus. Fed.
101 F2 **Klínovec** mt. Czech Rep.
93 G4 **Klintehamn** Sweden
89 D3 **Klintsy** Rus. Fed.
109 C2 **Ključ** Bos.-Herz.
103 D1 **Kłodzko** Pol.
100 C1 **Kloosterhaar** Neth.
103 D2 **Klosterneuburg** Austria
101 E1 **Kličze (Altmark)** Ger.
103 D1 **Kluczbork** Pol.
128 A2 **Klukwan** U.S.A.

M

Malaysia

108	A3	Maxia, Punta *mt. Sardegna* Italy
83	J2	Maya *r.* Rus. Fed.
147	C2	Mayaguana *i.* Bahamas
96	B3	Maybole U.K.
104	B2	Mayenne France
104	B2	Mayenne *r.* France
128	C2	Mayerthorpe Can.
140	B3	Mayfield U.S.A.
87	D4	Maykop Rus. Fed.
126	B2	Mayo Can.
118	B3	Mayoko Congo
121	D2	Mayotte *terr.* Africa
83	J3	Mayskiy Rus. Fed.
140	C3	Maysville U.S.A.
118	B3	Mayumba Gabon
137	D1	Mayville U.S.A.
151	C2	Mazagão Brazil
104	C3	Mazamet France
77	D3	Mazar China
108	B3	Mazara del Vallo *Sicilia* Italy
77	C3	Mazār-e Sharīf Afgh.
144	A2	Mazatán Mex.
146	A3	Mazatenango Guat.
144	B2	Mazatlán Mex.
88	B2	Mažeikiai Lith.
88	B2	Mazirbe Latvia
71	C3	Mazu Dao *i.* Taiwan
121	B3	Mazunga Zimbabwe
88	C3	Mazyr Belarus
123	D2	Mbabane Swaziland
118	B2	Mbaïki C.A.R.
121	C1	Mbala Zambia
119	D2	Mbale Uganda
118	B2	Mbalmayo Cameroon
118	B3	Mbandaka Dem. Rep. Congo
118	A2	Mbanga Cameroon
120	A1	M'banza Congo Angola
119	D3	Mbeya Tanz.
119	D3	Mbinga Tanz.
123	D2	Mbombela S. Africa
118	B2	Mbomo Congo
118	B2	Mbouda Cameroon
114	A3	Mbour Senegal
114	A3	Mbout Maur.
118	C3	Mbuji-Mayi Dem. Rep. Congo
119	D3	Mbuyuni Tanz.
139	D2	McAlester U.S.A.
139	D3	McAllen U.S.A.
128	B2	McBride Can.
134	C2	McCall U.S.A.
126	E2	McClintock Channel Can.
126	D2	McClure Strait Can.
142	B2	McComb U.S.A.
136	C2	McConaughy, Lake U.S.A.
136	C2	McCook U.S.A.
137	C1	McDermitt U.S.A.
134	D1	McDonald Peak U.S.A.
134	D1	McGuire, Mount U.S.A.
128	C2	McLennan Can.
128	B2	McLeod Lake Can.
134	B1	McMinnville *OR* U.S.A.
142	C1	McMinnville *TN* U.S.A.
137	D3	McPherson U.S.A.
123	C3	Mdantsane S. Africa
135	D3	Mead, Lake *resr* U.S.A.
129	D2	Meadow Lake Can.
140	C2	Meadville U.S.A.
66	D2	Meaken-dake *vol.* Japan
106	B1	Mealhada Port.
131	E1	Mealy Mountains Can.
128	C2	Meander River Can.
78	A2	Mecca Saudi Arabia
100	B2	Mechelen Belgium
100	B2	Mechelen Neth.
100	C2	Mechernich Ger.
100	C2	Meckenheim Ger.

106	B1	Meda Port.
60	B1	Medan Indon.
153	B5	Medanosa, Punta *pt* Arg.
73	C4	Medawachchiya Sri Lanka
107	D2	Médéa Alg.
150	A1	Medellín Col.
115	C1	Medenine Tunisia
134	B2	Medford U.S.A.
110	C2	Medgidia Romania
110	B1	Mediaș Romania
136	B2	Medicine Bow Mountains U.S.A.
136	B2	Medicine Bow Peak U.S.A.
129	C2	Medicine Hat Can.
137	D3	Medicine Lodge U.S.A.
155	D1	Medina Brazil
78	A2	Medina Saudi Arabia
106	C1	Medinaceli Spain
106	C1	Medina del Campo Spain
106	B1	Medina de Rioseco Spain
84	G5	Mediterranean Sea World
129	C2	Medley Can.
87	E3	Mednogorsk Rus. Fed.
83	L2	Medvezh'i, Ostrova *is* Rus. Fed.
86	C2	Medvezh'yegorsk Rus. Fed.
50	A2	Meekatharra Austr.
136	B2	Meeker U.S.A.
75	B2	Meerut India
100	A2	Meetkerke Belgium
65	B1	Meihekou China
		Meijiang China *see* Ningdu
62	A1	Meiktila Myanmar
101	E2	Meiningen Ger.
102	C1	Meißen Ger.
71	B3	Meizhou China
152	B3	Mejicana *mt.* Arg.
152	A3	Mejillones Chile
117	B3	Mek'elē Eth.
114	C2	Mekerrhane, Sebkha *salt pan* Alg.
114	B1	Meknès Morocco
63	B2	Mekong *r.* Asia
63	B3	Mekong, Mouths of the Vietnam
60	B1	Melaka Malaysia
53	B3	Melbourne Austr.
143	D3	Melbourne U.S.A.
108	A2	Mele, Capo *c.* Italy
131	C1	Mélèzes, Rivière aux *r.* Can.
115	D3	Melfi Chad
109	C2	Melfi Italy
129	D2	Melfort Can.
92	F3	Melhus Norway
106	B1	Melide Spain
114	B1	Melilla N. Africa
91	D2	Melitopol' Ukr.
101	D1	Melle Ger.
93	F4	Mellerud Sweden
101	E2	Mellrichstadt Ger.
100	C1	Mellum *i.* Ger.
152	C4	Melo Uru.
115	C1	Melrhir, Chott *salt l.* Alg.
99	C2	Melton Mowbray U.K.
104	C2	Melun France
129	D2	Melville Can.
51	D1	Melville, Cape Austr.
131	E1	Melville, Lake Can.

50	C1	Melville Island Austr.
126	D1	Melville Island Can.
127	F2	Melville Peninsula Can.
102	C2	Memmingen Ger.
61	B1	Mempawah Indon.
80	B3	Memphis *tourist site* Egypt
142	B1	Memphis *TN* U.S.A.
139	C2	Memphis *TX* U.S.A.
91	C1	Mena Ukr.
142	B2	Mena U.S.A.
114	C3	Ménaka Mali
		Mènam Khong *r.* Laos/Thai. *see* Mekong
105	C3	Mende France
116	B3	Mendefera Eritrea
145	C2	Méndez Mex.
119	D2	Mendī Eth.
59	D3	Mendi P.N.G.
99	B3	Mendip Hills U.K.
153	B4	Mendoza Arg.
111	C3	Menemen Turkey
60	B2	Menggala Indon.
62	B1	Mengzi China
131	D1	Menihek Can.
52	B2	Menindee Austr.
52	B2	Menindee Lake Austr.
52	A3	Meningie Austr.
104	C2	Mennecy France
140	B1	Menominee U.S.A.
120	A2	Menongue Angola
		Menorca *i.* Spain *see* Minorca
60	A2	Mentawai, Kepulauan *is* Indon.
60	B2	Mentok Indon.
50	B2	Menzies Austr.
100	C1	Meppel Neth.
100	C1	Meppen Ger.
123	D1	Mepuze Moz.
123	C2	Meqheleng S. Africa
108	B1	Merano Italy
59	D3	Merauke Indon.
52	B2	Merbein Austr.
135	B3	Merced U.S.A.
152	C3	Mercedes Arg.
127	G2	Mercy, Cape Can.
139	C1	Meredith, Lake U.S.A.
91	D2	Merefa Ukr.
116	A3	Merga Oasis Sudan
63	A2	Mergui Archipelago *is* Myanmar
110	C2	Meriç *r.* Greece/Turkey
145	D2	Mérida Mex.
106	B2	Mérida Spain
150	A1	Mérida Venez.
142	C2	Meridian U.S.A.
53	C3	Merimbula Austr.
116	B3	Merowe Sudan
50	A3	Merredin Austr.
96	B3	Merrick *h.* U.K.
140	B1	Merrill U.S.A.
140	B2	Merrillville U.S.A.
128	B2	Merritt Can.
53	C2	Merrygoen Austr.
116	C3	Mersa Fatma Eritrea
100	C3	Mersch Lux.
101	E2	Merseburg (Saale) Ger.
98	B2	Mersey *r.* U.K.
80	B2	Mersin Turkey
60	B1	Mersing Malaysia
99	D3	Mers-les-Bains France
74	B2	Merta India
99	B3	Merthyr Tydfil U.K.
106	B2	Mértola Port.
76	B2	Mertvyy Kultuk, Sor *dry lake* Kazakh.
119	D3	Meru *vol.* Tanz.
100	C3	Merzig Ger.
138	A2	Mesa U.S.A.

Mundrabilla

50	B3	**Mundrabilla** Austr.
119	C2	**Mungbere** Dem. Rep. Congo
75	C2	**Munger** India
53	A1	**Mungeranie** Austr.
53	C1	**Mungindi** Austr.
102	C2	**Munich** Ger.
155	D2	**Muniz Freire** Brazil
101	E1	**Münster** Niedersachsen Ger.
100	C2	**Münster** Nordrhein-Westfalen Ger.
97	B2	**Münster** reg. Germany
100	C2	**Münsterland** reg. Ger.
62	B1	**Mường Nhe** Vietnam
92	H2	**Muonio** Fin.
92	H2	**Muonioälven** r. Fin./Sweden
		Muqdisho Somalia see Mogadishu
103	D2	**Mur** r. Austria
119	C3	**Muramvya** Burundi
119	D3	**Murang'a** Kenya
81	B2	**Murat** r. Turkey
111	C2	**Muratlı** Turkey
50	A2	**Murchison** watercourse Austr.
107	C2	**Murcia** Spain
111	C3	**Mürefte** Turkey
110	B1	**Mureşul** r. Romania
104	C3	**Muret** France
142	C1	**Murfreesboro** U.S.A.
77	D3	**Murghob** Tajik.
155	D2	**Muriaé** Brazil
120	B1	**Muriege** Angola
101	F1	**Müritz** l. Ger.
86	C2	**Murmansk** Rus. Fed.
87	D3	**Murom** Rus. Fed.
66	D2	**Muroran** Japan
106	B1	**Muros** Spain
67	B4	**Muroto** Japan
67	B4	**Muroto-zaki** pt Japan
143	D1	**Murphy** U.S.A.
53	C1	**Murra Murra** Austr.
52	A3	**Murray** r. Austr.
128	B2	**Murray** r. Can.
140	B3	**Murray** U.S.A.
143	D2	**Murray, Lake** U.S.A.
52	A3	**Murray Bridge** Austr.
122	B3	**Murraysburg** S. Africa
52	B3	**Murrayville** Austr.
52	B2	**Murrumbidgee** r. Austr.
121	C2	**Murrupula** Moz.
53	D2	**Murrurundi** Austr.
109	C1	**Murska Sobota** Slovenia
54	C1	**Murupara** N.Z.
49	I4	**Mururoa** atoll Fr. Polynesia
75	C2	**Murwara** India
53	D1	**Murwillumbah** Austr.
115	D2	**Murzūq** Libya
81	C2	**Muş** Turkey
110	B2	**Musala** mt. Bulg.
65	B1	**Musan** N. Korea
78	B3	**Musaymir** Yemen
79	C2	**Muscat** Oman
137	E2	**Muscatine** U.S.A.
50	C2	**Musgrave Ranges** mts Austr.
118	B3	**Mushie** Dem. Rep. Congo
60	B2	**Musi** r. Indon.
123	D1	**Musina** S. Africa
140	B2	**Muskegon** U.S.A.
139	D1	**Muskogee** U.S.A.
128	B2	**Muskwa** r. Can.
74	A1	**Muslimbagh** Pak.
78	A3	**Musmar** Sudan
119	D3	**Musoma** Tanz.
96	C3	**Musselburgh** U.K.
88	B2	**Mustjala** Estonia
53	D2	**Muswellbrook** Austr.
116	A2	**Mūţ** Egypt
121	C2	**Mutare** Zimbabwe

66	D2	**Mutsu** Japan
121	C2	**Mutuali** Moz.
92	I2	**Muurola** Fin.
70	A2	**Mu Us Shadi** des. China
120	A1	**Muxaluando** Angola
86	C2	**Muyezerskiy** Rus. Fed.
119	C3	**Muyinga** Burundi
74	B1	**Muzaffargarh** Pak.
75	C2	**Muzaffarpur** India
144	B2	**Múzquiz** Mex.
75	C1	**Muz Shan** mt. China
119	C3	**Mwanza** Dem. Rep. Congo
119	D3	**Mwanza** Tanz.
118	C3	**Mweka** Dem. Rep. Congo
121	B2	**Mwenda** Zambia
118	C3	**Mwene-Ditu** Dem. Rep. Congo
121	C3	**Mwenezi** Zimbabwe
119	C3	**Mweru, Lake** Dem. Rep. Congo/Zambia
118	C3	**Mwimba** Dem. Rep. Congo
120	B2	**Mwinilunga** Zambia
88	C3	**Myadzyel** Belarus
62	A2	**Myanaung** Myanmar
62	A1	**Myanmar** country Asia
63	A2	**Myaungmya** Myanmar
63	A2	**Myeik** Myanmar
		Myeik Kyunzu is Myanmar see Mergui Archipelago
62	A1	**Myingyan** Myanmar
62	A1	**Myitkyina** Myanmar
91	C2	**Mykolayiv** Ukr.
111	C3	**Mykonos** Greece
111	C3	**Mykonos** i. Greece
86	E2	**Myla** Rus. Fed.
75	D2	**Mymensingh** Bangl.
65	B1	**Myŏnggan** N. Korea
88	C3	**Myory** Belarus
92	□B3	**Mýrdalsjökull** Iceland
91	C2	**Myrhorod** Ukr.
90	C2	**Myronivka** Ukr.
143	D2	**Myrtle Beach** U.S.A.
53	C3	**Myrtleford** Austr.
134	B2	**Myrtle Point** U.S.A.
89	E2	**Myshkin** Rus. Fed.
103	C1	**Myślibórz** Pol.
73	B3	**Mysore** India
83	N2	**Mys Shmidta** Rus. Fed.
		Mysuru India see Mysore
63	B2	**My Tho** Vietnam
111	C3	**Mytilini** Greece
89	E3	**Mytishchi** Rus. Fed.
123	C3	**Mzamomhle** S. Africa
121	C2	**Mzimba** Malawi
121	C2	**Mzuzu** Malawi

N

97	C2	**Naas** Ireland
122	A2	**Nababeep** S. Africa
87	E3	**Naberezhnyye Chelny** Rus. Fed.
59	D3	**Nabire** Indon.
80	B2	**Nablus** West Bank
121	D2	**Nacala** Moz.
63	A2	**Nachuge** India
139	E2	**Nacogdoches** U.S.A.
144	B1	**Nacozari de García** Mex.
74	B2	**Nadiad** India
90	A2	**Nadvirna** Ukr.
86	C2	**Nadvoitsy** Rus. Fed.
86	G2	**Nadym** Rus. Fed.
93	F4	**Næstved** Denmark
111	B3	**Nafpaktos** Greece
111	B3	**Nafplio** Greece

115	D1	**Nafūsah, Jabal** hills Libya
78	B2	**Nafy** Saudi Arabia
64	B1	**Naga** Phil.
130	B1	**Nagagami** r. Can.
67	C3	**Nagano** Japan
67	C3	**Nagano** Japan
75	D2	**Nagaon** India
74	B1	**Nagar** India
74	B2	**Nagar Parkar** Pak.
67	A4	**Nagasaki** Japan
67	B4	**Nagato** Japan
74	B2	**Nagaur** India
73	B4	**Nagercoil** India
74	A2	**Nagha Kalat** Pak.
75	B2	**Nagina** India
67	C3	**Nagoya** Japan
75	B2	**Nagpur** India
68	C2	**Nagqu** China
103	D2	**Nagyatád** Hungary
103	D2	**Nagykanizsa** Hungary
128	B1	**Nahanni Butte** Can.
76	A3	**Nahāvand** Iran
101	E1	**Nahrendorf** Ger.
153	A5	**Nahuel Huapí, Lago** l. Arg.
131	D1	**Nain** Can.
81	D2	**Nā'īn** Iran
96	C2	**Nairn** U.K.
119	D3	**Nairobi** Kenya
119	D3	**Naivasha** Kenya
81	D2	**Najafābād** Iran
78	B2	**Najd** reg. Saudi Arabia
106	C1	**Nájera** Spain
65	C1	**Najin** N. Korea
78	B3	**Najrān** Saudi Arabia
		Nakambe r. Burkina/Ghana see White Volta
67	C3	**Nakatsugawa** Japan
78	A3	**Nakfa** Eritrea
66	B2	**Nakhodka** Rus. Fed.
63	B2	**Nakhon Pathom** Thai.
63	B2	**Nakhon Ratchasima** Thai.
63	B2	**Nakhon Sawan** Thai.
63	A3	**Nakhon Si Thammarat** Thai.
130	B2	**Nakina** Can.
121	C1	**Nakonde** Zambia
93	F4	**Nakskov** Denmark
119	D3	**Nakuru** Kenya
128	C2	**Nakusp** Can.
75	D2	**Nalbari** India
87	D4	**Nal'chik** Rus. Fed.
115	D1	**Nālūt** Libya
123	C2	**Namahadi** S. Africa
77	D2	**Namangan** Uzbek.
122	A2	**Namaqualand** reg. S. Africa
51	E2	**Nambour** Austr.
53	D2	**Nambucca Heads** Austr.
75	C1	**Nam Co** salt l. China
62	B1	**Nam Định** Vietnam
120	A3	**Namib Desert** Namibia
120	A2	**Namibe** Angola
120	A3	**Namibia** country Africa
72	D2	**Namjagbarwa Feng** mt. China
59	C3	**Namlea** Indon.
53	C2	**Namoi** r. Austr.
134	C2	**Nampa** U.S.A.
114	B3	**Nampala** Mali
65	B2	**Namp'o** N. Korea
121	C2	**Nampula** Moz.
62	A1	**Namrup** India
62	A1	**Namsang** Myanmar
92	F3	**Namsos** Norway
63	A2	**Nam Tok** Thai.
83	J2	**Namtsy** Rus. Fed.
62	A1	**Namtu** Myanmar
100	B2	**Namur** Belgium
120	B2	**Namwala** Zambia
65	B2	**Namwŏn** S. Korea

62	A1	Namya Ra Myanmar	92	G2	Narvik Norway	150	B1	Neblina, Pico da mt. Brazil

Neuchâtel

Oss

Poprad

Qillak

Shark Bay

Sofia

Suiyang

U

Venice

Warrington

105	D2	Vittel France
108	B3	Vittoria Sicilia Italy
108	B1	Vittorio Veneto Italy
106	B1	Vivero Spain
144	A2	Vizcaíno, Sierra mts Mex.
110	C2	Vize Turkey
73	C3	Vizianagaram India
100	B2	Vlaardingen Neth.
87	D4	Vladikavkaz Rus. Fed.
89	F2	Vladimir Rus. Fed.
66	B2	Vladivostok Rus. Fed.
109	D2	Vlasotince Serbia
100	B1	Vlieland i. Neth.
100	A2	Vlissingen Neth.
109	C2	Vlorë Albania
102	C2	Vöcklabruck Austria
101	D2	Vogelsberg hills Ger.
119	D3	Voi Kenya
105	D2	Voiron France
131	D1	Voisey's Bay Can.
109	C1	Vojvodina prov. Serbia
92	J3	Voknavolok Rus. Fed.
		Volcano Bay Japan see
		Uchiura-wan
89	E2	Volga Rus. Fed.
89	F2	Volga r. Rus. Fed.
87	D4	Volgodonsk Rus. Fed.
87	D4	Volgograd Rus. Fed.
89	D2	Volkhov Rus. Fed.
89	D1	Volkhov r. Rus. Fed.
101	E2	Volkstedt Ger.
91	D2	Volnovakha Ukr.
90	B2	Volochys'k Ukr.
91	D2	Volodars'ke Ukr.
90	B1	Volodars'k-Volyns'kyy Ukr.
90	B1	Volodymyrets' Ukr.
90	A1	Volodymyr-Volyns'kyy Ukr.
89	E2	Vologda Rus. Fed.
89	E2	Volokolamsk Rus. Fed.
91	D1	Volokonovka Rus. Fed.
111	B3	Volos Greece
88	C2	Volosovo Rus. Fed.
89	D2	Volot Rus. Fed.
89	E3	Volovo Rus. Fed.
87	D3	Vol'sk Rus. Fed.
114	C4	Volta, Lake resr Ghana
155	D2	Volta Redonda Brazil
87	D4	Volzhskiy Rus. Fed.
92	⬚C2	Vopnafjörður Iceland
88	C3	Voranava Belarus
86	F2	Vorkuta Rus. Fed.
88	B2	Vormsi i. Estonia
89	E3	Voronezh Rus. Fed.
89	E3	Voronezh r. Rus. Fed.
91	E1	Vorontsovka Rus. Fed.
91	C2	Vorskla r. Rus. Fed.
88	C2	Võrtsjärv l. Estonia
88	C2	Võru Estonia
122	B3	Vosburg S. Africa
105	D2	Vosges mts France
89	E2	Voskresensk Rus. Fed.
93	E3	Voss Norway
84	H3	Vostochnyy Sayan mts Rus. Fed.
86	E3	Votkinsk Rus. Fed.
154	C2	Votuporanga Brazil
100	B3	Vouziers France
92	J2	Voynitsa Rus. Fed.
91	C2	Voznesens'k Ukr.
93	E4	Vrådal Norway
66	B2	Vrangel' Rus. Fed.
		Vrangelya, Ostrov i. Rus. Fed.
		see Wrangel Island
109	D2	Vranje Serbia
110	D2	Vratnik pass Bulg.
110	B2	Vratsa Bulg.
109	C1	Vrbas r. Bos.-Herz.
109	C1	Vrbas Serbia

122	A3	Vredenburg S. Africa
122	A3	Vredendal S. Africa
100	B3	Vresse Belgium
109	D1	Vršac Serbia
122	B2	Vryburg S. Africa
123	D2	Vryheid S. Africa
89	D1	Vsevolozhsk Rus. Fed.
		Vučitrn Kosovo see Vushtrri
109	C1	Vukovar Croatia
86	E2	Vuktyl Rus. Fed.
123	C2	Vukuzakhe S. Africa
109	B3	Vulcano, Isola i. Italy
63	B2	Vung Tau Vietnam
109	D2	Vushtrri Kosovo
74	B2	Vyara India
89	D2	Vyaz'ma Rus. Fed.
93	I3	Vyborg Rus. Fed.
88	C2	Vyerkhnyadzvinsk Belarus
87	D3	Vyksa Rus. Fed.
90	B2	Vylkove Ukr.
90	A2	Vynohradiv Ukr.
89	D2	Vypolzovo Rus. Fed.
89	D2	Vyritsa Rus. Fed.
91	D2	Vyselki Rus. Fed.
90	C1	Vyshhorod Ukr.
89	D2	Vyshniy-Volochek Rus. Fed.
103	D2	Vyškov Czech Rep.
86	C2	Vytegra Rus. Fed.

W

114	B3	Wa Ghana
100	B2	Waal r. Neth.
100	B2	Waalwijk Neth.
128	C2	Wabasca r. Can.
128	C2	Wabasca-Desmarais Can.
140	B3	Wabash r. U.S.A.
117	C4	Wabē Gestro Wenz r. Eth.
129	E2	Wabowden Can.
143	D3	Waccasassa Bay U.S.A.
101	D2	Wächtersbach Ger.
139	D2	Waco U.S.A.
115	D2	Waddān Libya
		Waddeneilanden is Neth. see
		West Frisian Islands
100	B1	Waddenzee sea chan. Neth.
128	B2	Waddington, Mount Can.
100	B1	Waddinxveen Neth.
129	D2	Wadena Can.
137	D1	Wadena U.S.A.
74	A2	Wadh Pak.
116	B2	Wadi Halfa Sudan
116	B3	Wad Medani Sudan
70	C2	Wafangdian China
100	B2	Wageningen Neth.
127	F2	Wager Bay Can.
53	C3	Wagga Wagga Austr.
137	D2	Wahoo U.S.A.
137	D1	Wahpeton U.S.A.
54	B2	Waiau r. Indon.
59	C3	Waigeo i. Indon.
58	B3	Waikabubak Indon.
52	A2	Waikerie Austr.
54	B2	Waimate N.Z.
75	B3	Wainganga r. India
58	C3	Waingapu Indon.
129	C2	Wainwright Can.
54	C1	Waiouru N.Z.
54	B2	Waipara N.Z.
54	C1	Waipawa N.Z.
54	C1	Wairau r. N.Z.
54	C1	Wairoa N.Z.
54	C1	Waitaki r. N.Z.
54	B1	Waitara N.Z.

54	B1	Waiuku N.Z.
119	E2	Wajir Kenya
67	C3	Wakasa-wan b. Japan
54	A3	Wakatipu, Lake N.Z.
129	D2	Wakaw Can.
67	C4	Wakayama Japan
136	D3	WaKeeney U.S.A.
54	B2	Wakefield N.Z.
98	C2	Wakefield U.K.
48	F1	Wake Island N. Pacific Ocean
66	D1	Wakkanai Japan
123	D2	Wakkerstroom S. Africa
103	D1	Wałbrzych Pol.
53	D2	Walcha Austr.
100	C1	Walchum Ger.
103	D1	Wałcz Pol.
99	B2	Wales admin. div. U.K.
53	C2	Walgett Austr.
119	C3	Walikale Dem. Rep. Congo
135	C3	Walker Lake U.S.A.
52	A2	Wallaroo Austr.
98	B2	Wallasey U.K.
134	C1	Walla Walla U.S.A.
101	D3	Walldürn Ger.
53	C2	Wallendbeen Austr.
49	G3	Wallis and Futuna Islands
		terr. S. Pacific Ocean
96	☐	Walls U.K.
98	B1	Walney, Isle of i. U.K.
99	C2	Walsall U.K.
136	C3	Walsenburg U.S.A.
101	D1	Walsrode Ger.
143	D2	Walterboro U.S.A.
120	A3	Walvis Bay Namibia
119	C2	Wamba Dem. Rep. Congo
52	B1	Wanaaring Austr.
54	A2	Wanaka N.Z.
54	A2	Wanaka, Lake N.Z.
130	B2	Wanapitei Lake Can.
154	B3	Wanda Arg.
66	B1	Wanda Shan mts China
62	A1	Wanding China
54	C1	Wanganui N.Z.
53	C3	Wangaratta Austr.
65	B1	Wangqing China
62	A1	Wan Hsa-la Myanmar
71	B4	Wanning China
100	B2	Wanroij Neth.
99	C3	Wantage U.K.
70	A2	Wanyuan China
70	A2	Wanzhou China
73	B3	Warangal India
101	D2	Warburg Ger.
50	B2	Warburton Austr.
52	A1	Warburton watercourse Austr.
75	B2	Wardha India
96	C1	Ward Hill U.K.
128	B2	Ware Can.
101	F1	Waren Ger.
100	C2	Warendorf Ger.
53	D1	Warialda Austr.
142	A2	Warmbad Namibia
135	C3	Warm Springs U.S.A.
134	C2	Warner Lakes U.S.A.
143	D2	Warner Robins U.S.A.
152	B2	Warnes Bol.
52	B3	Warracknabeal Austr.
53	C2	Warrego r. Austr.
53	C2	Warren Austr.
142	B2	Warren AR U.S.A.
140	C2	Warren OH U.S.A.
141	D2	Warren PA U.S.A.
97	C1	Warrenpoint U.K.
137	E3	Warrensburg U.S.A.
122	B2	Warrenton S. Africa
115	C4	Warri Nigeria
98	B2	Warrington U.K.

Warrnambool

X

Xapuri